Jessica Red

Jessica lives on the stunning

tion for the settings in her books

Sprocker Spaniel puppy, and an ever-growing collection of collectible teddy bears. Although if the puppy has her way, the collection will be reduced to a pile of stuffing and chewed limbs!

She's got several personas: HR Tutor, Internal Verifier, Writer, Write Romantic, Brown Owl, Chocoholic, and Mum. She spends far too much time in the chocoholic persona and often ponders going out for a run to offset the damage. Then she feels exhausted and has a Chomp instead!

'Dreaming about Daran' is the third book of the Whitsborough Bay series.

Visit her website: www.jessicaredland.com

Dreaming about Daran

Where do you go when it's your own past you are running from?

Jessica Redland

It's a So Vain Book

Published in Great Britain in 2016 by:
SO VAIN BOOKS Ltd
75 London Road
Oxford OX3 9BB

www.sovainbooks.co.uk
Email: info@sovainbooks.co.uk

A catalogue record from this book is available from the British Library

ISBN: 9781910869130

Printed and Bound in Great Britain by PrintOnDemand, Worldwide

Some friends come and go. Others stick around. To Susan who's been in it for the long-haul xx

Chapter 1

(Saturday 7th September)

'What the hell is that in the fruit bowl?' I cautiously leaned forward on Ben's sofa to get a closer look, hoping it wasn't an enormous spider about to scuttle over me.

'Apples, pears, kiwis and bananas,' Ben said. 'Don't tell me that you've reached the grand old age of 33 and you still can't identify your basic fruits.'

I raised my eyebrows at him. 'Ha ha. You're hilarious. You should be on stage, so you should.' I reached my hand out.

'Argh!' yelled Ben.

I snatched back my hand, screaming.

'Sorry. Couldn't resist,' he said, slumping back onto the sofa in hysterics.

'You eejit!' I whacked him with a cushion. 'You scared the life out of me! Is this what it's going to be like living with you? Because, if it is, I can check into a hotel for the next few months instead. Are you ready to say goodbye to that new kitchen?'

I work for a company called Prime PR, managing public relations campaigns for large corporates. I'd been promoted to Head of PR for the Midlands and North of England so needed to relocate from London to Leeds. Ben – or Saint Ben, as I called him – was the brother of my best friend, Sarah, and he lived in Leeds. He'd become my meal buddy for the past few years every time

I'd been to Leeds on business. Meeting up with a friend for some good craic was far more appealing than dining in a hotel restaurant surrounded by suits staring into space, eating meals for one. On my last trip, I'd moaned about the prospect of living in a hotel for a month or two while I found somewhere to rent and, being the saint he was, Ben immediately offered me his spare room. Grand idea. So I negotiated a deal where work paid me an allowance rather than putting me up in a hotel. It was cheaper for Prime and I could give Ben the allowance as rent to refit his prehistoric kitchen. Win-win. Of course, he refused to accept payment, but I wore him down eventually.

Ben put his hands up in surrender as I lifted the cushion to whack him again. 'Sorry. But you'd have done the same if it had been the other way round. You know you would.'

'Perhaps.'

'Definitely.'

I smiled. He was right. 'So, what is it, then?'

Ben reached into the fruit bowl, then held out the black object in the palm of his hand.

'It's a chess piece,' I said.

'What sort?'

I shrugged. 'I don't play chess. Boring game for boring people.'

'That's very judgemental, Clare. I'm sure lots of interesting people play chess.'

'Name one.'

Ben laughed. 'Okay, you've got me. But it's not the interesting bit I'm struggling with. I just don't know anyone who plays chess.'

'I take it you don't play?'

'No.'

'Then, why's there a chess piece in your fruit bowl?'

'Interesting story. I came home from work last Tuesday and, quite randomly, it was on the front doorstep.'

'With a note?'

'No note. Just the king on his own.'

'Very random. But do you know what's even more random? Why the hell it's in your fruit bowl instead of the bin.'

'It seemed like a good place for it.'

'But you don't know where it's been! It could have been peed on by a dog. Or worse!'

Ben looked at the king thoughtfully. 'Good point. Just as well it was between the bananas and kiwis, then, wasn't it? They've got skins.' He leaned forward and put it back.

'Ben! Put it in the bin!'

'No.'

'Ben!'

I reached forward, but he grabbed me and started tickling me. I squealed and leapt to my feet. I hate being tickled. I darted past him and into his kitchen. Thankfully, I was saved by the arrival of our Indian takeaway.

'Get your hands washed before you touch that food,' I ordered Ben.

He winked at me. 'I love it when you're bossy.'

I dug out some plates and we busied ourselves dishing up the food.

'Would you mind if we watch a film while we eat?' Ben asked.

'It's your house. Will you have a film in mind?'

'The Count of Monte Cristo's on and I've never seen it. My mate Pete said it's really good.'

'Is that the one with Jim Caviezel in it?'

'I think so. And Guy Pearce.'

'Ooh, two hotties. Grand. Count me in!'

'Your friend Pete was right,' I said, when the closing credits started rolling. 'Cracking film. What did you think?'

'I agree. The king thing was a spooky coincidence, don't you think?'

In the film, best friends Edmond and Fernand exchange a chess-piece king when one of them overcomes a challenge to symbolise who is 'king of the moment'.

I nodded towards the king nestled in his fruit bowl. 'Did you plant it there knowing it was in the film?'

Ben shook his head. 'Honestly, I've never seen the film or read the book. I didn't know about the chess piece. I genuinely found that bad boy sitting on my doorstep, just like I told you.'

'Are you sure?'

'Have you ever known me to lie?'

He made a good point. He was one of the most honest people I knew, although, unlike me, he was tactful with his honesty. Generous to a fault, ridiculously considerate of others and gifted in spades with patience, Ben definitely deserved his nickname of 'Saint Ben'. By contrast, I could be pretty blunt and to the point, not particularly patient and quite selfish. I was lucky he only called me 'Irish' because I probably deserved something a little less affectionate.

'Tell you what we can do.' He grinned at me, wrinkled his nose in a clear act of mischief, then reached for the king in the fruit bowl. He picked up a chilli pepper discarded from his curry in his other hand and said, 'If you eat the whole chilli, you win the king.'

So I did. Tears streamed down my face, my nose ran like a tap and my head felt as if it were about to explode. But that king was going to be mine.

'Oh my God! I can't believe you just did that.' Ben handed me a box of tissues. 'Serious respect to you, Irish.'

I gasped for breath and rasped, 'Wait till I tell your sister what you made me do.'

He laughed. 'You're king of the moment, Irish. He's all yours.'

And so it began.

Chapter 2

(Saturday 21st December)

'I now declare you husband and wife. You may kiss your bride.'

Sarah radiated happiness as Nick gently kissed her, then they turned to face the congregation. I put my fingers in my mouth and released a piercing whistle that echoed around the church. The vicar's eyes widened and he looked as if he were about to protest at my crassness in a place of worship. Bollocks to that. I whistled again, then started a round of applause, which everyone joined in with. I stared back at the vicar, challenging him to stop me, but he surprised me by smiling and joining in instead.

Sarah and Nick signed the register and posed for some photos. As it was only four days till Christmas and a bit on the nippy side, Sarah had arranged to have photos taken inside the church with the bridal party and immediate family members, before heading to their reception for group photos.

'Nice whistling,' Ben whispered to me, as we shuffled out of the pew to join the rest of the wedding party. He was an usher and I was a bridesmaid alongside Sarah's bestie since primary school, Elise, and Nick's sister, Callie. 'I thought the vicar was going to tell you off, though.'

'So did I. But he didn't scare me.'

'I don't imagine anyone or anything scares you, Irish.'

I laughed, but my stomach did a somersault. There were two

people who still scared me. I wasn't going to let them ruin my day, though. Time for a change of subject.

'I'm liking the morning suit on you,' I said, taking in the navy three-piece Ben was wearing. 'I don't think I've ever seen you in a suit.'

'That's probably because I don't own one. Don't need one for work.'

'It's just as well Lemony isn't here. She'd probably get ideas of dragging you up the aisle herself, after seeing you dressed like this.'

'It's Lebony, and you know it.'

'It's not even a name.'

'I've told you this before. She was conceived whilst her parents were working in Lebanon. They named her after it. Sort of. Yeah, okay, my girlfriend has a rubbish name, but that's not her fault, is it?'

'So, what's her excuse for missing your sister's wedding?'

Ben didn't get to answer the question, as the photographer shuffled us towards opposite sides of the line-up.

Sherrington Hall – an ivy-covered Georgian manor house perched on a clifftop about 12 miles south of Sarah's North Yorkshire coastal hometown of Whitsborough Bay – was pretty impressive as a venue. Sarah, a florist, had certainly pulled out all the stops to decorate it beautifully and achieve a balance between Christmas and nuptials. I'd been to loads of weddings in my time but never one so close to Christmas. Despite not being a fan of the festive period, I had to concede that the ambience created by swathes of ivy, bunches of mistletoe and church candles everywhere was pretty special. Champagne-coloured roses and teal flowers (no idea what type; not my specialist subject) matched the colours of our dresses and the men's waistcoats.

As Sarah and Nick cut the cake and giggled together after the meal, I smiled and had what Sarah would describe as a 'warm and fuzzy moment'. They were a good match. I liked Nick a lot, which was a good thing because I couldn't bear that eejit Jason, whom she'd lived with in London before finally seeing the light, ditching him and moving back home to Whitsborough Bay. Despite my cynicism about relationships and marriage, it warmed my heart to see Sarah and Nick looking so happy together.

Elise leaned towards me. 'Are those tears in your eyes, Clare?' she teased.

I cleared my throat. 'Tears? You talk bollocks, so you do! As if I'd cry at a wedding. Unless it was in sympathy for the poor buggers for ruining their lives and blowing their savings on what's effectively a big piss-up.'

'You can deny it all you want, but I know that's not how you really feel about marriage.' She nudged me gently. 'It'll be you one day, you know.'

I turned around to face her, confident that any tell-tale tears had retreated. 'Me? Married? Are you for real? Aside from the fact that I think marriage is a pile of shite, you have to be in a relationship to get married and, as you well know, I don't do relationships.'

'That's because you've never met the right person. I reckon your Nick's out there somewhere and you just have to open your heart up to finding him.'

I stared at her, wondering for a moment if she was just winding me up, but something told me she wholeheartedly believed what she was saying. 'Do weddings turn you a bit loopy, Elise? Never met the right person? Open my heart and I'll find him? Seriously?'

Elise smiled. 'Yes. Seriously. We're 10 days from New Year and I reckon you should make a New Year's resolution to actually have a relationship with someone. A meaningful relationship, that is, as opposed to just sex. Let someone in, for once.'

I shook my head as I topped up my glass of wine and took a sip.

'This sort of bollocks is one of the many reasons why you and I weren't friends until recently.'

Elise twiddled one of the auburn ringlets dangling from her up-do. 'Does that mean we're friends now?'

I'd walked into that one. I had to admit that, despite battling with her for a decade or so, I now really enjoyed Elise's company. It had taken a huge bust-up while planning Sarah's hen do, where we'd both said some nasty things – particularly me – to get us to face why we'd never hit it off and, ultimately, get over it and start behaving like adults. We'd probably have plodded along tolerating each other if I hadn't discovered Elise's secret and been there to support her as she came to terms with it.

I grinned back at her, a feeling of genuine affection flowing through me. 'Maybe,' I said. 'But I can easily scrub you off my very short and very exclusive friends list if you keep spouting bollocks like that. Anyway, why aren't you jaded and cynical like me, after what you've been through this year?'

Elise had discovered that her husband of 12 years, Gary, was gay and always had been. He'd managed to kid himself that their friendship was enough to make their marriage work, but his attraction to our friend Stevie's best mate, Rob, had been too strong, and Elise had walked in on them in the shower. Nightmare. In an effort to get over Gary, she'd started seeing Daniel, a rep from Sarah's shop. Turned out he was a two-timing git, too. Actually, in Daniel's case, he was a three-, four- or even five-timing git. The relationship ended, but Daniel had left Elise with a little more than memories of their time together. With her sister giving birth to twins and Sarah's wedding approaching, Elise was adamant that she didn't want to steal anyone's thunder by announcing her own news.

Personally, I think she was struggling to come to terms with what it meant. She'd been desperate for a baby, but having one as a result of a brief fling with a tosser like Daniel wasn't quite the way she'd planned it. Consequently, the only people who knew so far were Daniel (who, as predicted, couldn't care less), his brother, Michael (who had the hots for Elise and hated Daniel so wasn't exactly thrilled by the news), Stevie and me.

Waiting staff appeared with pots of tea and coffee. Elise entered into a conversation with one of them about which herbal teas they had, thankfully putting paid to any further discussion about marriage. Ben stood up and announced that he'd had enough wine and was going to get a round of beers in. He'd barely left the room before Stevie sat down in his empty seat beside Elise. I've no idea what he said, but it set her off giggling. I sat back and watched them chatting animatedly, sipping on my wine while my coffee cooled. If ever there was another perfect match, it was Stevie and Elise, but neither of them was ever going to make a move. Just as well I'd never been one for pussyfooting around things. I decided to corner her in the toilets 10 minutes later and pretty much order her to give him a sign that she saw him as more than friends. Whether she'd have the guts to go for it, only time would tell.

When we returned to the table, the conversation had turned to what everyone was planning for Christmas and New Year. Arse. Worst subject in the world, ever. Sarah's auntie Kay was telling everyone that she'd be managing Sarah's shop so would be looking forward to a takeaway and putting her feet up on Christmas Eve. Her new partner, Philip, looked towards me. Oh no! Here goes… 'What will you do, Clare?' he asked.

I gritted my teeth. Must try to sound light and friendly. 'Absolutely nothing.' He stared at me, frowning, and I realised I wasn't going to get away without explaining it. I took a deep breath. 'Christmas is family time. As far as I'm concerned, I have no family. Therefore, I don't do Christmas and I hate New Year with a passion.' There. I'd said it! I hoped nobody had noticed the shake in my voice.

‘What about you, Elise?’ Philip asked, quickly averting his gaze from me.

‘I’m going to my sister’s for Christmas. Can’t wait to spend it with my baby niece and nephew. My dad’s across from Spain at the moment, so he’ll be there too. Should be lovely. As for New Year, I haven’t really thought that far ahead. What about you?’

Everyone continued to chat about their plans while I shrank back into my chair, hoping nobody would try to bring me into the conversation. Surely my response to Philip had given the very clear message that Christmas and New Year were taboo subjects. The group discussion turned into a few individual conversations. Yes! The ordeal was over! Or was it? Ben turned to me and said, ‘If you’ve got no plans for Christmas, why don’t you join me at Mum and Dad’s? It’ll be strange with no Sarah.’

I was very aware of Elise listening and could almost hear her willing me to say yes. No doubt, she couldn’t bear the thought of anyone being on their own on Christmas Day. ‘Thank you, but no thank you,’ I said. ‘I’m fine on my own.’

‘New Year, then?’

‘No, again.’

‘Please.’

‘Why? Why would anyone subject themselves to hot, smelly pubs packed with obnoxious, drunk eejits, then pay five times the normal taxi fare to get back home? Assuming someone hasn’t already nicked their pre-booked taxi, that is. I can’t think of a more hideous way to spend an evening.’

‘And that’s not how we’d be spending it,’ Ben countered. ‘I’m going to a party at Pete’s house and it’s walking distance from mine, so you can crash in your old room.’

‘No thanks.’

‘Why?’

'Because it's New Year's Eve. I don't care whether it's spent in a pub, at a house party or at home in front of the TV. I still hate it.'

'But…'

'Ben! I suggest you drop the subject. Right now!'

Elise shuffled in her seat. 'What are you doing, Stevie?' she asked.

I didn't hear the answer, or anything else that was said, until a female voice made an announcement over the microphone about vacating the room so they could prepare it for the evening's entertainment. Desperate for some space away from the questions and judgemental looks, I grabbed my empty wine glass and a part-finished bottle. 'I'm going to freshen up,' I muttered to nobody in particular. 'See you later.' Without waiting for a response, I stormed across the room, through reception, then took the stairs two at a time until I reached my bedroom. Empty wine glass and bottle still in my hands, I pushed open the doors to the Juliet balcony and gulped in the cool night air, waiting for my heartbeat to return to normal and the butterflies in my stomach to settle. Every year. Every single year. They'd done this to me. They'd turned me into this. I hated this time of year, thanks to them. Hated it.

But I hated them more.

Chapter 3

My 20-minute time-out – and half a bottle of wine – calmed me down considerably. I returned to the bar feeling a bit childish for having stormed out earlier. It wasn't Philip's or Ben's fault that I hated Christmas and New Year.

'Ah! Here she is!' Stevie announced, as I joined him, Ben, Elise, Sarah and a few others in the bar. 'Your ears must have been burning, Clare. We were just talking about you!'

Anger flashed through me again. How dare they discuss me behind my back? 'Can't you just accept that some people don't like this time of year?' I snapped.

Ben flung his arm around me. 'Relax, Irish! That's not what we were talking about. I was just telling everyone that you can't resist a dare and how our last challenge nearly got me arrested.'

I relaxed against him. Phew! I didn't mind them discussing that. 'Will that be the challenge where you did a lap of the Indian with only a rapidly disintegrating poppadom to protect your dignity?'

'That would be the one.' Ben hung his head in mock shame. 'The worst part was that I ran outside straight into a passing PCSO.'

Gasps of horror came from the group. 'Oh my God! How do I not know about this, Ben?' Sarah demanded.

'It's a tad embarrassing.'

'Fortunately, the PCSO was female and clearly a huge Ben fan,' I said.

'*Huge* Ben? I didn't think you'd noticed.'

I grimaced and elbowed him. 'Gross! And not something you should be discussing in front of your sister, either!'

Ben laughed. 'Fortunately, I knew her through work so she let me off as long as I re-dressed immediately and disposed of what was left of the poppadom in the nearest bin.'

'So, what possessed you to strip off and streak in the first place?' Stevie asked.

'This.' Ben withdrew the king from his pocket.

'It's a chess piece,' Elise said.

'That's right. The black king.'

She shrugged. 'And that made you strip off and streak because…?'

'Have you seen the film *The Count of Monte Cristo*?' Ben asked her.

As Head of English and Drama at a local comprehensive, this was bound to be Elise's specialist subject. 'The 1975 version, the 2002 one, and I've read the book,' she said. 'Oh! I get it!'

'Well, I don't,' Stevie said. 'Care to explain?'

Ben and I took it in turns to explain how the king came into his possession, how it was used in the film and our very first challenge that evening.

'The king's gone back and forth several times since then,' I said, 'but Ben's had him too long this time. I need to win him back.'

'And I know how.' Ben dangled the king in front of my eyes. 'It doesn't involve stripping off, eating anything gross or doing anything embarrassing. I'd say it's the easiest challenge you'll ever have to face.'

'Doesn't sound like much of a challenge,' Stevie said.

'It is, because it's something she's already said no to.'

My heartbeat quickened. I knew where this was going.

'If you want to win the king back, you'll join me at that New Year's Eve party at Pete's and you'll stay until midnight.'

I felt all eyes on me.

'Ben! You know I hate New Year!'

'Do you think I liked stripping off and streaking round *The Taj Mahal*?'

'No.'

'Exactly. The point of the challenges is about facing your fears or doing things you hate. You'll hate this. It's therefore a challenge.'

I planted my hands on my hips. 'Why are you so keen for me to join you at this stupid party?'

He shrugged. 'No reason, other than I hate the thought of you being alone. Besides, it might be fun. And if it isn't, we can get drunk and pretend we're somewhere else on a different day of the year, if that makes you happy.'

I sighed. 'If I agree to come – and it's a big if – you promise we can leave at midnight?'

'As soon as the clock's struck 12, I'll declare you king of the moment and we're out of there.'

I sighed again and stared at the king sitting on his outstretched palm. Arse! I might have started off thinking of it as a scabby item that belonged in the bin, but my competitive streak had taken over after the chilli challenge, and winning had become an obsession. I needed him! 'I might live to regret this, but you're on. King's mine, Saint Ben. King's mine.'

'Oi! Saint Ben! Will you remind me again why I let you drag me here?' I gulped back the last couple of mouthfuls of cheap, warm Chardonnay out of a paper cup, shuddered, crumpled the cup and tossed it in the direction of the overflowing bin in the corner of

Pete's dining room.

Ben smiled. 'Because, Irish, you're desperate to get your mitts on this, aren't you?' He reached into his jeans pocket and pulled out the king. I tried to snatch it out of his hand, but he was too quick.

'You know it doesn't work like that. King's still mine if you don't make it past midnight.'

'Bollocks. You're a mean boy.' I gave him a playful shove as he put the king back in his pocket. 'By the way, can we put it on record that this is the crappiest house party ever?'

'It's not *that* bad,' Ben said. We both gazed around the large dining room. The table, pushed against the fireplace, housed empty tubes of Pringles, cremated sausage rolls, some wilted sticks of celery and about 30 or so discarded beer cans. In one corner of the room, a couple were eating each other's faces. In the opposite corner, another couple were having a domestic about who'd forgotten to renew the Sky subscription. Slumped on the floor between them, snoring loudly, lay a scruffy-looking twentysomething with 'I'm a twat' written across his forehead, a Poirot-style moustache and glasses. Ben laughed. 'I wonder how long it takes to remove permanent marker pen.'

'I think the clue is in the word "permanent", don't you?'

'Okay, it *is* that bad,' Ben admitted. 'Really bad. I'm sorry, Irish.'

'Home time?' I didn't want to lose the challenge, but this was torture. A chilli I could cope with; the house party from hell on the worst evening of the year was another matter.

Ben looked at his watch. 'It's only 11.20. Pete'll be insulted if we don't stay to at least see the New Year in.'

'Seriously? Pete's in the bathroom driving the porcelain bus and has been for the last hour. I don't think he'd know if *everyone* left before midnight.'

'Five past midnight, Irish. I promise. Please.' He looked at me with big, sad, puppy-dog eyes.

'You know that stupid expression gets you nowhere.'

He widened his hazel eyes even more and pushed out his bottom lip.

'Jesus. Stop it. I submit. I'll stay, but only because I've already suffered three hours of this so I may as well do another 40 minutes and embrace the stupid midnight thing. And win the king.'

'It'll be a worthy win.'

I poked him in the ribs. 'I hope you realise that the next challenge will be something you're going to really hate, just to piss you off.'

Ben grabbed two cans of lager from a box on the table and passed me one. 'Get one of these down your neck and quit moaning. I'm going to check on Pete. I won't leave you alone for long.'

'You'd better not.' I sighed as Ben left the kitchen. Everyone else seemed to be enjoying themselves… Well, everyone apart from Pete, the arguing couple and the body on the floor. Why couldn't I? That was an easy one. New Year's Eve was the day my life changed forever, thanks to *them*.

I sighed again and swigged on the warm lager. I really should have stuck to my guns and ignored Ben's stupid challenge this time.

Stomach rumbling, I peered into the tubes of Pringles, but they were all empty.

'Excuse me, but have you got a sticking plaster?' I turned around to see a tall man with a wild mop of dark hair beside me.

'No. Do I look like the sort of person who carries a first-aid kit in case of emergency?'

'Oh. It's just that I scraped my knee falling for you.'

I stared at him for a moment. On any other night, I'd have cringed at the cheesiness but turned on the charm offensive anyway. But this wasn't any other night. This was New Year's Eve.

'Please tell me you didn't just say that bollocks. You must be very pissed.'

He shook his head. 'Not pissed,' he slurred. 'Just intoxicated by you. I think you're the most—'

I put my hand up in a 'stop' gesture. 'Can I just stop you there?'

He waited expectantly. 'You were going to say something?'

'No. I just wanted to stop you there before I join Pete on that porcelain bus.'

He looked confused. He wobbled a bit and grabbed the table for support, knocking the empty Pringles tubes over in a domino effect. 'If I were to ask you out on a date, would your answer be the same as the answer to this question?'

I opened my mouth to hurl another insult, then smiled. I'd give him his due for that one. 'That's actually quite clever. Not so cheesy. I'm Clare.'

'I'm Taz.'

'What sort of name's Taz?'

'Short for Tasmanian Devil.' He gave a little growl.

I shrugged. 'Not getting it.'

'Because of the hair.'

'Ah. You'll be a friend of Pete's?'

'No. I've come with a mate who knows Pete. You?'

'Same. My friend works with him.'

Taz picked up a burnt sausage roll, squinted at it, then tossed it towards the bin in apparent disgust. Wise decision. It sounded like a stone as it hit the wooden floor.

'I've got a serious question for you,' he said. 'Was your dad an alien?'

I bristled at the mention of Da, even though I knew the line.

'Because there's nothing else like you on this planet,' he finished.

I squirmed. If I hadn't felt stone-cold sober, I'd probably have engaged in a little flirting with Taz and maybe tried to out-cheese him, but not tonight. I was on a countdown to midnight, then I was out of there.

I gave Taz what I hoped was a polite yet dismissive smile. 'Will you excuse me? I could do with some fresh air.' I stepped over the 'dead body' and headed into the kitchen. I closed the door to the garden firmly behind me, a clear message that I didn't want Taz to follow. I'd probably pissed him off by not responding to his lines, but who cared? I didn't invite him to talk to me; *he* was the persistent one. Being a lone female didn't make me fair game.

In the dim light emitting from the kitchen window, I could just about make out the shape of a swing in the middle of the lawn, where I decided to take a seat with my back towards the house, in the hope that I could shut out the sights and sounds of a hideous evening. I shivered as a cool breeze wrapped around me. Granted, it was mild for the time of year, but it certainly wasn't the weather for sitting on a swing in the dark wearing an LBD and no coat. I managed about five minutes before having to admit defeat. Shivering, I stood up and took a few steps towards the house, then smacked straight into someone.

'Sorry.' I stepped backwards and looked up. 'Taz? How long have you been there?'

'A few minutes.' He made no attempt to move. He just stood there staring at me.

I shivered again… but not from the cold this time. 'I'm just going in.' I moved to step around him, but he sidestepped in the same direction. I moved the other way, but he mirrored my move. 'That's not funny, Taz. Will you not let me past? I'm freezing. I want to go in.'

'Why did you walk away when I was talking to you?'

Crap. I *had* pissed him off. 'I needed some air, but I've had plenty now. Anyway, I didn't just walk away. I excused myself first.' I tried to step around him again, but he grabbed my arms, his rough hands digging into my bare flesh. I tried to wriggle free, but he tightened his hold and leaned closer. I could smell a mix of whiskey, cigarettes and pot on his breath.

'You're all the same, you women. Prick teases. You want a guy to tell you how beautiful you are and, when he does, you throw it back in his face.'

I wriggled again. Christ, he was strong. My heart started racing and I felt sick. 'You're the one who approached me.' I tried to keep my voice calm and steady. 'I didn't ask you to come over.'

'But you wanted me to. They all do.'

'Well, *I* didn't.' With all my strength, I sidestepped again, but he was far too strong. I couldn't shake him off. He pushed me towards the side of the house and pinned me against the wall by my wrists.

'Stop trying to fight it. You know you want it.'

'I don't—' He rammed his hand over my mouth before I could utter another word. The back of my head scraped against the rough bricks as I tried to wriggle free.

'Enough talking. It's time for action.' He ground his crotch against me. I closed my eyes, shuddering at the feel. 'You like that, don't you?'

He took his hand off my mouth and immediately thrust his lips against mine, ramming his tongue down my throat. I seized my opportunity and bit down hard. He released his hold with a yelp, then I drew my knee up between his legs. He cried out and dropped to the ground, clutching himself.

'You were right. It *was* time for action,' I yelled, as I legged it into the kitchen and slammed the back door.

'Clare? What's happened?' Ben ran towards me.

'We need to go. Now.' I glanced towards the back door, shaking.

'Who's out there?' Ben grabbed my hand. 'Clare? Who's out there?'

I glanced towards the door again. 'Not now. Where are our

coats?'

'Was it Taz?' Ben's jaw tightened.

'How...?'

'Right. That's it. Is he still out there?'

I nodded slightly. Ben grabbed the door handle.

'Ben. No. Leave it.' But I was too late. He'd already stormed out into the garden.

'Taz? Where are you, you piece of shit?' he yelled.

I ran after him. 'Ben!'

Taz had made it to his feet and was leaning against the same wall to which he'd pinned me moments earlier. He looked at Ben, then leered at me. 'Realised what you're missing and come back for more? No wonder you came looking for me if that's what you've been shagging. A dirty bitch like you needs a *real* man.'

'Don't speak to her like that.' Ben's fists were clenched by his side. My stomach churned. He'd never hit anyone in his life. He'd never win against Taz. The man was huge. And strong.

'Why? What you gonna do about it?' Taz squared his shoulders as he sauntered towards us.

'This.' Ben tried to punch him but Taz pre-empted it and grabbed his arm, bending it backwards. Ben gasped with pain.

'I think you were trying to do this.' Taz smashed his fist into Ben's face. 'That's how real men hit.' He let go of Ben, who fell onto his knees and then forward onto his hands.

'As for you.' Taz spat on the ground beside me. 'You're nothing special. Pretty minging, actually. I felt sorry for you on your own. That's all.' Then he disappeared into the kitchen, slamming the door.

I ran to Ben and put my arm around him. 'You're not minging,' he said. 'You're beautiful.'

'Ben, I don't give a shit about my looks. Are you hurt?' He looked up. I could see in the dim light that his cheek was badly swollen and his eye was already closing.

'We can go now, if you want,' he said. 'You were right. It's a pretty shit party.'

A nervous laugh escaped from me. 'We'll get some ice on this first. Then we can go. Can you stand up?'

He staggered to his feet with my help. 'Clare?'

'Yes?'

'Happy New Year! But the king's still mine, I think.'

'Yes, Ben. The king's still yours.'

Chapter 4

'Are you awake?' Ben poked his head around the door the next morning.

'I am if you have coffee,' I muttered, from under the duvet in my old room. 'I'm still asleep if you don't.'

'After living with you, I don't think I'd dare appear without coffee.'

I reluctantly pulled back the duvet and squinted at him, then sat upright, eyes wide open. 'Jesus, Ben! Your eye!'

'You should see the state of the other guy.'

'I did, and I seem to remember that he got off scot-free.'

Ben handed me the mug and sat down on the edge of the bed. 'It looks worse than it feels, although I do have a banging headache.'

'I'm not surprised. Will you not put some peas on that again?'

'I forgot to put them back in the freezer last night.'

'Ice?'

'I forgot to refill the tray.'

'Eejit.'

Ben tried to smile but winced. 'I suppose you think I was an "eejit" for coming to your defence last night?'

'You were and always will be an eejit, Saint Ben. I like that you tried, but will you just remember that you wouldn't be sporting that shiner if you'd listened to me and we'd left that party when I said.'

'I know.'

'An apology would be grand.'

'I'm sorry, Clare. As always, you were right and I was wrong.'

'I almost believe you,' I said. 'By the way, what made you think it was Taz who'd upset me last night?'

'I've met him before and can't stand the guy. He thinks he's God's gift, but he's really aggressive towards women when he's had a drink.'

'Why didn't you warn me?'

'I thought he'd gone. Pete hates him too. He threw him out before he started throwing up. I didn't know he'd come back until I saw the look on your face and I just knew. Sorry.'

'Not your fault. Now, will you get your fat arse off my bed so I can have a shower?'

Five minutes later, I stood under the steaming water. An image of Taz pinning me to the wall filled my mind, just as it had done when I'd tried to fall asleep. I lightly touched my throbbing, bruised wrists. He'd been so strong. What would I have done if he'd kept his hand on my mouth instead of kissing me? I shuddered. I'd have been powerless to stop him. Fear made my breathing quicken. I closed my eyes as the water flowed over me and tried to push aside the feeling of my head scraping against the wall, the rancid smell of his breath, the strength of his grip.

I delved deep into my memory banks, trying to dredge up a happy memory instead. A meadow. A ruined farmhouse. Strong arms around me, wanting me, protecting me. But there was something else there. Something wrong. Something…

Despite the hot water, goosebumps prickled my entire body. I turned off the shower, grabbed my warm towel off the radiator and quickly rubbed myself dry. What the hell was that? I shook my head. Nothing. It was a delayed shock response to what had happened with Taz. I didn't need to think about it anymore. I got away. I was safe.

Ben's black eye looked even blacker in full daylight. Damn. I knew it wasn't my fault, but I couldn't help feeling guilty. 'Thanks again for last night.' I nudged him playfully as we walked around his local park after lunch. 'You can add "rescuing damsels in distress" to your saintly repertoire. I'll never be getting the king back, at this rate.'

He indicated that we should sit on a bench. I didn't resist. I slumped beside him and sighed. 'Are you okay?' he asked. 'You're not yourself today. I know you don't like New Year, but it seems more than that.'

'That feckin' eejit Taz tried to attack me. Does there need to be more?'

Ben shook his head. 'No. It's just that you seemed to be fine before your shower and you've been jumpy ever since.'

'Have I?'

'Yes. If I didn't know better, I'd have said that either Norman Bates or the closet monster had been waiting for you in the bathroom.'

I shrugged. 'Taz scared me but nothing happened, other than a scraped head and some bruises. Something did happen in the shower, though, and I can't explain it. I was looking at my wrists and there was something, but I don't know what. Like a dream or…' I knew I wasn't making sense. I shrugged again. 'I don't know. I really don't know.'

'I'm not going to push it, but you just need to say the word and I'll be here for you.'

He meant it. I knew that. Sarah had always said he was a great brother – always looking out for her – and he'd done the same for me. I could trust him.

'So, what was *her* excuse for abandoning you this New Year?' I asked, eager to move the subject away from me.

'Lebony?'

'Unless there's another woman you're smitten with that I don't know about. Other than me, of course.'

Ben ran his fingers through his messy, dark hair and laughed. 'Lebony's in Vietnam at the moment and cash is tight.'

'When did you last see her?' As far as I could tell, she spent most of her time abroad on humanitarian projects and hardly any time with Ben. Apparently, her parents both worked for the *Red Cross* so it was in her blood.

'April,' Ben said. 'She came back to the UK for her grandma's 80th birthday.'

'April? Jesus, Ben, what sort of relationship is that?'

He gave me a wry smile. 'I think the common terminology is a long-distance one.'

'Duh. I know that. I just mean that there's long-distance and then there's what you and Lebony have.'

'I know it might seem strange to some people, but the relationship works for both of us. She gets to travel the world doing good, and I get to pursue my hobbies without feeling guilty that I don't give her enough time.'

'What hobbies?'

'Hospital Radio, the *Samaritans*, the *Food Kitchen*.'

'Jesus, Ben. You work for a charity and you spend all your spare time volunteering. Don't you ever do anything for you?'

'Those things *are* for me. I get a lot of satisfaction from them.'

'But you'd still get that sense of satisfaction if you ditched one of them and did something for you.'

'Like what?'

'I don't know. Take up base-jumping or something.'

'And a sensible suggestion would be…?'

I shrugged. 'Going to the gym, reading a book, playing football. Whatever it is that men in their late 30s do.'

'I *do* go to the gym. Can't you tell?' He flexed a non-existent biceps muscle at me. 'And late 30s? You cheeky nowt. I'm the same age as you.'

'And I look so much better for it.'

We sat in companionable silence watching couples and families wander around the park, enjoying the public holiday and the crisp weather.

'I've got something for you,' Ben said.

He passed me the king.

'We agreed you'd keep it,' I said, frowning.

'The deal was that you had to stay till midnight. By the time you'd iced my eye, it was after 12. And after what Taz tried to do to you…' He shook his head. 'He's yours. No argument.'

I took the king and placed him in my coat pocket. 'Thanks.'

'You're welcome.'

My iPhone bleeped a few minutes later. I dug it out of my bag.

✉ From Elise
I know you hate New Year, but Happy New Year anyway! I have the most amazing news. I'm moving in with Stevie! I have you to thank for that. I really do owe you big time. Hope you're having fun whatever you're doing xxx

I grinned. 'I don't believe it. He actually did it!'

'Who did what?'

'Stevie asked Elise to move in with him.'

'As in, a lodger?'

'No. As in, his live-in girlfriend.'

'Really? I didn't know they were seeing each other.'

'They weren't.'

Ben frowned. 'I'm all for a bit of romance, but how do you suddenly go from not dating to living together?'

'It's a long story. Maybe I'll tell you one day.'

'And since when did you and Elise become such good friends? You seemed really pally at Sarah's wedding.'

'Also a long story, and maybe I'll tell you that one day too, but I can't just yet so don't you be asking me.'

Ben shrugged. 'I've no idea what's going on, but that's the story of my life.'

I lightly punched him on the arm, then winced as my wrists hurt. 'Poor baby. Let's walk again. I'm getting piles sitting here.'

'Attractive,' Ben said.

'You know I'm irresistible to all men, women and small furry animals,' I quipped.

The sun – ahead of us and low in the sky – warmed my face as we walked along the River Aire. Despite the traumatic start, the walk and company were doing me good and the news from Elise had really made my day. The woman deserved a decent break. On top of my pep talk with Elise, I'd collared Stevie at Sarah's wedding and suggested that Elise needed a 'grand gesture' to show he was serious about her. I'm not sure what I had in mind, but they didn't come much more grand than moving in together. I looked forward to hearing the full details.

I wondered how Sarah would react, though. To my knowledge, she had no idea that Elise was pregnant or in love with Stevie, so that was going to be a shock when she got back from honeymoon. The fact that I – Elise's former archenemy – knew both things already wasn't going to go down well at all. I'd seen her glance across at us during the wedding with a look of confusion on her face, as if not able to comprehend how we'd turned from enemies into friends. For my part, I'd grown up. For Elise's, she needed someone, and I happened to be the someone who discovered her secret and promised to keep it. That hadn't been difficult. After all, I was better than anyone at keeping secrets.

Chapter 5

January the second fell on a Thursday, so most of my team had taken that day and Friday as holidays, excited at the prospect of a five-day weekend so soon after the Christmas break. Had I? Bollocks to that. Why prolong the torture of New Year into yet another day and let it eke into your weekend too? I was up and working on my laptop by 6.30am, thankful for a return to normality. Working was my domain, my comfort zone, the place where I was completely in control. Eejits like Taz couldn't get me at work. And I couldn't think about them, either. I was far too busy and important.

I was surprised when my iPhone rang at about 7.30 and my manager's name flashed up on the screen.

'Paul? I thought you weren't working today.' I stood up and wandered over to the full-length window and looked out over Leeds city centre. The view from the 14th floor of my rented apartment in *Orion Point* was pretty spectacular. I wasn't sure if I liked it best in darkness, like now, with twinkling lights, or in bright sunshine when I could see for miles.

'I'm not meant to be, but we've got a problem. I need you to clear your diary next week.' I loved that Paul was always straight to the point; none of the pointless chitchat that so many of my colleagues seemed to favour.

'Should be possible. Why?'

'What about this weekend?'

I turned away from the window, a sinking feeling in my stomach. 'No plans yet.'

'Good. Fabrian phoned. His dad died yesterday.' Fabrian was my European equivalent, who'd announced at our last team meeting that his dad had terminal cancer and would be lucky to make it to Easter.

'Poor Fabrian. You want me to cover for him?' I hoped Paul would say a simple 'yes', but I knew that he'd have waited until Monday to have that conversation, which meant bad news was on the horizon. Please don't let him say…

'You need to go to Ireland. Specifically, Cork.'

'No, Paul! Not Cork. Can't Rick do it?' Rick was my equivalent in the South.

'He's skiing.'

Bollocks! 'Surely there's someone else?' I sat down heavily at the dining table before my shaking legs gave way.

'There's nobody else, Clare. It needs to be you.'

'Can't it wait until Rick's back? He's covered for Fabrian before.'

'No. You know this is a key account and we've been teetering close to losing it. There's no way this meeting is getting delayed. You have to go.'

Cork. Of all the bloody places in Europe where we had clients, why the hell did Fabrian have to have meetings next week in Cork? I could have happily jetted off to Paris, Barcelona or Rotterdam. But Cork?

I closed my eyes and took a deep breath. I knew from the tone of Paul's voice that if I refused, he'd be issuing me with my P45. 'When will I need to go?'

'Saturday. There's a charity ball and we're hosting a table for them. You'll have Sunday to yourself. Maybe you can catch up with some family if you've still got any there.'

Family? Yeah, right. 'When can I fly back?'

'Fabrian had two days of meetings scheduled so I'd say Wednesday afternoon or evening, in case anything runs over. You can always work from the hotel if you finish sooner.'

'Okay.'

'We're counting on you, Clare. Some serious bridge-building is needed and I know you'll be perfect for the job. Margaret's working today so I'll get her to email you the details and sort out your tickets. Let me know how it goes.'

I bid him goodbye and ended the call. Pushing my laptop out of the way, I slumped forward and lay my head on the table. Jesus. Cork? Why me? Could this shitty New Year get any worse?

I felt sick during the train journey from Leeds to Manchester on the Saturday morning. I felt even worse during the flight from Manchester to Cork. I must have looked it too, as the old lady in the seat next to me reached into the storage pouch, handed me a sick bag and asked me if it was my first time flying.

'No. It's not the flight. I love planes,' I said. 'I just don't love the thought of who lives at the other end.'

'Oh. Boyfriend trouble?' Her eyes widened with curiosity. She had one of those kind faces: the sort of trustworthy person with whom you instantly felt at ease. She reminded me of Sarah's auntie Kay.

'Parent trouble,' I admitted. 'They threw me out when I was 16 and we haven't been in touch since.'

'So this will be the first time you've seen them in, what, a decade?'

I smiled. 'Thanks for the compliment, but it's been about 17 years.'

'You have a very youthful face, but your eyes tell of a greater maturity than your years.' She tilted her head to one side and stared at me thoughtfully. 'Yes, you've known some hard times, so you have.'

I swallowed on the lump in my throat and coughed. 'It was a long time ago. Anyway, I'm being an eejit because I'm not even going to see them. I'm here for business and I've got no intention of visiting them. Ever.'

The woman was silent for at least 10 minutes. I kicked myself for saying too much. She was probably only being friendly. She didn't need to know my life story. This was more than I'd ever shared with Sarah, so why open up to a stranger on a plane? Seriously, Clare, learn when to shut up!

'My parents threw me out too,' she said, eventually. 'I was 16, just like you.'

Oh. I hadn't screwed it up, after all. 'Really? Why?'

'I fell for a Protestant. You'd think I'd fallen for Hitler, the way they carried on.'

'Did you ever see them again?'

She shook her head. 'My da was killed in a fire at the factory where he worked 10 years later. I went to his funeral, but Ma gave out big time, so she did. I think she'd gone a bit funny in the head because she blamed me for the accident. Seems it was the onset of Alzheimer's. I took pity and tried to see her, but the nurses said I distressed her so I stayed away.'

'What about your man? Your Protestant man?'

'Oh, he's grand. We're still together. Four children, seven grandchildren and one great-grandbaby. I won't be having any regrets about him, but I do wish I'd confronted my da before he died, to understand why he cut me off without even listening to me. We all have to face our past sooner or later. This trip could be too soon for you, but maybe later?'

I shook my head vigorously. 'No chance. My family are dead to me. Sorry if that sounds harsh.'

'Throwing you out was harsh. But people can change. Sometimes.'

The captain announced our approach to Cork airport. We fastened our seat belts and prepared to land. People change? Not my parents. But was she right about facing my past? I shivered and pulled my jacket more tightly across my body. Perhaps. But not this weekend. The incident with Taz had been bad enough, without facing my past as well.

The hotel in Cork was nice. Comfortable. Warm. The charity ball that evening couldn't have gone better. I'd cast aside all thoughts of Ma and Da, and schmoozed like a champion. Paul had been right: I *was* the best person for the job. Even if Rick had been available, he wouldn't have had them eating out of his palm the way I had. Monday and Tuesday weren't going to be any problem. I'd handled clients who were far more disgruntled in the past. So why couldn't I sleep? I turned over and looked at the digital alarm by the bed: 03.17. Bollocks.

I peeled back the duvet and padded over to the drinks tray. Coffee wasn't going to help me sleep. Hot chocolate instead? I flicked the kettle on, then pulled on the fluffy hotel dressing gown.

Clutching my hot chocolate a few minutes later, I stood by the window and looked out at the lights of Cork reflecting in the River Lee. Very pretty. A stark contrast to the ugly thoughts in my head.

By the time I'd finished my drink, I knew how I was going to spend my Sunday. Ireland mainly held bad memories for me, but there was one place that held only good ones and I felt compelled to pay it a visit.

The first thing that struck me as I drove down the familiar roads towards Ballykielty was that absolutely nothing had changed. Trees were bushier, hedges were thicker, but there were no new housing estates or businesses to be seen. It was like entering the place where time stood still. The exterior of the village pub had changed colour from pale blue to cream, but the handful of shops and businesses looked the same.

I slowly drove through the village, tutting with disbelief at the familiarity of it all, then turned around and doubled back slowly. As I gazed out the windscreen, I realised I was drawing curious glances. I hit the accelerator, cursing my stupidity. I hadn't meant to actually drive into the village. What if someone had recognised me? I shook my head. There was no way they would, after all these years. To them, I'd just be a blonde in a hire car who'd got lost. Hopefully.

I left the village, then took a right at the crossroads instead of going straight over towards Cork. A few hundred yards later, I pulled into the entrance to Farmer Brady's field and got out of the car. My hands were shaking so much that it took several attempts to unlatch the gate. I had to skirt around three fields and through a copse before I came to it.

Looking at the dilapidated building in the middle of the meadow, I felt like a teenager again. A tree had sprouted out of the chimney and there were a few more loose piles of stones around the building, where it had crumbled, but it was still *our* place. Butterflies swarmed in my stomach as I stepped through the doorway. Sunlight filtered through the broken roof tiles creating dust bunnies and an ethereal sense. I half-expected Daran to tap me on the shoulder, then swing me around in a circle while showering me with kisses, like he used to. I stood for a few minutes with my eyes closed, taking it all in, my right hand wrapped tightly around the king in my coat pocket – trying to draw strength for this challenge that I'd set myself to acknowledge the past.

Opening my eyes, I took a deep breath, then brushed away some grass and mud, and sat down on the pile of stones that Daran had sat on when he first confessed his love for me. My eyes focused on something light-coloured in the corner of the room. It couldn't be… I stood up again and cautiously picked my way across stones and twigs to the corner of the room and tugged at the piece of material. It was dirty and damp, but it was definitely *our* blanket. I closed my eyes, smiling, remembering Daran's gentle touch.

Suddenly, a shiver ran through me, and a flash of something sped across my mind. I dropped the blanket, gasping for breath. What the hell was *that*? My wrists throbbed and my head thumped. What was happening to me?

I stumbled back across to the stones and sat down heavily, as a film of sweat covered my body. My eyes darted around the farmhouse; *our* farmhouse. And I knew at that moment that it hadn't been only ours, and that the memories there weren't all happy ones. But what…?

'So the rumours were true. You *are* back.'

I leapt up off the stones. Shit! 'Da?'

Chapter 6
Nineteen Years Earlier

'We have a very special guest for Mass this morning,' Father Doherty announced to the congregation. 'Daran McInnery is from Wicklow and has been studying in Cork. He's interested in becoming a priest and has asked to spend some time shadowing me whilst God and he decide if this is the right path for him. Daran, do you want to say a few words? They're a friendly lot. I'm sure they'll make you feel very welcome. Step up here, why don't you?'

I stopped playing with my long, blonde plaits and reluctantly looked up. I expected to see yet another old man with an expanding waist and diminishing hair. I certainly didn't expect to see a man in his early 20s with a full head of dark hair, a slim physique and a dazzling smile. I became aware of lots of murmuring and giggling in the congregation. I leaned over to my best friend, Orla Brennan, and whispered in her ear, 'I'll bet you anything you like that the Black Widow will be the first to make sure he feels welcome. Very, *very* welcome.' I glanced across at Mrs Shaughnessy. Widowed when she was only 21 and never remarried, she had a reputation as a man-eater. All the men in the village seemed to fancy her. Not surprising. With her shiny, blonde hair and flawless, youthful complexion, she looked more like a woman in her late 20s, although she was actually 40. I knew that because she lived opposite us and there'd been a 'Happy 40th Birthday' banner across her window a few months ago. I felt a bit guilty for giving her a nickname because she was actually really nice to me, but Ballykielty wasn't exactly the most exciting of places. Orla and I had to get our kicks somewhere.

Orla giggled, a little too loudly. A sharp dig in my back made me yelp. I didn't dare turn around and look at Da in the pew behind me. I didn't need to. I'd seen that disgusted expression in his dark eyes so many times that it was etched on my mind forever. I kept my eyes forward. Father Doherty gave me a stern look, but Daran McInnery just smiled.

And that dazzling smile was what started it.

Da commented that he'd never seen me so eager to go to Mass and perhaps I wasn't going to turn into a huge disappointment, after all. Well, with someone like Daran McInnery to gaze upon, who wouldn't want to go? For the first time ever, I felt captivated by the words of the Scriptures. Watching him speak with such passion made my heart beat faster. I hung onto every single word he uttered. Even that eejit Jamie Doyle, from two years above me at school, couldn't break my concentration, despite tugging on my plaits and trying to tickle my ribs with his grubby, scabby hands.

In mid-September, the village held a céilí in honour of Father Doherty's 30th year with our parish. Despite it being Father Doherty's event, Daran McInnery was the centre of attention, with a constant queue of fawning women begging him to dance. I'd been right about the Black Widow; she was by his side constantly. Medusa herself would have been proud of the stony stares she gave to any woman with whom he danced.

I leaned against the wall of the barn, playing with a loose thread on the hem of my dark-purple floral dress, kicking at some loose straw with my purple canvas pumps, and watching. Always watching.

After a hissed lecture from Da on being a 'miserable, sulky little brat' who had better 'stop bringing shame to this family and accept the next invitation to dance', I was forced into dancing with that gobshite Jamie Doyle. His breath smelled of alcohol and he kept placing his hand on my backside instead of my waist, then trying to make out he hadn't realised. Yeah, right. And he kept standing on my feet with his huge size-12s. God alone knew why, but my da seemed to think the creepy git was potential husband material for my sister, Nia, or me. Yuck. Over my dead body. Nia seemed to like him, though. I'd have thought that being in the same class as him would have put her right off. My other sister, Aisling, was lucky, as Da considered Jamie Doyle far too young for her. I wished, not for the first time, that I were much older. Closer to Daran McInnery's age, perhaps.

I danced with a couple of boys from my class, and with my da and my brothers, simply to avoid questions, but I couldn't take my eyes off Father-to-be McInnery. It seemed to me as though he was watching me too. Every time I danced, I could feel his eyes on me. And I liked it. A lot.

'Are you enjoying yourself, Father?' I asked, as I passed him on the way to dance with one of my brothers.

'That I am,' he responded, those green eyes burning into mine. 'But I'd be enjoying myself even more if you'd do me the honour of the next dance, Miss O'Connell.'

I smiled. Yes! Success! 'I might be free, Father.'

'I'm not a priest, yet, Clare. It's Daran.'

'Then I might be free, *Daran*.'

I might have only just turned 14, but I felt more like an 18-year-old. I was an early developer physically, as well as being very mature for my age. My sisters, Aisling and Nia, were six and two years older than me respectively, and my twin brothers, Keenan and Éamonn, were four years older. They were all devout Catholics, very sensible and very mature. Actually, I wasn't so sure about Aisling. She'd managed to escape to university in Limerick and – having spotted her unpacking some very sexy matching underwear when she'd come home for the holidays – I liked to imagine that she drank alcohol and danced topless while she was there and only pretended to be nun-like when she visited Ballykielty to keep the peace with Da.

I tried to be more like my siblings to please my parents, as being constantly scolded was no way to live, but I couldn't help it; there was an extroverted, fun-loving, boisterous woman inside me who refused to conform. I also wasn't convinced by the whole church thing, especially as Ma, Da and my siblings seemed to think Catholicism was code for 'no fun'. Daran McInnery seemed like fun, though, and I was very aware that I'd developed a huge crush on him – my first serious, stomach-flopping, heart-racing crush. It was killing me to play it cool.

'Would you be free for that dance now?' he asked, three dances later. 'Or are you too much in demand?'

'I'm hugely in demand, especially with that eejit Jamie Doyle, but I think you've waited long enough.' I took his hand and a tingle ran through my body at his warm touch. It was a very fast dance. We were both panting when we finished. He grabbed us some juice, then I followed him outside for some fresh air.

'What are you planning to do when you finish school next year?' he asked, after we'd gulped our drinks down and caught our breath. 'Will you be going to university?'

'University?'

'You must be in your Leaving Cert year, are you not?'

Not quite. I chose my words carefully. 'I'm studying hard. I'd like to be a midwife eventually. Babies are so cute and the thought of being the one who helps bring so many of them into the world must be such a blessing and so rewarding.'

'That's a grand vocation to want,' he said.

'My da doesn't think so.'

'Why not?'

'He believes a woman's place is in the home, being a good Catholic wife and producing a baby every two years or so, just like my ma.'

'I'm sure he only wants what's best for you.'

'Da only ever wants what's best for him and best for God.'

'Perhaps what's best for God is best for you too.'

I stood up and indicated that he should walk with me while I pondered his statement. 'I want to challenge you on that, but I can't think of an example of something that has displeased me but would have pleased God, so perhaps I've been unfair on Him.'

Daran laughed. 'Unfair on your da or unfair on God?'

I smiled. 'Both. I think. Are you from a large family, Father?'

'The oldest of eight. My father died young so I spent a lot of time helping my mother with my brothers and sisters.'

'I'm sorry about your da. That must have been hard.'

'It was, but my siblings were a great distraction.'

'Father Doherty said you're only looking into the priesthood.'

He nodded. 'I planned to become a religion teacher so I studied Religions and Global Diversity in Cork, then did a HDip in Education. I could have started teaching this term, but I couldn't help feeling that God had another path in mind for me, perhaps as a priest or an overseas missionary. The priesthood's a huge commitment. My priest in Cork is a good friend of Father Doherty. He arranged for me to spend some time with him to explore whether the priesthood is right for me. So here I am, exploring away, trying to work out what I want to do with my life.'

I stopped at a bench and indicated that he should sit beside me. The moon lit his silhouette. He looked like a model rather than a priest, and I longed to reach across and touch the curl of hair that kept blowing across his forehead and into his eyes. I sat on my hands. 'If you became a priest, you wouldn't be able to have a family of your own. Wouldn't you miss that?'

'A person can't miss something he's never had.'

'Fair point, but if you helped your ma, and you're the oldest of eight, you must know what it's like to soothe a baby and read a bedtime story to a toddler. Did you never want those things for yourself?'

'Right now, I want God in my life more than I want those things. Or at least I think I do. That's why I'm not rushing into any decisions. If I do join the priesthood, I'll be taking a solemn vow of celibacy and that's how my life will be.'

'Doesn't your mind ever wander and think about what it would be like to kiss someone and to press your body against theirs and make babies?'

I heard him gulp, but I couldn't see enough of his face in the darkness to discern his reaction. His shaky words conveyed his emotions, though. 'Emm… Well, er, Clare. It's like this… A priest… Well, it's just that… Okay, I sometimes *think* about it. Thinking is different from acting on… er… carnal desires. I… er… I think we'd better go back inside. I've cooled down now.'

How I resisted the urge not to reach up and kiss him at that moment, I'll never know.

Chapter 7

Present Day

'What in the name of God are you doing here, Clare?' Da growled. 'I thought we'd made it clear that you were *never* to come back.'

I cursed my stupidity. Damn stranger-hating village. Should have known I'd be spotted. Be brave. Be confident. You're not 16 anymore. You can handle him. 'It's great to see you too, Da,' I said, squaring up to him and standing tall. He looked old. And grey. And tired. I could take him.

But his strong, sharp voice still had the power to make me tremble. 'What do you want, girl? Why are you back?'

'I'm in Cork on business.'

'Business? Is that what you call it these days?'

My stomach twisted at the clear insinuation in his words. At least he'd stopped short of calling me the hurtful names he'd used 17 years earlier. Unable to think of a clever quip, I just stared at him and hoped he couldn't see me shaking.

'I hope you're not here to seek forgiveness,' he snarled. 'What I said back then still stands. You're dead to me, Clare. And to the rest of your family. You won't be welcome here again. Ever.'

He stared at me as if expecting a challenge. For years I'd dreamed of what I'd say to him if our paths crossed again. The scenes in my mind had ranged from a Harry Potter-and-Lord Voldemort-style stand-off with fireworks and demons (ending with me striking him down, of course), right through to an emotional reunion where he begged for my forgiveness and welcomed me back into the fold with open arms, and pretty much everything in between. But none of my scenes involved me standing in the ruined farmhouse, shaking like a small child who'd just seen the closet monster, completely dumbstruck.

'I expect you'll be leaving as soon as you've finished your trip down memory lane?'

I nodded.

'Good. Don't be coming back.'

'I won't.'

He turned to go, then stopped in the doorway. I shivered as he turned his dark eyes on me. 'He never loved you, you know. He just used you.'

'Daran?' My heart dropped into my stomach as I whispered the word.

Even in the gloom, I could see his face redden at the mention of Daran's name. 'Some priest in training he was. He was getting up close and personal with most of the parishioners. You just happened to be the youngest and stupidest.' Then he turned and left.

I sank to the floor. Daran sleeping around? No. He couldn't have. He wouldn't have. It was just Da striking out. Again. And it had worked. Seventeen years on and he still had power over me. Bastard.

Chapter 8

Seventeen-and-a-Half Years Earlier

After the céilí, I made it my mission to introduce Daran to the stunning countryside around our village. Well, someone had to. He seemed keen to accept my offer. As we walked across the fields and through the woodland, I'd chat to him about his family and his life in Wicklow. I'd also talk about my family, how Ma hated me, how I was always in trouble with Da, and how I felt I didn't fit in with any of their expectations of what a good Catholic girl should be. I also confessed that I was a Junior Certificate student, not Leaving Certificate. Apparently, he'd thought I was the second-youngest O'Connell and that Nia was my younger sister. Easy mistake. I'd always looked a lot older than her.

I knew it was cruel, given the career choice he was exploring, but I repeatedly painted a picture of what family life should be like – drawn from books and TV, rather than what I personally experienced from my own dysfunctional family – and what the love of a good woman, instead of just the love of God, might feel like. He laughed at first, but then he started to open up and talk about the family he'd dreamed of having before he'd started to think seriously about the priesthood.

Our favourite place on our walks was a ruined farmhouse in the middle of a meadow. It was so peaceful and so beautiful, with woodland on three sides and open fields on the fourth. Butterflies danced amongst wild flowers and birds chirped in the trees. I liked to imagine it was our home, although I didn't dare mention it to Daran in case I scared him off. I knew the boundaries. In all our conversations about family, I took care never to share my secret that he was the man who featured in my dreams.

He only ever asked me about boys once, roughly a year after the céilí. It was late September, a little after my 15th birthday, and we'd spent a few days basking in an Indian summer. Lying in the meadow outside our farmhouse, we'd been spotting shapes in the fluffy clouds that bounced across the cornflower sky.

'Why do you spend all your spare time with me, Clare?' He turned onto his side to face me. 'Do you not have a special boy in the village? Jamie Doyle, perhaps? He seems pretty keen on you.'

'Jamie Doyle's an eejit. He's not for me.' I shuddered at the thought, picturing his greasy, red hair and the way he always seemed to have white foam in the corners of his mouth as if he'd contracted rabies.

'He's not for you, is he not? Is there someone else who holds your heart, then?'

I turned onto my side too and gazed into his eyes. 'Yes, there is. There's someone who holds my heart so tightly that I don't think it could ever, or would ever, want to love anyone else.'

His eyes widened. 'And does he feel the same way about you?'

'I think he does, but he's torn because he has another love too. I keep trying to convince him there's space for us both in his life, but he's not ready to accept that. Not yet anyway.'

'Maybe he just needs time.'

'That's what I'm hoping.'

Daran turned onto his back again, staring at the sky. I hoped I hadn't said too much, but surely he'd have left if I had. I turned over and lay on my back again too. As I came to rest, my hand lightly touched his. He didn't pull away. We lay there in silence, hands touching, while my heart thumped faster and faster.

One Saturday afternoon towards the end of January, thick snow encased the meadow and weighed down the branches of the trees to the point where many had broken under the pressure. My heart leapt as I spotted footprints in the deep snow leading up to the farmhouse. Daran was early. Grand. I grinned as I stepped easily into his larger prints and danced across them, my breath hanging in the cold winter air.

'Daran?' I called as I approached the entrance. No answer. 'Daran?' I hesitated for a moment. What if the footprints weren't his? What if someone else had found our farmhouse? 'Daran? Is that you?'

'Yes,' came a hoarse whisper. 'I'm here.'

'Thank the Lord!' I walked through the doorway. 'I was starting to think that… Oh, sweet Jesus, what is it?' I ran across to him. He was slumped on a pile of rocks with his head in his hands. He looked up. His eyes were red and tears streaked his face. 'Daran? Are you sick?'

'I don't know what to do, Clare. I'm so confused.'

'Can I help?'

He shook his head. 'You're the problem.'

'Me. What have *I* done?'

'You've been you. Beautiful, funny, intelligent you.' He rubbed his cheeks and looked into my eyes. 'I can't stop thinking about you, Clare. I love you so much and every fibre of my body, mind and soul wants to be with you. I know it's wrong, yet it feels so right.'

'That's because it *is* right.' I knelt down beside him on the cold floor, grabbed his icy hands and kissed them.

He moaned softly at the gentle touch of my lips. 'You're too young.'

'I'm nearly 16. And I'm very mature for my age. You know I

am, Daran.'

'I know, but nearly 16 means you're still only 15, Clare. You may not look or act like it but, technically, you're still a child and I'm eight years your senior. I'm a qualified teacher who's considering becoming a priest. Neither of those scenarios allows for me falling in love with a 15-year-old. I made a vow to God to serve Him, whichever career path I took.'

'You can still serve God and be with me.'

'But I couldn't be a priest.'

I kissed his hands again. 'You could do missionary work. That was one of your options, wasn't it? I could go with you. I know it's hard for you, but it's hard for me too. I love you too, Daran. I want to be with you forever. I want to kiss you and hold you and make babies with you.'

He let out a shaky sigh. 'I can't believe I'm going to say this, but I think I want all those things too. With you. Which means I can't become a priest. I didn't expect…'

'You didn't expect to fall in love, but it happened. We can't control who we fall for.'

'But your age…'

I placed my fingers across his mouth. 'My age is just a number. I'll be 16 on September the fifth. Not that I'm saying we need to rush into anything if you don't want to. I'm telling you because it means I'm officially an adult in September.'

He shook his head. 'Not in Ireland. The age of consent here is 17.'

'Perhaps, but we can pretend we're in England or somewhere else in Europe. Did you know that the age of consent in Spain is 13? And it's 14 or 15 in a stack of other European countries.'

Daran smiled despite his clear angst. 'You've done your research.'

'I had to know what I was up against – 15, 16, 17 – they're just numbers, and they mean different things in different countries, so don't start thinking we'd be doing something wrong because I'm not too young in so many places. Places that God created. All those countries class me as an adult.'

He stroked my cheek. I closed my eyes as I trembled at his touch.

'What about God?'

'It's not me or Him, you know. You can have us both in your life. He won't abandon you for choosing me instead of the priesthood, Daran. He'll bless you for choosing love instead.'

Daran wiped his eyes. 'You make it sound so simple.'

'It is! You love me. I love you. You love God. That's all there is to it. We can make this work, Daran. We really can. Besides, if He really were calling you to be a priest, you wouldn't have spent two years living in Ballykielty exploring it, would you? You'd have joined the seminary and started your studies.' I stroked his face and he leaned into my hand with his eyes closed. He looked so serene, so perfect, that I couldn't help myself. I leaned forward and gently kissed his lips. His mouth parted slightly as though he were about to speak, but no words came out. I expected him to pull away, but he didn't move. I kissed him again and again until he started to kiss back, gently at first, then more urgently. He entwined his fingers in my long, loose hair as he kissed my lips, then my neck, then back to my lips again.

Finally, he pulled away. 'I'm sorry, Clare. I shouldn't have done that.'

'You should.'

'No. I shouldn't. Because my thoughts were taking me much further than a kiss and I can't allow them to do that. Not yet. I'll walk you back to the village. Now.'

I cried myself to sleep that night, although the words 'not yet' gave me hope that, one day, he'd change his mind. And I'd be waiting for him.

Three agonising days passed with no word from Daran. I went to our farmhouse every evening and waited for hours. On the fourth evening, he appeared in the doorway, unshaven, dark bags under his eyes.

'I've barely slept,' he said. 'I thought it would be easier if I stayed away from you.'

I remained slumped on the pile of stones, terrified that he'd come to end it before it had even started. 'Easier for whom? You or me?'

He shrugged. 'I don't really know.'

'Has it been easy for you? Because it certainly hasn't been easy for me waiting here for you night after night, not able to come round to your house in case anyone sees me, worried that something might have happened to you.'

'Something *has* happened to me. I've made a decision. I finally know what I want to do with my life.'

My heart sank. He'd chosen the priesthood. 'You're leaving, aren't you?'

Daran took a few steps towards me. 'Why would I go and do something stupid like that when all I want to do is be with you?'

In a fraction of a second, I was in his arms, the place I'd dreamed of being since the day he'd been introduced to our congregation. As he kissed me and ran his hands through my hair and down my back, I knew he'd been worth the wait.

Chapter 9

Present Day

'How were the meetings?' Ben heaved my case into the boot of his old Focus early on Wednesday evening.

'Grand, thanks.'

He slammed the boot shut. 'Did you charm the pants off them?'

'Of course.'

We got into the car and belted up.

'So you've saved the day?' Ben asked.

'They're still a client.'

'You might want to tone down the enthusiasm a bit.'

I gave him a half smile. 'Sorry, Ben. It's been a tough trip.'

'Because it involved going back to Cork?'

'No. It's because Fabrian had stupidly…' I sighed. I couldn't lie to Ben. 'Yes. Because it involved going back to Cork.'

Ben started the engine. 'Remember I'm here if you ever want to talk about it.'

'I know. I appreciate it.'

He manoeuvred his car out of Leeds train station. 'I'm going away in the morning, Irish. I won't be back till the end of next week.'

'Oh.' I felt quite uncomfortable at the thought of Ben not being around for a curry and a gossip. 'Last-minute holiday?'

He laughed. 'I wish. Our charity has set up an office in Birmingham and I've been asked to train the new recruits and help them plan their first big fundraiser.'

'You won't be back for the weekend?'

'Unfortunately not. I need to work then too. You can phone me if you want to talk, though.'

'Seriously, Ben, I'm just grand. You have great craic on your little jolly and don't you be worrying about me.'

'Going to work in Birmingham is hardly a jolly.'

'You know what I mean. I don't need to talk about New Year or Ireland, or anything else. I really don't. Stop raising your eyebrows at me. I'm grand. Honest. What is this obsession with people wanting to talk all the time? Sometimes, things just need to be left alone.'

'Okay. Message coming through loud and clear.'

I stared out of the window in silence for the rest of the journey. If I'd opened my mouth to speak, I might have begged him to stay because, for the first time ever, I felt as if I might actually need to talk to someone about my past. And if I started talking about it, I might never stop.

I abandoned my suitcase by the door of my apartment, headed straight for the fridge and poured myself a glass of wine. A very large one.

Unlocking the patio door, I stepped out onto the balcony and sat down, breathing in the icy night air. The cold metal of the chair under my legs made me shiver, but I needed to be outside. I hoped the wind and the cold might help clear the fog in my head.

I took a glug of my wine, then another. What a hideous start to the new year. Could anything else go wrong? I stared out at the cityscape and tried to focus on the sounds of a distant siren, honking horns, laughter, music; anything but the confrontation with Da, his suggestion about Daran's infidelity, and whatever the hell had happened in the farmhouse right before he'd appeared.

I'd thrown myself into preparing for my meetings when I'd got back to the hotel on Sunday and had worked solidly since then. But now, back in the quiet of my apartment, the questions wouldn't go away. Could Daran really have slept around or had Da just said that to torment me? I wouldn't put anything past him.

A knock on the door made me jump. I reluctantly wandered back into the lounge. 'Who is it?'

'Lydia from next door. I've got a recorded-delivery envelope for you.'

Bollocks. I couldn't face anyone. 'I'm just out of the shower. Will you leave it outside and I'll get it in a few minutes?'

'Are you sure? I can wait until you're decent.'

'I'm sure. Thanks for taking it in.'

I stared out the peephole. When I was confident she'd gone, I yanked my door open, grabbed the envelope and quickly shut it again. I looked at the large, brown, cardboard envelope in my hands. Work. How odd. They'd never sent me anything by recorded delivery before. I wandered into the lounge and ripped open the envelope. Inside was another envelope but a paper one this time, with my name and the London head-office address typed on it. I couldn't make out the postmark. I opened the paper envelope and removed a stiff sheet of A4 cream paper with a fancy letterhead on it and the address of a solicitor's in Truro. My stomach churned. There could only be one reason why that particular solicitor's firm would be contacting me.

Dear Ms O'Connell

We've tried to contact you on several occasions by telephone but have been unable to track down a correct number for you and must therefore write instead.

At Bowson, Higgs & Crane, we represent the estate of Mrs Nuala Sheedy, who passed away on 18th October. St Joseph's Catholic Church in Truro has been the beneficiary of Mrs Sheedy's personal effects and finances. However, Mrs Sheedy requested that this letter be passed on to you, her great-niece.

We are unaware of the contents of the letter. However, if we can be of further assistance to you, please do not hesitate to contact the office and ask for me, quoting Mrs Sheedy's name.

Yours sincerely
Angela Crane

I was right. So, the old bat was dead. How did I feel about that? Like I needed a drink! I poured another large glass of wine, then leaned against the fridge, sipping on it. What was in the letter? A plea for forgiveness, perhaps?

Setting my glass down on the worktop, I retrieved Great-Aunt Nuala's letter from the bottom of the solicitor's envelope. A drawing of some Rosary beads draped over a Bible filled the bottom-left corner of the small, peach envelope. How very Nuala. I stared at the envelope. Could I be arsed? Not really. 'Do you know what, Great-Aunt Nuala, I don't want to hear it. Not tonight. Not after what Da said about Daran. You can wait until tomorrow. You're already dead so what difference does it make? It's been a long few days. I'm off to my bed.'

I retrieved my suitcase, tossed the letter onto the coffee table as I walked through the lounge area to my bedroom, unpacked and got ready for bed.

But sleep wouldn't come. Every time I closed my eyes, I

pictured that damned peach envelope and Great-Aunt Nuala's immaculate script. What if it wasn't what I expected? 'For feck's sake,' I cried, hurling back the duvet and storming into the lounge to get the letter.

I jumped back into bed and ripped open the envelope.

12th June

Dear Clare,

I'm dying. I have terminal leukaemia. The doctors have given me until next spring, at a push. I think Christmas is more realistic, but I don't mind. I'm 76 and more than ready to meet both the Lord and my husband, who joined Him far too early.

As you'd probably expect, I've spent a lot of time in Confession, preparing for the end. I have a lot to confess and my priest, Father Finnegan, has been very generous with his penance. I feel blessed and forgiven for all but my greatest sin. I have confessed this to Father Finnegan, but I cannot meet the Lord without confessing to you.

Reaching the end of the page, I slumped back against the pillow. 'Exactly as predicted. Please forgive me, Clare, for I have sinned, but only because you sinned first.' I ran my fingers through my bob. 'I'm a bloody eejit for expecting anything else.'

I sighed and reluctantly turned over the page, bracing myself for a load of religious babblings.

This is going to come as a huge shock to you and I can do nothing to soften the blow: Shannon did not die. It was a lie.

I sat upright, gasping for breath. WTF? I reread the sentence again and again, my heart beating so fast, I thought it might burst. She wasn't dead? What? How? I rubbed my eyes and blinked a few times before reading the rest.

> She was adopted as planned, but by a different family from the one you met, so you could never trace them if you ever had doubts about her 'death'. It was your father's idea, but I am equally to blame, as I willingly played my part, believing I was doing the right thing. You were so young, Clare, and you'd committed such a cardinal sin against God and the Holy Catholic Church, but Father Finnegan – and old age – has helped me realise that the future of your baby was not my choice, or your father's choice, to make. It should have been your decision, despite your youth. I now accept that we were very wrong to force you into giving up baby Shannon. We were even more wrong to tell you that she had died, poor little mite.
>
> I don't expect your forgiveness. I would find it hard to forgive anyone who had done such a wicked thing to me. I do, however, hope to belatedly repair the damage we've done. Your father knows nothing of these actions. I lost touch with my nephew five years ago when I was first diagnosed with this disease, confessed my sins and realised the error of my ways. I enclose a photo and all the details I know, just in case you wish to track her down. I believe Shannon would have turned 16 today. Perhaps she is ready to meet her birth mother? Whatever you decide, may God be with you.
>
> I have one more confession. Daran McInnery wrote

to you many, many times via your priest, Father Doherty. At my insistence, he destroyed the letters. Your sister Aisling also tried to make contact. I returned her letters, unopened. I know now that I had no right to do either of these things, not that this will bring you any comfort.

I go to my Maker with my conscience at peace now and hope that one day you can perhaps understand, even if you can't forgive. At the time, I genuinely did believe it was for best for you, Clare, but I realise now that your father and I were thinking of ourselves, not what was right for you and your daughter.

God bless you on your journey, should you wish to find young Shannon.

Great-Aunt Nuala

I dropped the letter. Jesus Christ! She's alive? After all these years, Shannon's alive? They lied to me? Why would they lie? I'd agreed to the adoption. My hands shook and my heart raced as I snatched up the letter again and scanned it for an answer – '… so you could never trace them'. What difference would it make if I had? I closed my eyes tightly and muttered, 'Same as keeping her in the first place. Same reason I was banished to Cornwall. Disgrace to the family. Damn them. Damn them all. She was *my* baby. It was *my* choice. *My* body. *My* choice.'

I opened my eyes again and reread the letter. 'Photo. Where's the photo?' I rummaged through the sheets of the letter. It wasn't there. Stay calm. It'll be here. Think. The envelope! It'll still be in the envelope. So where the feck's the envelope? Not in the bed.

I found it on the floor, and relief flowed through me when my fingers touched something inside. I sat on the floor, leaned against the side of the bed and gazed at the image. A pretty, blonde baby with green eyes and pudgy cheeks grinned at the camera. She must have been about five or six months old. I turned the photo over. A scribble in blue biro on the back stated: *Shannon at 6 months. Thank you for our beautiful gift.*

I flipped the photo back over and stroked her face with my fingertip. 'I'm sorry I didn't keep you. I wanted to. I can remember the day you were born, as if it were yesterday. And the pain when they took you away was not a patch on the pain that I felt when they told me you'd died. Because, while you were alive, there was hope that we'd find each other one day, then we'd track down Daran and be a proper family. He'd have wanted that. He loved me and he was true to me, whatever Da says. I'm sorry, Shannon. I'm so sorry they gave you away.'

For someone who'd barely shed a tear about my past in 17 years, the outpouring of grief was overwhelming. I gasped for air as my body shook and tears rained down my cheeks, soaking my PJs.

I awoke in the early hours of the morning slumped on the floor beside my bed, cold, damp, disorientated and clutching the photo of Shannon. The first thought in my mind was that I needed to talk to someone. Desperately. But with Ben out of town and Sarah still on honeymoon, who could I turn to?

Chapter 10

✉ To Elise
Do you have any plans this weekend? I need to talk to someone. Is there any chance I could meet you in Whitsborough Bay? Please!

✉ From Elise
Are you OK? Do you want to talk now? I've got 10 mins till break's over. Just tried to call you but got voice-mail. Worried about you! No plans for the weekend xx

✉ To Elise
Sorry for not answering. Don't want to discuss it on phone. Please don't worry. I'm fine. Just received some unexpected news and I need to talk through my next steps with someone. And no, I'm not pregnant! Can we meet at a quiet café at 10.30am on Sat?

✉ From Elise
There's a café called The Stuffed Bun a couple of miles down the coast. It's lovely and really quiet first thing. Google it for directions. It's easy to find. See you then, but call me if you need me before xx

I should have asked Elise to meet me sooner – 10.30am? What was I thinking? I'd pulled into the car park an hour early and the place was closed up. The staff hadn't even arrived at that point. A heavy frost had settled overnight and blankets of snow covered the higher ground. I had to keep the engine running and the heating on full blast while I waited.

One by one, staff members arrived. I think they must have taken pity on me, all alone in my car, because the door opened at about 10.15 and one of them beckoned me to come in.

'Sorry,' I said, yanking the door shut behind me to stop the heat from escaping. 'I'm meeting a friend at half past and I'm way too early.'

'It's no problem,' the waitress said, smiling. 'If you want food, I can't help you until we open at half past, but I can offer you a drink.'

'Thank you. A large latte, please.'

I took a window seat and slowly stirred my drink, staring out at the grey sea pounding the distant shore, as I wondered what I'd say to Elise. Where could I start to talk about a past that had been buried for 17 years? A past that I'd refused point blank to ever discuss with Sarah, even though I trusted her implicitly.

Elise was right next to the table before I even noticed her. 'Elise! Sorry. Miles away.'

She unwrapped a long, fluffy turquoise scarf before sitting down opposite me. 'You look like you've got the weight of the world on your shoulders.'

I sighed. 'I may well do. I'm hoping I can unburden some of the pressure on you.'

'Unburden away.'

I stood up. 'Let me get you a drink first and then I'm going to tell you a little story that will make your hair even curlier than it is already.'

'Sounds intriguing.'

'More sad than intriguing, but definitely a big surprise.'

I walked over to the counter and ordered a hot chocolate and a piece of shortbread. As I placed them in front of Elise, I searched for the right words. 'I found out something this week that has completely thrown me and I need some advice on what to do next.' I sat down. 'To get the advice, I'm going to have to talk about my past and, as I'm sure you already know, I *never* talk about my past, so this is going to be really difficult for me.'

Elise snapped her shortbread in half and wiped her fingers on a napkin. 'I'm all ears. Just like you were for me last year.'

'Thanks. Okay, here goes…'

'You must have been terrified, being pregnant at 16,' Elise said, when I'd told her the first part of my story – my relationship with Daran.

'I was. Not of having the baby, but of telling Da. I knew he'd go ballistic so I kept it quiet. I had no sickness and no fatigue so there were no physical signs of pregnancy. My parents found out, though.'

'How?'

'To this day, I don't know. I was so careful. I wanted to do right by my baby so I started taking folic acid. I travelled to a town miles away to get the tablets, but all I can think was that someone still managed to see me and word got back. The only other thing I can think of is that Ma noticed I wasn't having periods. It could have been anything, but I got home from a walk with Daran on New Year's Eve to find Ma, Da and Father Doherty waiting for me in the living room, looking very serious. A couple of suitcases and some boxes stood in the middle of the room. Da ordered me to put on the clothes that Ma had laid out on my bed, then come back downstairs immediately. His voice was calm, but his face was puce. I knew that he knew. I nearly wet myself with fear. As soon as I got to my bedroom, I could see it had been stripped bare of my belongings.

My drawers and wardrobe were empty and the black woollen dress and thick tights that I wore for funerals were laid out on my bed.'

My eyes filled with tears as I relived that memory. Those faces staring at me. Judging me. Hating me. I didn't want to start crying again. I bit my lip and stared out the window at the sea. Elise remained silent, waiting for me to continue.

'I changed as quickly as I could and ran back downstairs to face the firing squad. Ma couldn't look at me. She just sat in the chair, arms folded, lips pursed, shaking her head. It was Father Doherty who spoke. He wasn't angry. He just sounded disappointed. He wittered on about sinners and threw out a stack of quotes from the Bible. I wasn't listening. I was too scared to concentrate. Then Da asked who the father was. I couldn't tell them. They'd never have understood. I said "I don't know", which was like lighting the touch-paper. Da obviously assumed I'd been sleeping around. He went absolutely ballistic. For a God-fearing man who never swore, I heard words spew from his mouth that I'd never even heard before. I was called everything, from a harlot to a temptress to the village bike to Jezebel herself, before he told me I'd brought disgrace on the family and I was no longer his daughter.'

Elise gasped and reached for my hand as the tears started to flow.

'He said he never wanted to see me or hear from me again. I know he was upset and ashamed, but what parent says something like that to their youngest daughter?'

Elise shook her head. 'No parent should ever behave like that. It's appalling. Parents should be supportive, not judgemental. Mind you, with my mother, I know what a bad parent can be like. And don't get me started on Gary's evil mother. I'm so sorry, Clare. What happened next?'

'I was sent to live with Da's aunt Nuala in Truro. There was no talk of me returning. Father Doherty seemed shocked at that part and tried to convince them to have me back after the baby was born, but they both refused. It got pretty heated. He started talking about forgiveness, but Da just hurled back at him everything he'd said about sin. He couldn't win. I got a letter from Ma a month later telling me that they knew who the father was. Apparently, Daran had been asking after me and they'd noticed he seemed overly surprised and concerned that I'd moved to the UK to help an elderly relative. It wouldn't have taken him long to work out that I was pregnant and that I'd been sent away because of it. So he went to Father Doherty and confessed his sins. He was removed from the county and given strict instructions never to contact me or else face legal consequences for having sex with a minor. Apparently, my parents didn't judge or blame him because I'd clearly been – and I quote – "the harlot who'd chased and hounded a celibate man until he was powerless to resist your advances". That was the last contact I had with either of them.'

'Oh, Clare, I don't know what to say. I had absolutely no idea you'd been through anything like this. I knew you weren't close to your family, but I never imagined this.'

I wiped my tears and blew my nose. 'Nobody knows. Not even Sarah. It hurts too much to think about it. It's one of the reasons I don't do Christmas and New Year. It reminds me of being with Daran, then having our happy bubble burst on New Year's Eve.'

'I don't blame you,' she said. 'So what happened to the baby?'

'It was a baby girl. Shannon. She was born on 12th June. She was beautiful. Absolutely beautiful. But I only got to hold her for a few minutes before they took her away. Da and Great-Aunt Nuala had arranged for her to be adopted. I'd had to sign some paperwork to give her to the Flannerys – a good Irish Catholic family from Exeter. I kept telling myself it was for the best, but best for whom? Me? Shannon? Or my prejudiced family? I tried to convince Great-Aunt Nuala to let me keep her, but she gave me an ultimatum: give Shannon up and she'd put me through school, college and university, or keep her and she'd throw me out with no money.'

'What sort of ultimatum is that?' Elise cried. 'It didn't give you any real choice.'

'I know. I knew I couldn't support Shannon because I had no money, no qualifications, no job and no prospect of getting one. I'd had to pack in my Leaving Certificate exams and was going to have to start my GCSEs in England from scratch, two years later than everyone else. I had a lot of studying ahead of me. I figured that if I let her get the right start in life with a family who could provide for her, I could try to find her once I got my education and a job. I knew I could never fully be her mother, but perhaps I could still be in her life.'

'And you never found her?'

'I never looked. She died. Or at least that's what they told me. Post-birth complications or something. She supposedly died a few hours later, but I got this letter yesterday.'

I reached into my bag and passed Great-Aunt Nuala's letter to Elise. She scanned down the contents and I watched as her jaw dropped open. 'Wow! And you thought she was dead for, what, 16-and-a-half years?'

I nodded. 'This is her at six months.' I passed Elise the photograph.

Elise smiled. 'There's no doubting she's yours. Absolute image of you. She's beautiful, Clare.'

'I know. So now you know the huge skeleton in my closet. Only, it turns out it's not really a skeleton, but a young woman now. And while I'm confessing everything, I have another biggie that you may as well know. I hope you believe me that I wasn't the village bike at age 16, as my father so nicely put it, but I want you to know that I've never been the village bike since then…'

She shrugged. 'I don't judge, Clare. I know I've made snide comments in the past, but I haven't meant them. How many men you've had sex with is up to you.'

I laughed. 'That's just the point. I haven't had sex with any. Well, obviously I did with Daran, but he was my first and only.'

'But why…?'

'Why do I make out that I sleep around?' I wet my finger, picked up some sugar granules off the table and dropped them into my empty cup. 'It's easier that way. I created a persona to protect myself from my past, based around the person my parents clearly thought I was. If you make out that you don't do relationships, people want to know why. If you make out that you don't do relationships because you prefer one-night stands, people don't question it. They see it as a lifestyle choice. Which begs the question why I don't do relationships. Quite simply, it was because I loved Daran so deeply that nobody else stood a chance. Every moment we were apart hurt.' My tears started again. 'Sorry. I can't stop crying now. It's like a dam has just burst.'

'Are you going to try to find Daran?' Elise asked.

I shook my head. 'No. I thought of him constantly for years after I moved to Cornwall. I'd dream about how different things could have been if I'd told Daran I was pregnant or if I'd stood up to Da. The thing is, I don't even remember why I didn't tell Daran. I've been racking my brain and it feels like there was a reason, but I just can't put my finger on it.'

Elise shrugged. 'It was a long time ago and you've been through so much since then.'

'I know. It's so strange, though. It's not the only thing I can't remember. I was going to take the morning-after pill after we… you know… but I don't remember taking it. Considering I ended up pregnant, I'm guessing I didn't, but I don't understand why. I don't get it because there are some things I remember so vividly and other things… Well, it's like there's a thick fog hanging over parts of my past and I can just see shapes, but I can't convert them into anything tangible.' I smiled at Elise. 'Sorry. That sounds like absolute bollocks, doesn't it now? Hindsight's a great thing.

'I know now that I should have stood up to my da, but the man terrified me. He still terrifies me. I saw him on Sunday and I was completely defenceless all over again. I didn't put up a fight on Sunday and I didn't put up a fight when I was 16. I let him put me on a plane and send me to England, away from Daran. I wrote to Daran every other day until Shannon was born. I sent the letters to Father Doherty and begged him to pass them on. I'm assuming he didn't, since he destroyed the letters that Daran wrote. The only thing I do know is that we could have been really happy together if I'd been a bit stronger and pushed a bit more. But I can't try to recover what we had nearly two decades later. I just can't.'

Elise shook her head again. 'What a waste.'

I sat back in my chair and looked out the window again. 'Father Doherty used to say Confession was good for the soul. I do admit that I'm feeling a little relieved just now.' I looked back at Elise. 'What should I do?'

She took a deep breath. 'Crikey. Where do I start? That was a lot of unexpected information that I can't believe you've been carrying around for half your life.'

'I know. And now I expect you to solve all my problems.' I smiled. 'Thanks for listening.'

'You're welcome. You've been there for me and baby Bean so it's the very least I can do. Firstly, I'd say don't beat yourself up about any of this. You couldn't have prevented what happened. Making you put Shannon up for adoption was cruel, and to tell you she'd died was unforgivable.' She rubbed her own stomach, as if to reassure her baby that she was safe from imminent adoption. 'Secondly, I suggest you drop the sex-mad persona and just be you. If you don't want a relationship, you don't have to have a relationship, but you don't have to make out that you have a different one every week, either. Thirdly, I think you should confront your parents. I don't mean you have to fly to Ireland to see them, especially as it sounds like things with your dad didn't go well on Sunday. You could write to them instead. You don't even have to post it, but I think it would do you the world of good to get down on paper what you think of them, to help box it off and move on.'

'Did you do that to your mum?' Elise had a very volatile relationship with her alcoholic mother, who, even before the drinking, had resented the disruption that Elise and her sister had created by being born.

Elise nodded. 'My counsellor, Jem, suggested it. I've written loads of letters in my time. I've never sent any. Mind you, when I saw her between Christmas and New Year, I gave her a piece of my mind, then walked out on her, so I think I've finally had my opportunity.'

'Good for you.' I pondered on what she'd said. 'That's all good advice, so it is. To be fair, I think I've naturally dropped the man-eater act since getting promoted last year. It didn't fit so well with the responsible-professional image and, to be honest, I don't think anyone's noticed. Anything else?'

'I think you should start looking for Shannon.' Elise smiled. 'But you'd already decided to do that, hadn't you?'

I smiled too. 'Was it that obvious?'

'The way your eyes lit up when you spoke of her was a big clue. I don't think you really needed my advice, did you? I think you just needed to tell someone, after all these years.'

Very astute. 'The advice was good, though. An added bonus, perhaps. I liked the bit about ranting at the parents. I really will do that, but on paper, like you suggest. I never want to set foot in Ireland ever again. I didn't want to go at the weekend, and I definitely didn't want to go to Ballykielty, but I felt drawn to *our* place. Never again.'

'Are you sure you don't want to find Daran? What if Shannon wants to know who her dad is.'

'Christ! It never even crossed my mind. If I find Shannon, I'm not expecting it to be easy. If she takes after me in personality as well as looks, she'll be a tough cookie and will give me a hard time for abandoning her. Quite rightly so. She might not want to hear the sorry story of my past. I really hadn't thought beyond her reaction to me, but you're right: she might want to know about Daran. I don't think I'm ready to find him yet, though. It's going to be emotional enough finding Shannon. I think adding Daran into the mix will tip me over the edge.'

Elise looked around. 'It's getting busy in here. I know it's freezing, but I'm well wrapped up and I've got some extra layers in the car if you need any. Do you fancy a walk along the beach and we can talk some more? Unless you feel you're talked out.'

'I've been quiet for half my life and, now that I've finally opened up, I feel like I could talk for Ireland. Are you sure you can cope?'

She smiled. 'Anything to help you get through this. But Bean needs another shortbread first.'

'And I need a strong coffee.'

Chapter 11

Sixteen-and-a-half years earlier

I gazed around the farmhouse at my handiwork and smiled. I'd liberated a couple of rectangular straw bales from a nearby field, opened one up and spread the straw across the corner of the room that I'd come to think of as 'kissing corner'. I'd found an old picnic rug tucked away at the back of the shed at home. Resting on top of a thick blanket of straw, it would be perfect for what I had planned. The second bale acted as a table. Having only turned 16 that day, I knew there was no chance of being served alcohol anywhere local, so we'd have to pretend with fizzy white grape juice out of plastic picnic beakers.

I'd chosen my outfit carefully to avoid awkward clothing-removal disasters. The short, cream summer dress had buttons all the way up the front, which could be swiftly undone to reveal a cream and red lacy bra-and-panties set that I'd liberated from Aisling's drawers, the little minx. Surely Daran wouldn't be able to resist it.

As a good Catholic, he was a firm believer in 'no sex before marriage', but I could tell with each passing day and every touch that holding back was getting harder and harder – literally! I was determined to change his mind.

'I'm so sorry I'm late. I was worried you might have gone.' Daran picked me up and spun me around, kissing me, as he always did.

After he'd admitted his feelings for me in January, he'd told Father Doherty that he didn't think life as a priest was the right path for him, but he was still just as committed to learning about and serving God. Father Doherty had been very understanding and had asked if he'd like to stick around and continue to help him out, in return for further guidance on the Catholic faith. Daran jumped at the offer. After Easter, he also secured a position teaching religious studies at the local comprehensive. Naturally, we had to keep our relationship quiet or he'd have been dismissed. Fortunately, Orla Brennan was seeing a Protestant in Ballyshelty, so we provided constant alibis for each other. She didn't know who I was seeing, just that he was older than me and that our relationship wouldn't meet with anyone's approval. She was convinced he was married and I let her continue to think that.

'Where were you?' I asked.

'I joined Father Doherty while he read the Last Rites to Carrig Murphy.'

I stepped back, still holding onto Daran's arms. 'Oh no. Is he dead now?' Carrig was one of the village's oldest residents and liked by all, but he had suffered a stroke at the start of the summer and had gone downhill rapidly.

'Not yet. He's unconscious, though. His wife said she wanted to stay with him alone, but she wants me to call back and say another prayer every couple of hours.' He cupped my chin and gave me a gentle kiss on the lips. 'I'm sorry, Clare, but I've only got about an hour and a quarter.'

'And I've got to go out for that meal with the parents anyway. Oh no, I haven't. That's what normal parents would do to celebrate the birthday of a child they love, whereas mine have barely acknowledged the day. Ma tossed a card at me. No gift. Just a card.'

'I'm sorry they're so cruel to you. It breaks my heart to see it.'

I shrugged. 'I'm used to it. Anyway, I don't want to waste any of our precious time talking about them. Seeing as time is tight, we'd better get on with things.'

Daran nodded his head towards the 'table' and makeshift bed. 'What's this? Are we moving in now?'

'It may or may not have escaped your notice, but I have reached the grand, old age of 16 today. I'm an adult, and I'm ready to do everything that adults do.'

He wrapped his arms around me. 'We've talked about this. You know that I can't do that, Clare.'

'Are you trying to convince me or yourself?'

He laughed. 'Me! You know I want you, but it's not how I was brought up.'

'I respect you for that and, if this were just a casual thing, I wouldn't even consider taking that step. But it's not a casual thing, is it? I love you, Daran. I want to be with you till the end of forever. For me, this is just the next logical step. You've already got my heart, my mind, my soul. The only thing you don't have is my body and I want you to have that too. I'm more than ready. Aren't you?'

He fixed his green eyes on mine. I could tell he was really struggling to find more reasons not to consummate our relationship. Since he'd started teaching, he'd talked a lot more about the different religions he'd studied for his degree. They all had different views on relationships, sex and marriage, and, even though I knew his love for God was unfaltering, I knew he was starting to question whether everything about the Catholic faith was right.

'I want to give you your birthday present,' he said.

I grinned. 'I didn't see you bring anything in.'

'My gift isn't big in size, but it's big in meaning. Close your eyes and hold your hands out.'

I did as he instructed. I could hear his shallow breathing, smell soap and shaving balm, feel the light touch of his fingers, as he gently placed something into the palm of my left hand. A shiver of longing ran through me at his touch. It took a hell of a lot of willpower not to drop whatever he'd given me, hurl myself at him and rip his clothes off.

'Open your eyes,' he whispered.

I opened them, looked down and gasped. 'A Claddagh ring?' I picked up the shiny, silver ring with my right hand. It was a very simple yet beautiful design with a heart-shaped sapphire.

'It's your birthstone. It's only a sterling silver ring, though, and a fake sapphire. I promise I'll buy you a better one as soon as I can.'

I shook my head. 'There's no need, Daran. It's absolutely perfect.' My heart raced. I had to ask the question: 'Which way will I wear it?'

He took the ring from me and smiled so tenderly that I feared I might cry. Not wanting to make an assumption, I put my right hand out towards him (right hand, point of heart towards the wrist = in a relationship) but he shook his head and lifted my left hand to his lips, gently kissed it, then slipped the ring onto my fourth finger, with the point of the heart towards my fingertips. A perfect fit. I stared at him, then the ring, then at him again.

Daran got down on his bended knee in the straw. 'When I came to Ballykielty, I never imagined I could love another human being as much as I love God. Then I met you. You showed me a future I'd never considered and you taught me that I can be committed to God's work but also have a family. I love you, Clare, and I want to be with you till the end of forever too. Will you marry me?'

I did cry at that point. My lips trembled and great, fat tears splashed down my cheeks. Daran leapt to his feet and wrapped his arms around me. 'Was it too much?'

'No. It was perfect, and the answer's yes.'

He stepped back so he could look into my eyes. 'Really?'

'Really. They're happy tears. Honestly.' I wiped my cheeks and passionately kissed my fiancé.

'I think we're ready for the next step,' I whispered, nibbling his ear.

'I'm still not sure.'

I moved my kisses down to his neck, untucked his shirt from his jeans and ran my nails up his bare back. 'We're engaged, aren't we? That's nearly married.'

Daran's breathing quickened. 'Nearly married isn't the same as married,' he whispered.

'I'm just as committed to you right now as I will be when we're married, so what's the difference?' With shaking hands, I undid his shirt buttons. My eyes widened at seeing his naked torso for the first time. Not quite a six-pack but certainly toned. He caught me looking and smiled ruefully. 'Pathetic, isn't it? I've been working out at home. Five hundred crunches a night before prayers. I didn't want to disappoint you if… when…'

So he'd been thinking about it as much as I had. He gasped as I kissed his chest and my kisses went lower and lower. I wanted to unzip his jeans and continue my kisses down there – the way I'd read in a Jackie Collins novel that Orla Brennan had stolen from her older sister – but I wasn't brave enough. Instead, I worked my way back up to his neck, then gently steered him towards the makeshift bed. He didn't protest as we lay down on the rug and I slipped his shirt off.

'I'd like to give you an engagement gift,' I said.

Holding his gaze, I undid the top two buttons of my dress, revealing my bra. His breathing quickened even more, sending a ripple of electricity through my body. 'I want you, Daran.' I undid the rest of my buttons and he gasped.

'Clare! That's playing dirty.'

I giggled. 'That's what I'm hoping for.' I slipped out of my dress completely and reached around to unclasp my bra. I eased it off my arms and let it slip to the floor. 'I think you might be a bit overdressed,' I said.

Daran propped himself up on one arm as he lightly traced his other hand down my face, neck and arm, gently skimming my breast and sending another fizz of pleasure through me. 'I do want you too, Clare. You have no idea how much.'

'Then, why wait? We love each other. We're engaged. I don't know what else I can say to convince you it's okay to do this.'

When Daran didn't respond but continued to stroke me, touching more of my breast with each hand movement, I knew he didn't need much more convincing. I'd done enough talking. Actions spoke louder than words, didn't they? I reached down and, with fumbling fingers, undid the belt and zip on his jeans. He didn't protest. I slipped my hand inside, hoping I'd learned enough from a combination of biology books and Ms Collins to do things right.

Daran groaned as I touched him through his underwear.

This was potentially the point of no return. 'Do you want me to stop?' I whispered. 'Because I will if you really want me to. It's just that I don't think you do.'

I caressed him and he groaned again. 'Will I stop?'

'No! Don't stop. Oh, Clare! That feels so… I've never done this before. It might be quick.'

'If it's quick, it's quick. We can always do it again. Lots of times, I hope.'

Daran kissed me. 'Are you sure this is what you want?' he asked.

'Yes! You?'

'May God forgive me, but yes. I really, really do.'

'Then you're wearing too many clothes.'

He wriggled out of his jeans, then we lay side by side in only our underwear, gazing into each other's eyes. 'I know I'm meant to do things to you before we… you know,' he said. 'But I'm so turned on right now, I might not be able to hold out if I do them. If I have an accident, I'll have ruined our first time.'

'Daran, believe me, I'm ready for you right now. I don't think you need to do any of those things. Lie down and stop worrying.' I lifted my hips up and wriggled out of my panties, then carefully pulled his boxers down. He was right: from the research I'd done, he was very, very turned on.

I straddled him and slowly lowered myself down, letting out a little squeal as he entered me.

'Are you okay? Does it hurt?'

'A bit. Ow! Oh, but it feels good too. Oh my God. Daran! Are you okay?'

'I'm incredible. Oh, Clare! But this is going to be so quick.'

It was, but it was also incredible. I collapsed against Daran's chest, trembling from the new sensations. 'Are you okay?' I asked, feeling him trembling too.

'I'm in shock. I've never… you know… even as a teenager… so that was… that was…' He shook his head. 'Why was I even considering a life in which I'd never get to do that?'

I laughed. 'I take it you enjoyed it.'

'Immensely.' Then the grin slipped from his face. 'What if there's a baby? You're too young for that.'

I held him tightly and snuggled against his bare chest. 'I know you won't like this, Daran, but I'm going to go on the pill. I know someone in Ballyshelty who knows someone who can get me it. They've already got me the morning-after pill for what we've just done. I know it's not the Catholic way but—'

'It's grand,' he said. 'It's your body, Clare. It's your choice. Sure I can hardly preach about the Catholic way after what I've just done.'

'No regrets?' I asked, looking into his eyes.

'Just one.'

My heart thumped. 'Dare I ask?'

He smiled. 'That it didn't last longer. It will this time, though.' He pulled me closer and kissed me, then rolled me onto my back so he could trace kisses down my body from tip to toe, then back again. By the time he entered me for the second time, I was burning with desire for the man I loved, who now had my heart, mind, soul… and body.

Chapter 12

Present Day

'Are you sure you'll be okay?' Elise asked, as we stood by her lime-green Beetle in the car park of The Stuffed Bun. 'You're welcome to stay with Stevie and me.'

I smiled as I shook my head. 'I appreciate the offer but I'm not being a gooseberry.'

'You won't be. Stevie won't mind.'

I shook my head. 'Thanks, but no thanks.' I rubbed my hands together. 'It's feckin' freezing. Get yourself home and get your lovely man to warm you up. I need to go back to Leeds and think about what to do next.'

Elise opened her car door. 'You're sure?'

'I'm sure. Be off with you!'

'I really don't think you should be alone at a time like this.'

I laughed. 'You know me. Hard as nails. It takes more than my past catching up with me to knock me down.'

Elise raised an eyebrow at me.

'Go!' I said. 'That's an order.'

'You're not as hard as you like to make out. You don't need to pretend you are.'

My throat tightened and tears pricked my eyes. I reached out and hugged Elise, whispering into her hair, 'Thank you for today.'

'Any time,' she whispered back. 'I mean that.'

We released each other and she eased herself into the driver's seat. 'Go and find your daughter, Clare. Keep me posted. I'm here for you.'

'I know.' I waved her off and walked back to my car. I started the ignition and turned the heating up full blast but didn't set off. I actually felt quite shaky. Seventeen years. I'd kept my past hidden for 17 years. More than half my lifetime. But, Christ, it had felt good to finally share it with someone.

Elise had been amazing. She'd listened and she hadn't judged. She'd asked lots of questions, but she seemed to have a gift for asking the right ones; the ones that made me think about what I wanted to do, instead of the sort that were clearly about getting the juicy gossip from the situation and – let's face it – '16-year-old gets pregnant by former-priest-in-training-turned-teacher' is pretty scandalous stuff. We'd talked for hours and it really had done me the world of good. It felt as though the cobwebs on the skeletons in my closet were being blown away. If I'd known that a chat to a friend could have so easily lightened the burden I'd carried for 17 years, I'd have done it long ago.

I took a swig from a bottle of Sprite in my bag, ran a brush through my tangled hair, then pulled out of the car park. It was fine: I could do this. I was fine on my own. I was used to it.

But as I got closer to Leeds, a feeling of unease overcame me. Bollocks. Elise had been right. I really didn't want to be alone. What choice did I have, though? I could hardly turn around and drive an hour and a half back to Whitsborough Bay and ask to stay the night. Elise and Stevie needed to make the most of their moments together before the baby arrived. Plus, I felt absolutely shattered and in danger of falling asleep at the wheel if I drove for much longer. If only Ben hadn't gone away for work. I didn't feel the need to talk; I'd done enough of that with Elise. I did feel the need for company, though. An evening stretched out in front of the TV with him, a film, a takeaway and some trivial banter would have been perfect. Instead, I had a sparse, soulless rented apartment and silence to return to. I pictured Ben's cosy lounge and knew what I was going to do.

There were no lights on at Ben's house, but I still rapped loudly on the door knocker a few times, just in case his plans had changed and he'd unexpectedly returned home for the weekend. When I felt confident that the house really was empty, I let myself in with the spare key that Ben had suggested I hang onto, as long as I pinkie-promised him not to break in and steal the king whenever it was in his possession!

I hadn't realised I was quite so tense until I shut the door behind me and a wave of relief washed over me. A small two-up two-down mid-terrace, with film posters on the walls rather than pictures, and piles of books, CDs and DVDs everywhere, it reminded me of student digs, but without the dodgy smells and stains. It was homely. It was safe. It would be my haven for the evening and I'd head back to *Orion Point* in the morning.

Coffee. I dumped my handbag in the hallway, wandered through to the kitchen with a carrier bag of provisions from the local *Spar*, filled the kettle and popped a bottle of wine into the fridge for later. While I waited for the kettle to boil, I went upstairs. I poked my head around Ben's bedroom door, just in case, but his room was empty. In my former room at the front of the house, I drew the curtains, then undressed and pulled on a pair of fleecy pyjamas and slipper socks that I kept there.

Ten minutes later, I was curled up on the sofa with a coffee and a film. Thirty minutes after that, my Indian takeaway arrived. I cracked open the wine and dished up my meal. It had definitely been the right decision to come to Ben's. It was just a shame that he wasn't there.

Sunday dawned and I still couldn't bring myself to go back to my empty apartment. Even though Ben's house was empty too, it felt different.

I had a long soak in the bath, then borrowed a pair of Ben's PJs and his dressing gown, and retreated to the sofa to watch back-to-back films.

A text came through shortly after I'd had some lunch:

✉ From Sarah
We've landed safely! At Manchester station waiting to get train home. Can't believe nearly 3 weeks are over already. Should be home by 5. Catch up soon xx

I tapped in a response:

✉ To Sarah
Welcome back from honeymoon! Hope you had an amazing time. Loads to tell you. If you're not too tired, give me a call when you're settled xx

When 5pm arrived, my stomach did a somersault. Sarah would be home now. She could call at any moment. I tutted at myself. Eejit. She'd surely check in with her parents and Nick's mum before ringing me. And she might not even ring me if she was shattered. Which she probably would be, given that she'd have flown through the night.

I rolled off the sofa and headed into the kitchen, where I distracted myself by preparing an omelette and some salad. Once I'd eaten it, I couldn't stop fidgeting. I kept picking up my phone, putting it down, picking it up again. Despite half-expecting her call, I still managed to jump when Sarah's name flashed up on the screen. She was my best and oldest friend. It was ridiculous that I felt nervous about speaking to her. When I'd been with Elise the day before, she'd told me that she'd confessed to Sarah about her pregnancy before Sarah left for her honeymoon.

Apparently, they'd had a huge argument about keeping secrets. Sarah had been particularly hurt that they'd been best friends since the age of four and Elise hadn't felt she could tell her such life-changing news, yet I – the enemy – knew. If she'd reacted that badly to a secret Elise had kept from her for five months or so, how was she going to react to something I'd kept from her for the 13 years since we'd met on our first day at Manchester University?

As I accepted Sarah's call, I toyed with whether to wait until I saw her face to face before telling her about my past, but I felt I owed it to her to tell her sooner rather than later.

It was the world's worst phone call. I'd imagined all afternoon how it would go and nowhere in my imaginings had I called her a 'selfish eejit', yet that's exactly what I did. I lost it. I'd gone for the pleasantries first – how was Canada/what was the best thing you did/favourite place/was it cold? and all that malarkey – but she gave really brief answers before changing the subject to Elise and Stevie. They'd just visited and told her they were moving in together. She was thrilled they'd got together but worried that they were moving in too soon. And, speaking of moving in together, apparently her auntie Kay and Philip were also setting up home. Kay was putting her cottage, *Smuggler's View*, on the market, which had shocked and upset Sarah.

I should have left my confession for another time. I should have accepted that she'd already had an overload of surprise information that evening and was never going to be able to process what I said. Yet, I just blurted it all out. It was the first opportunity to tell her, and I didn't want her getting upset later that I hadn't opened up to her as soon as I'd started talking about my past.

I'd like to say she was supportive. I'd really like to say that. But all

I got was: 'What made you confess all this to Elise? When did you two become the best of mates?'

We argued. Nasty things were said by both of us that couldn't be unsaid. She slammed the phone down on me in tears.

In bed that night, I lay there staring at the ceiling, replaying our conversation, and I felt sick. I could see her point. It had to hurt that she'd tried to be there for me for all those years and I'd refused to open up. I'd thrown strops and stormed off every time I let something minor slip about my past, and Sarah had handled it with support and compassion for years, never pushing me but always making it clear that she was there for me whenever I was ready. To have me finally open up to my former nemesis had to be a slap across the face with a wet kipper – especially after Elise had confessed that I knew about her baby first, and about her and Stevie. Yes, I could definitely see why she reacted the way she did, but surely she could see that the letter from Great-Aunt Nuala was the catalyst for me needing to open up. Call it the straw that broke the camel's back. If she'd been here, of course I'd have gone to her first.

If I'm honest, Ben would have been my second choice, not Elise, but he'd been away and it wasn't something I wanted to confess for the first time over the phone or via social media. Sure, in an ideal world, I wouldn't have told Sarah over the phone, but there was no going back. I just hoped we could recover from it.

Chapter 13

I sat at the dining table back at *Orion Point* on Monday morning, staring at Shannon's photo and the list of information about her and her adoptive parents that had accompanied Great-Aunt Nuala's letter. Elise had been right: I was always going to try to find her.

I sighed and put Great-Aunt Nuala's letter down. I was meant to be working from home but I couldn't concentrate. Between the letter and the call with Sarah, my mind was on anything but sales figures and promotional strategies. Coffee.

Feeling a bit calmer, with a dose of caffeine flowing through my veins, I closed down my spreadsheet, opened Google and typed in: *how would I find a baby given up for adoption?* I scanned down the list of results. 'UK Birth Adoption Register' – seemed like a good starting point. I clicked into it. 'Information on what to do if you were adopted in the UK.' No. I wasn't the one who was adopted. Ah, 'Information on what to do if you gave a child up for adoption in the UK… Unfortunately, under UK law, it is illegal to try to make contact with an adopted child, at least until they turn 18 years of age.' Feck. She's only 16.

I scrolled further down the page, clicking on various related websites, but nothing seemed helpful. Then I spotted a link to an adoption-search message board. Interesting. I clicked on it and waited a moment for it to load. A stack of messages appeared. I started scrolling through, but it was going to take forever. There had to be some sort of search facility. It wasn't in an obvious place but I found one and entered her name: Shannon O'Connell… No! Shannon Kitteridge. I triple-checked the spelling on Great-Aunt Nuala's note before I pressed 'return'. Surely there couldn't be many Shannon Kitteridges out there? A pageful of messages loaded and my heart leapt, then sank again. All Shannons. No Kitteridges. Bollocks!

I tapped my fingers on the keyboard, then returned to Google and typed in: *Shannon Kitteridge*. A record of a Shannon Kitteridge living in Bognor Regis came up. With shaky fingers, I clicked on it and the first thing I noticed was the age guide of '65-plus'. Bollocks again! I returned to my Google search, but there was nothing. Absolutely nothing. I slumped back on the sofa, arms folded. What next?

As my eyes scanned the table, I clocked the letter from Bowson, Higgs & Crane. They'd offered to help, hadn't they? I reread the letter. It was probably just a polite standard line in all their correspondence, but what the heck? I dialled the number and quoted my great-aunt's name.

'Hello, Ms O'Connell, this is Angela Crane. I was your great-aunt's solicitor. Am I right in thinking you've received her letter?'

'Last week. You said to call you if you could help me…?'

'Of course. What's your query?'

'It's a long shot…' I explained about the content of the letter.

After I'd finished, Angela said, 'Unfortunately, under UK law, it's illegal to search for a child you've given up for adoption until they've turned 18 and are therefore classed by law as an adult.'

'I'm aware of that, and Shannon won't be 18 for another 18 months. Is there anything else that can be done?'

'I'm assuming you've Googled her name?'

'Yes.'

'And those of the adoptive parents?'

'Muppet! I never thought of that. Thanks, Angela.' Before she could respond, I hung up. I quickly typed in the names of Paul and Christine Kitteridge, plus Northampton, where Great-Aunt Nuala had said they lived. The search revealed several newspaper articles. I'd found them! I'd definitely found them. Oh. They were both dead. I picked up the phone and called Angela again.

'I think we got cut off,' she said, a little sharply.

'I'm sorry. I hung up in my excitement. Are you by a computer?'

'Yes. Why?'

'I know this may seem a little unusual, but can I ask you to Google something and see what you make of it? You can bill me for the time I've taken up.'

There was a pause and a sigh. 'Okay. You have my attention, but only because my 10 o'clock has failed to show. What do you want me to Google?'

'Paul and Christine Kitteridge of Northampton.' I heard her tapping on a keyboard. 'Click on the article a few results down that says "Tragic couple leave daughter" and tell me what you make of it.'

The line went quiet. As I waited impatiently for her to speak, I scanned down the article again. They had to be the same family. Just had to be.

'Hi, Ms O'Connell. It would seem that these are the same people who adopted your daughter, given the use of her middle name and the suggestion that she was adopted. The problem is, it gives no indication of where she went next. Foster care is most likely, as it says that neither Mr nor Mrs Kitteridge had siblings.'

'So, what do I do next?'

'All I can suggest is that you make contact with Social Services in Northampton. They may not be able to help, given the law, but they'd be your best starting point. Because Shannon's adoptive parents are deceased, it puts the law into a different context, but the law is there to protect the child as much as the parents, and the fact still remains that Shannon is under 18. I wish I could help further but I'm not a specialist in this area. Would you like me to recommend someone who is?'

My heart sank. It was over. Well, for now anyway. 'I might come back to you on that.'

Angela gave me her email address in case I did want a recommendation, then wished me luck again before hanging up. I reread the article. Shannon's adoptive mother had been active in fundraising for breast cancer after her mother had died from it. Sadly, she developed the disease herself – a particularly aggressive form – and was dead within a year, leaving behind an adopted 10-year-old daughter. Then, three years later, her adoptive father dropped dead from an aneurism. Absolutely tragic.

I shook my head, sent the article to print, emailed a copy to Elise to get her take on it (I was still sulking too much to share it with Sarah), then phoned in sick. It was partly true. My head throbbed and I felt emotionally drained. Very emotionally drained.

'Hi, Elise,' I said, turning down my music on Saturday morning.

'Are you driving?' she asked.

'Yes, but I'm on hands-free.'

'Where are you?'

'About 20 minutes from Whitsborough Bay. I told Sarah about the skeletons in my closet on Sunday. To say she was upset that I hadn't confided in her sooner would be the understatement of the century. We haven't spoken since, although we've exchanged a few curt texts. I don't need the stress of falling out with my oldest friend right now, so I've invited myself over to make my peace and find out about Canada.'

'Stevie and I went round on Sunday too and told her about moving in together,' Elise said. 'She was pretty shocked about that.'

'She told me. Apparently, Kay went over there too and she had news. I don't think Sarah was expecting to come back to so many revelations!'

Elise laughed. 'Is she expecting you?'

'No, but I thought I'd surprise her in the shop and hope she doesn't have plans for tonight. Why?'

'I wondered if you wanted to meet me first to chat about the article you sent me.'

'You don't mind me taking more of your time?'

'Of course not. That's what friends are for.' There was a pause. 'There's also something I need to tell you.'

My stomach lurched. 'Are you okay? Is the baby okay?'

'We're both fine. It's something else, but it's not a conversation for the phone. Could you come to the house?'

'Sounds serious. I'm just pulling into a lay-by. You can give me the postcode for my sat nav.'

Half an hour later, I pulled up outside Elise and Stevie's home – *Bramble Cottage* in Little Sandby. I gave Stevie a quick hug. He'd actually been my friend before he'd met Elise. When Sarah had moved back to Whitsborough Bay, we'd double-dated Stevie and his best mate, Rob, after Sarah joined an online dating agency. Stevie and Sarah had hit it off immediately, but the chemistry was missing, so they'd become friends rather than a couple. Ironically, Rob had then got together with Elise's husband, Gary, and Elise had finally hooked up with Stevie. Talk about partner-swapping. Seriously. You couldn't make this stuff up!

Stevie made drinks, then muttered some excuse about work before heading upstairs.

'Spill,' I said, sitting down on the sofa. 'I can't stand the suspense.'

'Please don't be mad at me. I know you said you didn't want to find Daran but it was such a romantic story, and curiosity got the better of me, so I Googled him.'

My heart thumped and I felt a little light-headed. I slumped back in my seat. 'Elise! What did I say to you just last Saturday?'

'I know. I was being nosy and I had no plans to share my findings with you. Only, I think you should know what I found out.'

I sighed. 'If you're going to tell me he married a nun and spawned the next von Trapp family, I'm really not interested. It was 17 years ago.' I realised as I said it that I absolutely didn't want to hear that he'd got married. That was what we had wanted. It wasn't right to think that he'd done that with someone else.

Elise bit her lip. 'After he left your village, he went to Thailand to do some sort of missionary work.'

'And he shacked up with a ladyboy?' It felt inappropriate to say it, but after a decade and a half of trying not to think about Daran, discussing him like this was a bit overwhelming, and humour was the only defence mechanism I had in me.

Elise shook her head. 'He was there in 2004.'

'So?'

'Christmas, 2004.'

'So?'

'Boxing Day, 2004. Thailand.'

My hand went to my mouth. 'The tsunami?' I whispered.

Elise nodded. 'I'm so sorry, Clare.'

My mouth went very dry. 'He's dead?'

'I found this article online.'

Elise handed me a crumpled piece of paper, but my eyes couldn't seem to focus on the words. 'What does it say?'

She perched on the edge of the coffee table. 'Do you want me to read it to you?'

I reached for the Claddagh ring I now wore on my right hand and twisted it around and around my finger. Somehow I found the strength to nod.

Catholic Online
16th January 2005

A service was held yesterday in the Church of St Paul the Apostle in Dublin to commemorate the thousands who tragically lost their lives during the tsunami that hit Thailand, Indonesia and the surrounding area on 26th December, 2004, or during the days that followed.

Amongst those specifically remembered was humanitarian Daran Seamus McInnery. Mr McInnery had been working tirelessly with local communities in Sumatra for three years, having previously supported community work in Counties Wicklow and Cork.

Mr McInnery was the eldest of eight siblings. His three sisters and four brothers all attended the service, along with his mother. His father had passed away shortly after his youngest sister was born.

I felt funny, as if I were swimming in glue, unable to move or breathe or think straight. I listened to Elise's fuzzy words, my mind saying over and over, 'It might not be him,' but the facts were there: the middle name, the communities in Ireland, the seven siblings, the deceased father. It was definitely him. The last thing I heard was Elise shouting for Stevie to help her. Then the room went dark.

'Do you know what would happen to us if anyone ever found out?' Daran kissed my forehead as he wrapped his arms more tightly around me. I leaned back into his embrace.

'What could they do? Order us to stop being in love?'

'They could order it, but it would never happen. I know I've said it before but I really will love you until the end of forever, Clare. I hope you know that.'

'And I'll love you longer than that, you great big eejit.'

'I'm serious, though,' he said. 'There'd be consequences. Big ones. For both of us. They'd send me away. You too.'

I stroked his strong forearms. 'Then I'd jump in me da's car and chase after you.'

'You can't drive.'

'I can, so. I can drive a tractor.'

'I hate to break it to you but a car is slightly more complex to drive than a tractor, so it is.'

'You'd better start teaching me to drive your car, then, just in case we need to make a swift getaway.'

I lay in Daran's arms in silence, trying to imagine life without him. 'I really would follow you,' I said. 'To the ends of the earth.'

He kissed my forehead again. 'You know where I'd really like to go?'

'Where?'

'The Far East. Places like Thailand, Malaysia, China, Vietnam, The Philippines.'

'Why there?'

'It sounds daft, but I had a dream many years ago where I was standing on a beach in Indonesia and it was like paradise on earth. A small boy came up to me and asked me to help his family. He led me to a village, where he lived in a shack – corrugated iron and bits of wood hammered together. It was a world away from what I knew, yet I felt God's presence more strongly than I'd ever felt it before.'

'I could come with you,' I said. 'Let's leave this place. Run away. Be together where nobody knows us and nobody will judge us.'

Daran turned my face gently and kissed me. I melted into his kiss as always. 'I want to take you up on that right now. I really do. But you need to finish school first. Do you hear me?'

'Why?'

'Because an education opens doors. It's only two more years. It'll fly by. You'll see. But finish your education. Do you hear me, Clare? Do you hear me?'

'Do you hear me, Clare? Can you hear me?'

'Daran?' I whispered.

'It's Stevie. You fainted.'

'Drink this.' A glass was pressed against my lips and I took a sip of cold water, then another. I opened my eyes. Elise and Stevie were both crouched on the floor in front of me.

'How long?'

'A few minutes,' Elise said. 'You had us really scared there. I was about to call for an ambulance. Should I still do that?'

I took another couple of sips of water. 'Bollocks to that. I know I like drama but that's going a bit far, even for me.' I sat slightly forward on the sofa. 'I was dreaming about Daran. He told me he wanted to go to the Far East to help the communities there. I was going to go with him when I finished school. I'd forgotten about that conversation.'

'It looks like he got what he wanted,' Elise said.

'Except the part where he did it with Clare.' Stevie handed me the glass of water. 'I'm sorry.'

I sighed. 'I'm sorry too. He was a very special person.' I took a few more sips of water. 'I can't believe he's gone.'

Elise took my hand. 'Did I do the right thing in telling you?'

I nodded. 'Can I read it myself?'

Elise handed me the article. I read it over and over again and shook my head as tears streamed down my cheeks. Still the same words. Still the same message. Still gone. I wiped my tears again and looked at Elise. 'Hard as it was to hear, I'm glad I know. I told you last Saturday that I hadn't thought about Daran much over the last five years or so, and I really haven't. But this week I haven't stopped thinking about him. I'm sure I'd have searched eventually, so I'm glad I know.'

'What are you going to do now?' Stevie asked.

'You're not the only one who's been going mad on Google. I found out this week that Shannon's adoptive parents are dead. Seems there's a lot of it going around. I've been away all week with work so haven't been able to do anything about it, but I'm going to call Social Services on Monday and find out my options for tracking her down, especially as she's officially an orphan now. After that, there's something very important that I need to do.'

'What's that?' Elise asked.

'Go back to Ballykielty and confront my da.' I winced as I felt my nails digging into my palms, but I couldn't unclench my fists. 'I thought about writing that letter you suggested, Elise, but it wouldn't be enough. I need to look him in the eye. I'm owed an apology and I'm owed a hell of a lot of answers. When I saw him a couple of weeks ago, I crumbled before him, but I didn't know that Shannon had lived or that Daran had died. I hold him personally responsible for both of those things and, even if I get no answers, I want him to know what I think of him.'

Chapter 14

Elise opened the door to Sarah's shop, *Flowers and Gifts,* and the little bell tinkled. She'd rung Sarah to explain what had happened. From listening to Elise's end of the conversation, Sarah had been a bit funny about why I was at Elise's but had come around when Elise had explained that I'd been on my way to see Sarah and that she'd hijacked me.

Sarah put down the bouquet she was making and rushed over, looking very worried. 'Clare! Are you okay?'

I nodded. 'I'm grand. Embarrassed, but grand. I don't think I've ever fainted before.'

'We've had a pretty chilled afternoon,' Elise said. 'I got Gary to pop round and give her a once-over, but he says she's fine and should just rest for a bit.' Elise's ex was a GP, a handy person to call on in circumstances like this.

'Am I okay to stay at yours tonight?' I asked.

'Of course. You know you're welcome any time. Cuppa?'

'Coffee, please.'

'Are you stopping?' she asked Elise.

'I've got to go. I'm off round to our Jess's for tea. See you later, Clare.' She gave me a hug and left the shop.

'So, what happened?' Sarah asked. 'Elise said it was something to do with Daran, but she didn't say what.'

I was about to tell her but the door opened and several customers came in. 'You need to get on with your work,' I said. 'Do you mind if I have my drink out the back? I'll tell you everything when we get back to yours.'

After tea at Sarah's, Nick went to the pub with Stevie, leaving Sarah and me to talk. I opened up to her properly for the first time ever. I told her about my brothers and sisters, how strict Da was and how Ma had always acted as if she hated me. I talked in detail about the Mass where I first saw Daran and how our secret relationship had developed. The more I spoke, the more the memories tumbled out.

'You're really going back to Ireland to confront your dad?' she asked, when I'd finished. 'Do you want me to come with you?'

'You'd do that?'

'Of course. You've always been there for me. I want to be there for you.'

'Thank you. That means a lot, but this is something I need to do on my own. I may need you when I get back, though.'

'I'll be here. When are you going?'

'I might fly out on Thursday night and confront them on Friday. If I chicken out, I've still got Saturday.'

'You're absolutely sure you don't want some moral support?'

'I'm sure. Besides, you've got a business to run. I know you're the boss but you've been away for three weeks already. Another few days would seriously be taking the piss, wouldn't it now?'

She laughed. 'You might have a point.'

It was after 3am before we finally called it a night. As I brushed my teeth, it struck me how great a friend Sarah had been over the years and how much I'd taken her friendship for granted. It must have been really difficult to deal with my mood swings and my refusal to talk about the past, yet she'd put up with it for 13 years. I vowed never to take our friendship for granted again.

Chapter 15

'What the hell are you doing here? You're not welcome.'

'Hello, Ma,' I said.

Her pale-grey eyes flashed with hate and bitterness. Her dark hair, streaked liberally with grey, was pulled back into a bun that emphasised the hard angles of her jaw and cheekbones. Frown lines creased her forehead. There was no evidence of laughter lines. My stomach churned and my first instinct was to turn around, jump into my hire car and speed back to Cork. But my need for answers was greater than my fear. Somehow, I mustered the strength to keep my shoulders back, my head held high and my voice steady. 'I'd like to say it's great to see you but that would be a lie.'

'You cheeky… What do you want?'

'I want to speak to Da and I'm not leaving until I do.'

'He's not here.'

'We both know that's a big fib. I saw him at the window just now. You might as well let me in because I'll only stand here and make a scene if you don't.'

'You wouldn't.'

'Is that a challenge?'

I stood on the doorstep, arms folded, holding her stare.

'Let her in, Maeve,' shouted Da from the living room.

Ma turned her back on me and yelled, 'She's not welcome here.'

'I didn't say she was welcome. I said let her in, woman, before the neighbours see her.'

Ma shook her head and narrowed her eyes at me but stepped back and held the door open. 'You'll not be wheedling your way back into his affections, you know. He hates you.' She practically spat the words.

I took a deep breath as I followed her into the living room. I didn't want to be part of their lives, but hearing that Da hated me still hurt.

'So, you came crawling back.' Da glared at me.

I couldn't help looking around me. The room had been wallpapered and there might even have been a new carpet but everything else was still the same, from the gold-coloured sofa with tassels around the base to the huge-backed TV, to the dresser covered in decorative plates depicting Jesus and Mary, and wooden crucifixes.

'You're not the prodigal daughter, you know.' He folded his newspaper and tossed it onto the floor before standing up. 'There's no forgiveness in this house.'

'I never expected to be welcomed back. And I wouldn't want to be. As for your forgiveness, I don't want it and I don't need it.'

'I'm not going to invite you to sit,' he said.

'I don't want to sit.'

'And you needn't think I'll be offering you any tea,' Ma said.

'I don't want a drink, either. All I've come for is some information, then I'll be out of your lives forever.'

Da scowled at me. 'As far as we were concerned, you were already out of our lives forever. Yet somehow you're here for the second time this month.'

'All I want to know is why you were so quick to disown your youngest daughter.'

Ma let out a high-pitched sound like a hysterical laugh. Da

shook his head. 'I should have thought that would be obvious,' he said. 'You brought shame to your family and damaged a good man's name with your whoring ways.' The bitterness with which he spat out the last words cut through me. The years hadn't softened him at all.

'We were in love.'

He stamped his foot on the floor like a child having a tantrum. 'Blasphemy.'

'It's *not* blasphemy. Daran was young, I was young and we loved each other. *You* made it into something dirty.'

'It *was* something dirty. You seduced him, so you both had to pay the price.'

'Why were you so quick to believe it was *me* who seduced *him*?

'I used to watch you, and how men and boys reacted to you. You weren't studious like Aisling or plain like Nia. You were precocious and curious. As a toddler, it was refreshing. As a growing woman, it was dangerous. Your ma and I always knew you'd let us down. You brought shame on our family name.'

'How? How could I have caused shame when nobody knew about the baby?'

'It wasn't just the baby,' Ma cried. 'It was everything about you. The way you dressed, the way you spoke, the way you flicked your hair. Everything about you said "harlot" and, to be sure, look what you became: Jezebel herself.'

Watching her eyes flash with hate and the colour in Da's cheeks darken with each word, I realised it was pointless and that they weren't worth it. Why had I thought for even a second that we might have a sit-down conversation tinged with regret and sadness, instead of a slanging match? Clearly, their opinion hadn't changed from the day they'd disowned me. It seemed that time had deepened their hatred instead of easing it. 'Seventeen years haven't mellowed either of you, so I'll be going soon. Before I do, I want to know two things.'

Da crossed his arms. 'The first will be…?'

'Why did you get Great-Aunt Nuala to say that my baby had died?'

A flicker of something flashed across his eyes. Doubt, perhaps? 'The baby *did* die,' he declared, holding himself upright and strong.

'Bullshit,' I said. 'Shannon's alive, and you know it.'

He visibly flinched when I used her name. He probably hadn't realised I'd named my daughter. His granddaughter. 'How do you know?' he snapped.

'Nuala wrote to me on her deathbed. She couldn't live with the guilty secret on her conscience. She told me why *she* went through with it. I want to know why *you* did. I was giving her up for adoption. I wasn't about to return to Ireland with my baby in tow to bring shame on you all, so why take it that step further?'

'Because.'

'Because what?'

'Because I had no choice.'

'That's bullshit too. Why did you do it?' I yelled. 'Why did you tell such an evil lie?'

'Because.'

'That's not an answer, and you know it. Why?'

'Because I wanted you to feel what I was feeling.' He uncrossed his arms and clenched his fists by his side. I sensed it was taking all his willpower not to strike me.

'What does that mean?'

'The day I found out about your treachery, you became dead to me. I wanted you to know what it felt like to lose a child.'

'I wasn't dead.'

'You were. You are. I told you back then that you were dead to me and I meant it. Now leave this house and, this time, don't ever return.'

I stared at him. I wanted to say more but my legs were shaking, my heart was racing and I was desperate to leave. After all these years, he still terrified me and I hated that he had that sort of power over me. Ma was less terrifying – possibly because there'd never been any love lost between us – but I still squirmed in her presence.

'I'll go,' I said, hoping my voice sounded confident. 'And don't you worry, there's nothing for me here anymore without Daran. I won't be back.'

He followed me to the door. 'Like I give a damn what you do with your life. You're not my daughter. I don't care about you or anything that happens to you. Why is that so hard to get through your thick skull?'

I opened my mouth to speak but I couldn't form any words.

'Not that I'm remotely interested,' he said, 'but what was the other question?'

'What?'

'You said you had two questions to ask me. What was the second one?'

'It was… er…' I tried to stand tall and force out the words, but the two hateful pairs of eyes boring into me were too much. And it didn't matter. I was going to ask him how he lived with himself knowing what he'd done, but I could see the answer right in front of me. Quite easily. He hated me. Really hated me. When he'd said I was dead to him, he'd really meant it.

He planted his hands on his hips. 'Great second question, Clare. I bet you're really glad you flew home to ask that. I think we're done here, so we are.' He pointed to my hire car parked outside the house. 'Get in that thing and get out of here. I never, ever, EVER want to see you again. Is that clear?'

I nodded. Crystal clear.

I made it four miles outside Ballykielty before I had to pull over and give way to my emotions. Facing him again had been terrifying, and I'd managed to let him intimidate me and throw me out yet again. I hadn't had the last word. I hadn't stood up to him. For Christ's sake!

Just as I'd dabbed my eyes and blown my nose, a battered silver Micra pulled up in front of me and a woman with shoulder-length dark hair got out and strode towards my car. Oh Christ, who was this now? Someone to escort me to the airport and make sure I didn't bring more embarrassment to the village? She knocked on the window. I reluctantly opened the door and got out, preparing myself for a torrent of verbal abuse at best, or a slap at worst.

'Clare? Is it really yourself?' said the woman.

'Who's asking?'

'Your big sister.'

I did a double take. 'Aisling?'

She nodded and her face crumpled as the tears fell. 'I thought I'd missed you.' She grabbed me and hugged me tightly. 'Can you forgive me for not coming after you? I'm your big sister. I should have protected you, but I did nothing. It doesn't mean I haven't thought about you every day since you left. I failed you, so I did. I'm so very sorry, Clare.'

I wrapped my arms around her and stroked her hair. 'I don't think there's anything you could have done. I don't think he'd have let you.'

She released me from her embrace but kept her hands on my shoulders and stared into my eyes. 'I can do something now, though. Can we go for a drink?'

I followed Aisling in my car as she drove through various villages and towns to the outskirts of Cork and a pub called *The Burnt Whiskers*. 'I'm friends with the owner,' she said, when we got out. 'Nobody from our village knows about this place. We'll be safe to talk properly with no risk of Ma or Da appearing.'

And talk we did. For the next three hours, we talked non-stop. At six years my senior, Aisling was approaching 22 when I was thrown out. She'd been living in Limerick at the time, completing the final year of a science and teaching degree, so we didn't see much of her except during holidays and, even then, she had a part-time job working in a lab in Cork, so she was barely around.

She'd been home that Christmas but had been out at a New Year's Eve party when it happened. She'd woken up the next morning to find my bedroom empty and hear the news that I'd moved to Cornwall.

'It was the oddest thing, Clare,' she said. 'They never breathed word about it. I had to ask why your room was empty. When I say "empty", I mean completely empty. There was no furniture or anything.'

I gasped. 'No furniture? They'd gutted my room?'

Aisling nodded. 'It was like you'd died and all trace of you had been wiped out. They told me that you'd been worried about Great-Aunt Nuala being on her own after a fall and had asked to move to England immediately so you could look after her.'

I shook my head. 'She hadn't had a fall. She was fit as a fiddle back then. Did you buy that excuse?'

'No. I asked why they'd let you put your education at risk like that, because you'd surely have to go back two years and start your GCSEs. Da went mad at me for questioning him. I was told it was none of my business and I should drop the subject or I could get the next train back to Limerick and see how I managed the rest of my degree with no financial support.'

'That was harsh.'

'He's a harsh man, Clare, as you've experienced first-hand. I tried to quiz Nia about it. All she'd say was that Father Doherty came round, then she and the twins were sent out to visit friends.

When they came back, you were gone and your room was empty. I asked her whether she thought your sudden departure was something to do with your secret boyfriend but—'

'You knew I was seeing someone?'

'Someone kept stealing my underwear and I couldn't imagine it was Nia or Ma.'

I clapped my hand over my mouth. 'Jesus! I'm sorry. I had no money to get my own. I didn't mean to keep them.'

She laughed. 'It's fine. I found it quite funny. Anyway, Da chose that very moment to walk past and overhear me. He got really jittery and insisted that you'd never had a boyfriend and had always wanted to study in England. One more word and I could join you.'

'I'm sorry you got into trouble.'

Aisling smiled. 'Don't be. I could handle myself by then. Moving to Limerick was the best thing I ever did because I got free from his control and found out who I was. I discovered I had a voice and opinions and a life that wasn't controlled by him and the Church. But I also wasn't stupid. I needed his financial support to finish my degree so I dropped the subject at home. I did my Miss Marple bit out of earshot, though. I discovered that Daran McInnery had been whisked away from the village and nobody seemed to know why. Rumours ranged from his ma being ill to an inappropriate relationship with a married woman, but a million little things suddenly made sense – I just knew that he was your secret boyfriend and that both of you leaving wasn't a coincidence.'

'Did you say anything when you'd made the connection?'

She laughed. 'I must like to live dangerously. I confronted Da. He denied it, of course, but his eyes gave him away. You might remember that I'd always been close to Father Doherty. I might have made out that Da had confirmed the relationship. Believing I knew everything, Father Doherty mentioned the baby. I'm so sorry for what Ma and Da did to you, so I am.'

'Father Doherty was there too, you know.'

Aisling nodded. 'He told me. He also said it was the worst thing that he'd ever experienced. Da had led him to believe that you'd have the baby, it would be adopted, then you'd come home and continue as before. He had no idea they were going to cut you off forever or he'd never have helped them.'

'To be fair, he did try to stop them but there was no reasoning with either of them. They told me I was dead to them and would never be welcome in their lives. Ever. Something they reminded me of again just now.'

Aisling closed her eyes and shook her head. 'You were 16. I know you were mature, but you were still only 16. What were they thinking?' She reached out and took my hand across the table. 'I want you to know that I wrote to you as soon as I knew. I wrote every week for six months, then every month for four years, but my letters were returned unopened. I kept hoping one might slip past her so I kept going.'

'What made you stop writing?'

'She wrote to me and told me you'd left Cornwall and that she had no idea where you were, so I might as well save myself the postage. I should have tried to find you but I was married by then, had a baby, and life just got in my way.'

'I'm an auntie?'

She smiled. 'Twice over. Torin is 10 and Briyana is eight, but I've separated from their dad now.'

'Oh no! I'm sorry.'

'Don't be. Finn and I were friends who tried to make a marriage work, which was fine until he met someone he wanted to be more than friends with. You can imagine what Da had to say about that.'

'I bet he thought it was your fault.'

'Of course. Apparently, I didn't know how to keep my man

happy so it was no wonder he looked elsewhere.'

'Sounds just like Da. What about Nia, Keenan and Éamonn? Do they know what happened to me? Do they care?'

She shrugged. 'There was no point in talking about it at the time. Keenan and Éamonn were mini versions of Da back then, although they've both changed since. Nia was too scared to talk about it. She married someone just like Da, poor thing. She isn't allowed to wear make-up, to work, to have an opinion, or do anything that would make her a real person. I don't really see much of her, but I do see the boys from time to time.'

'Did any of them know about the baby?'

She shrugged. 'I don't think so. If they did, they never mentioned it. Father Doherty told me the baby died. I'm sorry about that.'

'She didn't die,' I said. 'They lied about that too.'

A tear trickled down Aisling's cheek, and she swiped at it when I told her about Great-Aunt Nuala's letter and my findings about her since then. 'Just when I think that man can't get any lower… Oh, Clare, you must have been to hell and back. And poor Daran. I liked him.'

My heart raced at the mention of his name. 'We were going to get married. He gave me this, although I wear it on the other hand now.' I stretched out my hand with the Claddagh ring on it.

'It's beautiful,' she said. 'He must have really loved you to give up joining the priesthood, which makes the whole thing even more tragic.' She bit her lip. 'Oh Christ! You do know about him…?'

'Yes. A friend Googled him and found out about Thailand. Discovering that he'd died and Shannon had lived made me determined to confront Da, which is why I was at the house today. I wanted answers. Fat lot of good it did me, though. I let him get to me again and bollocksed the whole thing up. Stood there like a right eejit, quaking in my boots.'

'I'm sure you didn't bollocks it up. Did you get any answers?'

'Yes. I didn't like them, but I got them.'

'Then it's mission successful or mission partly successful, isn't it?'

I smiled at my sister. 'I suppose so.'

'Purely selfishly, I'd say it was very successful because, if you hadn't visited them, I'd never have spotted you and I'm absolutely thrilled to finally catch up.'

'Thank you. Me too.'

'If your man, Daran, had still been alive, would you have tried to pick things up with him?'

I shook my head vigorously. 'No. It's been too long. I still love him. I always will, but there'd have been so many regrets niggling away that I don't know if we'd have made it. I thought about him constantly for years, though. I ached for him. I wrote long letters to him and posted them without Great-Aunt Nuala's knowledge. I didn't know where to post them, though. The only place I could think of was care of Father Doherty. Ma had threatened to call the Guards if I tried to contact him, but they obviously hadn't knocked all of the rebellion out of me, as I wrote anyway. I have no idea if Father Doherty delivered them. I suspect not because Great-Aunt Nuala said she told him to destroy the letters that Daran sent me. I wonder if he did.'

'Only one way to find out.' Aisling knocked back the last of her orange juice and stood up. 'Let's go now.'

'Where?'

'To see Father Doherty and ask him about the letters.'

My eyes widened. 'He's here?'

Aisling pulled her coat on. 'He's in a retirement home about 10 minutes away. I visit him every few weeks. He sometimes asks about you, but I've never been able to tell him anything. He'll be delighted to see you.'

'Really? I know he tried to convince Da not to disown me but he still believed I was a sinner.'

'I think you'll find that old age and retirement have had a profound effect on our former priest. Come on.'

I followed Aisling into the car park. 'Follow me. Are you ready to face your past now?'

Was I? I'd already made one failed attempt this morning with the parents but, as Aisling pointed out, I *had* got some answers, even if I didn't like them. I'd also had an unexpected serendipitous moment in finding a sister who'd never stopped caring and trying to find out what had happened. Could Father Doherty hold more answers?

I opened the door of my hire car. 'I'm ready. Bring it on!'

Chapter 16

'Are you sure it's okay for me to turn up unannounced?' Seeing Father Doherty had seemed like a good idea in the pub but now, in the car park of the retirement home, it didn't seem such an enticing plan. I'd already faced two of my demons and it hadn't been pleasant. Was I strong enough to face the third?

'And here was me thinking you were a strong, confident woman,' Aisling said.

'I am. I'm just thinking of Father Doherty. I don't want him to drop dead of a heart attack at the sight of me.'

Aisling laughed and grabbed my hand. 'I think you'll be pleasantly surprised.' I followed her along a carpeted corridor until she stopped outside a door with the number 36 on it and a simple wooden cross. 'Are you ready to face himself?'

I drew a deep breath. 'As ready as I'll ever be.'

She knocked on the door, then turned the handle. 'Father Doherty? Are you home? It's Aisling.'

'Aisling? Is it yourself? Come in, child, come in.'

She pushed the door wide open and we stepped into a small hallway. We walked past a couple of closed doors, then into an open-plan lounge/diner/kitchen. He was reclining in an armchair by the window with a glass of sherry on a table beside him and classical music playing.

'I've brought someone to see you.' Aisling pushed me forward. 'Someone from your past.'

He looked in my direction expectantly and frowned. He removed his glasses, opened his mouth, replaced his glasses, then closed his mouth. Still staring at me, he pressed his feet on the recliner to bring the chair to an upright position, then shuffled towards me. 'It can't be,' he said. 'Is it yourself, young Clare?'

I nodded.

He reached out his hands and took both of mine in his, then brought them to his mouth and kissed them. 'I always prayed that I'd have a chance to meet you again one day and now the Lord has delivered you to me. Come and sit. Please.'

I looked at Aisling and she nodded encouragingly. I sat down on a two-seater sofa next to Aisling as Father Doherty shuffled back to his armchair.

'It really is you?' he said.

I finally found my voice. 'It really is me, Father. How are you?'

'Blessed,' he said. 'Blessed to see that you have grown into a fine young woman after everything your parents and I did to you. I have dreamt I could make amends for so many years and now here you are like an angel of mercy, so you are.'

'I'm confused, Father,' I said. 'You seem pleased to see me.'

'Of course I am, my child.'

'Why?'

'Because you've never been far from my thoughts for nearly two decades. I've longed to make sure you're well and to ask for your forgiveness for the part I played in your exile. Tell me, how is the child? She'd be, what, 16 now? Does she look like you?'

'You don't know, do you?'

'Don't know what?'

'Why do you think my da sent me to Cornwall?'

'So you could have your baby away from the gossip and rumours in the village and give her a better start in life.'

I looked at Aisling but she shrugged and mouthed, 'I thought he knew.'

I took a deep breath as I looked back towards Father Doherty. 'Da arranged for Shannon to be adopted, but they told me she'd died shortly after she was born.'

'She died? Oh no, child. That's too tragic.' He closed his eyes.

'She didn't really die, though, Father,' I added quickly. 'It was just a ploy to stop me finding her. She was adopted by another family, which I only found out a week ago, when I was sent a confession letter that my great-aunt Nuala wrote before she died.'

He opened his eyes. 'Oh my goodness! I should have realised something was afoot when your da didn't want to talk about his grandchild. He told me that he was in touch with you and had offered you the chance to return, but you loved it in Cornwall and wanted to stay.'

More lies. How could someone who claimed to be such a devoted Catholic lie as easily as breathing? I sat forward. 'Can I ask you a question, Father?'

'Of course.'

'What happened to the letters I sent you for Daran? Did he ever get them?'

He sighed, then stood up and shuffled out of the room. I heard the sound of a cupboard opening, then he reappeared holding a cardboard box. 'Here.' He handed the box to me.

I opened the lid. On the top lay a large bundle of letters in various pastel-coloured envelopes, tied together with a piece of string. 'My letters. You kept them! I take it Daran never saw them?'

'I'm sorry, child. Daran was a good man from a good family. I wanted to protect him, and them, from scandal. If word had got out that he'd impregnated a minor…' He shook his head. 'I'm afraid your da threatened to contact the Guards if I acted as any sort of conduit between the two of you. I felt I had no choice. What good would it have done for anyone if he'd been arrested? It could have ruined both of you, and I only wanted what was best for you and the child.'

I pulled out another bundle from underneath. 'These are for me. This is Daran's writing. You didn't destroy them?'

'Your great-aunt asked me to, but I couldn't do it.'

I stared at the bundles of letters, my emotions in turmoil. 'Did Daran know you had letters from me?'

'Yes.'

'Did he know his letters never made it to me?'

'Yes.'

'Then why did he write?'

Father Doherty looked at me with watery eyes. 'For the same reason that you wrote to him for all those years.'

I gently placed the bundles back in the box. It had been my way of keeping our love alive. It had also been my way of coping. If I hadn't been able to hide away in my room for hours and write, I'm not sure I'd have got through it. It was comforting to know that Daran had done the same. It was further evidence that Da's claims that I hadn't been the only one were absolute bullshit. He wouldn't have written dozens and dozens of letters if I'd meant as little to him as Da had tried to make out. And he wouldn't have given me the Claddagh ring. I twiddled it again.

'We were going to get married,' I said. 'He proposed to me on my 16th birthday. He gave me this.'

'I know.'

I stopped fiddling with it. 'He told you?'

'He asked me to hear his Confession. Oh, child, you do know what happened to him, don't you?'

I nodded. 'I know.'

He sighed and shook his head. 'Tragic. Absolutely tragic. I

blamed myself for my part in him being in Thailand that day.' He leaned forward in his chair. 'He really loved you, you know. All I could think of in that memorial service was how I should have been strong and asked God what to do about the two of you, rather than being led by your da. If I'd done that, things could have been very different.'

We sat in silence for a while. I riffled through the letters, tears running down my cheeks, although I didn't open any. I didn't feel strong enough.

'Your kids?' I asked, turning to Aisling suddenly, wiping the tears away. 'Who's got your kids?'

'Don't you be worrying yourself about that. They're with Finn's mother. They stay there on a Friday night so I can have some me time, now that Finn's living in Manchester. I'm free all night. I'm here for you.'

A glass of water was pushed into my hands. I hadn't realised Father Doherty had got up. I sipped it slowly.

Father Doherty looked at me with the saddest eyes I've ever seen. 'May I say a prayer?' he asked.

'I don't believe in God,' I said. 'I never felt He had a place in my life after He took my baby. Or supposedly took my baby.'

'I can understand why you'd feel like that. I shouldn't have suggested it.'

He seemed to have aged 20 years since we'd entered his flat. I sighed as compassion overcame me. 'Actually, a prayer might be good. Thank you.'

'You're sure?'

'I'm sure.'

Aisling and I bent our heads and he placed a hand on each as he prayed for Daran, Shannon and forgiveness. 'May you give back to this child what she thought was lost and help her find a way back to happiness and contentment,' he finished. 'Amen.'

'Amen,' we both whispered.

'We should go,' I said. 'Can I have these?'

'The letters are yours, my child. They always were. I'm sorry they're with you too late.'

'You weren't to know. I blame my da for all of this. Not you. So if it's forgiveness you want, you have it. Part of me wishes you had passed on our letters, but I have no doubt that Da would have called the guards on Daran. What good would that have done anyone? You did the right thing in the circumstances.'

A flicker of what I could only describe as peace passed over the old man's face. 'What you do next is entirely up to you, Clare, but I implore you to draw a line in the sand and move on. What's done is done and we can't change the past, but you have a chance for a new future. Find Shannon and don't waste a further thought on your father. He'll be judged by the Lord when the day comes. You don't need to waste the energy on judging him yourself, so you don't.'

Aisling and I hugged him goodbye, then left his flat and walked to the car park in silence.

'Thank you,' I said to her, when we reached the cars. 'I'm glad you made me do that.'

'I told you he'd changed,' she said. 'What happens next?'

I shrugged. 'I don't know. I feel drained.'

'I'm not surprised. Will you be reading the letters, do you think?'

I screwed my nose up. 'Not sure I'm strong enough for it today. Do you know what? I never cry, but I've barely stopped since finding out about Shannon. If I start on these today, I think I may unleash the Hoover Dam.'

Aisling smiled and patted my arm. 'The main thing is that you have them. You'll know when the time is right. Will you go back tomorrow?'

'Probably. I booked a Sunday flight in case I bottled seeing the parents today, but the deed is done so I'll see if I can change it for the morning.'

'I understand if you want to head home, after what you've been through today, but I'd love it if you'd stay. I know a couple of kids who'd be thrilled to spend a day with their long-lost auntie Clare.'

'They know about me?'

Aisling grinned. 'Not the full family scandal, but they know I have a baby sister who lives in England whom I lost touch with. They'll be thrilled.'

'You're sure it wouldn't be too complicated for you if I joined you?' I said.

'It would be a pleasure.'

'If I spend the day with you, I have one condition.'

'Name it.'

'We don't talk about the past. I've had my fill of history today. Tomorrow I just want to focus on getting to know my big sister, my nephew and my niece.'

'You're on.' She flung her arms around me. 'Jesus, Clare, I'm so glad you came back. The rest of the family may be bloody eejits but I want my baby sister in my life.' Her voice cracked. 'I hope you want me in yours.'

The tears started again. 'Of course I do. You're the only family I have.'

'You get three of us for the price of one. Not bad, eh?'

As I drove back to my hotel, I glanced at the box of letters on the passenger seat and shook my head. What a day. Of all the ways I'd played it out in my mind, I certainly hadn't expected to end it having gained a sister, a nephew and a niece. For the first time since I was 16, I had a family. I had real-life blood relatives who wanted me in their lives. Most unexpected.

Chapter 17

'Will you stop passing me from one department to the next?' I snapped on Monday morning. 'I've been on the phone for 40 minutes and I'm going around in circles.'

'It's illegal for a mother to try and find out about her adopted child before they're 18,' said the woman on the end of the phone. She had a strong Glaswegian accent, but something about her tone told me I might finally be speaking to someone more senior and with more common sense than the others I'd been passed around so far.

'Will I tell you something? You are the eighth person to tell me that this morning and, as I said to the other seven, I'm very aware of the law already. However, I would like you to listen to what I'm saying to you about the circumstances of my enquiry, instead of repeating the words that I've already found online. Will you do that? Please?'

There was a pause and a sigh. 'Okay, Ms O'Connell. I'm listening.'

At last!

'I see,' she said, when I finished. 'Quite an unusual set of circumstances.'

'I know. Thank you for listening to them.'

'You're welcome. I'll tell you what I'm *not* going to do, Ms

O'Connell. I'm not going to pass you onto anyone else. I'm also not going to lie to you. I don't know the protocol in this case, as it's unusual. What I *am* going to promise you is that I'll personally find out what we can do in these circumstances. May I take your phone number and assure you that I will call you in an hour's time? I suspect I won't have an answer in an hour, but I'll definitely call you to update you on my progress. Would that be acceptable?'

'That would be far more acceptable than any other offer I've had today,' I said. 'Thank you.'

'My name's Valerie Sinclair. I'll call you back within the hour.'

And she did. But only to tell me that she'd hit a few brick walls and was unable to get hold of the people she needed to speak to. She asked me to leave it with her and promised me she'd come back to me by the end of the week. Let the waiting commence.

I put the phone down and made myself a coffee, glad that I'd booked a long weekend off, because my mind was on anything but work.

Despite the hideous confrontation with the parents, the weekend had ended up being pretty special. I'd had a long soak in the bath, then ordered room service on the Friday evening, before falling asleep in front of the TV. I met Aisling, Torin and Briyana for lunch on Saturday, then spent the day with them. The avoid-the-past pact worked well. Despite the six-year age difference, Aisling and I seemed to have loads in common. She was a strong, confident woman who also had a very fragile relationship with our parents because she wasn't afraid to challenge their views and opinions. She worked in the local comprehensive as a biology and chemistry teacher from Monday to Thursday and usually spent Fridays doing shopping and housework so she could devote her weekends to her kids. Torin and Briyana were an absolute joy to be around: funny and vivacious yet polite at the same time. They immediately accepted their 'long-lost auntie Clare' as someone they felt comfortable being around.

All too soon, it was time to fly back to the UK, start my search for Shannon and hope that she wasn't harbouring a 16-year-long hate vendetta towards the woman who had abandoned her at birth.

I sighed as I pressed the intercom button at around seven on the Friday night of that week. 'Yes?'

'Ah! You *are* alive. Can I come in?'

'It's not really convenient, Ben. Sorry. You should have called first.'

'I tried, but someone has been ignoring my calls.'

'Sorry, Ben, but I have loads to do. I'll call you next week.'

'Okay.'

I returned to the dining table and the pile of letters from Daran. A two-day trip to Newcastle, followed by a day in Edinburgh, had provided a welcome distraction but now, with no news from Valerie Sinclair (bloody typical) and no plans for the evening, I felt that it might just be the right time. I hoped that the years apart really had helped me get over him and I wasn't about to rekindle strong feelings that had lain dormant but not forgotten.

A knock on the door made me jump. I peered through the spyhole: Ben stood in the corridor looking at his watch. I reluctantly pulled the door open. 'I thought I said it wasn't convenient.'

'And I thought that was rude, so I decided to ignore you. Someone was leaving so they let me in. What are you doing?' He walked past me and into the apartment.

'Won't you come in and make yourself at home?'

'I fully intend to,' he said, heading for the sofa. Then he stopped and turned around. 'I'll stop now. You know I'm nowhere near that cheeky. If it really is inconvenient, I'll leave, but I'm worried about you. I haven't seen you since before my trip to Birmingham. You haven't returned my calls or texts; you haven't put anything on Facebook…'

'I hardly ever put anything on Facebook.'

'I know, but you've put even less than your usual very little.' Ben grinned. 'So the Facebook thing is rubbish, but you definitely haven't returned my calls or texts. I just wanted to come round to say that I'm here if you want to talk about what happened at New Year, what happened on your trip to Ireland, or anything else for that matter. Or if you just want someone to share a curry and a cold beer with.' He looked so sincere and so keen to help.

'How did you know I'd been to Ireland again?'

Ben shrugged. 'I didn't. I was talking about after New Year.'

'Oh.'

'You've been again? When?'

'This weekend just gone.'

'Oh. Two trips to Ireland in the space of two weeks sounds like a story…'

Feck it. It was time to let Ben in too. 'Why don't you sit down?' I said. 'You're making the place look a mess.'

He smiled as he took a seat on the sofa. I curled up on the other end. 'I went to Ireland at the weekend to confront my da about why he kicked me out when I was 16. I know the fact that I was pregnant with the local trainee priest's baby wasn't exactly welcome news, but sending me to Cornwall and telling me I was dead to him was a bit harsh, don't you think?' I watched Ben's expression carefully. If he was surprised or shocked, he gave nothing away.

'Definitely a story,' he said. 'Do you want to tell me it all from the beginning?'

'I may be able to help you find Shannon,' Ben said, when I'd finished.

'How?'

'You know what I do for a living?'

'Saintly stuff?'

'Ha ha. What do I really do?'

I shrugged. 'Fecked if I know. Other people's jobs bore me senseless. You do something with a charity.'

Ben raised his eyebrows and cocked his head to one side.

I frowned. 'You do, don't you? I'm sure I'm right. I'm buggered if I know what sort of charity it is, but you definitely work for one, so stop winding me up.'

Ben laughed. 'Yes, I do work for a charity. We help find missing persons, but I focus particularly on young people who have probably run away from home. Consequently, I have a really good relationship with Social Services, adoption agencies and various other parties that could help.'

'You really find missing people?'

Ben nodded.

'Why didn't you tell me?'

'I swear I've told you loads of times.'

I studied Ben's face and realised that, although I'd spent a lot of time in his company over the years, I'd never bothered to really take the time to talk to him. It was always good craic being out with Ben, but that was mainly because we took the mickey out of each other all night. Suddenly, I could see him as a very interesting person and I regretted all the times I must have switched off or cut him short. Was I really that bad a person? 'I'm sorry,' I said.

'For what?

'For not listening to you. Tell me more about your job. And I'm not saying that just because I want to know how you can help me. I'm genuinely interested.'

As Ben talked about his job and the families he'd reunited over the years, I became filled with admiration for him. Although I'd jokingly called him Saint Ben over the years, he really was a saint, someone who genuinely did good and made a massive difference to the lives of others. It must be amazing to feel like that. My own career in PR seemed pretty insignificant. A few hours' work from me could increase a client's Twitter following, put a positive slant on a bad-news story and increase the cash in the shareholders' pockets. A few hours' work from Ben could reunite a family, take a teenager off the streets or save a child from abuse. They simply didn't compare.

'If your contact comes through with information first, you keep the king,' Ben said. 'But if I get answers first, I get him.'

Bollocks. I suspected I was going to have to hand the king over. But, right now, information on Shannon was far more important, and I had every confidence in Ben that he was going to come through for me. He always did.

Shortly after he left, a text came through:

✉ From Aisling

Saw Da this morning. He banned me from being in touch with you. I told him where to stick his opinion. The kids can't wait to see their auntie Clare again and I'm dying to spend more time with my baby sister. This time 3 weeks, we'll be with you. Hurray for mid-term break! Any news on Shannon yet? xxxx

✉ To Aisling

No news. Hoping next week will bring something. Not a very patient person ;-)

I smiled at the thought of Aisling and the kids coming to stay. I wouldn't have predicted that at the start of the year.

I returned to the letters. Picking up the first envelope in the pile from Daran, I stroked my finger lightly over his curvy writing, a lump blocking my throat. I shook my head and returned the letter to the box. I wasn't ready, after all. I wasn't sure if I ever would be.

Valerie Sinclair phoned me first thing on Monday with an apology. She'd been off sick all week, but she said she'd definitely get onto it and come back to me by the end of the week. Ben rang at the end of the day to tell me that he'd had some good conversations but had come up with nothing concrete yet. He also promised a deadline of the end of the week. He was definitely going to win the king.

Chapter 18

'I've got news.'

I buzzed Ben in and stood with the door wide open, waiting for him to come up in the lift, my heart thumping uncontrollably.

'What is it?' I said, ushering him into the lounge area. I could tell by the anguish in his eyes that it wasn't good news.

'I'm so sorry, Clare. There's no easy way to say this so I'm just going to have to blurt it out. Shannon was in a car crash a few days ago.'

'She's dead?' I whispered. 'She really is dead this time?'

He shook his head. 'No, but it doesn't sound good. Apparently, she's in a coma. She was on the M1 when a lorry jack-knifed and hit the car she was travelling in.'

'Are you sure?'

He reached into his jeans pocket and pulled out a couple of sheets of A4 paper, which he unfolded and handed to me. 'I'm sure.'

I scanned the words on the computer printouts of newspaper articles about the accident but found myself struggling to take it all in. 'Jesus wept! The driver was her boyfriend? And he's…?'

'Okay, I think.'

'Where on the M1 did it happen?'

'Close to Junction 43.'

My eyes widened. 'Junction 43? But that would mean…' I couldn't bring myself to say the words, in case I was wrong.

'It would mean that they were rushed to *Jimmy's*. Clare, your daughter's in Leeds.'

'Can you not drive any faster? I knew I should have driven.'

Ben indicated to change lanes. 'You don't know the way, which is why I'm driving and, no, I can't drive any faster. There's a red light, in case you hadn't noticed. And stop biting your nails.'

'I'm not.'

'Yes, you are. I can see you out of the corner of my eye.'

'I'm not biting my nails,' I insisted. 'I'm nibbling the skin around them.'

'Urgh. Don't do that! You'll hurt yourself.'

'I can't help it. I'm full of nervous energy.'

The lights changed and Ben did his best to accelerate, but the flow of traffic wouldn't allow him to get up to more than 20mph.

He gave me a sideways glance. 'You know I'm normally an optimistic person, but you do realise we probably won't be able to see her, don't you? Stop biting!'

I sat on my hands. 'I know, but I can't just sit in that apartment knowing she's in the same city as me and doing nothing about it. I'd be climbing the walls.'

'Just as long as you're prepared for the reality.'

'It's worth a try.'

My stomach twisted and turned as the car edged ever closer to *St James's University Hospital,* affectionately known locally as *Jimmy's*. What if we were too late? What if she'd already passed away? No. I mustn't think like that. It could have gone the other way. She could have come out of her coma. How amazing would that be? But what if she refused to see me? How would I feel if I'd been given up for adoption and my biological mother turned up

16 or 17 years later? Would I want to see her?

'Are you ready?' Ben took my hand as we dashed across the car park. He'd already found out that she was in the Intensive Care Unit. I gripped his hand tightly as we made our way up lifts and down a maze of corridors.

'What now?' Ben whispered.

'Would I be right in thinking they only let family in?'

'Yes.'

'Piece of piss, then. I'm family.'

Before Ben could protest, I'd marched up to the nurses' desk. A large, matronly woman with curly, grey hair looked up. 'I've just heard that my daughter's been in an accident,' I announced.

'Name?'

'Shannon O'Co… Kitteridge. Shannon Kitteridge.'

'You're her mother?'

'Yes. I've been abroad. I've just got back or I'd have been here sooner.' I hated the way the lies tripped off my tongue but, over the years, I'd got used to telling white lies to hide the truth about my past. I heard Ben gulp beside me.

'And you are…?' she said, glancing at Ben.

'Shannon's stepdaddy,' I said.

'I'll need to get a doctor to speak to you before you can see her. Give me a minute. You can take a seat over there.' She pointed to some plastic chairs nearby, then picked up a phone.

'What if she's calling Security?' Ben hissed once we'd sat down.

'We're hardly a threat, are we?' I whispered back. 'We're sitting down like good children, patiently waiting for the doctor.'

'I don't like telling lies.'

'Neither do I, but needs must. Besides, the only lie was about you being her stepfather. I *am* her mum, even if only biologically.'

Six or seven excruciatingly slow minutes passed while we

waited. Eventually, a petite Indian woman appeared, holding a clipboard. 'Mrs Kitteridge?' she asked, barely glancing up from her paperwork.

Ben and I both stood up. 'Clare,' I said, avoiding another lie or an awkward explanation.

'I'm Dr Maahi Kaur. I'm treating your daughter.' She flicked through a few sheets of paper on the clipboard, then tucked it under her arm and looked at me for the first time, with a gentle smile. 'There's no mistaking the family resemblance.'

My stomach did a somersault. Shannon looked like me? I knew from the photo of her at six months old that she'd inherited the blonde hair, but I had no idea how she'd developed.

'And you're the father?' Dr Kaur asked, turning to Ben.

His cheeks reddened slightly. 'Stepfather.'

Dr Kaur nodded. 'Shannon has been in a serious RTC. She's suffered a severe head trauma, broken arm and broken ankle. The ankle and arm will mend, but the head trauma is the greatest concern. In cases like this, it's always vital to do our best to reduce any swelling that could cause damage to the brain. She's therefore in an induced coma to allow this to happen.'

Brain damage? I gripped onto Ben's arm. I had questions. Lots of questions. I needed to be strong. 'How long is she likely to be in a coma?'

'It's hard to say. The swelling has gone down, which is a positive sign, but her young body has been through such a lot that we don't want to bring her round too quickly.'

'She will pull through, though?'

I held my breath as I waited for Dr Kaur's response.

'We would expect so. She's young, healthy and strong. She's definitely a fighter. What we can't say is whether there will be any lasting damage until she comes round. All head traumas carry risks. We do our best to reduce those risks, but there are no guarantees. Do you have any other questions?'

I shook my head. I probably did. I probably had loads. For now, I just wanted to see my little girl.

'Nurse Wilson will direct you to Shannon. Please ask her if you think of anything else.'

'Thank you,' I whispered.

We followed Nurse Wilson down a corridor and into what appeared to be a private room.

'All the tubes and monitors can be pretty scary to see,' she warned. 'She's actually doing better than you might think from looking at them all.'

But I wasn't looking at the tubes and monitors. I was looking at the baby girl who'd grown into a beautiful young woman. Long, blonde hair was scraped back from her forehead. Bruises and small cuts covered her face, but I could still see that she was the spit of me when I was her age. It was uncanny.

'I'll leave you to it.' Nurse Wilson shuffled out of the room.

'The doctor was right,' Ben said. 'She's just like you.'

I stared at Shannon for a while, searching for any similarities to Daran, but it was hard to tell amongst the injuries and tubes. Please let her be all right. Please. Please don't let me find her, then take her away from me.

'How does it feel, seeing her after all these years?' Ben whispered.

'Like I'm in a dream. I can't get my head around it. She was a tiny baby, and now…' I shook my head. 'Do you think she'll be okay?'

'I thought the doctor sounded quite positive.'

'Did you? I hope you're right.'

I stared at Shannon again, unsure whether to talk to her or touch her hand. I turned to Ben. 'I don't know what to do now that we're here. I feel like an intruder.'

‘In what way?’

I started to chew on the skin around my thumbnail again, and Ben gently slapped my hand away. ‘If Shannon had wanted to find me, she could have. I know that I have no legal right to look for her until she’s 18, but she could have searched me out at any point and she hasn’t. As far as she’s concerned, I’m a stranger who abandoned her at birth and wants nothing to do with her. I don’t have a right to be here, Ben, staring at her while she’s in a coma fighting for her life. She doesn’t get to choose whether she’s ready to meet me or not. It’s not fair on her. In typical “me” style, I’ve just barged back into her life without thinking through the consequences. I’ve lied to a nurse and a doctor, and I’ve dragged you into that lie.’

‘Don’t worry about me. I wanted to come. What do you want to do, then?’

‘I think we’d better go. I really shouldn’t be here.’

‘No, you shouldn’t,’ said a man’s voice. ‘So why the hell *are* you?’

Chapter 19

Bollocks! We'd been sprung! I spun around, heart thumping, expecting to see a security guard or even a policeman. Instead, I found myself face to face with a broad-chested Zac Efron lookalike of roughly 17 or 18, leaning on a pair of crutches. He shook a dark fringe out of his piercing, blue eyes. Just like Shannon, his face was covered in tiny cuts and bruises, and he had some Steri-Strips across his right cheek. He had to be the boyfriend.

'Hi. My name's—'

'I know who you are.'

'You do?'

'My leg may be busted, but my eyes still work.'

'I'm Clare.' Too many years in PR kicked in and I walked towards him with my hand outstretched.

'Callum.' He showed no sign of returning the handshake, although, to be fair to him, his movement was slightly impeded by the crutches. Could I have been any more of an eejit? I let my hand dangle by my side again and shuffled backwards slightly. 'Shannon's fiancé,' he added.

'Oh! Congratulations.' It seemed a bit of a cheesy thing to say in the circumstances, but what was the protocol for the first time the absent mum meets the fiancé of the daughter she thought was dead?

'How did you find her?' he asked.

I glanced towards Ben.

'I did some research,' Ben said.

'Who are you, like? The police?'

Ben shook his head. 'Just a friend. I'm Ben. Hi.'

Silence.

'We came as soon as we found out,' I said.

'Really? How kind of you to rush to your daughter's side in her hour of need. Except, it's not her first hour of need, is it? It's not like you gave a shit when her parents died and she was in and out of foster homes. She needed you then. She doesn't need you now. She's got me. I'm her family now. I'm, like, all she needs.'

Ouch. 'I'm sorry she's had it tough. But there's a good reason why I've only just appeared.'

Callum flicked his hair out of his eyes again. 'Don't tell me. Let me guess. You've been living overseas? No, that's not it. Erm … You've been working on your career and it's taken this long to earn enough to buy a home for you and Shannon?' He shook his head. 'No, that's not it either. I know! Your husband and kids wouldn't understand if you admitted that you'd shagged the local priest and got knocked up at 16?'

I gasped. 'You know about Daran?'

'Shannon's family – her *real* family – didn't keep secrets from her. She knew she was adopted, and she got it. What she didn't get was why you never tried to find her when her dad died. She wrote to you every week for months and—'

'I didn't get any letters.'

'Liar! You ignored her at first, like, but then you wrote back, telling her that you were happily married with two little kiddies and you didn't want a mistake from your past to ruin your perfect life. Can you imagine what that did to her? She'd just lost her parents and now her biological mother had rejected her for the second time.'

I felt sick. Great-Aunt Nuala. She must have written back. Or Ma. Or Da.

'Where did she send the letters?' I whispered.

'I don't bloody know. Does it matter, like?'

I shrugged. 'Probably not. Any of them could have done it. The point is that I never got any letters and I certainly didn't write to Shannon.' I stood up a little straighter. 'You've said your piece, Callum, and now it's my turn. I want you to sit down and rest your leg, though.'

'I'm fine here and I'm not interested in your excuses. You can leave.'

I folded my arms and fixed my hardest stare on him, reminding myself that he wasn't Da; he was an angry teenager who'd been through a traumatic experience and I didn't need to be afraid of him. 'I'm not going anywhere till you've heard me out. Sit down.'

'No!'

'Bollocks to you. Stand, then. I don't care. But you *will* listen. If you still want me to go after you've heard me out, I'll go, although please know that I'll be back. Now that I've found her, I'm not walking away that easily.'

Callum looked as if he were about to object but sat down anyway in the seat next to the bed, no doubt grateful at being able to relieve some of the pain.

'Right. Good. Glad you've seen sense. You said that Shannon's family never lied to her. Well, Shannon's very lucky because mine did nothing *but* lie to me. There's an incredibly good reason why I never tried to find her, and it has nothing to do with being married with kids, because I'm *not* married and the only child I have is right there fighting for her life. The reason why I never tried to find her is that, until three weeks ago, I believed that she'd died two hours after she was born. How's that for a good excuse?'

Callum's mouth opened and he looked from me to Ben and back to me again, as if searching for signs that I was winding him up. 'You've just made that up!'

'I wish I had.' I yanked open my bag, rummaged for a moment, then thrust Great-Aunt Nuala's letter into his hands. 'Imagine my surprise when this arrived.'

Callum looked at the letter and shrugged. 'You want me to read this?'

'Be my guest. You can see first-hand what a delightful family I have.'

I watched Callum's eyes widen as he read the letter, then went back to the beginning and reread it. He put the peach sheets back into the envelope and handed it to me, keeping his eyes on Shannon the whole time. He took hold of her hand and kissed it. 'I think I should tell them. You would if you were awake and you'd just read that.'

My heartbeat quickened. What could he possibly tell us? If it was something serious about her injury, Dr Kaur would have told us already, wouldn't she?

Still holding Shannon's hand, Callum twisted around and looked at me. 'I need to show you something.'

He lifted the crutches up and heaved himself out of the seat. 'Follow me.'

'Where are we going?'

'You'll soon find out.'

'But what about Shannon?'

'Not being funny, but she isn't going anywhere, is she?'

In silence, Ben and I followed him along a corridor, down in a lift, along another corridor and up in another lift. I'd stopped looking at the various hospital signs, as most didn't mean anything to me and those that did conjured up terrifying possibilities of serious surgery and terminal illness.

'Back so soon?' A young redheaded nurse with a Geordie accent looked up from some paperwork as Callum hopped towards the nurses' station. 'Did youse leave summat behind?'

'No. I found something. A couple of unexpected visitors. Are we okay to…?'

She nodded. 'Oh, aye. You know your way.'

'Thanks, Kelly.'

I followed Callum into a small room containing four plastic cribs, three of which contained babies. He stopped by the first one on the left and nodded towards the sleeping baby.

'Shannon and me have a little surprise for you. This is Luke. Your grandson.'

Chapter 20

'Sweet Jesus!' I looked over at Ben as he fastened his seat belt. 'I certainly wasn't expecting that. You really didn't know?'

'Of course not!' He started the engine. 'You don't seriously think I'd keep something huge like that from you, do you?'

I shook my head. 'No.'

Ben reversed his car out of the parking space. 'Where to now? My place? Your place? The pub?'

'The offie, then yours. Can I stay over?'

'Of course.'

I watched his profile as he concentrated on finding the exit of the hospital car park, noticing the way his cheekbones tightened and his nose wrinkled each time someone pulled out in front of him. I'd have beeped my horn and screeched expletives, but Ben was definitely more in control of his emotions. 'I'm glad you were with me, Ben. Tonight was above and beyond. Thank you.'

He glanced in my direction. 'Any time. And it wasn't above and beyond. It's what friends do for each other. Besides, you're going to need a lot more looking-after going forward.'

'What do you mean?'

I stared at him as he waited to pull onto the main road.

'You can pretend you're concentrating on the traffic till the cows come home, Saint Ben, but you'll have to explain a comment like that, so you will.'

A van driver flashed us out. Ben pulled onto the main road, grinning.

'Will you just come out with it, you eejit? I know you're dying to.'

'I have no idea what you're talking about.'

'You liar!' I lightly nudged him in the ribs. 'I know exactly what's making you laugh just now, and you're a mean boy.'

Ben laughed out loud. 'I'm sorry. I can't help it. I know it's completely inappropriate, given how poorly Shannon is, but I can't not acknowledge that you're a grandma. Granny Irish. That's hilarious!'

'It's not! It's bloody terrifying!'

'I can't help picturing you with a blue rinse, brogues and a shopping trolley. A tartan one. Ooh, and a Yorkshire Terrier tucked under your arm.'

'Ben!'

'Perhaps one of those plastic headscarf things and horn-rimmed specs dangling from a chain.'

'Christ, Ben! Could you be more stereotypical about the elderly? Next you're going to suggest I'll have yellow teeth and smell of wee.'

'If the cap fits…'

'Ben! If you weren't driving this car…!'

But I had to admit, it was pretty funny. Petrifying, yet funny. Thirty-three years old and already a grandmother. Imagine Ma and Da's faces if they knew! It would be all 'like mother, like daughter'. Maybe I'd feel brave enough to confront Da again one day and tell him. I shuddered. It wasn't going to happen. The man still terrified me. There was no way I'd be able to face him again, even though the expression on his face would be absolutely priceless.

'Do you think Callum meant what he said about wanting me to

be part of Luke's life?' I said.

'Of course he did. I know he was angry when he first saw you, but wouldn't you be, in his situation? He clearly loves Shannon and, in his eyes, you'd abandoned her when she most needed you. Now he knows that's not true. He seems like a really decent lad.'

'I know. She's picked well there.' I stared out of the window for a while. 'What will I do if Shannon's not as understanding as Callum when she wakes up?'

'You'll work that Irish charm and bring her round in time.'

'And what if she doesn't come round?'

'I'm sure she will. You'll just need to be patient with her.'

I shook my head. 'No. I meant what if she doesn't come round, as in: what if she doesn't wake up?'

'She will.'

'What if she doesn't?'

Ben stopped at a red light and turned around to look at me. 'Then we'll cross that bridge together. Come on, Clare. This isn't like you. You're always the strong, positive one. I know this evening has been a hell of a shock, but you've got to think positively. Shannon's made it through the worst part already. I know she's not out of the woods yet but she's well on her way. She's already battled her way through the thick forest of thorns and now she's just got a little copse to navigate through.'

I had to laugh at his analogy. 'Did you just make that shite up?'

He smiled. 'Yes. Did you like it?'

'It was dire. But I get it, and you're right. I guess I'm just not feeling so strong at the moment. It's been a hell of a year so far.'

'Then it can only get better, can't it?'

I nodded. I hoped he was right.

'I know what will make you happy,' Ben said, as we paused at another set of lights. 'Although he's still in your possession, the king's now mine, isn't he?'

'Feck.' I delved into my bag to retrieve him. 'I thought you said you were going to make me happy?'

'I hadn't finished. Officially, I'm the recipient of the king for finding Shannon before your contact, but I want to give him straight back to you.'

'Why? What have I done that's so special?'

'What have you done? You absolutely rose to that challenge. You dashed straight to the hospital, not caring whether or not you got a bad reception. You blagged your way in; you turned around your daughter's hostile fiancé. And you let me get away with a load of ageist jokes. Definitely king of the moment. Although, you do realise I'm going to go all out to win him back, don't you?'

Chapter 21

✉ To Elise and Sarah
Sorry to do this by text. I wanted to update you both and I don't have the energy for a phone call tonight so please don't call me back. Three pieces of news. Great news: Ben found Shannon and I saw her tonight! Bad news: she's been in a car crash and is in an induced coma while her body recovers. She should pull through OK. Unexpected news: I'm a granny. Yeah, I know! Ben's already done all the jokes. Will call tomorrow night or over the weekend xx

✉ From Elise
Oh my goodness! That's a lot of information in one text. Sitting on my hands to stop me from picking up the phone to find out more. Wonderful news about finding Shannon, although I'm so sorry to hear the circumstances. Keeping everything crossed. She has a baby? I'm assuming we're talking a baby, given the ages...? Boy or girl? Sorry. Too many questions! Won't be offended if you don't text back. Speak tomorrow. Hugs xxx

✉ To Elise
Ha ha ha. It's OK. Definitely a baby! Luke. Shannon & her fiancé Callum were on their way to Gretna Green to get married before he was born. Hit by jack-knifing lorry. They had to deliver Luke by C-section. Miracle he's still with us & healthy. I promise to call tomorrow with full details. At Ben's now. Need a bottle of wine and time to get my head round it all xx

✉ From Sarah
OMG! You've certainly had a busy evening. I'm here for you when you're ready to talk xx

I lay on my old bed in Ben's spare room that night, with the lights off and the curtains open, watching the rain pelting against the window. Despite the best part of a bottle of wine swimming around my bloodstream, I couldn't relax and switch off. Vivid memories swirled around my head of Shannon being born and placed in my arms for a few brief moments, before the midwife whom Great-Aunt Nuala had hired reached forward and took her away, whispering that it was for the best that I wasn't given any time to get attached. No time to get attached? What did she think had been happening during the nine months she'd been growing inside me? The next time I saw her had been this evening: a grown woman lying on a hospital bed – her poor young body cut, bruised and hooked up to machines – believing that her own mother had rejected her at birth and then again years later. If she'd inherited any of my fire or my ability to hold a grudge, she certainly wouldn't accept me with open arms.

My heart actually ached for all the missed years, and a streak of hatred towards Da flowed through me again. When I'd reluctantly agreed to the adoption, I'd always known I was unlikely to see her until she turned 18, and that I'd have to live with the hope that we could be reunited again, knowing that it might not happen if Shannon chose not to get to know me. That had been hard enough. What sort of monster would take that glimmer of hope away? I just didn't get it. He must have really hated me to do that, but why? Why did my own father hate me so much? I accepted that Daran and I getting together could be seen as scandalous in a small, narrow-minded community like Ballykielty, but he'd covered it up and he'd sent me away. He'd made it clear I wasn't welcome back and I'd had no intention of returning. He'd removed his problem. He'd punished me for what he perceived to be my crime. So why punish me further by telling me she'd died?

I picked up my iPhone from the bedside table and looked at the clock: 3.17am. Sleep! I needed sleep! Reluctantly, I rolled out of bed and closed the curtains. Maybe a bit less light would help. I needed to stop focusing on Da because, for every moment I wasted thinking about him, I was letting him control me, and he'd done that for far too long. I needed to stop thinking about the wasted years with Shannon and focus on the future with her. Which meant a future with Luke. I smiled at the thought of that tiny little boy in his hospital-loaned blue babygrow, as he'd curled his hand around my little finger and kicked his dumpy legs. I might not have had a chance to be there for my own baby, but I had an opportunity to be there as my grandbaby grew. Daran's grandbaby.

As I lay on my back, staring at the ceiling and twiddling my Claddagh ring, I imagined Daran looking down on Shannon and Luke, and smiling at the legacy he'd left behind. Christ! Looking down on them? I didn't believe in all that bollocks, after what had happened to me.

'Do you believe in God?' Daran had asked me, about a month after my 16th birthday. 'I mean, really, truly believe in God.'

Although the day had been mild for early October, the darkness had brought a chill to the air. We were going to need to rethink our farmhouse love nest very soon. I shivered slightly and pulled a blanket over us as I stroked my hand over his bare chest. 'You won't be hurt, whatever the answer is?'

'Nothing you say or do could ever hurt me, Clare.'

'Even though you believe in God and love Him with all your heart?'

He kissed the top of my head. 'Not with all of my heart. I did. But then I met you, and you took my breath away and stole my heart.'

My eyes filled with tears. I couldn't speak. Instead, I reached up and stroked his face, then gently kissed him, my body full of love and longing for this man who had chosen me over the priesthood. I straddled him. 'One more time, then I'll answer your question. But, for now, just know that I really and truly believe in you and the fact we're meant to be together. Always.'

'You'll be wanting my answer,' I said, as I lay beside Daran later, panting.

He laughed. 'You can get your breath back first. And you don't have to answer the question if you don't want to. I think I know the answer and I'm fine with it, so I am.'

I propped myself up onto my elbow. 'Amazing kisser. Incredible in bed. Will you be adding psychic powers to your list of skills?'

Daran propped himself up on his elbow too so he could look into my eyes. 'You really think those things about me?'

'Of course. Of the 47 lads in the village I've slept with, you're definitely the best.' I winked at him.

He grinned. 'So are you. Out of the 47 women I've slept with. Although, Mrs Shaughnessy was pretty special so that's some tough competition there.'

I laughed and threw a handful of straw at him. I'd told him about my bet with Orla Brennan on the first day we'd seen him.

He'd admitted that she'd flirted with him, but he thought she was just lonely and got a kick out of a bit of male attention. Trust him to see the good in every situation.

I lay back and stared at the dilapidated ceiling. 'I really am going to answer your question, Daran. I think beliefs are something that an individual develops as they grow and learn, rather than something that can be thrust on them by others. Religion has been thrust on me. In fact, it's been rammed down my neck by my parents. Instead of the presence of God being presented as a beautiful thing, it's been used as a bribe and a threat.'

'What do you mean?'

'If any of us were naughty, we'd be told that God was watching us and would punish us. If we hurt ourselves, we'd be told that it was God getting His revenge for our wicked thoughts or actions. We were made to believe He was judging us and that we needed to constantly work harder to make Him happy, as though He were always displeased. I found myself wishing He didn't exist. I hated the idea of this grumpy, old man watching over us, tutting every time I got a word wrong in my school spelling test or slopped gravy on my shirt.'

Daran held me closer and stroked my hair. 'Is that what you still think?'

I sighed. 'When I met you, you talked about a different God. A God who was in the flowers, in children laughing, in a kiss. A God who cared, and understood, and forgave. What I'm struggling with is how two people can interpret the same God so differently. Is that because He doesn't exist and they believe what they want to, or is it because He does exist and what He is depends on the beauty or ugliness inside the believer?'

'I don't know your da very well, but from what I do know and from what you've told me, I think he's a man who hides behind religion to control others and manipulate them into doing what he wants them to do. The God I know and love doesn't sit in judgement. He guides and supports us through good times and challenging times. If you want to imagine Him watching over us and tutting, I think it's safe to say that it's your da he's tutting at for his behaviour.'

'I like that thought.' A cold breeze ruffled my hair and I pulled the blanket more tightly across my body.

'It's too cold to stay here,' Daran said. 'We need to get you dressed and back home, where it's warm.'

'I know a way we can warm up,' I said.

'Again?'

'I've already told you, you're an amazing kisser and incredible in bed. Or should that be on a pile of straw and an old blanket? I can't resist you.'

'That makes two of us,' Daran said, as took me in his arms again.

'I hope God wasn't watching us while we did that!' I said, as I pulled on my panties after quite a frantic session. Our lovemaking was becoming more adventurous each time, as we became more familiar with each other's bodies and what turned us on. 'What you did with your tongue just now was pretty X-rated. I don't think He'd have approved one little bit, although I did. You have a massive thumbs-up of approval from me, so you do.'

Daran laughed. 'I wasn't sure I was doing it right.'

'Oh, you were!'

'Thank you. Let's say that God approves of our love for each other and, contrary to what your da says, I don't think He's watching us every single second, so perhaps He missed the performance this time. Speaking of which, what time is it?'

I glanced at my watch. 'Jesus, Daran! It's half eight. Weren't you meant to be meeting Father Doherty at eight?'

His eyes widened. 'Where did the time go? Actually, I know the answer to that. Crap! I'm going to have to run. Are you up for it?'

'You be going. I need to find my runners. I'll blow the candles out and tidy up a bit.'

'You'll be okay on your own? You've got a torch?'

'I'll be fine and, yes, I've got a torch. I've been here in the dark on my own a million times. I'm perfectly safe.'

'I love you.'

'I love you too. Now, run! And make sure you get that straw out of your hair.'

Daran kissed me, then ran across the farmhouse, pulling on his jumper with one hand and trying to knock straw out of his hair with the other. I finished pulling on my clothes and hunted around for my running shoes. As I bent over to tie the laces, a feeling of unease crept over me. Heart racing, I slowly turned around to face him.

'That was quite a show the two of you put on again. You know what's going to happen now, though, don't you?'

'Clare! Are you okay?'

I squinted under the bright light.

'Ben?'

'You were crying for help.'

My heart was thumping, I was drenched in sweat and I was crying. 'Bad dream.' I pushed my hair out of my eyes and wiped my wet cheeks.

Ben knelt on the floor beside me. 'Can I get you anything? Some water, perhaps?'

I nodded. He held my gaze for a moment, then squeezed my arm gently. He flicked the bedside lamp on, putting the main light off as he left the bedroom.

I sat up and hugged my knees up against my chest. I'd been dreaming about Daran and the night he'd asked me whether I believed in God. That had actually happened. It was a real memory, not a dream. But what about what had happened next? That hadn't happened. Why had I gone from dreaming about Daran and a real event into a horrible nightmare? Because that's what it was. A nightmare.

Wasn't it?

Chapter 22

✉ To Callum
Looking forward to seeing you all again tonight. Do you need anything? Does Luke?

✉ From Callum
I'm OK but would be cool if you could get some clothes and nappies for Luke. His are all borrowed from hospital. Laters

✉ From Ben
Good luck tonight. Are you sure you don't want me to get my Samaritans shift covered?

✉ To Ben
Don't you dare! You've done enough already. I'll call you tomorrow

Looking at the pile of carrier bags in the boot of my car, I chewed on my thumbnail and hoped I'd chosen well. I'd dashed around several high-street stores in Leeds city centre at lunchtime, realising I knew absolutely nothing about babies and what they wore. Tiny Baby, Early Baby, New Baby, First Size, Newborn, 0-3

Months, Less Than 5.5lb, 5-7lb. And don't get me started on the nappy choices... Argh! Who knew there were so many options for what appeared to be exactly the same thing? No wonder so many new mums suffered from postnatal depression. As if having a new life to take care of weren't scary enough, a trip to the shops would absolutely tip them over the edge! I'd finally settled on a combination of Newborn and 0-3 Months clothes, a similar size in super-absorbent nappies and a bottle of pretty much everything in the Johnson's Baby range. It'd be grand.

I lifted the bags out of the boot, shoved a fluffy, cream teddy bear under my arm and headed into *Jimmy's* to meet Callum on the maternity ward, as agreed, before going to see Shannon.

Luke was awake. God, did we know it! My shoulders tensed as his cries pierced through me.

'Jesus!' I said, when I'd greeted Callum and been introduced to Kelly, the nurse gently rocking Luke. I recognised her as the same nurse from the evening before. 'He's got a good pair of lungs on him, so he has.'

Kelly smiled at me. 'Believe it or not, he's pretty quiet compared to some of the bairns we meet. And just youse imagine what it's like when they all cry at the same time. It's mental, man!' She reached for a bottle of milk and gave it a shake. 'Are youse ready?'

Callum had propped his crutches against the wall and was settling into a chair beside Luke's crib. He draped a cloth over his arm. 'Ready.' Then he looked at me. 'Unless you'd like to…?'

I shook my head quickly. 'You're settled now. And your little man is starving, so I wouldn't want to delay his tea.'

Callum reached out for Luke, then the bottle. 'In that case, you can be on nappy-changing duty.'

Bollocks. Was it too late to ask to feed him instead?

'I'll leave youse to it,' said Kelly. 'Just shout if youse need owt.'

'Thanks, Kelly.'

'You look like you've been doing this all your life,' I said, watching Callum's natural ease with admiration.

'There were babies in some of my foster families. I got used to them.'

I took a seat beside him. 'How long were you in foster care?'

'Since I was six.'

'What happened to your parents?'

'My mum's dead and I don't know who my dad is. I don't think my mum knew, either.'

'Sorry.'

He shrugged dismissively. 'Shit happens. She had loads of boyfriends when I was young. They were all tossers. One used to hit us. My teacher spotted it and I ended up in care, like. Mum stayed with him. He used to beat the crap out of her, but she blamed herself for his moods and wouldn't leave him, because she supposedly loved him. He got her into drugs. It was a bit of pot at first, but it got more serious when he started dealing.'

Callum paused to wipe away some milk that had dribbled down Luke's chin. 'When I was 11, she overdosed, and that was that.'

The question popped out before I had engaged my brain. 'Deliberately?'

He played with Luke's pudgy hand before he answered. 'They don't think so. We'll never know for sure. There was no, like, note so the verdict was accidental death. She'd have died young anyway 'cos of the drugs.'

'Did you ever see her after you were placed in care?'

'A couple of times a year for the first few years, but she was so drugged up that she didn't really know who I was. Not exactly what you'd call a responsible adult. The visits stopped. I wasn't bothered. I'd, like, got used to life without her.'

'Sounds like you had a tough childhood.'

Callum shook his head. 'It wasn't so bad. My foster families were cool. Life was better than it would have been with Mum. And if I hadn't been in care, I'd never have met Shannon.' His eyes lit up at the mere mention of her name. He stroked Luke's head. 'And we'd never have had you, would we? I know you might think we're young to have a baby, but I had to grow up a lot quicker than most kids my age. Shannon says I act like I'm 38 instead of 18. Says she's going to buy me a pipe and slippers.'

I smiled. As if I'd judge anyone for having a baby young! I wanted to ask more. I knew first-hand what it was like to be abandoned by your family, but I had no idea what it was like to be brought up by strangers. Plus, I'd only had four years with Great-Aunt Nuala before I left for university, whereas Callum had spent most of his life living with strangers. How had that affected him? How had it affected Shannon? How would it affect how she felt about me?

'So, what's in the bags?' Callum asked, lightening the mood.

'Ah, yes! I got a bit carried away.' I jumped up and began unpacking bags, showing Callum the various sleepsuits and outfits I'd bought. I picked up the teddy. 'And this fella is baby-safe and washable. His name's Phyllis… or something. Hang on.' I checked his label. 'No, it's Philbin, apparently. Strange name for a bear. You can change it if you want. I'm sure he won't mind.' I placed the bear at the end of the cot.

Callum laughed. 'I'm not going to steal his identity, poor bear. Philbin it is.' He handed me Luke's part-empty bottle and held his hand under Luke's chin while he rubbed his back. Luke released the most enormous belch, making me giggle.

'Good boy,' Callum said. 'Ready for more?' He popped the bottle back into Luke's mouth and looked up at me. 'Shannon'll be gutted. She wanted to feed him herself but, like, we don't have much choice.'

At the mention of breastfeeding, a flashback hit me of my own swollen breasts post-birth, and no baby to feed. It suddenly struck me as odd that they hadn't let me at least give her one feed, but clearly they had other plans for a fake death and ongoing deception. I needed to change the subject before I got wound up with regrets again.

'What's she like?' I asked.

'Shannon?' His eyes lit up again. 'She's awesome. She's really brainy. She got 10 A-stars or As in her GCSEs. She had a place at sixth-form but deferred a year when we found out about Luke. She's a great friend and, like, dead funny. She can go quiet and likes to be on her own when she's got stuff to think about. She's ace at giving advice, even if she's not always good at taking it. She's feisty and opinionated and, now that I've met you, I know where she gets that from.'

'Feisty and opinionated? Me? What would possess you to say something like that?'

Callum laughed. 'No idea.' He removed the bottle from Luke's mouth. 'Nice work, Luke. Let's hear some more burps, then Grandma can change your nappy and dress you in some of those new clothes that don't smell of hospital.'

He passed me the bottle and manoeuvred Luke into burping position again. 'Do you mind me calling you "Grandma"?'

'No. Although, I'd be lying if I said it was going to be easy getting used to it. I do feel a bit young to be a grandmother, but I guess that's what happens when you have a child young and they have a child young too.'

'Would you prefer "Clare"?'

I shook my head. 'It's not right. It seems vain and as though I'm ashamed of being pregnant so young, which I'm not. Grandma's fine. As long as Shannon's okay with it. I'm conscious that she might not want me in her life.'

'She probably won't at first, but she'll go quiet and spend some time thinking about it, then she'll decide it's right for her and right for Luke. Anyway, I'm his dad and I want you to stick around. I never had a proper family, like, and neither has Shannon since her dad died. If there are real family members who want to be involved – ones who aren't into drugs – then I want them to be around Luke.' He blew his fringe out of his face and wrinkled his nose. 'You do want to stick around, don't you?'

'Of course I do! As I said last night, I'd always hoped I'd see her again when I agreed to the adoption. I never wanted to give her up in the first place. With no money, no home, no family and no education, I didn't have many options. I thought adoption would be best for her.'

Callum nodded. 'It probably was. I didn't know Paul and Christine, but Shannon said they were awesome parents.'

Luke produced a couple of loud belches. 'Nice ones!' Callum said. 'High five!' He placed his fingertips against Luke's palm. 'Let's give you to Grandma for a change.'

Bollocks. I was going to have to tell him. 'I feel like a right eejit saying this, Callum, but I don't know how to hold a baby.'

He frowned. 'Really?'

'Yes. Really.'

'You've never held a baby before?'

'Never.'

'You don't have friends or family with babies?'

'No! Why's that so hard to believe? I don't have any family. Actually, I have my big sister Aisling now, but her kids are school-age. I wasn't in contact when they were babies. I don't have a huge circle of friends and none of them have had kids yet. My friend Elise is pregnant, so I guess I'll hold hers at some point, but I genuinely haven't held a baby since Shannon was born. Back then, a midwife placed her in my arms but whisked her away minutes later saying…' My voice caught in my throat, and tears filled my eyes. 'Anyway, I don't know what to do. Can I watch you instead?'

'Slight problem with that plan.' He jerked his thumb towards the crutches behind him. 'You'll have to do it. Don't look so scared.'

'What if I drop him?'

'We'll just have to hope he bounces.' Callum laughed. 'I *am* joking, you know. How about you get out everything you need and then I'll pass Luke to you?'

'You don't think we should call Nurse Kelly instead?'

'Oh dear, Luke, looks like Grandma is a fraidy cat. She's scared of a six-pound, three-ounce baby.'

'I'm not scared of *him*. I'm just scared of… Okay, you've made your point. What do I need?'

How hard was it to remove a baby from his clothes, change a nappy and re-dress him? Jesus! How was it that I could negotiate incredibly tough business deals with stroppy chief execs and instigate challenging recovery plans when a client had experienced a PR disaster, yet I couldn't remove a baby's arm from a sleeve?

'I don't think he's had a dump, so you've got it easy with your first change,' Callum said.

'Easy? There's nothing easy about any of this.' I wiped the sweat off my brow with the back of my hand.

He laughed. 'It'll get easier. I promise. Oh, and you might want to…'

I screamed and stepped back, spluttering, as a flow of warm urine spattered across my face and down my white shirt.

'Oops! Too late.'

I grabbed at the sleepsuit that I'd removed, wiped my face and dabbed helplessly at my top. 'Did he do that deliberately?'

'It often happens when baby boys are exposed to the air. I was about to say that you might want to put a tissue over him, just in case. Sorry.'

'You're sure it wasn't a dirty protest for my incompetence?'

'I'm sure.'

I turned back to Luke. 'Right, you! Listen and listen good! When you're older and you bring girlfriends home, I'm going to be telling them all about how you peed on your grandma the second time she met you. You'll pay for this, young man. You mark my words. This'll come back to haunt you, so it will.'

Callum laughed. 'If it's any consolation, it happened to me, like, the first time I changed a boy's nappy. Think of it as Luke marking his territory. You're now officially his property.'

When I'd finally sorted everything out, I was able to sit down and have a cuddle. It was my first opportunity to relax and properly look at my grandson. As I stroked his chubby cheeks and bald head, an overwhelming sensation of love and protectiveness enveloped me, just as it had that first time I'd held Shannon. Tears rushed to my eyes, and my throat tightened.

'It's pretty special, isn't it?' Callum said.

I nodded, not daring to speak.

'You said you got to hold Shannon?'

A couple of tears sprang loose as a feeling of déjà vu hit me. 'Only for a few minutes before they took her away.'

'Must have been rough.'

'It was, but I managed to hold it together, convincing myself that she had a far better life ahead of her than I could give her. Then they told me she'd died. I lost the plot at that point.' I took a deep breath, shuddering again at the memory of that horrendous moment. I'd cried pretty much solidly for a fortnight. Great-Aunt Nuala told me to toughen up and accept my penance at first, then she got worried and called the doctor, who prescribed some happy pills. I didn't need tablets; I needed my baby. Disgusted by their lack of understanding, I flushed the tablets away and vowed never to let them see me being weak again. Until I got the letter from

Great-Aunt Nuala, that had been the last time I'd cried.

'How is Shannon?' I asked. 'Any improvements?'

'They reckon there've been some, but it's still too early to bring her round. Luke'll fall asleep again soon. We'll go and see her as soon as he does.'

'Okay.' I hoped he'd be quick about it. My arm was killing me. My little six-and-a-bit-pound bundle was beginning to feel more like 60-and-a-bit pounds, although I suspected that was my fault for holding him all wrong. I was too scared to adjust him in case I dropped him, though. 'Tell me more about how the two of you met,' I said. 'You said earlier that you met Shannon in a foster home.'

Callum nodded. 'When her dad died, Shannon was 13. Her mum… adoptive mum… had died three years before. She had no aunties or uncles, like, so she was sent to an emergency foster family – the Hendersons – which was where I was placed. They're this awesome couple. Completely bonkers. They couldn't have kids of their own so they started fostering. She'd inherited the family business – a large guesthouse on the outskirts of Northampton – and quite a lot of money, so they ran it as a sort of children's home.

'I'll never forget the first day I saw Shannon. I'd been with the Hendersons for a couple of years and, as the longest-standing foster kid, I was always the one who welcomed newbies and helped them settle in. I got home from school one day and Mrs Henderson told me that we had a new girl, who'd gone to explore the grounds. I couldn't find her at first. I was worried she'd done a runner, like, but I eventually found her in the treehouse talking to two wooden boxes. Turns out they contained the ashes of Paul and Christine. She told me that her dad hadn't been able to bring himself to say goodbye and scatter her mum's ashes, and she was glad about that because it meant that she could scatter them together. I asked her if she was going to do that now, but she said she wanted their ashes to be scattered somewhere where they could always be with her. She knew her stay with the Hendersons was temporary. They were already committed to two brothers moving in a fortnight later so they didn't have space to keep her. She said that she'd probably go to loads of different foster families, but she had a plan. She was going to…'

'She was going to what?' I asked, when Callum stopped and looked away.

'She was going to contact her real mum and hopefully go to live with her.' He grimaced. 'Sorry. I'm not saying that to have a dig.'

'It's grand,' I said brightly, my stomach twisting with guilt. 'Go on.'

'Well, as you now know, she wrote loads of letters to you but heard nothing back at first. She did move around a lot, but she was really positive about it because she was convinced she'd find her birth mum and they'd live happily ever after together. Sorry. Again, that's not a dig. Anyway, we became, like, best mates and often met up on weekends. She was so much fun and nothing seemed to get her down. She threw herself into everything she did: schoolwork, friendships, dance classes, learning the guitar. I struggled at school so she helped me with my maths and science. She taught me to play the guitar, although I refused to let her teach me ballet!' He paused and smiled. 'Didn't think a pink tutu was quite the look for me, like. Anyway, I found myself wanting to be with her all the time and I soon realised I wanted to be more than friends. I'd never had a girlfriend before, and I had no idea whether she felt the same way about me, so I kept quiet.

'When you wrote to her and said you wanted nothing to do with her… or at least when we thought it was you who'd written… she was gutted. It was like someone had taken a fire extinguisher and put out her spark. She'd moved to yet another foster family that week and claimed that nobody loved her or wanted her in their lives. I told her that I did. She said I was only saying that because we were friends and that I only needed her in my life to get through my GCSEs and would dump her after that. I had a go at her, telling her exactly how I felt about her. She had a go back at me, asking why the hell I hadn't said anything before then, because she felt exactly the same way and hadn't dared make the first move. We were inseparable after that.

'I passed my GCSEs, thanks to her, and I started a plumbing apprenticeship. I wouldn't have had the courage to apply if it hadn't been for Shannon, but she's one of these people who believe you can achieve anything. She says the only barriers you face are the ones you put up for yourself.'

I felt a surge of pride in my daughter, who sounded wise beyond her years.

'When we found out about Luke, she was so excited. We'd talked about getting married and having kids at some point. It was earlier than expected, but she prayed about it and said it was God's plan that we have children sooner.'

I felt my pulse race and my stomach churn again. 'She prayed about it?'

'We both did.'

'You're Catholics?' I was aware that I was saying the words through gritted teeth, but I couldn't help it.

'Shannon is, and I'm a Methodist.'

Of course she was. As if Great-Aunt Nuala and Da would allow her to be placed with a family who weren't practising Catholics. Great. Just great.

'Our faith was one of the many things that united us,' Callum continued. 'And I have to say, I don't know how I'd have got through the past few days without God's love and support.'

'Luke's asleep,' I said, relieved of the opportunity to shift the subject away from religion. 'Will I put him in his cot?'

I somehow managed to lay Luke in his cot without waking him up. Miracle. I shoved the shopping bags in the cupboard before reaching for my coat and bag. 'Will we go in to see Shannon now?'

'In a minute. There's something I need to ask you first. Actually, it's something I'd like you to do for Luke and me, if you can.'

'Okay.'

'You might want to sit down for this one.'

My stomach twisted again. I sensed that a request for something a little more significant than shopping for nappies and sleepsuits was on its way. 'O-kay.'

'I don't think it's fair on a healthy baby like Luke to be stuck in hospital. I'd like you to look after him.'

Chapter 23

'You're sure he wasn't winding you up?' Ben took another slurp of his coffee and pulled his duvet more tightly around his body as he curled up on one end of his sofa. I felt a bit guilty. After lying awake all night worrying about Shannon and thinking about Callum's proposition, I thought I'd been generous in waiting until nine before banging on Ben's door, instead of turning up at six like I'd wanted to. With everything that had happened, I'd forgotten about his nightshift at the *Samaritans*. I offered to come back later, but he insisted I come in and spill the beans.

I shook my head. 'No. He was deadly serious. I understand his logic. Shannon's incapacitated and, even when she awakes, she's likely to have weeks, if not months, of recovery ahead of her. He can't do much on his crutches. Apparently, he's also got a couple of cracked ribs so he's on strong painkillers. Meanwhile, poor Luke has started his life stuck in hospital, with limited human contact.'

'How did you leave it with him?'

'That I'd think about it. Seriously, Ben, I did not see that one coming. I don't know what to do, which, as you know, is very rare for me.'

Ben smiled. 'Rare? I'd suggest non-existent! Okay, let's start with the basics. What stopped you from saying yes immediately?'

'Only a-trillion-and-seven things.' I started counting them off on my fingers. 'One: I have no idea what to do with a baby. Couldn't even change a nappy yesterday. Two: I have a full-time job with frequent travel. Three: I rent a one-bedroom apartment with a "no children or pets" policy. Four: Shannon might not like it. Plus a-trillion-and-three other things. Stop laughing at me.'

Ben put his mug down on the carpet. 'Sorry. It's just that you're so cute when you get all stressed like this.'

'Cute?' I threw a cushion at him. 'Kittens are cute. Babies are cute… sometimes. I'm not.' I looked around for something else to throw.

'I concede!' Ben raised his hands in the air. 'Cute might have been the wrong choice of adjective. It's just that you're normally so in control and it's reassuring to see that you occasionally have vulnerable, clueless moments like the rest of us.'

'You should have seen me in the hospital with Luke yesterday. Jesus, was that a picture of clueless vulnerability or what?'

Shrugging the duvet off, Ben reached for his mug and stood up. 'Sorry, I need a top-up. You?'

I shook my head. 'Still on this one.'

He returned a few minutes later with another drink. 'Where were we? Oh yes, a-trillion-and-seven reasons not to say yes immediately. Let's just ignore all those issues for the moment. What's your gut feeling? What do you want to do?'

'I want to be looking after Luke. Of course I do! He's my grandson. But—'

'Don't revert to the objections yet. Let's focus on the positives. That was a pretty strong declaration that you want to do it. Aside from the fact that he's your flesh and blood, why do you want to look after Luke?'

I took a swig of my coffee as I thought for a moment. 'Because

I missed out on looking after Shannon when she was a baby. This would be like getting a second chance. I want to do it for me, and I want to do it for Shannon.'

'Then you should do it. I'm not sure about the trillion-and-three objections you didn't list, but we can definitely overcome the four you did.'

'What? The four absolutely enormous objections?'

'The only barriers in your way are the ones you put up for yourself.' Ben frowned. 'Why are you looking at me like that?'

I smiled. 'That's the exact phrase Callum used in the hospital yesterday. Apparently, it's the phrase that Shannon lives by.'

'It's a sign! Alleluia!'

Ben was saved from having anything else thrown at him by my phone ringing.

'Hi, Callum!' I said.

'How soon can you get here? Shannon's taken a bad turn.'

Ben pulled up at the entrance to *Jimmy's*. 'You go to her. I'll park and find you later.'

I leapt out of the car and power-walked to the ICU. As soon as I entered the waiting room, I spotted Callum slumped in a plastic chair, pale-faced. A cold chill crept over my body. I was too late. My feet felt as though they were rooted to the spot.

Callum looked up. 'Clare!'

'Is she...?'

He ran his hand across his stubbly chin. 'She's critical... infection from one of the lines... don't really know... couldn't take it in.' His speech was slurred and he appeared to be struggling to focus his eyes on me.

'Callum? Are you all right? Callum? Shit! Nurse! Help!' I tried to catch him as he fell towards the floor, but he was too heavy. 'HELP!'

Ben put his arm around me as we walked back to his car a little after eight that evening. 'They'll both pull through. The doctor said so. Callum's had a successful op and Shannon's over the worst.'

I relaxed against him, grateful for both the physical and emotional support. 'I know. It was just a hell of a shock. Hadn't they both suffered enough already?'

Callum's appendix had ruptured, or burst, or whatever it is they do, so he'd been rushed to have that removed while another team of doctors fought to stabilise Shannon. It had been a terrifying day. I sighed. 'It makes one decision for me, though. I'm definitely going to look after Luke.'

Ben squeezed my shoulder. 'But you'd already decided that, hadn't you?'

Chapter 24

✉ From Elise
Is everything OK? I've tried to call several times but it goes straight to voicemail. Getting worried. Hope all's well with Shannon and Luke xx

✉ From Sarah
Where are you? You didn't call on Friday so I've been texting and calling you but no response. Hope you're OK. Can you call me? xx

✉ To Elise and Sarah
Really sorry. Phone's been off. Been at Jimmy's. Shannon took a bad turn, then Callum collapsed with appendicitis, but they're both over the worst. Traumatic couple of days. On my way back from Northampton with all their belongings. They were meant to be moving into a rented house when they got back from Gretna Green. Eejit landlord's given it to someone else and their foster places have been filled so, on top of all the other bollocks, they're homeless! Also got Luke's cot, buggy and a pile of other baby crap cos he's going to be staying with me.

Don't ask! Not worked it out yet. Promise I'll call for a catch-up soon, but got lots to sort out. Off to London 2moro. Not sure my boss is going to appreciate the immediate 'maternity' leave request but will worry about that tomorrow! Hope you're both OK xx

✉ From Sarah
OMG! Let me know if you need any help with anything. Keep me posted xx

✉ From Elise
Stevie and I are on our way to Leeds. Sounds like you're going to need help unpacking and putting up a cot. He's just made Bean's so he's pretty useful. We've packed the tools! Text me your postcode xx

'Why do you keep looking backwards?' Ben asked, as we headed up the M1 towards Leeds shortly after lunch on the Sunday.

I twisted back around in my seat to face forward. 'My last experience of moving was when I relocated to Leeds. My stuff filled a small lorry. It just seems a bit sad that there are three of them and their stuff doesn't even fill a Transit van.'

'It's a big van, though,' Ben said. 'Bear in mind that you had some furniture and they don't. And you've had twice as long to accumulate stuff. How much did you have when you were their age?'

I pictured the two suitcases and a couple of boxes in Ma and Da's lounge, ready to be banished with me. 'Not much.'

We travelled in silence for 10 minutes or so.

'The Hendersons seemed like nice people,' Ben said.

I nodded.

'It was good of them to store Shannon and Luke's things for them.'

I nodded again.

'Come on. Out with it,' he said.

'Out with what?'

'When you're quiet like this, it means something's bothering you. What is it?'

I folded my arms. 'It's not fair.'

'What's not?'

'That eejit landlord evicting them like that.'

'Hey! We've been through this already. He was a friend of the Hendersons, and Callum explicitly instructed him to rent it out to someone else. Callum doesn't know when they'll be out of hospital and there's no point him paying rent while he isn't working. You heard what Mrs Henderson said. She offered to pay the rent, but Callum refused. He said he didn't want to be worried about mounting debts or letting anyone down. It was his choice, Clare. His choice. Besides, you can't evict someone who hasn't even moved in. They haven't lost any money. They've got their deposit back. So uncross your arms and feed me some wine gums. Not green ones, though.'

I pushed a green one into his mouth and he grimaced. 'You're a mean girl, Irish. Very mean.'

'Yeah, but you still love me, so you do.'

He glanced across at me briefly. 'If you say so.'

Elise and Stevie were already waiting on the pavement outside *Orion Point* when Ben pulled up right outside the entrance and put on the hazards.

'I'm not going to be much help lifting and carrying,' Elise said, 'but I can keep everyone in drinks.'

'All help is appreciated. Thank you, both of you.'

'What floor are you on?' Stevie asked.

'The 14th.'

'Please tell me there are lifts and that they work.'

I laughed. 'Thankfully, yes, although they're not very big so we'll have to do several trips.'

Elise held doors open while we filled the lift with the first load, then Elise and I travelled up together while Ben and Stevie emptied the van. I left Elise in the apartment in charge of drinks and travelled back down for the next load.

'Surprise!' The lift doors opened to reveal Sarah and Nick.

'Jesus! You scared me! What are you two doing here?'

'We figured you might need some help, but it looks like someone beat us to it.'

'The more the merrier,' I said, trying to ignore the slight edge to her voice. 'Thank you. It means a lot.'

Sarah put her arms out. 'I know you don't do hugs often, but I'm thinking now might be a good time for one.'

I nodded, tears suddenly pricking my eyes. 'It's been a shitty few days.'

'I bet it has,' she said.

'Excuse me!' said a woman's voice. 'Any chance of getting to the lift?'

I let go of Sarah and wiped my eyes. 'Sorry.' I stepped aside. 'We're just moving some stuff in.'

'So I see.' The woman was in her mid-to-late 40s, immaculately dressed from head to toe in winter-white Ralph Lauren. Her glossy, black hair was pulled back into a chignon, and a slash of raspberry across her lips matched the raspberry-coloured Mulberry bag she carried. Wow! I'd always thought I was stylish, but I looked like something out of the Matalan sale next to her. Actually, in my present house-moving gear of jeans and an old t-shirt, I probably looked like something from a jumble sale.

'I'm Clare, 14th floor. I think you might live above me.'

She looked me up and down, and I swear her lip curled in

disgust. Without offering her name in return, she looked pointedly in the direction of the flatpack cot resting against the wall. 'You rent from Daryl Smithers, don't you?'

I nodded. 'How did you know?'

'Daryl's a friend of mine. A good friend.' She stepped into the lift and gave me a frosty stare. 'I trust the cot is a gift and you're not about to move a baby into the building, because I do believe that would be a breach of your rental conditions?'

Holy crap! 'Of course. Just a gift.'

'I thought so.' The lift door closed.

Sarah whistled. 'Delightful neighbour you've got there.'

'And a hideous problem I've got now.'

'Why's that?'

'My lease strictly states "no pets and no children".'

'Oh. What are you going to do?'

'Move Luke in and hope he turns invisible and never cries. Yeah, I know. I'd better start packing because I'm about to be evicted.'

Ben dumped a couple of suitcases next to me. 'You're not still angry at Shannon's landlord, are you? He didn't evict them.'

'I know. I was just telling Sarah about it, though.'

Ben pointed towards the pile of belongings in the lobby. 'That's everything except Callum's bike, which I'll store in my shed, so I'm going to move the van. Stevie and Nick are moving their cars to the visitor spaces.'

'Okay.'

'Why didn't you tell him about that woman?' Sarah said, as soon as the door had closed.

'Because I know him too well. If he gets wind of me being kicked out, what will he do?'

'Offer you his spare room again?'

'Exactly. Only, it wouldn't just be me this time, would it? It would hardly be fair to lumber him with a newborn baby too. I'll just have to find somewhere else to live. If Frosty Knickers grasses on me, that is. I may be able to get away with it.'

Sarah smiled reassuringly, but I knew that she knew Frosty Knickers was going to have her eye on me and would be running straight to Daryl the minute she got so much as a sniff of a dirty nappy. Bollocks!

I'm one of those annoying people who don't get nervous. I thrive on the pressure of deadlines, challenging targets, important presentations, difficult customers and awkward negotiations. Yet I found myself actually trembling the following morning as I slowly made my way down the corridor of our London HQ to meet with Paul and our HR manager, Sabina. I felt exactly the same way as when I'd confronted Da, which was ridiculous, as I'd always had a good relationship with Paul. Some of my colleagues found him difficult, describing him as a 'control freak', 'awkward bastard' and 'bully', but I loved his direct, straight-talking, no-nonsense approach. He rewarded loyalty and he was financially generous towards those who, like me, exceeded their targets and added value to the business.

Unfortunately, he was embarrassingly old-school when it came to women and careers. I swear he'd only promoted me because he was certain I'd never settle down and have children. I therefore suspected he'd take my news as an act of disloyalty and treat me with the same contempt he'd shown to my colleagues, although I hoped that the results I'd delivered would have earned me enough brownie points to get the flexibility I needed.

I could hear raised voices as I approached the meeting room. Through the glass panel next to the door, I could see Paul pacing up and down, looking like a bear with a sore head. Sabina kept shaking her head and indicating that he should sit down and, I suspected, calm down. Bollocks! Taking a deep breath and standing tall, I knocked on the door, then entered the lion's den.

Sabina smiled warmly. 'Come in, Clare. Take a seat. Would you like some water?'

'Yes, please.'

Sabina poured me a drink from an iced jug on the table. 'Paul was just about to take a seat, weren't you, Paul?' Her voice was friendly yet firm.

Like a chastised child, Paul pulled out a seat, sat down and glowered at me.

'Thank you for coming, Clare,' Sabina said. 'I understand that you emailed Paul last night asking to change this morning's monthly review to a discussion about going on maternity leave. Is that correct?'

'It is.' I wished Paul would stop glowering at me.

'And I understand that your request is to start that leave with immediate effect? Is that right?'

'Yes.'

Sabina smiled. 'Okay. We'll explore the details in a moment. Before we do, Paul and I are a little concerned. As employers, we have a duty of care to ensure that all of our employees are safe at work and, for pregnant women, there are procedures we'd normally follow. I'm very conscious that we haven't been able to follow these because we had no idea you were pregnant, Clare.'

'Oh. Well, I'm not pregnant.'

Paul's eyes widened. 'You've already had the baby?'

'No. My daughter has.'

His eyes widened even further and he leaned forward. 'So, what the hell are you requesting maternity leave for?'

Sabina stared at Paul and gave a little cough. 'I think you'd better explain, Clare.'

I tried to stick to the bare facts, but it was still very uncomfortable laying my past out on the table when I'd never opened up to Paul or any of my colleagues about my life before Prime PR.

'I'm sorry to advise you that you're not eligible to take maternity leave,' Sabina said, when I'd finished. 'That's only available to mothers who have either given birth or who have adopted a child.'

'Oh.' I could have kicked myself for having not even thought to Google maternity rights. Awkward.

Paul pushed his chair back. 'That's that, then. No maternity leave. Can we get on with your review now?'

Sabina frowned at him. 'There are other options we can explore, though. Clare's facing a unique scenario and, as her employer, we want to try to find a way to support her.'

'She can take some holiday leave, then. In March. Late March. The next six weeks are pivotal for the new Elatryx product launch.'

'Late March? I need time off now, Paul. Six weeks' time won't work for me.'

'And right now doesn't work for Prime. You and your team have loads of work on, and I expect you to deliver. You can't take maternity leave. Sabina said so. I've offered you holidays. I think that's very reasonable. I'd grab the offer if I were you.'

'There are other options,' Sabina insisted. 'We need to explore them.'

I was still trembling. I had a horrible feeling that this was going to end badly. I tried to keep a friendly tone to my voice as I offered a compromise. 'I don't mind working from home for a week or two to finish things off and do a handover.'

'How's that going to work?' Paul demanded. 'The odd day at home is fine, but it's not sustainable. What about meeting clients? Are you going to strap the baby to yourself and take him with you? Leave him in the car and hope he doesn't cry? Dump him—'

'Paul!' Sabina snapped, stopping him from digging himself a deeper hole. She turned to me. 'That sounds like a reasonable compromise and a great starting point. We can explore how practical it is in a moment. Before we do, how long do you think you might need away from work?'

I tried to avoid eye contact with Paul. 'Hard to say. It depends when Shannon regains consciousness and how much support she'll be needing. Callum will be off his crutches eventually, but he won't be able to cope with a baby on his own. Plus, they have nowhere to live. Could be three months, but could be six or more.'

'Six or more? You've got to be fucking kidding me!'

I flinched at the volume of Paul's voice and the expletive.

'Paul!' Sabina cried. Her face was pale and I would have bet my life that, like me, she was trembling. 'I suggest you remember that this is a place of work and that one of your team has come to us with a very reasonable request. Unexpected? Yes. But she could hardly plan for something like this, and it's our job to find a way of making this work for both parties. How about we take a break for 10 minutes while everyone calms down, then we can return and discuss the request without the expletives?'

Paul shook his head. 'As far as I'm concerned, the meeting's over. She…' He pointed at me. 'She needs to think about where her priorities lie. The way I see it, there are two options: holiday or the highway.'

I stared at Paul for a moment in astonishment. To think that I'd once respected and admired him for being a strong and confident leader, who wasn't afraid to push his team to reach challenging goals. Now, all I could see in front of me was the control freak, awkward bastard, bullying manager my colleagues saw. As if in a film montage, I recalled the snide comments, withering putdowns and public humiliations for failure to meet targets. I recalled the long hours, the no-praise culture, the extensive travel and being forced to go to Ireland when it was clear I didn't want to. He was just like my da! A feeling of calm swept through me. I smiled, nodded and stood up.

'What are you grinning at?' Paul demanded. 'This isn't funny. You've let me down, Clare. I thought you had it in you to go far. Believe me, it's the last time I promote a bloody woman.'

Sabina gasped. She opened her mouth to speak but I beat her to it.

'No, Paul. Not funny. Quite tragic, actually. It's tragic that you are a prehistoric, misogynistic bully. It's tragic that I used to look up to and respect you, when you're really not worthy of that respect. It's tragic that you think a female has to work 50 times harder than any man to impress you. It's tragic that you'll probably walk away from this with no consequences and you'll take it out on the team I leave behind. The exceptionally talented team, that is, who work their arses off every day and would appreciate a thank-you once in a while.'

'They get a bonus. That's their thanks. Ungrateful little—'

'I haven't finished! You asked me to think about my priorities. For the last eight years or so, Prime PR has been my life. It's been my number-one priority, and I've more than shown that through the accounts I've won and the millions in revenue I've generated. My priorities have now changed. I have a daughter, her fiancé and a grandson who need me and, if I'm honest, I need them too. Holiday or the highway? It's a no-brainer. I'll take the highway. I'll put that in writing, hand over my laptop and leave the building. Thanks for being so supportive.'

Paul's face was purple. I half-expected steam to come out of his ears, like a cartoon character. Sabina, on the other hand, looked as if she was having to stop herself from leaping up and cheering.

'I take it you're resigning with immediate effect?' she said, eyes twinkling.

'She can't,' Paul yelled. 'She's on three months' notice. She has to work it.'

Sabina nodded. 'Contractually, she does. But given that she mentioned her potential case for constructive dismissal…'

'What? She never mentioned that.'

Sabina frowned. 'Sorry, Clare, am I having a senior moment and getting my wires crossed with a different meeting? You did just say that you felt you had been given no choice but to tender your resignation, given the refusal of your manager to consider any other options for your request, didn't you?'

I nodded. 'That's right. I think a tribunal would be very interested in the sex-discrimination discussion too…'

'Well, that went well,' I said to Sabina, after Paul stormed out of the room, slamming the door. 'Thank you for doing that. I hope you won't be in trouble.'

She smiled and shook her head. 'I got offered a new job on Friday. I'm just waiting for the contract to come through, then I'll be handing in my notice too.'

'Congratulations!'

'Thanks. I can't wait to get away from Paul. Everyone else at Prime is lovely, but most of my challenging cases have been because of him. Mind you, it's all been great employment-law experience!' She gathered her papers together and stood up. 'I hate to do this, but I'm afraid I need to play Big Brother and stand over you whilst you write your resignation to make sure you don't acquire any of Prime's intellectual property.'

'I understand. Thanks for everything. I can't quite believe I'm leaving. It wasn't the outcome I expected, but it feels right.'

'What will you do afterwards?' she asked, as we walked back to my hot desk.

'I don't know. I've been saving for a house deposit for years so I'm financially sound. My focus can therefore be purely on my family for however long they need me, without worrying about money.'

'Then, I'd say make the most of your time off and really think about what you want out of life. I reckon you'd be amazing at running your own business.'

'Really?'

'I've always thought that. My mum runs a catering business and I see a lot of her qualities in you. You're passionate, driven, focused, organised, great with people and brilliant at self-promotion. You'd be an amazing success.'

It wasn't something I'd ever considered, but I liked the idea. I liked the idea a lot. 'Maybe I will.'

She smiled. 'I bet you will. But enjoy your family for now. It's a lovely story, to be reunited after all these years. I hope Shannon recovers quickly.'

'So do I, Sabina. So do I.' I sat down on my chair and fired up my laptop. 'I guess I'd better write my resignation letter, then.'

Chapter 25

My cheeks burned and tears of frustration dripped onto Luke's jacket as he screamed, his face bright red and his hands balled into tiny fists, flailing about angrily. It was about 4pm. After saying my goodbyes and leaving the office – clutching my handbag and a carrier bag containing my mug and a few other personal effects – I'd caught the train back to Leeds, picked up my car and driven to *Mothercare* at the suggestion of Paul's PA, Margaret. She'd pressed a piece of paper into my hand. 'I've written the essentials on here and the stuff that's a waste of money. I've got five kids and eight grandchildren. If you need any advice, please call me. I've written my home number on there too.' She grabbed me and pulled me into a bear hug. I just hoped that Paul didn't take out his fury at me on her, poor woman.

'I'm sorry, Luke,' I cried. 'I'm trying. I just can't seem to…'

'Are youse okay?'

I twisted around to see Nurse Kelly hovering near the boot of the car. 'Jesus! Are you a sight for sore eyes.' I wiped the tears off my cheeks.

A flicker of recognition crossed her face. 'You're our little Luke's nana!' she said.

'Yes. And I'm an eejit. He's coming home with me and I never thought to read the car-seat instructions. I've faffed that much, I've made him cry.'

'Aw, divn't worry. They seem more complicated than they are. Youse'll soon get the hang of it. How's aboots I…?'

I stepped back, gratefully. 'Be my guest.'

She crouched down by the back seat and lifted Luke out of his car seat. 'Ah! I don't think he's crying just because youse couldn't do the car seat. He's crying because he's got a stinky bot. How's aboots I do it quickly?'

How had I not realised? Great start. I lifted the changing mat I'd just purchased out of the boot and found some wipes, a nappy and a nappy sack. Incredibly, Luke's cries had stopped. Nurse Kelly was obviously one of those baby whisperers. I wondered if I could bribe her to come home with me and teach me her secrets. Or kidnap her.

After Luke was changed, in ridiculously quick time, she helped me fasten him back into his seat.

'Firstly, it needs to be the other way round. Aye. That's it. And you see them clips…?'

Five minutes later, we were on our way.

As soon as I pulled into my parking space at Orion Point, I realised I'd messed up yet again. I had a boot full of baby stuff that would probably take me a few journeys had I been on my own. Problem was, I wasn't on my own. I couldn't leave Luke in the car while I traipsed back and forth, and I couldn't leave him in the apartment either. Bollocks! I was going to have to do at least six journeys with Luke in his car seat, with every journey putting me at greater risk of bumping into Frosty Knickers.

Luke decided to demonstrate exactly how many decibels his cries could reach at 2.37am. My hands shook so much while I tried to mix his formula that I dropped the first bottle. Why was it that a small amount of liquid could multiply exponentially when spilled?

I could have sworn that at least 10 pints of formula had covered the cooker, the worktops, the cupboards, the kitchen floor and my PJs. Unravelling an entire kitchen roll, I threw it across the floor and units in an effort soak up the liquid as I made another. And all the while, Luke screamed. And screamed. And screamed. There was no way on this earth that Frosty Knickers hadn't heard.

The very next day, I was served with my eviction notice. How had I suddenly become homeless and jobless, with a baby to look after and not the faintest clue how to do it? Jesus wept!

'Are you absolutely sure about this?' I said to Ben the following evening.

Ben slammed the boot of my car shut. 'I'm sure. And I was sure the 786 previous times that you asked me.'

'It's a huge thing,' I protested. 'He wakes up in the middle of the night and his screams register high on the Richter scale.'

'Oh, well, in that case…' Ben opened my boot again.

'I'm serious, Ben. I know you'd do anything for anyone, but this is seriously above and beyond.'

He shut the boot. 'I know what I'm letting myself in for, Irish, and I genuinely want to help.'

God knows what I'd done to deserve such a good friend. 'I promise I'll find somewhere else for us to live as soon as possible, but thank you for now.'

'There's no rush.'

'You won't be saying that at three in the morning.'

Ben smiled. 'I mean it. There's no rush.'

'I have a thank-you gift for you.' I reached into the pocket of my jacket. 'You're about to rise to the biggest challenge of your life so far. King of the moment, Ben.'

He shook his head. 'No. You keep him. You've packed in the job you love and given up your apartment for a grandchild you never imagined existed. You're king of the moment, Clare. What you've done is nothing short of amazing.'

I pushed the king into his pocket. 'I'll be offended if you don't take him. What you're doing for us is nothing short of amazing. I mean that, Ben, and you know I'm not generous with the compliments. Or the hugs. But you definitely deserve one of these.' I wrapped my arms around Ben and squeezed tightly. He squeezed back and, for a brief moment, I found myself closing my eyes and melting into his arms. I didn't want to let go. I'd never understood why Sarah was so fond of hugging everyone. I'd oblige occasionally when there was good news or she was upset, but I'd never really got it. Perhaps it was because Ma and Da had never hugged me. There'd been no physical displays of affection towards anyone in our family. Of course, Daran had held me, but that had been different. We'd been in love. There had been chemistry and longing. I hadn't understood the need to hug friends. Clinging onto Ben, I suddenly got it. It felt as if all the stresses of the past month or so were seeping out of my body and into his, making me relax and feel that I wasn't on my own.

Ben squeezed a bit more tightly and placed a gentle kiss on the top of my head, then suddenly let go. Damn! I'd been enjoying that.

'I think I can hear Luke,' he said, looking towards his house.

I cocked my head. 'I can't hear anything. He only fell asleep 10 minutes ago. He'll be dead to the world for ages yet.'

'I'm sure I heard crying. You'd better check on him anyway. You grab that case and I'll bring the rest of your stuff in.'

I shrugged but grabbed the case and went inside. Luke was in the dining room, away from the chaos my belongings had brought to the lounge, snuggled in his carrier, lips pouting, eyes flickering, but definitely sound asleep. I knew he wasn't crying. I wandered back into the dining room and surveyed the mess.

Daryl Smithers had issued me an ultimatum: leave at the end of the month and lose my bond for breaching the terms of our rental agreement, or leave within 24 hours and he'd return my bond and the rent I'd paid for February. I didn't have much choice. I didn't have time to seek legal advice, although, let's face it, I probably didn't have a leg to stand on because I had breached the terms of my rental contract. I didn't want to deplete my house-deposit savings too much while I was out of work, so I couldn't risk losing the money. I reluctantly accepted his offer and asked Ben if I could take him up on his kind invitation after all. Ben's mate Pete (the host of the New Year's Eve disaster) had generously offered his garage as temporary storage for my bed and a few other bits of furniture, and had sent his brother and dad to collect it all in a van. I got the impression that he'd heard about what Taz had done and this was his way of making up for what had happened at his house while he'd been out of action.

Ben appeared with the last few boxes. 'Déjà vu,' he said.

'Except this time there's two for the price of one, and no allowance for a kitchen refurb. Not such a great deal.'

'Kitchen's already done, thanks to you,' he said. 'So the allowance wouldn't be needed anyway.'

'I'll pay you rent.'

He shook his head. 'There's no need.'

I planted my hands on my hips. 'Bollocks! I may not have a regular salary anymore, but I do have money. If you won't take payment, you might as well put all my crap back in the car 'cos we'll not be staying.'

'Okay, okay. Keep your knickers on. We'll work something out.'

'Grand. Glad that's settled. Now, go and earn that rent I'll be paying you by making me a coffee.'

Ben laughed. 'Definitely déjà vu!'

We settled into a routine over the next week or so. Ben continued with his day job with the missing-persons charity, but he temporarily stopped his volunteering shifts. How guilty did *I* feel?

'We'd better move out, Ben. It's not fair that you're changing your life for us.'

'You once asked me why I didn't do anything for myself. I said I already was. I get a kick out of helping others and it doesn't matter what form that takes. Right now, it's more important to me that I'm here for you and Luke. I want to do this more than I want to do my volunteering and that's my final word on the subject.'

'She's a lucky girl.'

'Who is?'

'Lebony, of course. I think they might have broken the mould when they made you.'

He held my gaze for a moment, then smiled. 'You do realise it's a façade? I'm really a selfish misogynist who's luring you into a false sense of security before unleashing my evil plan for world domination.' He touched his lip with his little finger, like Dr Evil from the Austin Powers films. 'Speaking of Lebony, I'd better go and Skype her.'

So that was that. I was back at Ben's playing mum – a role I should have been allowed to adopt more than 17 years ago. I had the days on my own, looking after Luke, and the evenings with Ben's extremely welcome support. I went to Jimmy's every day to sit by Shannon's bedside, hoping for news, and to see Callum. Sometimes Ben would accompany me again in the evening, and other times I'd go on my own and leave Luke in his capable hands. He tried to make out that he struggled with changing nappies, found it challenging to dress Luke and had the frequent bottle-assembling spillage disasters that I had, but I knew he was only saying it to make me feel better. He was a natural with Luke. What did make me feel a little better was when I 'accidentally' forgot to warn him about the urine risk and Luke gave Ben the same welcome he'd given me. Hilarious!

Callum's recovery was slower than expected. He'd been given some penicillin-based antibiotics and it transpired he was allergic to the stuff. He swelled up and developed a painfully itchy rash all over this body, poor lad. Shannon, on the other hand, was doing very well. She'd fought off the fever. The cuts and bruises had healed, leaving behind a few tiny scars that were only noticeable if you knew they were there. Dr Kaur assured us that her internal wounds had healed too. The swelling on her brain had reduced and, two weeks after the accident, they started talking about bringing her round. I was elated yet also terrified at the thought. I'd become extremely close to Callum and had learned so much about my daughter from him. I'd learned that her favourite colour was yellow because it represents hope and happiness and her favourite passage in the Bible was: 'And there I will give her her vineyards and make the valley of trouble a door of hope' (Hosea 2:15). I knew that fairground carousels terrified her, yet she loved rollercoasters and once went on The Big One at Blackpool Pleasure Beach 10 times in a row. She was allergic to cats, she once dyed her hair green by accident and she dreamed of running her own school of dance. I'd even watched videos of her playing the guitar and dancing. The guitar playing was good and she had a sweet singing voice, but what a talented and versatile dancer she was. She could do ballet, Latin, ballroom, contemporary and street, although Callum told me ballet was her main passion. I knew all of these things about her. I'd had a snapshot into her life through the power of social media. I felt as if I actually knew her as a person, yet she didn't know me from Adam. Worse than that, she hadn't given me permission to explore her past. She hadn't Facebook-friended me and shared the videos with me. What if she regained consciousness and hated that Callum had let me into her life in this way?

On Saturday morning, Aisling arrived. She'd flown to Manchester the evening before to drop Torin and Briyana off at their dad's, then caught a train to Leeds first thing in the morning. He was going to bring them across on the train on Thursday so I could see them. Ben had offered to swap rooms so that Aisling and I could share his double bed, but I put my foot down. It wasn't fair to kick him out but it also wasn't fair on Aisling to be disturbed by Luke. Being in the lounge on an inflatable mattress wasn't going to provide much protection from his screams, but it would certainly give her more chance of sleep than being in the same bedroom. When the kids arrived, though, the three of them would need to check into a hotel. There was no way three adults, two kids and a baby could spend two nights in a two-bedroom house with only one bathroom.

'This is my big sister Aisling,' I said to Callum, on the Sunday afternoon. I screwed my face up. 'I guess that makes her your auntie-in-law-to-be, if there's such a thing.'

They exchanged greetings, then I passed Luke to his daddy for cuddles. When he was settled, Callum reached for my hand. 'Tomorrow's the day,' he said.

'Shannon?'

He nodded with vigour. 'They're going to bring her round.'

'Oh my God!' Aisling said. 'That's amazing news. Will she be okay? Do they know?'

Callum shrugged. 'They're hoping so, but there are no guarantees. You'll be here, won't you, Clare?'

'I'd love to, but I don't know if I should be one of the first people she sees.'

'I'd like to say don't be daft, but I talked to Dr Kaur about it. She says that Shannon will be, like, very disorientated, and it's going to be confusing enough having a bunch doctors and nurses staring at her without introducing anyone else. She wants me to be the only one she sees at first. She's not likely to be awake for very long. When she wakes up again, we can prepare her to meet you. I'd still like you to be here, though.' Callum squeezed my hand.

'Of course I'll be here. Should I bring Luke?'

'Dr Kaur says yes. Shannon might ask for him and she doesn't want her thinking, like, she lost him in the accident and we're fobbing her off. It's better that he's around if she asks about him.'

I couldn't sleep that night. I curled up in my duvet, listening to the wind battering the windows, staring at my sleeping grandson, curled up in his cot. Up until that point, I'd focused mainly (and very selfishly) on how Shannon might react towards me when she came round. I'd pushed aside the thought that she might not come around in the way we hoped. What if she had brain damage? What would that mean for Callum and for Luke? I lit up my iPhone for a moment so I could see the time: 03.38. They were planning to take her out of the induced coma in the morning so, in less than 12 hours, we'd know either way.

Shannon's favourite verse from the Bible kept popping into my mind: God making the valley of trouble into a door of hope. She'd certainly walked through the valley of trouble. Could hers and Callum's faith in God bring a door of hope? I thought about Daran. He'd have liked that verse. It might even have been one of his favourites too. The more I thought about it, the more familiar it sounded. What would Daran have done in this situation?

I slowly eased myself into a sitting position on the edge of the bed, clasped my hands and bent my head. I sat like that for a few minutes, watching the steady rise and fall of Luke's chest. Then I did something I hadn't done since they told me Shannon had died nearly 17 years before. I closed my eyes and I prayed.

Chapter 26

✉ To Elise
Hope all goes well with the midwife today. Let me know. Off to hospital shortly. They're bringing Shannon round this morning. Moment of truth x

✉ From Elise
Oh my goodness! Thinking of you all. I'm sure she'll be OK. Please let me know as soon as you can. Nervous about midwife. Praying my blood pressure has gone down. Hoping that handing over the reins on the school play will have helped. Glad it's half term. I'm exhausted. Bet you are too! xx

✉ To Elise
I am! I've forgotten what sleep is! Good luck xx

'Feeling brave?' Aisling asked, when I'd pulled into a parking space at *Jimmy's.*

'Shitting a brick! But I have to put on a brave face for Callum.'

Aisling squeezed my hand. 'I know it's a cliché, but what will be will be.'

'I know.'

'I prayed for her last night,' I said, as we walked across the car park. 'That's something I never thought I'd do again.'

'Must be contagious,' Aisling said. 'Because I did too.'

'Let's hope that there is a God, then, and that He was listening. Luke surviving that crash unscathed was a miracle. We need another one for Shannon.'

'You look done in,' Ben said, as we bathed Luke together that evening.

'I am. I feel like I could close my eyes and sleep for a year.'

'Why don't I have Luke in my room tonight and give you a chance to sleep through?'

I shook my head. 'I can't ask you to do that.'

'You didn't ask me. I offered. And if you get bolshy about it, I'm going to lock you in the shed with Callum's bike and do it anyway, so quit it with the protests.'

'Ooh, I love it when you turn all alpha male on me.'

Ben laughed. 'I don't think anyone could ever accuse me of being alpha male.'

He gently sponged Luke's legs. 'When do they think you'll be able to speak to her?'

'Maybe tomorrow. Maybe the day after. I'm just so relieved that the early indications are good.' Shannon had opened her eyes a little before 10am that day. Callum told me she'd been very disorientated, as we'd been warned, but she'd known who he was. She knew her name and date of birth, she could remember a lorry veering towards the car but she couldn't remember the actual impact. She'd then tried to reach for her stomach, no doubt panicking that something had happened to her baby. Callum had reassured her that they had a healthy baby boy, but she was asleep again before they could fetch him from me. She'd awoken again in the afternoon and had managed to stroke a sleeping Luke. Callum admitted that he'd cried seeing Luke finally being held by his mum. He showed me a photo of the moment, which made me cry too.

Dr Kaur had told Callum that whatever it was they looked for when they shone a light in her eyes was looking good. He couldn't remember the technicalities, not that it would have made sense to me if he had.

Ben lifted Luke out of the bath and wrapped a bright-yellow hooded towel around him. 'Don't you dare pee on me again, young man, or I'll be lodging an official complaint with your mummy when she's ready for visitors.'

The hood on Luke's towel slipped down as Ben stood up with him. 'Ooh, look, Grandma! I think we might be finally growing some hair. And, if Uncle Ben isn't mistaken, I do believe we may have a little ginger baby in the family.' Ben kissed Luke's head, then pulled the hood up again. 'Are you okay, Irish? You've gone pale. I didn't have you pegged as a ginger-phobe.'

'I'm not. I'm… It's…' I sat down on the edge of the bath. It was there again. Shapes. Shadows. Swirls. Something. Just as I'd felt when I'd stood in the farmhouse before Da appeared. I shook my head, trying to dislodge the feeling. 'I'm just exhausted. Ignore me.'

'You look terrible.' Ben looked genuinely worried. 'I think you should go to bed right now before you keel over.'

'We need to move the cot. And I can't abandon Aisling.'

'Aisling will understand, and don't worry about the cot. I'll sleep in your bed and you can sleep in mine. I changed it on Saturday, if you can cope with almost-clean bedding.'

'You haven't made a crusty mess since then?'

'I don't even want to think about what you might mean by that. No, I haven't! Bed. Now.'

I nodded, kissed Luke's cheek, kissed Ben's too, grabbed

a fresh pair of PJs from my drawers, then gratefully retreated under Ben's duvet.

Sleep overcame me pretty much instantaneously. As I drifted into dreams later, I was back at the farmhouse. And there was something in the shadows. Or someone.

Chapter 27

'Are you decent in there? Can we come in?'

I opened my eyes as Aisling pushed open Ben's bedroom door and appeared with Luke cradled in one arm and a mug of coffee in her other hand.

'Morning,' I mumbled. 'Or is it afternoon already?'

She smiled as she put the coffee down on Ben's bedside drawers. 'It's just gone 8.40am. Ben's gone to work. He had a pretty good night with Luke and he says he hopes you got the rest you deserved. How are you feeling?'

'Still pretty tired,' I yawned, as I wriggled into a sitting position. 'I had bad dreams last night.'

'I'm not surprised. Your head must be mashed after all the disruption and worry lately.' She handed Luke to me for a cuddle. 'I've popped some toast in for you so I'll just get that. Quick shower and we should be at hospital for 10 at the latest.'

I nodded. 'Sounds grand. Will you put some Nutella on my toast? I could do with the energy boost.'

'One round of Nutella toast coming up,' Aisling said.

'Two rounds?'

'Greedy yoke!'

'I don't know how you cope with the traffic around here,' Aisling said, as a driver cut me up on the way to the hospital. 'It's so busy.'

'D'you think so? I'm used to London traffic, so this is grand by comparison.'

'I couldn't do it,' she said. 'My blood pressure would be sky high.'

'Arse! Blood pressure. Elise. Can you get my phone out my bag and see if I've got a text from her?'

Aisling reached behind her for my handbag and found my iPhone.

'The code's 2409.'

Aisling tapped in the numbers. 'No texts.'

'Bollocks. Can you send her a text for me?' I dictated what I wanted to say, then explained the situation.

✉ To Elise
I'm hoping no news is good news. Let me know how it went xx

As we crossed the car park 10 minutes later, my iPhone began ringing. My stomach clenched as I saw the name.

'Stevie? Is Elise okay?'

'Not really. She's in hospital.'

I stopped walking. 'Jesus! Is the baby okay?'

'Hopefully. Her blood pressure was really high so the midwife sent her to hospital for monitoring. They did all sorts of tests and checks, and apparently she's got pre-eclampsia too.'

'Pre-what-ia?'

'Pre-eclampsia. I don't really know the details, but I know it's not good for baby or mum. It's fairly common, though, so they know what they're dealing with. She had another scan and Bean's fine, but they'll keep monitoring her and Elise.'

'Is Elise okay? I mean, is she upset or stressed?'

'She's putting on a brave face.'

'What if her blood pressure keeps rising?'

'They'll put her on medication.'

I swallowed hard as I formed the next question. 'What if this clampsie thing gets worse?'

There was a pause before Stevie said, 'We could be looking at a premature birth.'

I put my hand over my mouth. Poor Elise! 'How far along is she?'

'She'll be 30 weeks on Thursday.'

'Ten weeks early? Christ, Stevie, is that far enough?'

'I don't know. I'm trying not to think about it. I'm about to leave for the hospital again now, but I wanted to call you and Sarah first to let you know what's going on.'

'What did Sarah say?'

'I got her voicemail so I left a message. I'll try her again later. I'd better go.'

'Okay. Send Elise my love and keep me posted.'

We said our goodbyes and I hung up. I turned to Aisling. 'It never rains but it pours.'

'She'll be grand – 30 weeks isn't so bad. Most babies are fine from that point so try not to worry. Focus on Shannon for now and you can get an update on Elise later.'

Callum was waiting for us in the corridor outside the ward.

'What's wrong?' I asked, panic filling me as I took in the serious expression on his face. 'She's okay, isn't she?'

'She's fine. Actually, she's doing really well.'

'So, why the serious face?'

'She wanted to see Luke so I had to explain why she couldn't.'

'So she knows…?'

He nodded. 'She knows. The bang on the head hasn't knocked the feistiness out of her.'

'Feck!'

Aisling placed a comforting hand on my arm. 'It was probably just a shock since she thought you wanted nothing to do with her.'

'Did you tell her I didn't send that letter? Did you tell her I didn't even know she was alive?'

He shuffled awkwardly. 'I kind of didn't get the chance before—'

'Before what?'

He wrinkled his nose and shuffled a bit more on his crutches, suddenly appearing fascinated by his shoes. 'Before they had to sedate her.'

Aisling's grip on my arm tightened. I took a deep breath. 'That bad, eh?'

'Sorry.'

'No, Callum. It's me who's sorry. I never meant to cause trouble between you two.'

He shrugged. 'It was just the shock. I told you that she's a thinker. She'll strop and sulk for a while, but she'll think it through and she'll come round.'

So my worst-case scenario had come true. Actually, it was worse than that. She'd reacted so badly, she'd had to be sedated. Christ alive!

I glanced down at my grandson. 'What do you want to do about Luke?'

Callum glanced down at Luke too. 'Same as before. We're both stuck in here and it's not the right place for him. God will show Shannon that it's the right thing for Luke to be with you, like he showed me.'

I squirmed at the mention of God but didn't say anything. If He existed, He owed it to me to bring her round to wanting me in their lives. Although, speaking of bringing her round, had He brought her safely out of her coma? If Daran had been here, he'd have said it was God's work, and I wouldn't have argued with him. God had always seemed very real to me when I was with Daran. Everything had seemed very real to me when I was with Daran. But if God had loved Daran as much as Daran had loved Him, why had He taken him in the tsunami? Immediately, Daran's voice echoed around my mind with his answer: 'Yes, but what about all those He saved?' I'd challenged Daran on where God had been during various natural disasters, crashes or terrorist attacks, and that had always been his answer: 'What about those who were delayed on their way to work/missed that train/weren't in that area? He saved them, didn't He?' He made a compelling argument.

I felt as if a part of me were missing when I left the hospital without Luke. Aisling draped her arm around me. 'She just needs time. It'll be grand.'

Would it be? I, of all people, knew what it was like to hold a grudge.

'How about we go shopping?' she said, when I remained silent. 'Ben said there's a shopping centre near here. White Dove or something?'

Shopping was the last thing I felt like doing, but it struck me that when Aisling had booked her flight for the school holidays, she hadn't signed up to all of this. Granted, she'd expected to have to amuse herself during the day, as I'd have been working. Instead, I wasn't working, but she'd been subjected to disturbed nights and days spent hanging around a hospital waiting room instead. The least I could do was treat her to a nice lunch and a bit of retail therapy.

'*White Rose*,' I said. 'It's about five or six miles from here. Shopping it is, then.'

A spot of shopping would probably do me the world of good. I didn't shop often but when I did, I splurged. I'd just have to be a bit more careful with the budget this time.

I found myself in *Zara* an hour later, stroking a gorgeous, short, ivory wrap dress with embellished shoulders and waistband, and a low back, imagining how it would look with my nude Louboutins. 'What do you think of this?' I said to Aisling, holding it against my body.

'Absolutely gorgeous. I saw that in *Practical Parenting* last week. It's what all the mums wear when changing dirty nappies and burping their babies.'

It took me a moment to register what she'd just said. 'Jesus! What an eejit I am! When will I ever have a chance to wear something like this with Luke around?' I quickly hooked the dress back onto the rail. 'Mind you, if Shannon gets her way, I won't be allowed to be part of Luke's—'

'Stop right there,' Aisling said. 'I won't be letting you wallow in this. Shannon's angry and that's understandable. When she calms down, Callum will explain what really happened. She won't suddenly become your BFF and start calling you Mum, but she *will* want to build a relationship. It'll be slow. There'll be hiccups. But it will be a relationship. Callum will make sure that happens. You heard what he said. He's only going along with it just now because he doesn't want to jeopardise her recovery.'

Aisling steered me out of *Zara* and towards a coffee shop, where she ordered two large cappuccinos. 'You'll probably need to accept that Luke's going to be at the hospital during the day,' she said, as we took a seat. 'But you'll get him back in the evenings.' Callum was moving off the ward and into a visitors' room, but he couldn't have Luke with him while still on crutches.

I tipped a packet of sugar into my coffee. 'What am I going to do with myself during the day?'

Aisling shrugged. 'I know you resigned, but could you go back to work? Part time, I mean, after you've done the hospital drop-off?'

I shook my head. 'From what I understand, they've already replaced me.'

'That was quick.'

'Internal promotion. They've even backfilled his position.'

Aisling studied my face for a moment.

'What?' I asked, feeling self-conscious. I wiped my mouth with a napkin. 'Froth?'

'No. You're grand. If they'd granted you leave to look after Luke, you wouldn't have returned, would you? You're thinking of doing something else?'

I smiled at my big sister. 'How did you know that?'

'There's a twinkle in your eye. You're scheming about something.'

'It's just a seedling of an idea at the moment and it might not grow. When I left, our HR manager said she could imagine me running my own business and the more I've thought about it, the more I like the idea.'

'I could see you as a successful young entrepreneur,' Aisling said. 'Doing what? PR still?'

I nodded. 'PR, marketing, social media… But maybe on a smaller scale. Local companies, rather than big corporates, so I don't have to do the travel.'

'Sounds grand. Here in Leeds?'

I shrugged. 'That'll be the unknown element. I want to be near Shannon, Callum and Luke, if they'll let me. I'm not sure if they'll want to go back to Northampton, stick around Leeds or go somewhere else.'

'Do you have a preference?'

'I really don't mind. I'll follow them anywhere. Well, anywhere as long as it's not Ballykielty!'

Aisling laughed. 'Can't imagine why you wouldn't be dying to move in next door to Ma and Da. They'd make you so welcome!'

She took a slurp of her drink. 'Have you heard from your man? Stevie, is it?'

'Jesus! I haven't checked my phone.' I dug it out of my bag. Sure enough, Stevie had texted me.

✉ From Stevie
Elise and Bean OK but BP still rising ☹ Will give it a few days before they decide on inducing birth. Elise is bored but says she has another story idea so taking her in some paper later. Hope Shannon's OK xx

'Everything okay?' Aisling asked.

'I think so.' I took a sip of my coffee while I gathered my thoughts. 'If she's anything like me, Shannon won't change her mind about seeing me within the next few days. Do you fancy a trip to the seaside tomorrow after we drop Luke off? I need to visit Elise, which means the inside of yet another hospital, but I promise that the rest of the day will be devoted to you.'

'Will you buy me an ice cream?'

'It's February.'

'It's the seaside. Which means ice cream.'

I laughed. 'Okay. There's an old-fashioned ice-cream parlour on the seafront. Sarah took me there once. It does amazing sundaes.'

'Sold,' she said. 'When we've finished these, what would you say to us getting you some sensible baby-friendly clothes? We passed a *Penneys* earlier. Or, what do you call it in England? *Primark*?'

'Wash your mouth out!'

'Have you been in *Primark* lately?'

'I've *never* been in *Primark*.'

'Then you don't know what you're missing. I love your clothes, Clare. They're gorgeous and you always look amazing, but designer skirts and dresses with three-inch heels are not practical with a baby.'

True. I'd become increasingly exasperated with my wardrobe since I'd started looking after Luke. I actually only owned one pair of jeans and two T-Shirts, and I felt so much more comfortable with Luke when I was wearing them. Maybe it was time to change my wardrobe.

'I'll give it a go. Reluctantly. As long as we can visit *Paperchase* first. I want to get something to cheer Elise up. And I'll need to be psyching myself up for the most dramatic makeover of my life. Or should that be make-under?'

Aisling nudged me in the ribs. 'Neither. It's just a transition into the world of parenting. It doesn't need to mean sweatpants and shapeless, beige sweaters. You can still have colour; you can still have dresses. You just probably don't want to spend as much on them. And you might want to invest in a few pairs of flat shoes.'

Chapter 28

'Welcome to Whitsborough Bay,' I said, as I pulled into a parking space on The Headland. 'Looks like we've got the perfect weather for a trip to the seaside.'

We both stepped out of the car and breathed in the fresh sea air. Fluffy clouds danced across a cornflower-blue sky, and gulls squawked as they swooped down in search of discarded chips and doughnuts. I reached into the back seat for my coat and scarf. The sun felt warm against my cheeks, but it was still February and there was definitely a winter chill in the air.

'What do you fancy doing?' I asked Aisling. 'We've got three hours till visiting time. If we go left out of here, we can walk around The Headland. It's about 30 to 40 minutes and it brings us out at North Beach and *Hearnshaw Park*. If we go right, we're at South Beach in a few minutes, which is the touristy part we drove through. We can get a coffee whichever direction we go.'

Aisling pondered a moment, looking left, then right, but there wasn't much to see, as the road curved all the way around The Headland, so it was just the North Sea straight ahead or a wide path left and right. 'What do you recommend?'

'Left. I prefer North Beach.'

'Is there somewhere to grab some lunch?'

I nodded. 'There's a couple of cafés and a bar that Sarah says does good food.'

'Left it is, then.'

'So,' Aisling said, when we'd crossed the road and set off. 'You and Ben? What's the story?'

I pulled a face at her. 'There's no story. He's a friend.'

'Is he, now?'

'Eh, yeah!'

'You don't think that what he's doing for you goes a bit above and beyond friendship?'

I laughed. 'For most people, yes. For Saint Ben, no. He works for a charity by day and volunteers by night. Luke and I are his current volunteering project. He's just being a good friend.'

'Friend? You're codding yourself.'

I stopped and leaned against the thick stone wall between the path and the sea. 'What brought this on? Did he say something?'

Aisling smiled. 'No. But I've seen the way he looks at you, so I have.'

'Bollocks! He's got a girlfriend and he's devoted to her.'

'Ah, yes, the mysterious Lebony. Don't you think it's convenient that she's on the other side of the world?'

'Not really. In fact, not at all, poor Ben.' I shook my head and started walking again. 'You've been reading too many romance novels. Ben doesn't see me as anything other than a friend and, even if he did – which he doesn't – it would be bugger all use because I don't think of him in that way. He's my best friend's brother and he's a good friend and housemate. There's never been anything more and never will be.'

'You go on convincing yourself of that.'

'Aisling! What's got into you? Ooh, I know! You've seen me *looking* at him too. Men and women *never* normally look at each other so it *must* mean we're harbouring deep, secret desires for each other.'

'I'd say your man Ben is, but your feelings for him are a bit too deep for you to acknowledge just yet.'

'Bollocks! The reason I haven't acknowledged them is because they're non-existent.'

'That's what you think.'

I shook my head again. Where the hell had this conversation sprung from? 'Even if I did have feelings for Ben – which I don't – and even if he didn't have a long-term girlfriend – which he does – it would be pointless anyway.'

'Why?'

'Because I have no intention of letting anyone in ever again. I've been there and got the battle scars.' I twiddled my Claddagh ring as images of Daran filled my mind once more. 'It's too painful when it ends.'

'But that was an extreme set of circumstances and it only ended because of Da. If he hadn't interfered, you'd still be together now, wouldn't you?'

'I'd like to think so, but who knows? What if he'd started resenting me for taking him away from the priesthood? What if he'd started to hate having to share his love for God with me?'

'And what if he realised that the priesthood was never his calling and a life with you was? And what if he was such a wonderful person that he had plenty of love for you *and* God? From what you've told me, you were made for each other. You'd have made it.'

We wandered in silence for a moment, only breaking it to say 'good morning' to a dog-walker and an elderly woman pushing a buggy.

'Did you think you and Finn were made for each other?' I asked eventually.

'Of course I did.' She sighed. 'Fair point. *I* believed we'd survive forever, but we didn't.'

'There you go, then. It's all heartache and I don't believe it's worth it.'

'Lots of relationships end, but there's always a reason. For Finn and me, the reason was that we should never have got married in the first place. *I* thought we were made for each other, *I* was the one who believed in us, and *I* was the one who loved him so deeply that I couldn't imagine life without him. Finn didn't feel the same. Don't get me wrong: he certainly cared about me. He might have even loved me a little bit, but it was more of a platonic love. As soon as he met someone who was the real thing, he was off and I couldn't blame him. Deep down, I knew it would happen eventually.'

I frowned. 'Really?'

'On our wedding day, I half-expected to be jilted, but he was there at the altar looking absolutely gorgeous… and absolutely petrified. I kept expecting him to stop the Mass because he couldn't go through with it. When he didn't, I kept telling myself that I needed to do the right thing and stop the ceremony myself, but I selfishly couldn't do it. I managed to convince myself that he had to love me a bit if he was willing to go through with the wedding. If a seed of love was there, perhaps it would grow into something bigger. So we both said "I do" and I spent the rest of our marriage wondering if each day was the day when he'd announce "I don't".'

'Jesus, Aisling! You never told me that. From what you'd said, I thought you'd been happy together until the affair.'

'That's what I let everyone think.' She pulled a tissue out of her coat pocket and wiped her eyes. 'I've never told anyone the truth. Even Finn doesn't know that I knew how he felt all along.'

'Then how do you know you were right about him?'

'Because I asked him. He denied it at first, but I told him he was an eejit if he thought I couldn't tell when he was lying, after he'd given me three years of lies while sneaking around with *her*. I told him he owed it to me to be honest for once, so it all came out. In return, I *wasn't* honest. I didn't let on that I'd known he'd had doubts all along. I played the part of the hurt wife who'd known about the affair and had come to terms with it already, and only turned a blind eye for the sake of the kids. I pretended I was relieved that it was out in the open and we could end the sham marriage and both start afresh. I told him everything he needed to hear to keep the split amicable for the sake of the kids so that…'

'So that what?' I asked, when Aisling didn't continue.

'So that I could still have him in my life.'

I stopped walking again and looked at my big sister. 'Oh no! You're not still…?'

She leaned on the wall and stared out at the twinkling sea. 'Pathetic, isn't it? He never loved me, he had an affair for three years, then left me for her, he left Ireland and moved to Manchester to be with her and, even though they split up and he didn't come running back to me, I'm *still* head over heels in love with the man and would do anything for him. I think that makes me the eejit, doesn't it?'

I sat on the wall beside her and put my arm around her. 'No. I think it makes him the eejit for not realising a good thing when he had it.'

She dabbed at her eyes again. 'He is one. But I'm an even bigger one because, ever since he split up with *her*, I've let him… you know.'

'Friends with benefits? Jesus, Aisling, are you mad?'

'Madly in love?' She shook her head. 'I know! You don't need to lecture me. I lecture myself about it every day, so I do. Because of the kids, I was always going to have to see him, so it was going to be harder to try and get over him. I know that sleeping with him is just taking me deeper and deeper into this mess, but he's so attentive when we're together that I can almost kid myself that he loves me. Almost.'

She put her head on my shoulder and we sat like that in silence for five or six minutes, listening to the gulls, a gentle sea breeze tickling our faces with locks of our hair.

'I don't know about you, but I'm ready for that coffee,' Aisling said, standing up and stretching.

We set off walking again. 'What happened with Finn and *her*?' I asked.

'Ironically, it was the same as what happened with Finn and me, only he was the one in deep this time. Turns out she was a big, fat coward and thought that accepting a job in Manchester would bring a natural end to the relationship. Stupid cow hadn't counted on him following her. She strung him along, house-hunting and everything. They even put a deposit down on a new build. His money, of course. They exchanged contracts and, the day before completion, she dropped the bombshell that she didn't want to be with him anymore.'

'Bitch.'

'I know! He was devastated. There he was, stuck with a house they'd chosen together, miles away from his kids, and no girlfriend anymore.'

'Could he not have moved back to Cork?'

'His job had gone, not that he'd have wanted to return to it even if it hadn't. Going to Manchester was a good career move for him – better company, big promotion – and he loves his job, so he decided to make a go of it.'

'What about the two of you? Any chance?'

'I'd have him back like a shot, but only if I could be sure that he'd woken up one day and realised he loved me as much as I loved him. Chances of that? Zero to none.'

'I'm sorry.'

'Not your fault. We can't control who we fall in love with.'

I smiled. 'No shit. A potential priest would *not* have been top of my list!'

'And the opinionated, underage daughter of a stroppy, controlling, religion-obsessed bigot probably wasn't top of his list, either. Yet it worked because you both felt the same way about each other. That's why it didn't work with Finn and me, or Finn and *her*. It's why it didn't work with your friend Elise and her ex-husband…'

'That, and the fact that he's gay.'

Aisling laughed. 'True. And that's why it won't work between you and Ben. Yet. Because, at the moment, he's smitten but you're not. It'll grow, though. It'll definitely grow.'

'Seriously, Aisling. Do you want me to push you over the sea wall? Will you stop trying to matchmake Ben and me. We're just friends.'

'For now.'

'Forever!'

'Hmm. Anyway, I'll drop the subject for now. Would that be a coffee shop I can see ahead of me like a shimmering oasis?'

'It might be.'

'Then, coffees are on me for talking about Ben. I should have realised it was too soon.'

I shoved her towards the sea wall. 'Final warning!'

As we continued to walk around The Headland towards the café, a feeling of unrest settled upon me. She was completely and utterly wrong about Ben, wasn't she? I certainly didn't feel anything for him, other than friendship and a tremendous amount of gratitude. He'd never given any indication that he felt anything for me, either, had he? I racked my brain. No! He'd always been clear about his devotion to Lebony and, let's face it, that had to be a huge amount of devotion, to keep a relationship going across such a distance. Aisling was way off. Given her revelation about still sleeping with Finn, she needed to get her own love life under control, instead of inventing romances between other people that didn't exist. What was she thinking?

Chapter 29

'What's this?' Elise asked, as I handed over a sparkly, lilac gift bag at the start of visiting hour. Aisling had decided to explore *Hearnshaw Park* rather than join me.

'Stevie said you'd been working on your stories,' I said. 'I thought these might be helpful.'

She carefully emptied the contents of the bag onto her bed and began unwrapping little packages. I'd bought her a selection of notebooks, pens, a planner and Post-it notes in different shapes and colours.

'Clare, that is so thoughtful,' she said. 'Thank you so much.'

'How's the writing going?'

'Really well. Including some work I did at the back end of last year, I've now managed to edit five of the nine books I'd written in my teens and come up with an idea for the 10th. One of the originals had a pretty weak plot so I've got some ideas for solving the problems with that too.'

'Sounds good. Did you say they're fantasy books?'

Elise nodded.

'I'd love to read them. I'm a fan of that genre.'

Elise bit her lip. 'That's very kind, but you don't have to. They're actually aimed at the young-adult market.'

'Doesn't mean I won't enjoy them too. I've read plenty of YA fantasy books in my time. Some of them are better than the adult ones.'

'I'd love another opinion, if you really don't mind. Gary's read them and he says he loves them, but he's not a reader so he can't compare me to what else is out there. Are you sure you've got time?'

'To be honest, I could do with the distraction. I don't know how long it'll be before I can see Shannon, and I can't stop thinking and worrying about her. Aisling is here at the moment, the kids will join us tomorrow, but I'll be on my own from Saturday afternoon with just my thoughts and my guilt for company.'

'How are things going with her?'

'When she heard I'd put in an appearance and had been looking after Luke, she had such a strong reaction that they had to sedate her.'

'Oh my goodness, Clare! That's awful.'

'Not the best. I felt so sorry for Callum having to deliver that little gem to me.' I coughed. 'I'm parched. Is there anywhere I can get a drink? Then I'll tell you about it and you can tell me the latest on Bean.'

Elise pointed. 'There's a water fountain and some cups over there near the nurses' station. I'd offer you some of mine but it's been here all day and could probably do with changing.'

'I'll do it.'

When I returned to the ward with fresh water, Elise had another visitor.

'Sarah!' I put the jug and cups down. 'Elise didn't tell me you were coming.'

'She didn't know. Auntie Kay offered to cover the shop so I could nip over. How are you? I didn't know you were coming to Whitsborough Bay.' Sarah might as well have added the missing words 'and that you clearly weren't planning to visit me afterwards' because her intention was very clear. Awkward.

It felt just like the hideous phone call we'd had after Sarah returned from her honeymoon, and I absolutely didn't want to go down that road again, especially after we'd had such a good talk when I'd stayed over at hers. It was time to change the subject. 'How's the shop?' I asked.

'Fine. A bit quiet after the Valentine's Day rush, but it will soon be Mother's Day.'

'Are you okay?' I asked, noticing that Sarah's eyes had filled with tears.

She sniffed and dabbed at her eyes with a tissue from her pocket. 'Sorry. Think I'm getting a bit of a cold. Watery eyes. Do you mind if I have some of that water?'

I picked up the jug and poured her a cup. 'Are you sure you're okay? You don't look too good.'

'Just a bit tired. It's been busy at work. I'll go and find another chair.'

Elise caught my eye as Sarah headed towards the nurses' station. 'Is something wrong with her?' she asked.

I shrugged. 'Not that I'm aware of, but I'm not buying the "tired" thing. There's something else.'

'I think so too. Whatever it is, she obviously doesn't want to talk about it. Maybe she'll let us know later.'

'The nurse is going to bring one over,' Sarah said, returning to the bed. 'So, how's Shannon doing?' She looked from Elise to me, then back to Elise. 'Or have you already discussed this?'

'No,' I said. 'I only got here about 10 minutes ago. So, the update is that she came round on Monday but was in and out of sleep. She was more with it yesterday and asked for Luke. Callum told her about me, and she hit the roof and had to be sedated. Physically and mentally, they're pleased with her progress so that's really positive. Doesn't look like the knock on the head has had any lasting damage. Emotionally, it's clearly not so good. It's going to be a long road. It's just another reason to be angry with my da. That man has such a lot to answer for.' I unclenched my fists and tried to relax. The mere mention of him made my blood boil.

'I'm sure he'll answer for it one day,' Elise said. 'Changing the subject slightly, how's it working out with Luke?'

'It hasn't been without its challenges. I've lost my job and I've been evicted; I've got baby sick on most of my clothes, and I still haven't quite mastered feeding, burping or changing him. But the cuddles are worth it.'

'I still can't believe you're a grandma,' Sarah said. 'And that you've walked out of the job you loved to take on parenthood, just like that. That's such a huge commitment. Are you sure about it?'

'It's different and it's unexpected, but what sort of person would I be if I'd refused to do it? I'd have kept Shannon if I'd had any choice but I wasn't given one, as you know.'

'I didn't mean it like that,' Sarah said.

'What did you mean?'

'Just that… well… er…' Sarah's eyes filled with tears again.

Elise bit her lip. 'What I think Sarah means is that she's known you for nearly half your life and she'd always believed you didn't like children. We know now that it was a defence mechanism but it's quite a contrast – from thinking you were someone who avoided babies at all costs to seeing you actually bringing up your grandson. Is that what you mean, Sarah?'

Sarah nodded, her red cheeks showing her embarrassment.

I relaxed and smiled, realising I was unfairly channelling my anger at Da towards Sarah. 'Sorry. Ignore me. I'm just a bit stressed by the whole Shannon situation. Do you want to see a photo of them?' I dug in my bag for my iPhone and thrust it under Elise's nose.

She smiled. 'Aw, she's just like you. And Luke's a little baldie!

How cute.'

'He's started to get hair now. Looks like he may be a redhead.' As I said the word, an involuntary shiver rippled through me and that strange feeling was there again. What the hell was it?

'Really? Is Callum a redhead?'

I shook my head. 'Callum's dark.'

'Maybe the red comes from further back in the genes.'

'Maybe.'

Elise handed the phone to Sarah, who took it without a word. I frowned as her eyes filled with tears again. She cleared her throat and handed it back. 'They're gorgeous, Clare. I can't wait to meet them.' She fished a tissue out of her jeans pocket and blew her nose. 'I think it's time I headed off.'

'But you've just got here,' Elise protested.

'I know. I'm sorry. I'm definitely coming down with something and I don't want you to catch it, Elise. It's the last thing you need right now.' She stood up and picked up her bag. 'Keep me posted. Both of you.' Then she left.

'Was it just me or was that really strange?' Elise said, as soon as Sarah had gone.

'Very strange,' I agreed. 'Although, I think I was a bit snappy with her and I didn't mean to be.'

She nodded. 'You were a bit, but I'm sure she'll understand it's not about her but about your situation. Do you think I should phone her later and ask her what's going on?'

I shook my head. 'You've got more than enough on your plate at the moment.'

'And so have you. I'm sure she'll tell us what's wrong if she needs our help. Remember how she was with Jason? It took her a year to admit that she wasn't happy with him and the first we knew of it was when she dumped him. She likes to work things through in her own mind.'

I nodded. I felt uneasy about it, though. Yes, Sarah hadn't let on that she'd had doubts about Jason, but she'd learned from the experience. When she moved back up to Whitsborough Bay and wasn't sure whether Andy or Nick was the one for her, she'd really opened up and seemed to find it valuable talking to Elise or me about her concerns. What if she didn't think we were interested anymore? What if she thought we had each other now and didn't need her? Surely she wouldn't think that. It was childish. Sarah wasn't a childish person. She'd always wanted Elise and me to make our peace. Surely she was happy that we had. But that feeling of uneasiness wouldn't go away.

Chapter 30

✉ From Elise
Hi everyone. Baby's on the way! BP's continued to rise and pre-eclampsia's getting worse so they induced me early this morning. Waters have just been broken and everything seems to be happening. She'll be 31 weeks tomorrow so scared but excited about early arrival. Been taking steroids to build her lungs so hopefully she'll be OK. Stevie or I will text with news and a name when she's born xx

Jesus! Thirty-one weeks. Elise must be terrified. After visiting her in hospital the week before, I'd Googled it and it seemed that 30 weeks was the magic number for a very high survival rate so the odds were in her favour, as long as there were no further complications.

I strapped Luke into his car seat. 'Are you ready to visit Mammy and Daddy?' He stared at me and blew some bubbles. 'I'll take that as a yes. When you're with your mammy today, will you ask her to stop sulking and accept that what happened 17 years ago was completely out of my control? I just want to see my daughter and try to make up for all the lost years.' Luke blew some more bubbles. 'Good boy! I knew you were the man for the job!'

I tried to relax as I drove to *Jimmy's*. Again. To drop Luke off. Again. To face Callum's slumped shoulders, the bags under his eyes and that apologetic expression. Again. It had been nine days since she'd woken up. Nine bloody days, yet she still point-blank refused to talk about me, never mind meet me. It broke my heart that she refused to let me in. If she had her way, I wouldn't get to see Luke and I certainly wouldn't be the one providing a roof over his head, but Callum had put his foot down. She wasn't well enough to look after him – neither was he – and the hospital had already done their bit.

'Let's take it as a good sign that she only had to be sedated the once,' I said to Luke. 'Did you have words with her and tell her that I'm not so bad?'

'You look exhausted,' I said to Callum, who was waiting for me on the seats near the nurses' station as per our usual routine: 10am drop-off, pick-up two hours later.

'I had a bad night. I think I'm also suffering from a lack of fresh air.'

'If you can get hold of a wheelchair, I don't mind pushing you around outside for a bit, if that would help.'

'Tempting, but I'd better take Luke in to Shannon. She's been asking where he is.'

Argh! Must control temper. Must not snap. 'She's been asking where he is? I'm… what?' I glanced at my watch. 'Two minutes late. Two minutes. And that's only because your son decided it would be a good time to fill his nappy moments before we were due to set off. Only, when I say "fill his nappy", I don't really mean that. I mean his nappy, his dungarees and his T-Shirt. Christ alone knows how something so small can generate so much. It was like a sewer had exploded in there! So I had to strip him, wash him and start again. Then, guess what? I realised that I had shit all over me too so I had to get changed. And then we must have caught every feckin' red light this side of Leeds. So I'm sorry I'm late by two whole minutes and have failed my daughter yet again. You'd better rush Luke to her side immediately and I'll be on my way, rushing home, then rushing back again so that Luke and I are out of your hair by dinnertime, exactly as demanded.

'I've left my job, I've been evicted and I've done everything she's asked, yet she still won't even grant me five minutes of her time. I get that she's angry. I get that she was let down. I get that I wasn't there when she needed me. What *she* needs to get is that I was forced to give her up, I was told that she was dead and I didn't write that letter telling her I wanted nothing to do with her.' Yeah. Did really well controlling my temper there.

'Feeling better?' Callum asked.

I stared at the floor, feeling very sheepish. 'Yes. Sorry. I wasn't having a go at you, Callum. I just needed to vent. The whole situation's getting to me.'

'I know. I'm surprised you didn't do it sooner.'

I smiled. 'You should hear the road rage on the way home each morning. The air is blue!'

He smiled back at me. 'I can imagine. Anyway, the reason that Shannon was wondering where Luke was had nothing to do with her being demanding or thinking you were late. It was about her being anxious and nervous and wanting to get it over with.'

'Get what over with?'

'She's had her sulking and thinking time, and she's ready.'

'For what?'

'To meet her mum.'

I was absolutely shitting a brick as I held Luke close to my chest with one arm and wielded the baby carrier with the other. I had no idea what to expect. Would she rant at me, releasing 17 years' worth of pent-up frustration? If she did, would I be able to control my temper, or would my frustration at Da project onto her and ruin any relationship before it had even started? Or would she give me a chance to explain?

And, if she did, was 'I had no choice' a good enough excuse for agreeing to the adoption? I had, after all, had a choice. I could have said no.

Shannon had been moved onto a ward with six beds in it, five of which were occupied.

'She's on the far left,' Callum whispered, as he hobbled beside me on his crutches.

She had her eyes closed as we approached her bed but opened them when Luke sneezed, showering my neck and T-Shirt with snot. Great. Might as well have kept the pooey top on. I placed the baby carrier on the floor, grabbed a tissue from a table at the foot of the bed, and wiped Luke's nose and my neck. All the while, I was aware of Shannon's eyes on me.

'Hi,' I said, turning to face her. 'Somebody wants cuddles from his mammy.'

Shannon moved her arms so I could nestle Luke into one. She smiled at him and lightly kissed his head. 'Thank you.'

'You're welcome.'

'So, you're my birth mum.' Her voice was low and gentle, devoid of any discernible accent. It threw me. For some ridiculous reason, I'd expected her to have an Irish accent like me. Of course she wouldn't have! What had possessed me to think that?

'It would appear so. How are you feeling?'

'Sore. Tired. Grateful to be alive. Speaking of which, Callum tells me you thought I was dead.'

I nodded. 'They told me you'd died shortly after you were born. That letter you got? It wasn't from me. I knew nothing about it until Callum told me.'

'He told me that too.' She nodded towards a seat on the other side of the bed. 'You'd best pull up a pew and start from the beginning. You might need to do it in two parts, though. I get tired easily.'

I did manage to get through the story before Shannon's eyes started to get droop. 'I'd better go,' I said. 'Will I leave Luke with you and come back later?'

'No. Stay,' Shannon whispered, before surrendering to sleep.

'Do you want to see if we can get that wheelchair?' Callum asked, reaching for his crutches. 'I could do with some air. Shannon will probably be out for an hour or so.'

Fifteen minutes later, Callum and Luke were bundled up in coats and blankets, ready for a push around the grounds. Luke was due a feed so one of the nurses had heated up his bottle in readiness.

'That seemed to go well,' I said, as we left the building.

'It went very well. I knew she'd come round.'

'What happens next?'

'With you and Shannon?'

I shook my head. 'With everything: Shannon and me, the three of you, hospital, where you live. Everything!'

He adjusted Luke's hat to cover his ears better. 'You and Shannon will continue to talk and get to know each other. She might still have stroppy moments but the hardest part is over. Me and Shannon will get married at some point, but the priority is getting her better. And me. They think I've got a urine infection so I'm having more tests.'

I stopped pushing the wheelchair and moved around it so I could face him. 'No! Really? That's not fair. Haven't you been through enough already?'

'You'd think so, wouldn't you?'

'Is that why you had a bad night?'

'Yes.'

'That's bollocks. Sorry, Callum.'

He shrugged. 'Could be worse. At least I'm in the right place to get it sorted out.' Luke's face crumpled and he let out a loud squawk. 'Looks like someone's ready for his feed.'

I resumed pushing as soon as Luke was settled with his bottle.

'What else did you ask me?' Callum said. 'Oh yeah, where we'll live. I don't know. There's nothing left for us in Northampton. No home. No job.'

'What about your apprenticeship?'

'Gone to someone else.'

'No! Why did they do that?'

'Because I told them to. It wasn't fair to ask them to hold my place when I had no idea when I'd be able to return. Even when I'm better, Shannon won't be, so I'm going to need to be around for her and Luke. For now, this place is our home. I'm back on the ward being monitored so it's not costing us anything again.' He took the bottle out of Luke's mouth. 'Can we stop for a minute while I burp him?'

Luke released a few impressive belches, then we set off again. 'You know you don't need to worry about money, don't you? I have savings. I can help.'

Callum shook his head. 'There's no need. We've got the money back from the house we were going to rent, and Shannon gets, like, an allowance from her parents' estate. It'll be tight without me earning but we'll manage. Besides, we only need to scrape by till a year come June.'

'Why? What happens then?'

Callum twisted around to face me, frowning. 'Shannon's 18th, of course. She'll inherit half a million. Actually, it might be closer to £600,000.'

I stopped pushing. 'You're kidding?'

'Her parents… her *adopted* parents… were loaded. The house was paid off, they both had life assurance, savings, pensions and all sorts of stuff like that. It all went into a trust fund until Shannon's 18th, with a monthly allowance till then.'

'That's amazing. You can buy a house outright if you choose the right place to live. You'll be financially stable for life.'

'I'll still work, you know. I'm no sponger. And Shannon still wants to go to college so I definitely want to bring in some income while she's studying. I'd like to put some of the money aside for Luke's future.'

'From what I've learned about you, Callum, I know you're definitely not a sponger. So your challenge isn't money – it's location?'

Luke finished his bottle and we stopped again for Callum to burp him. 'I don't know where we'll live,' he said. 'It'll depend whether we need to stay close to *Jimmy's* or not. I don't know Leeds, but it probably wouldn't be in my top 10 of places to live. Or Shannon's. In fact, it probably wouldn't be in my top 50. Nothing against Leeds – I'm sure it's a lovely place – but big cities aren't us. The Hendersons were out in the country and Shannon was brought up in a village.'

'If you could live anywhere in the country, where would you go?' Please don't say you want to move abroad, and definitely don't say you want to move to Ireland!

Callum pondered for a moment. 'I don't really mind. It would need to be in the north. Shannon's inheritance is loads, but I know it won't buy us much down south. It would need to be a town or village. It would need to have a decent school for Luke. Shannon quite fancies living near the sea. I've never really thought about it, but why not try something different, after spending my whole life living miles from the coast? What I *really* want is to find somewhere that Shannon can properly call home. She's carried those wooden boxes around with her for years. I want her to find somewhere to scatter the ashes.'

'So, you want northern, coastal, not too big, reasonable house prices, decent schools and somewhere that feels like home?'

Callum ran his fingers through his hair. 'I said I didn't mind but it looks like I do, when you list it like that.'

'I know the perfect place.'

'You do?'

'Yes. Whitsborough Bay.'

Chapter 31

✉ From Stevie
She's here! Melody Hope. Born at 3.42pm by C-section as her heart rate had started to drop. She's tiny - 3lb 9oz - but mum and baby are doing well. Melody on special care baby unit. Elise resting. Will report back with news #prouddad #firstselfie

Tears filled my eyes as I clicked into the image attached. Stevie, wearing a surgical mask, blue paper gown and hat, was closest to the camera, the joy clearly radiating from his eyes. I could guarantee the grin beneath that mask was enormous. On the right, Elise's head rested on a pillow, her auburn curls hidden beneath a paper hat too, and a clear oxygen mask over her face, showing the biggest smile ever. Wrapped in a white towel, a tiny, red, wrinkly baby nestled between them, eyes tightly shut, fists in tiny balls under her chin.

'Hi, Melody Hope,' I whispered, gently touching her image with my finger. 'You be a good girl now and grow quickly so you can go home with your parents.'

✉ To Stevie
Beautiful name for a beautiful baby. Congratulations

to you both. Send my love to Elise. Can't wait to meet Melody xx

I resumed my task of emptying the tumble dryer, very relieved to hear that Melody had arrived safely. I loved her name. It was very Elise. She'd said she had a shortlist of six names, and that she and Stevie had a favourite amongst them but didn't want to tell anyone in case they changed their mind. I wondered whether Melody had been the favourite because I knew from personal experience that names could easily be changed. Ma had often told me that I was going to be Siobhán if I was a girl and Fergus if I'd been a boy. Thank God I hadn't been a boy. I hear 'Fergus', I think 'bogeyman'! Mind you, I hated the name Siobhán too, although I hadn't escaped it entirely, as they'd made it my middle name. Ma said that when I arrived, I'd screamed so loudly and flailed about so much that they'd decided Siobhán was too classy a name for me and that I needed a straightforward, one-syllable name. As Sarah would say, how rude! I'm not sure why Ma told me that story, but it was her favourite one to reel out every time we heard news of a birth and confirmation of the baby's name. I suppose it was just another excuse to put me down.

I Googled my name five or six years ago, when it suddenly struck me that they might have given me a name that meant something nasty, but the definition had been something like: *cheerful, friendly, likely to have an emotional life, good talker, self-promoter, rarely worries, bold, independent, inquisitive, knows exactly what she wants.* I'd have said that was pretty accurate… if I believed in bollocks like that. At least it hadn't said something like: *spawn of Satan, evil, trouble, likely to bring disrespect on her family, sinner.*

I dropped the baby monitor into the basket of clothes, picked it up with one hand, then grabbed my mug of coffee with the other, before heading into the lounge to fold everything. I dropped the basket on the floor and slumped onto the settee, feeling drained. I lay back against the cushion for a moment. What a day! Shannon finally speaking to me. Elise having the baby. I hadn't realised I'd been so tense about those two events.

The sound of a key in the lock startled me.

'Were you asleep?' Ben asked, poking his head around the door.

I rubbed my eyes and sat up, 'I must have been. I swear I only closed my eyes for a moment.' I looked at the clock on the wall. 'Bollocks. Forty minutes ago. I'd better check on Luke. He'll be awake any minute.'

'I'll do it. I need to go up to get changed anyway.'

'Thanks.' I rolled my stiff shoulders, then reached for the basket. I probably still had time to fold the washing before Luke awoke.

'He's still asleep,' Ben said, when he reappeared in a fresh T-Shirt and jeans 10 minutes later. He sat down beside me on the sofa. 'How was today? Is she still refusing to see you?'

'No. I was finally granted an audience.'

'Oh my God! How was it?'

'A bit awkward at times, but it was such a relief to see her. She looks—' I rolled my eyes as a loud squawk filled the room. 'No rest for the wicked. I'll tell you later. Have you got any plans tonight?'

'I've got to Skype Lebony at seven, then I'm all ears.'

As I made my way upstairs, I thought about my conversation with Aisling. She absolutely had it all wrong. Ben emailed and Skyped Lebony on a regular basis. He was just as committed to making their long-distance relationship work as he'd always been. I was just a friend. In fact, I was probably more like another sister to him. Aisling probably just liked to fantasise about happy-ever-afters for other people, given that she couldn't have her own, thanks to her little obsession with Finn.

'Has your auntie Kay sold Smuggler's View yet?' I asked Ben, after we'd put Luke to bed later that evening.

'I spoke to her at the weekend and she's had two viewings but no offers. The housing market's slow at this time of year. Why? Are you thinking it might be a good home for Shannon and Callum?'

I shrugged. 'I'm not sure it would. I see them more in a 1930s semi with a big garden or maybe even a new build. I was thinking for me.'

Ben's eyes widened. 'You're leaving Leeds?'

'I'm jobless and I'm homeless. It's not like there's anything to keep me here, is there?'

'Thanks a lot!'

I shoved his leg. 'Don't sulk. You know I don't mean it like that. If I were to copy your sister and write the pros and cons on some Post-its, seeing you would be top of my reasons to stay in Leeds. Problem is, I'm not sure there'd be any other Post-its on that column.'

'Not even the shops?'

I thought about the bags of *Primark* purchases and how much more comfortable I'd been in leggings or jeans and T-Shirts, and casual dresses. 'Not even the shops. I like Leeds. I – it's an amazing city, – but my priorities have changed. If they'll let me, I want to be where my family is and, from what Callum's said, Whitsborough Bay would seem a sensible place to settle.

'Do you want me to have a word with Auntie Kay?'

'Not just yet. I don't want to be my usual impulsive self, put plans in place, then discover that by "north", they actually mean Scotland. Or that they don't want me with them.'

'I'd miss you,' Ben said. 'You and Luke, that is. I've got used to having the little man around.'

'We'd miss you too, but it's not like we wouldn't see each other again. You are, after all, his step-granddaddy, or whatever lie it was we told the nurse on that first day.'

'We? What's with the "we"? I think it was you, young lady, who were the big, fat fibber that day.'

I laughed. 'I can't believe it was only four weeks ago. So much has changed in such a short space of time.'

'Feels like longer.'

'It certainly does.'

We sat in companionable silence for a while, listening to the clock tick and sipping on our drinks.

'I always imagined you'd choose to settle in a swanky apartment with a shiny kitchen, white walls and minimalist décor,' Ben said, after 10 minutes or so. 'Like *Orion Point*.'

'So did I, but it never felt like home. It had a spectacular view but it lacked soul. I really liked *Smuggler's View* when Sarah was living there. I really like it here too. There's something safe and cosy about older properties.'

'Is that why you stayed here while I was in Birmingham?'

I gasped, as colour rushed to my cheeks. 'Jesus! How did you know that?'

'The old lady next door, Mrs Astell, asked if you'd moved back in or if you'd just been house-sitting while I was away.'

'I'm so sorry, Ben. I meant to say something. It was after I got the letter and told Elise everything. It was such a huge thing for me, opening up to someone after so many years of silence. I couldn't face going back to *Orion Point* on my own. I should have asked, or said something afterwards, but things went a bit crazy.'

'I'm not mad at you. I'm glad you like it here. I just wish I hadn't been away that weekend so I could have been here for you.' He smiled at me and his dark-brown eyes twinkled with warmth. For a moment, I thought I saw a flicker of something. No! Aisling couldn't be right about him, could she?

'You're a good friend, Ben,' I said, placing a slight emphasis on the word 'friend'.

'Any time.' He was still looking at me tenderly. Arse. I had to nip this in the bud.

'I don't think I've ever had a proper male friend before,' I said. 'Any male I've got pally with has always turned out to have another agenda of getting into my knickers, so it's so refreshing that we can have this, knowing that it will never be more than friendship.'

Ben grinned. 'You think I fancy you, don't you?'

I blushed again. Where the hell had *that* come from? I'd *never* blushed before and now I'd done it twice in one evening. 'No. It's just that—'

'It's just that your sister's planted the idea in your head and now you're overanalysing every comment, every glance and every touch.'

Realisation dawned. 'She said something to you too?'

'She quizzed me about it when you were in the shower one morning.'

'I hope you told her she was way off and you were very happy with Lebony.'

'What do you think?'

'Phew! I can relax again now.'

'Am I *really* that undesirable?'

I threw a cushion at him. 'Stop fishing for compliments. I suppose you're not too bad-looking, if you're into that whole "boy next door with sad puppy-dog eyes" kind of thing.'

'Ooh, don't push it with the praise.'

'What about me, anyway? How come you've never tried it on with me? Am I *really* that undesirable too?' I playfully flicked my hair and pouted. 'I thought I was irresistible to all men, women and small furry animals.'

Ben laughed as he stood up and reached for my empty mug. 'Just as well I'm immune to your charms, then, isn't it?'

'How can that be?'

He shook his head at me, grinning. 'Look, you know I think you're gorgeous but I have a girlfriend, so let's just say that I can enjoy looking at the goods; I just can't sample them, which works out perfectly for everyone. No friendships are tested and no partners are made jealous. Win-win. Night, Irish.'

'Night, Saint Ben.'

As I lay in bed shortly afterwards, gazing across the room at Luke sleeping peacefully in his cot, I thought about my conversation with Ben. What must he have thought when he'd discovered I'd stayed for the weekend? How embarrassing! And even more embarrassing was the revelation that Aisling had interrogated him about his feelings for me. I didn't like to dwell on what she might have actually asked him. I'd be having words with her when I next spoke to her. What was her game? It could have gone horribly wrong, because I couldn't have continued to live with Ben if I thought he saw me as more than a friend.

Chapter 32

✉ To Sarah
I'm coming over to visit Melody this afternoon. I can't stay long as I need to be back for Luke. I know it's a Saturday, but do you have time for a coffee late pm?

✉ From Sarah
Would love to see you but Cathy & Jade are away for the weekend so I'm really short-staffed. I've had to send Briony home with a high temp and Josh isn't very experienced yet. Mum's here but we have a 60th birthday party to prepare for so I might not be able to give you much time. Sorry ☹

✉ To Sarah
Sounds chaotic. I won't add to it. Laters

'She's absolutely gorgeous, Elise. Congratulations, both of you.' I hugged Elise and Stevie, then gazed into the incubator again. 'I'm not convinced that the tube-up-the-nose fashion she's currently sporting will catch on, but she's working the look pretty well just now.'

Elise laughed. 'With us as parents, I don't think she's ever going to be fashionable, is she?'

'What are you saying?' Stevie indicated his usual wardrobe of jeans and a T-Shirt with a cartoon of a sheep drinking a pint of beer. 'I'll have you know, this T-Shirt is only six years old.'

'And you bought it in *Sainsbury's*,' Elise said. 'Not that there's anything wrong with supermarket clothes, as I own loads of them too, but it's not exactly leading-edge design, is it?'

Stevie shrugged. 'Fair point. Can I get you a coffee, Clare?'

'Stevie, you're a legend. Black, strong, no sugar, please.'

When he'd left the room, I turned to Elise. 'Does the twat know?'

Elise rolled her eyes. 'Daniel?'

'Unless there's a list of twats who could be the father?'

She shook her head. 'One's enough, thank you. I texted him yesterday.'

'Any response?'

'What do you think? Kay and Philip stopped by this morning with some gifts. Philip had contacted him to check if he'd heard, but he said he didn't care, as the baby wasn't his anyway. If that's the attitude he still wants to take, it's fine by me. As far as I'm concerned, Stevie's Melody's dad.'

'What if he wants to be in her life later?'

'The door will always be open for him, but I'm not going out of my way to try and get him involved. I don't want or need any money from him, so that should make things easier.'

Stevie returned with the coffee and I took a grateful gulp. Luke now only woke up twice a night for a feed and settled quickly afterwards, but I didn't. My mind would start whirring. Sometimes it was worries about the future, sometimes it was a list of chores I needed to do, and sometimes it was a song or TV theme going around my mind on a loop. I never used to struggle to sleep. What was that all about?

'I come bearing gifts, as you might have noticed.' I unknotted a bin liner to reveal a shiny, pink 'It's a girl!' helium balloon, then handed over a packed gift bag.

Elise grinned. 'Thank you, but when have you had time to go shopping for all of this?'

'Luke and I went to a retail park for a spot of late-night shopping on Thursday. I've got all the receipts, if you don't like anything or already have it. Apologies that none of it's wrapped. I forgot to buy wrapping paper.'

Stevie and Elise took turns delving into the huge bag, pulling out soft toys, teethers, babygrows, dresses in various age ranges, blankets and bottles of baby products. 'This is too much, Clare. You've spent a fortune.'

'It's grand,' I said. 'I'll admit I might have got a bit carried away, but it was exciting. It was quite therapeutic buying things for a baby girl when I didn't get the chance to do it for Shannon, and boys aren't quite as much fun to buy for.'

Elise started to carefully place everything back in the gift bag. 'How's it going with Luke?'

'I'm still a bit worried I'm going to break him when I change him, but I don't feel as completely clueless as I did before.'

'I think most first-time parents are clueless,' Elise said. 'I thought I was pretty good with children but when my sister's twins came along, I realised I'd had hardly anything to do with babies. I could confidently hold one, but I didn't know how to change a nappy or make up a feed. Our Jess made sure I had plenty of practice on the twins.'

'Same here,' Stevie said. 'I've never been round babies either. The first time I held one of Jess' twins, I thought I was going to drop him, and I was convinced that I was going to hurt him when I tried to change his outfit one day. I'm still learning but I feel a lot more confident now.'

So it wasn't just me being an incompetent eejit? Phew. I'd assumed Elise would be an absolute natural at it all, like Callum and Ben. I finished my coffee and dropped it into a nearby bin. 'So, have you had any other visitors?'

Elise nodded. 'Our Jess came yesterday afternoon and her husband dropped in that evening. My boss, Graham, and his wife, Beth, nipped in very briefly this morning before Kay and Philip, but that's it. Dad's flying over on Tuesday or Wednesday.'

'No Sarah?'

Elise glanced towards the incubator and shook her head. 'No. No Sarah.'

'She's texted,' Stevie said. 'She replied to the group text about Melody's arrival to say she was thrilled for us and hoped Melody would be home really soon, but there was no mention of visiting. Are you going to see her while you're over?'

'I texted her to say I could pop over after visiting time but couldn't stay long because I've got to get back for Luke. I got this gibberish response about staff being on holiday, off sick or inexperienced. Who's Briony?'

Elise shrugged. 'Not heard her mentioned before.'

'Me neither,' Stevie added.

'Well, apparently Briony is ill, whoever she is. It seemed to me like she didn't want me there, but she didn't want to say it outright so there were all these excuses. You know how she babbles when she's nervous? Well, she was babbling on her text message, if that's possible.'

Stevie shook his head. 'I don't know what's going on with Sarah lately. I'd invited her to start running with me again, but she's had an excuse every time. I've suggested cinema trips but she's turned those down too. I've hardly seen Nick, either.'

I looked towards Elise. 'Have you seen or heard from her since the awkward hospital visit?'

She shook her head. 'No. A couple of texts to ask if I was okay but nothing more.'

'There's something going on,' I said. 'Under normal circumstances, I'd drive over to the shop and drag it out of her, but I have too much going on at the moment and I don't have the energy to keep asking her what's wrong.'

'I feel the same,' Elise said. 'We've got bigger things to worry about right now and it's a bit easier for Sarah to come and visit us, rather than the other way round. I understand that a Saturday is difficult because of the shop but if she doesn't show up tomorrow, I'll be very unimpressed.'

A young nurse opened the door. 'Sorry to interrupt, but you have another couple of visitors and I'm afraid we only permit two at a time, plus parents.'

'Sarah and Nick?' Elise asked, sounding hopeful.

'Gary and Bob, I think they said.'

'Gary and Rob. Okay. Thank you. Could you ask them to wait a moment, please?'

The nurse nodded, then closed the door.

Stevie hugged Elise. 'She'll come soon.'

I picked up my bag. 'I'm sure she'll visit soon too. Gary and Rob have perfect timing 'cos I need to get back to Leeds. I'll try to get back over again soon.' I blew a kiss in the direction of the incubator. 'Bye, Melody. Hurry up and get out of that incubator so Auntie Clare can have hugs.'

As I drove back towards Leeds, I reflected on our conversation about Sarah, and how I was more likely to pick up the phone to Elise or Ben these days rather than her, despite that huge heart-to-heart we'd had. How had that happened? Had I pulled away from Sarah or had she pulled away from me? If Elise was feeling it too, surely it was the latter? But did I have the time and energy to do anything about it? No. Did that make me a useless friend? Did it mean I was taking her friendship for granted again – something I'd sworn I wouldn't do?

Could there be something going wrong with the shop or with her marriage already that she didn't want to face up to? Surely not. The shop was thriving, and she and Nick were besotted with each other still, weren't they?

An uneasy feeling settled over me as I joined the A1 towards Leeds. I *was* being a useless friend. I was all wrapped up in Shannon and Luke, and full of criticism for Sarah for not being more supportive, but what if she was facing something even bigger in her life that she needed my support on?

I drummed my fingers on the steering wheel as I slowed for some gobshite lorry driver to pull out and inch his way past another lorry uphill. Why did they do that? Back to Sarah, though. What could be going on in her life that was bigger than me discovering that my daughter hadn't really died at birth, that her father had been killed in the tsunami, that she'd been in a serious car crash, and that she had a son who needed my care?

The lorry finally pulled back in and I pressed my foot on the accelerator. Sarah had occupied enough of my thoughts. I'd make another attempt to find out what was going on, but I'd wait until next week. She knew where I was if she really needed me, didn't she? Why should I be making all the effort?

Chapter 33

I have no idea where the next two weeks went. Well, actually I do. They flew by in a frenzy of hospital visits and babysitting.

Callum's urinary tract infection cleared up but his immune system was so low that he picked up something else (I've lost track of what), which wiped him out, so he was on strict bed rest and hooked up to a drip. Meanwhile, Shannon continued to improve. Dr Kaur was very impressed with her. They'd got her up and about surprisingly quickly after they'd woken her up, but she'd still had a broken ankle and arm, which meant she was limited with her movement. Five weeks after the accident, she was ready to put weight on the ankle.

Her first steps on her damaged ankle were very tentative. Physically, I could see she was exhausted, as she clung onto the railing in the physio room. Emotionally, I could see that it was worse. I recalled the footage of her dancing and was pretty certain she was petrified she'd never be able to dance again. I didn't know how to broach the subject, though, so I took Dr Kaur aside and asked her outright.

'The fact that she's a dancer will make her rehabilitation easier,' she assured me. 'Her legs will be used to hard work. Because of the accident, though, the muscles have forgotten what that feels like and they're objecting to it. If she's determined – and I can see that she's that kind of woman – there's no reason why she won't fully recover and dance again to the same standard. The broken ankle has healed nicely because she's had complete bed rest and she didn't damage her legs in the accident. She just hasn't used them for a while.'

Shannon cried after that first intense physio session. She'd been strong in front of us but, when she was alone on the ward, the tears fell. I only knew because I realised I'd left Luke's teddy, Philbin, on her bed so returned to get it. She wasn't quick enough to wipe the tears away.

'I know it hurt today, but it will get better,' I said, passing her a tissue.

'And you'd know because you were in a coma and woke up to discover that your legs had forgotten how to work?'

'No.'

'You're a doctor, then, are you?'

I gazed at her and saw so much of me in her, desperate to strike out at anyone, in order to keep the pain at bay. 'You'll dance again,' I said. 'I know it.'

Another tear slipped down her cheek. She didn't need a pep talk from me. She needed her alone time to think.

'I'll see you tomorrow, Shannon. Don't give up. And don't forget that stuff about God making the valley of trouble a door of hope.' Without waiting for her reaction, I left the ward. Callum was adamant that her faith was strong. Maybe that was what she needed to get her through this. It wasn't my thing but if it worked for her, so be it.

The next day, she seemed a lot more positive and apologised for snapping. It was her first apology to me. Things were looking up.

Sure enough, a week of physio did wonders for her. By the end of the second week, Callum was up and about again, encouraging and supporting her, and the improvements were incredible.

I visited Whitsborough Bay twice during that fortnight. The first time was an evening so I texted Sarah a couple of days before, knowing the shop would be closed. I got another garbled message back about meetings and stocktakes and Christ knows what. I didn't bother contacting her the following week. I was going to be over there during shop opening hours, which gave me an easy excuse. To be honest, I couldn't face a third rejection.

Melody was doing really well, putting on weight and sleeping less. Sarah still hadn't visited. I could see how hurt Elise was. There'd been several texts, each with a different excuse: she'd had a cold and didn't want to pass it on to Melody; she'd had a stomach bug and couldn't risk passing that on either; Nick had picked up the bug and she was worried about still being contagious. And so it went on. She'd posted a new baby card through their letterbox one evening but hadn't knocked. Stevie had actually been in, and his car was on the drive, so he'd felt pretty miffed that she didn't seem to have five minutes to say hello and ask after Melody. Elise, who always tried to see the good in everyone and every circumstance, suggested that it might not have been Sarah who'd dropped off the card, but her words lacked conviction and I could tell she felt totally let down by Sarah's absence.

Shannon and Callum made a decision that it wasn't fair on Luke to spend his days cooped up in hospital, especially as that had been the reason why Callum had asked me to look after him in the first place. We therefore settled into a routine: one full day there without me, the next evening with me, a morning without me, another evening with me, then back to the start again. I liked the new arrangement. It was far better for Luke to get out in the fresh air, and it was good for Shannon and Callum to get time alone with him so they could bond with their son. It also helped my relationship with Shannon. I could tell her about the places Luke and I had been. She lapped up all the minute details, like the colours of the leaves on the trees, the feel of the breeze on our cheeks, the cries of other children in the park and so on. I think she liked to imagine she was the one pushing the pram and behaving like a 'normal' mum.

On the Sunday, two weeks after Shannon had started her intensive physio, I was due an evening visit. A mild mid-March day had dawned, with blue skies and a warm sun.

'It's gorgeous out there,' Ben said, as he washed up after breakfast and I dried the dishes. 'Do you fancy making the most of a full day with Luke and taking a run through to Whitsborough Bay?

'To see Elise?' I asked. I clocked his frown and quickly added, 'Or Sarah?'

He reached for the tea towel and dried his hands, then leaned against the sink. 'You can tell me to mind my own business, but she's my sister so I have to ask. What made you say "Elise" first? I thought Sarah was your best friend, yet you hardly ever mention her these days.'

'She is, but I can't work out what's going on in Sarah World at the moment. I've tried to spend time with her, but she seems to be avoiding me. She's avoiding Elise too. Don't think she wants to be our friend anymore.' I flinched. Even to my own ears, the reference to 'Sarah World' sounded extremely bitchy and the rest of the statement sounded downright childish. Clearly, Ben thought so too.

'Have you tried to find out what's going on in "Sarah World", as you so beautifully put it?'

I snatched the tea towel back off him and picked up a mug to dry. 'Don't get stroppy with me, Ben. It was just a flippant comment.'

He folded his arms and shook his head. 'I don't know what's going on between the three of you, and I don't really want to get involved, but I also don't want to hear any talk about you not being friends anymore. If you think my sister hasn't been there for you, it might be because she has things going on herself, and she could easily say that you haven't been there for her either.'

'Don't be cryptic, Ben.'

'I'm not being cryptic. I'm just making a point. I know you have lots on at the moment, and so does Elise. But perhaps Sarah does too.'

I put the mug and tea towel down and folded my arms as well. 'Is she sick? Is that what you're trying to tell me? I mean, properly sick, rather than just a cold?'

'No.'

'Problems with the shop?'

'No.'

'Problems with Nick?'

'No. It's not that either.'

'Then, what is it?'

'It's… Sorry, Irish. I can't tell you. It's not up to me to say anything. But I really think you should—'

But at that moment, Luke woke up and screamed. The unfinished conversation hung in the air while I brought him downstairs to feed him, doing my best to avoid eye contact with Ben as I prepared Luke's bottle. Eventually, Ben left the room, muttering something about taking a shower, and my shoulders relaxed. Well, that had gone well!

In true Saint Ben style, he came back downstairs 15 minutes later, apologised for interfering and for lecturing me, and insisted that we still go to Whitsborough Bay and forget the conversation had ever happened.

'So, how's Lebony?' I asked, as I pushed the pram along the North Beach promenade after a walk around *Hearnshaw Park* followed by a late lunch outside a beachside café. The sun had brought everyone out. Cyclists, dog-walkers and families jostled for space along the wide pathway, and the beach was as packed as on a summer's day. Many of the brightly coloured beach chalets had their doors wide open, with children dashing in and out brandishing buckets and spades or body boards, and parents or grandparents making lunch or lounging on deckchairs with a book, e-reader or the Sunday papers. I smiled as I took in the scene, thinking how much Shannon and Callum would love living in Whitsborough Bay. It was so perfect for families.

'She's good,' Ben said, bending to chuck a rogue Frisbee back to a couple of teenagers on the beach. 'She's in France at the moment.'

'France? That's a little normal for her, isn't it? I thought she wasn't interested in anywhere that wasn't famine- or disease-stricken.'

'The charity she currently works for is French so she's doing some training with them.'

'Oh.' I realised I wasn't really interested in hearing more about Lebony. I still hadn't met her, but I'd heard a lot about her from Sarah over the years. Sarah didn't like her because she never seemed to have time for Ben, even when she was in the UK. Visiting him was like an afterthought. Sarah said she was too nice, too perfect and too passionate about changing the world, without being aware of the impact she had on those she left at home. I was inclined to agree and found myself disliking her too. And then I'd feel like a right bitch for thinking that, because we needed people like Lebony. So much was wrong with the world and I was full of admiration for anyone who felt compelled to do something about it; something more than making the occasional charitable donation. I guess, in that way, she was a lot like Daran. I just wished she'd either end it with Ben or spend a little more time with him. He made out that he didn't mind, but he always got a sad, distant look in his eyes when her name came up.

'You're imagining living here, aren't you?' Ben said.

I smiled. 'Is it that obvious?'

'I see the way your eyes are darting about everywhere, as if you're seeing the place for the first time and sussing it out.'

I indicated that we should sit on a bench that had just that second been vacated. I lifted Luke out of his buggy so he could see what was going on. 'I laughed when Sarah moved back here,' I said. 'I couldn't understand why someone who'd lived in Manchester, then London, could possibly want to move back to a small town by the sea. When I first visited, I was pleasantly surprised. It was very Sarah, but it wasn't me. I still wanted my bright lights, big city. When I got the promotion at Prime, Sarah suggested I live here, and I laughed at her again. On a practical note, it would take too long to drive to my main clients from the coast, but I couldn't imagine myself living here either.'

'And you can now?'

'I think so. I thought I liked being surrounded by designer clothes shops, nice restaurants and trendy bars, but I prefer a night out at your local Indian, or a night in with a takeaway and a film. My expensive wardrobe suddenly seems impractical and uncomfortable, and I'd rather go shopping for clothes for Luke than anything for me. I think this young man might have completely changed me, in more ways than my wardrobe choices.' I pointed to my outfit: charcoal leggings, grey Uggs, a burgundy tunic top, nipped in at the waist, and a sparkly, silver scarf.

'I like the outfit, by the way,' Ben said. 'I like your new wardrobe style a lot. I actually think it's more the real you, not that you didn't look amazing in your old outfit choices.'

'It feels more like the real me. I used to dress like this when I was younger, before I was kicked out. I consciously changed my clothes and cut my hair to separate myself from the past. I guess the real me couldn't really disappear.'

'And the real you is a small-town girl at heart? I actually think you started to change last year, before you knew about Shannon or Luke. When you lived with me first time around, I'd offer to go out to bars and restaurants, and you were always keener to stay in or go local.'

I thought for a moment. 'You could be right. I hadn't—'

My phone began ringing, cutting me off. 'I pulled it out of my jacket pocket. 'It's Aisling. Do you mind…?'

'Be my guest.' Ben reached for Luke as I connected the call.

'Hi, Ash, how's it going?'

'Not good. I'm sorry to do this over the phone, but Da's had a heart attack. A serious one.'

The squeals of children and the squawks of seagulls, which had been so loud moments ago, seemed to mute. The scene before me on the promenade and the beach paled and blurred as I fought to form the words. 'He's dead?'

'Not yet, but it's not looking good. He's asking for you, Clare. I know you owe him nothing but—'

'I'll be there. Bollocks. I'm in Whitsborough Bay now. I might not get back in time for a flight tonight, but I'll get there as soon as I can. Do you think he'll…'

'I don't know, Clare. He's really sick.'

Chapter 34

I spotted Aisling as soon as I made it through arrivals the following morning, clutching a small suitcase. I hadn't a clue how long I'd be staying. I probably should have packed more clothes, but it would have to do.

Aisling looked exhausted. 'Am I pleased to see you,' she said, holding me tightly. 'Ma's driving me crazy. If she doesn't calm down, she'll take a heart attack herself, so she will.'

I followed her out to her car. 'So, what happened?' I asked, as we pulled out of the car park.

'It's been building up for ages. The man's a bloody eejit. He's been in a right state since your trip home, spouting on about sinners and repentance. The kids don't see much of Ma and Da. They say the house smells funny and they're scared of Ma, but I subject them to a visit every couple of months. We saw them the weekend after you were here and Da commented on how much Briyana had grown since Christmas. She responded by asking him if he thought she'd grow up to be as tall and beautiful as her auntie Clare.'

'Shite. I bet he hit the roof.'

'Ma spilled her cup of tea all over the carpet. Da turned purple and suggested we'd probably been there long enough. The poor kids could hear the yelling as we got back into the car. They hadn't a clue what was going on, and I couldn't think of a way to explain his behaviour off the top of my head. I made up some fib about him not feeling well and being angry that he felt so unwell that he couldn't enjoy their visit. I visited again a couple of weeks ago without the kids and told them we'd all seen you over the school holidays. I wanted them to get over it before the kids saw them again, and I didn't want to risk one of them mentioning anything about Shannon or Luke. I wasn't sure if you wanted him to know your news.'

'I don't, so thanks for doing that. Was he purple again?'

She concentrated on the traffic for a moment as she guided the car out of the airport and towards Cork. 'I actually thought he was going to keel over clutching his heart at any moment. His mouth kept opening and closing, and no words came out. Ma called me a few choice words and threw me out. I haven't seen or spoken to them since.'

'Jesus Christ! I'm so sorry, Aisling. That sounds hideous.'

'It wasn't the best craic I've had, but it was inevitable at some point.'

'If that was two weeks ago, what happened to bring on the heart attack? Or was it just a build-up of rage?'

'It was coming for a while, and it wasn't helped by Keenan going round on Saturday night and announcing that he's getting divorced.'

'No! I thought you said he was a strict Catholic like Da.'

'I thought he was, but I've spent so little time in his company since the kids were born that I had no idea how much he'd changed. He took Éamonn with him for support, which makes me think he must have changed too.'

'So I'm not the only sinner in the family, then?'

Aisling shook her head. 'Nope. Five kids, two divorcees, and one supporting one of those. Mind you, you still hold the crown for being a wicked harlot. Keenan and I are sadly no contest for you there.'

I laughed. 'I'm very proud of that. Will I have that carved on my gravestone? "Here lies Clare O'Connell. Wicked harlot. And proud!"'

Aisling laughed loudly. 'I'll have to outlive you now, just to be able to see that.' She shrugged her shoulders and rolled her head as if letting the tension ease away. 'You're a tonic, little sister. An absolute tonic.'

We drove in silence for a while until I realised she hadn't finished the story. 'You said you didn't think that Keenan's news had helped. Does that mean something else happened too?'

'Yes! Sorry. I didn't explain that very well, did I? So, we have him angry with you since, well, since forever. We have him furious with me for spending time with you. We have him livid with the twins, and then the straw that broke the camel's back was that he went and paid a visit to Father Doherty after Mass yesterday. I hadn't told him about you seeing the Father and him handing over the letters. I hadn't been hiding it deliberately, but it just didn't seem like information to share and he hardly ever visits Father Doherty. I'm assuming he wanted his guidance on the divorce situation, so he pays him a visit, no doubt expecting support and understanding. Instead he gets a sermon on how wonderful you are and how he should seek forgiveness. He storms out, drives home and collapses an hour later.'

'Christ!'

'I know!'

We pulled into the visitors' car park of *Cork University Hospital* and walked towards the entrance. 'Tell me honestly,' I said, 'Why do you think he's asked for me?'

'To clear his conscience.'

'Do you *really* believe that?'

She hesitated and lightly touched my arm. 'I want to. I really do.'

My stomach churned. She clearly thought exactly the same as me: he wanted to say his piece before he met his maker, and his piece wasn't going to be about making peace. It was going to be about him getting the last word in. Would I let him, or would I finally tell him exactly what I thought of him, knowing that it could finish him off?

I'd carefully selected my outfit. I didn't want to give them any ammunition to accuse me of dressing provocatively, so I wore a pair of tailored boot-cut black trousers, a ruched turquoise blouse that revealed no cleavage and a pair of low-heeled boots. From the withering look Ma gave me, I might as well have danced down the ward wearing fig leaves on my privates and flowers in my hair.

'The good Lord alone knows why he's asked for you, you dirty harlot.' She rose from beside his bed and narrowed her eyes at me.

'Hello, Ma. It's lovely to see you too.' My voice might have sounded confident but I didn't feel confident inside. I felt like a 16-year-old girl being judged all over again. I hated that the pair of them still had that effect on me.

'Will we get some tea, Ma?' Aisling said, grabbing Ma's shoulders and steering her out of the ward.

I gasped as I took in the sight before me. When I'd last seen him just two months earlier, he'd looked older, of course, but he'd still been a big, strong, formidable character. Lying on the bed in front of me was an old man with grey skin and sunken features. If I'd walked into a room full of beds, I'd never have picked him out as my da. Wires connected him to various bleeping machines, and I wondered fleetingly what was keeping him alive: the machines or sheer willpower in wanting a final standoff with me.

I glanced at the chair that Ma had just vacated. Sitting would bring me down to his level. It would take me closer to him. It would imply a relationship: that I wanted to be close because I cared. I pushed my shoulders back and stood tall. 'You wanted to see me.'

His eyes flickered open and he turned his head slightly. 'You're here.' It was uttered as a statement: no relief, no sentiment. Just as well I hadn't sat down.

'I'm here. I thought Aisling might need me.' *Cheap shot but you deserve it. 15-love.*

'Why would she need *you*?' *Ooh. 15-all.*

'Because, try as you might to turn my whole family against me, she had the intelligence and integrity to bother to find out the truth.' *30-15, I believe.*

The beeps on the heart monitor quickened. He closed his eyes for a moment and exhaled deeply a few times until they steadied. I glanced towards the door, my heart racing too. Should I just leave? He meant nothing to me, but he was a human being and I didn't want to be the cause of his death.

'You found her.'

I turned back to Da. 'Who?'

'You know who.' The strong voice was back. Demanding. Accusing.

'Oh. Would you be referring to Shannon? My daughter? Your granddaughter? Did you know that was her name? Shannon Máire. Beautiful Irish name, isn't it, for a beautiful Irish girl?' *40-15.*

He stared at me, his dark eyes flashing with the same contempt I'd seen in Ma's. 'You say that as if I'd care. You should know that she means *nothing* to me. NOTHING! You're *not* my daughter so she's *not* my granddaughter.' *Ouch! 40-30.*

I straightened my shoulders again and narrowed my eyes at him. 'Why did you ask for me?'

'To order you to stop bringing shame on this family.'

'To *order* me?' I slammed my handbag down on the floor in

disgust. 'I don't take orders from you and haven't done since you threw me out.'

'Maybe not directly, but I've still controlled your life. I made you give up your bastard, didn't I?' *Deuce.*

'Oh, that reminds me. Did you know that my bastard had her own little bastard?' His eyes widened and the heart-monitor beeps quickened again. *Advantage, Ms O'Connell.* 'Yes, I thought that might shock you. A little boy called Luke and he's absolutely gorgeous. You might have sent my fiancé away from me and stolen my opportunity to be a mother to his child, but you can meet your God knowing that Daran McInnery lives on in his grandson. I may not have been a mother, but I'll be the best grandmother ever.' *Game, Ms O'Connell.*

'You're lying,' he said.

'No, that's what you do, Da. I'm nothing like you.' I picked up my bag and grabbed my iPhone. I opened the photos on a recent shot of Shannon cuddling Luke and thrust the phone into his eyeline. 'Gorgeous, aren't they? My family, who, despite everything you did, I'm reunited with.'

'More shame on the family,' he spat.

'I don't know why you're getting so het up about it. You told me two months ago that you had no daughter and you've just reiterated it now. You're absolutely right too. You *don't* have a daughter because I don't recognise you as my father. That means that you don't have a granddaughter or a great-grandson. I, on the other hand, have a family who love me unconditionally and, whatever challenges or issues Shannon or Luke face in the future, I'll be there for them without judgement or prejudice. Because that's what families do. But, hey, you'd know that if you'd ever been part of a loving family, wouldn't you?'

'Family? What do you know about family?'

'Loads of things, and none of it was learned from you. I'm not the one who brought shame on the family. You and Ma did that by your actions towards me before you knew about Daran, after you knew about him, and every moment of every day ever since.'

He stared at me, breathing heavily, but I could see that the fight had gone out of his eyes. Whether that was down to fatigue or recognition that the words I spoke were true, I'll never know.

I put my phone back in my handbag and hoisted it onto my shoulder. 'What I suggest you do is forget about me from now on. Put your energy into getting yourself better and repairing your damaged relationship with Aisling and the twins, and Nia if you've damaged that too. They're your family. I'm not. So what I do from now on should make no difference to you.' I shook my head and turned to go. Then I turned back. 'I feel sorry for you, Pádraig O'Connell. I just hope your God can forgive you for your sins because I can't. Goodbye.' Without another glance, I strode out of the ward and out of the hospital. Game, set and match, Ms O'Connell.

Chapter 35

The call came through at 5.47am the following morning as I lay fully dressed on top of my bed in *The River Lee Hotel*. 'He's dead, Clare,' Aisling said, in a tone that reflected relief rather than sorrow. 'I can't believe he's died on St Patrick's Day of all days.'

The significance of the date hadn't been lost on me either. 'I want to say I'm sorry…'

'I know. And I understand. Look, Ma's lost it so I can't talk just now. I'll call you later and we'll meet. Promise me one thing.'

'What?'

'You won't go home. I want you here. I *need* you here.'

'I promise.'

I lay back on the pillows, staring at the hotel ceiling, clutching my phone to my chest. 'Wherever you are right now, I hope you've found your peace,' I whispered. 'Because I don't think you ever found it in this lifetime, did you, Da?' A tear slid down my cheek, then another, and soon my cheeks were slick with moisture.

Why was I crying? Regret? I certainly didn't regret what I'd said the night before. I'd maintained my dignity while my parents had continued the name-calling. Tempted as I'd been, I hadn't told him what I thought of him – I'm not that heartless – although I had deliberately given him facts that I hoped would hurt him. Relief? I tossed the feeling around my mind. Was I relieved he was gone?

Not really because, although his actions from 17 years ago had had a major impact on my life, I'd blocked thoughts of him from mind until recently, so he hadn't been on my radar enough for me to be relieved that he was no longer around.

I turned onto my side, staring towards the curtained window. What was it, then? Loss? I certainly wasn't going to miss him. You can't miss something you never had. Maybe that was it. Maybe I was mourning never having had a father, Shannon not knowing her father and Luke not knowing his grandfather or great-grandparents. But at least Shannon had had her adopted dad, and Luke would have Ben. I sat up and wiped my cheeks. Luke would have Ben? Where had that come from? Ben was just a friend; he wasn't a father figure. Obviously, I'd meant Callum. I looked at the clock: 6.23am. I needed some fresh air. I wasn't thinking straight.

🖂 To Aisling

Hope Ma's calmed down. I'm out for a walk but I've got my phone with me. I'm here for you xxx

It was a few hours before Aisling called, suggesting that we meet up for tea and saying she had a surprise for me: Keenan and Éamonn wanted to join us!

The pub was heaving with St Patrick's Day revellers. Green and white bunting and flags hung from the ceiling and the bar. All-day drinkers wearing leprechaun hats and ginger beards brushed shoulders with those who'd had to work the bank holiday but had stopped off for a swift drink or two on the way home.

'Clare? Is that you? I barely recognised you.'

'*I* did. It's the eyes. I remember those green eyes.'

The four of us stood awkwardly in a small gap near the bar. Hug? Shake hands? What was normal in these situations?

I looked at Aisling for reassurance and she nodded encouragingly.

'I'd have recognised you two,' I said, 'but I must confess that I don't know which is which anymore.' As boys and young men, they'd been identical, although, being their sister, I'd never mixed them up. Now they'd both changed. You'd have put them as brothers, but not necessarily twins. One wore dark designer jeans, a designer shirt, was freshly shaved, smartly coiffed and wore contact lenses. The other wore old, worn blue jeans and a cheap T-Shirt with a couple of small holes in it. His hair curled up at the collar of his shirt and was flecked with grey. Glasses couldn't hide the dark circles under his eyes, which fitted well with a few days' growth on his chin. I suspected he was the soon-to-be-divorced Keenan. I was right.

'Quick! Grab that table!' Éamonn called, pointing to a table by the window about to be vacated by a gaggle of leprechauns. Aisling practically launched herself at it. We took our seats and an awkward silence descended on us again. The pub door opened and I half-expected a collection of tumbleweed to blow through and spin past us. I was about to make a flippant comment about that to try to break the ice when I saw Keenan remove his glasses and rub his eyes. At that moment, I registered what they'd been through that day and that the silence was more about that than it was about meeting me again. I might have detached myself from Da years previously, but they hadn't. They'd lost their father that morning and were probably hurting like hell.

'I'd ask "tough day?" but I'm guessing that would be a daft question,' I said.

Keenan gave me a weak smile. 'One of the toughest.'

'Look, I really appreciate you coming to meet me, but I understand if you'd rather not do the big reunion thing tonight. You all look exhausted.'

'We are,' Éamonn said. 'But it's nothing a bit of food won't fix. I'm absolutely starving. I need to order some food pretty damn quick. Apologies if that's rude.'

I smiled. 'I understand. I'm pretty hungry myself.'

The three of them grabbed menus from the holder on the table. They'd probably barely touched food for the past two days.

'It's been a long time,' Éamonn said, after we'd ordered our meals. 'You look great, Clare. Aisling says you're a PR manager or something like that?'

I nodded. 'I was, but I'm taking some time off at the moment.'

'Oh. To do what? Are you going travelling or something?' Keenan asked.

I glanced towards Aisling, who shook her head and said, 'It's your news to share, but I think they'll be pleased.'

'What's going on?' Keenan said. 'Oh. You're pregnant?'

I laughed. 'Are you saying I'm fat?'

'No. Just…'

I laughed at his red cheeks. 'I'm so not pregnant. You have to be having sex with someone to get pregnant.' I laughed again at both their shocked expressions. 'Sorry. Way too much information to share with my brothers who I haven't seen for 17 years. No. I'm not pregnant, but I am bringing up a baby at the moment. It might be back-story time…' They listened in stunned silence as I told them my side of the story, from my relationship with Daran right through to reuniting with Shannon and looking after Luke. It took every bit of diplomacy I could muster to avoid painting Da in his true colours, but it wasn't right to speak so ill of him when he was only just cold, and I had no idea what their relationship had been like until the recent divorce debacle.

My twin brothers were obviously pretty astute, though. 'It's good to hear your side at last,' Éamonn said, 'and thank you for not dwelling on the part Da played. I think I can fill in the blanks.'

'Sorry. I tried.'

'We appreciate it.' Keenan rubbed a hand across his stubble. 'So, that would make us both… what?… uncles and great-uncles?'

I thought for a moment, 'Yes. Shannon's uncles and Luke's great-uncles.'

'That's pretty special,' Éamonn said.

'It sure is,' Keenan agreed.

Another silence descended, and I let it rest for a while so that they could chew over the implications of family lost and family found. I studied their pale faces. I could see so much of Da in them, in terms of physical looks, but there was something in the way they held themselves that reminded me more of myself: someone who'd taken a battering but was trying to prove to the world that they were strong and could take whatever else life threw at them. I saw it especially in Keenan. As if aware I was focusing on him, he said, 'I take it Aisling told you I'm getting divorced?'

'Yes. I'm sorry. I think it's time for your back-stories now.'

We spent the next three hours in the pub eating and chatting, until the live music started and it became impossible to talk. We dwelled very little on our childhood, instead focusing on the paths our lives had taken since. I liked them, but I didn't feel the same instant affinity with my brothers that I'd felt with Aisling, despite them being closer to my age, at four years older than me compared to her six. I knew I held some wariness towards them from what Aisling had told me about them being very religious and, despite the impending divorce, it was clear they did hold strong Catholic beliefs and were struggling to understand why I… shock, horror… had no man in my life to provide for me. I held my own, though, and made it very clear that I had been and always would be fiercely independent and, if they judged that, then they needed to pause a moment and think about why I'd become that way.

When we said our goodbyes, I suspected we wouldn't become the closest of siblings, but a truce had certainly been called, and they clearly had an interest in getting to know their new family members.

'The wake's probably going to be Thursday and Friday and the funeral Saturday,' Aisling said, after the twins had gone. 'You'll be coming?'

'I don't know whether I should. I won't be welcome.'

Aisling shrugged. 'I can tell you right now that, from Ma's perspective, a dose of the clap would be more welcome than you at Da's wake.' She smiled and I laughed at the crudeness of her comment – the sort of thing I'd come out with.

'I half-want to come to make sure he's really dead. And I want to be there for you. But I don't want to turn it into a circus.'

Aisling pulled me into her embrace and whispered, 'You do what's right for you. Don't mind the rest of us. If you decided to pelt spoons at his coffin, nobody could blame you.'

I stepped back. 'Why would I pelt spoons?'

She shook her head. 'I've no idea. It's the first thing that came into my head and it's one of the worst turns of phrase ever.' She hugged me again. 'I've got to get back to the kids, but let's talk again tomorrow. Oh my God! Speaking of kids, I haven't asked you where Luke is. Has Ben got him? Will you have to go home before the wake?'

'It's okay. Callum's moved back into a visitor's room at *Jimmy's* and he's off his crutches now so he can have Luke with him. I miss him, but it'll be good for them to have some family time. Maybe they'll decide where they want to live and whether they want me to move near them. Life feels a bit on hold at the moment.'

'I bet it does!'

I caught a taxi back to the hotel, where a wall of sound hit me the moment the sliding doors opened. A St Patrick's Day event was in full swing in the bar, with live music and laughter. I hesitated for a moment in the lobby. Not that long ago, I'd have joined the party, not caring that I was on my own. I'd have chatted and flirted and slipped away before any expectation that it would go further. At that very moment, though, I was aware of being alone and I didn't like it at all. Somehow, I'd gone from being fiercely independent and happy in my own company to someone who longed to be surrounded by my family and friends. My arms ached for Luke. I missed Shannon's sharp tongue, her zest for life, and the softness in her eyes when she let her guard down and allowed a moment of closeness to pass between us. I missed Callum's eternal optimism and his passion for his family.

Crossing the lobby, I caught the lift up to my floor. Without switching my light on, I crossed the bedroom and looked out over the River Lee. Yes, I'd admit it, I missed Ben too. As a companion, though, not anything else. I closed my eyes and pictured a typical Saturday night in his cosy terrace, curled up on the sofa with a takeaway and a bottle of beer, watching a film, an easy banter flowing between us. I'd have done anything at that very moment to open my eyes and be there with him.

Chapter 36

'Clare? Is that yourself? Come in, child, come in.' Father Doherty shuffled back to let me pass the following morning.

'These are for you,' I said, handing him a large carrier bag bursting with fresh fruit and vegetables. 'And because that's all very healthy, I have a little treat too.' I handed him a chocolate orange.

'My favourite,' he said. 'How did you know?'

'I asked the warden.'

He smiled, but tears glistened in his pale eyes. 'I don't deserve your company or your kindness.' He lowered himself into his armchair and I sat on the sofa.

'You know I've forgiven you,' I said. 'Because you asked and you apologised. Which is more than I can say for the guiltiest party.'

Father Doherty nodded. 'I heard about your da. How do you feel?'

'I don't know. I cried when I found out, but not because I'm sad that he's dead. I'm not glad, either. I'm not sure what I am.'

'You don't have to know at this moment. You may not know how you feel for a long time to come. He didn't ask for forgiveness, then?'

'I didn't think he would. He called for me so I jumped on a plane like an eejit. I suspected there'd be an ulterior motive and there was. He knew I'd been searching for Shannon and wanted me to stop bringing shame on the family.'

Father Doherty's shoulders sagged. 'He never did. Oh, Clare. I'm so sorry, child. What did you say?'

'That he needn't be concerned, when he'd already told me last time that I was no daughter of his. Then I told him about Shannon's baby.'

His eyes widened. 'You found her and she has a baby? You have a family?'

'It seems that I do.'

Father Doherty listened attentively while I told him everything that had happened. When I finished, he sat back in his chair and closed his eyes. He kept them shut for so long, I thought he'd fallen asleep.

'Father?' I whispered. 'Father?'

He muttered, 'Amen,' then opened his eyes. 'Sorry, child, but I felt a prayer was needed for your poor Shannon, who has had far too much suffering for one so young. I'm so happy for you. You've found your little girl, thanks be to God, and she has a child of her own. You may have lost one family, but you've gained another. I believe it's God's way of putting right for you the wrongs that others – including myself – have done to you.'

I was about to retaliate and say I didn't believe in God, but I stopped. A wave of comfort swept over me. Whether there was a God or not, I did believe in the concept of karma and that was essentially what Father Doherty had just described. Very comforting.

I drove back to the hotel a couple of hours later, abandoned the car I'd hired that morning and walked along the river into Cork. A dull, grey sky threatened rain, and a cold wind pushed my hair across my face and tickled my nose. I bought myself a sandwich and coffee and headed for *Bishop Lucey Park*. I shivered as I sat down on a bench, feeling the cold metal through my dress. Office workers scuttled past on their lunch breaks, and women pushed babies and toddlers in prams and buggies. I watched for a while before digging out my iPhone and calling Sarah. My conversation with Ben on Sunday morning was niggling at me. I wanted her in my life, I needed her in my life, and it was time to reconnect. Unfortunately, the only connection available was with her voicemail. I hung up without leaving a message. 'Sorry I'm a lousy friend, hope your health/business/marriage/everything else is okay. By the way, my da's dead' didn't seem like an appropriate message to leave.

It was pointless calling Ben; he wasn't allowed to take personal calls at work. Elise would have her mobile switched off on the ward and, if Stevie wasn't with her, he'd have work to do so I didn't want to disturb him. I thought I might manage to catch Aisling on her school lunch break but I got her voicemail instead, so I left a message telling her that I was definitely going to the wake, even though I knew Ma would make a scene.

I looked at my watch. I hadn't caught Aisling on her lunch break, but was it worth trying Ben in case he was on his? No such luck.

'Hi, Ben, it's Clare. Just thought I'd let you know that the old git is dead. I'm going to the wake tomorrow and the funeral on Saturday, although I suspect my ma will throw me out of the wake and have Satan on hand to brandish a pitchfork at me if I turn up to the funeral. I expect I'll be back on Sunday afternoon, so maybe we can do a curry and get pissed or get pissed and do a curry. Or just get pissed, because I think I need to. I've texted Shannon and Callum to let them know. I know it's a big ask, but I'd be really grateful if you could visit them and let me know they're okay. Bye.'

I put my phone back in my bag and opened my sandwich. A woman in her late 60s ambled past pushing a buggy as I took my first bite. She was clearly the granny. I doubted anyone would imagine I was the granny when they saw me out with Luke. Next to her, an older man – presumably her husband – pushed an older lady in a wheelchair. She must be the great-grandmother. How sweet. It was a shame that my ma would never get to enjoy that role, or at least not with my side of the family. Then it hit me. Christ! What about Daran's mother? She'd lost her son, but did she have any idea that she had a granddaughter by him? If she did, she certainly wouldn't know that she also had a great-grandson. Father Doherty must have met her at Daran's memorial service. Perhaps he had her contact details.

I finished my sandwich and drink. It was time to shop. I had a funeral and a wake to attend, and I stupidly hadn't packed anything black.

Chapter 37

I twisted and turned so I could see the black skater dress from all angles in the full-length mirror on the wall of my hotel bedroom. Not bad. Not that he deserved black, but I didn't want to make a scene by turning up in head-to-toe scarlet, especially as that's probably what Ma and her cronies expected. Mind you, I'd snuck in some colour to show I wasn't really in mourning. The dress had an Aztec-style embellishment in red, burnt orange, turquoise and green across the waistband, and I'd teamed it with a red silk scarf. Ha!

For the funeral, I'd purchased a classy below-the-knee shift dress with a square neck and capped sleeves… and a hot-pink belt around the middle teamed with hot-pink stilettos. Double ha! He wasn't worth the expense, but I was!

I ran my brush through my hair, then, in another streak of rebellion, applied some bright-red lipstick. Picking up my handbag and coat from the bed, I took one last look in the mirror and nodded approvingly.

By the time I'd descended to the hotel lobby, my confidence had well and truly evaporated. I glanced towards the hotel bar to my right and had to fight the urge not to walk right in, sit in a corner and drink myself into oblivion. Maybe offering Father Doherty a lift had been my way of ensuring I went through with it.

'Are you nervous, my child?' I pulled out of my space outside his retirement home.

'I am, Father. The whole extended family will be there, along with most of the village, and I don't know who knows what. I'm a pretty strong person, but even the strongest would hesitate at being thrown into the lion's den.'

I could see him nodding in my peripheral vision. 'I wish I could offer some words of comfort and suggest you're exaggerating what it will be like…'

'I know.' I turned my head slightly and smiled. 'I've been through worse.'

'Hindsight is a wonderful thing,' he said. 'And I know that everything we do is all part of God's plan, but I do so wish that I'd known then what I know now and guided your father to show forgiveness and compassion, instead of stirring up accusations of sin.'

'Please don't punish yourself, Father. Even if you'd done that, I don't think he'd have listened.'

'Perhaps you're right.'

I laughed. 'If we're going to remain friends, I think you'll find I'm always right.'

Father Doherty laughed too. 'I'd like to be friends. You're a wise woman, Clare O'Connell.'

'Well, before he started spouting hell and damnation at me, I was tutored by a pretty good priest.'

'Thank you.'

'And, even though he decided against the priesthood, Daran taught me well too. He taught me so much about the world, about myself, about the person I wanted to be…' I tailed off, as the words stuck in my throat.

Father Doherty lightly touched my hand on the steering wheel. 'I know,' he said softly.

We left the city behind and headed into the countryside towards Ballykielty. I didn't like the silence. It gave me too much time to think about what I was about to face. 'I wondered something yesterday,' I said. 'Daran's mother. Did she know about me?'

Father Doherty paused for a moment before answering. 'I can't be certain, my child, but I know they were very close.'

'Do you know where I might find her?'

'Assuming she hasn't moved since he died, yes, I do.' He fidgeted in the pocket of his cardigan. 'Oh, now, what's this, then? I do believe this is the address of a certain Mrs McInnery. Just how did that get in there?'

I gasped. 'How did you know?'

'I had a feeling that you'd be thinking of family and your thoughts might naturally stray to Daran's. Another chance to grow that family of yours, so it is.'

I linked arms with Father Doherty as we walked slowly along the lane packed with cars. I knew that he knew my grip was more for my benefit than his. I felt sick as we turned the corner and walked down the driveway of my childhood home.

Aisling was on door duty. She hugged Father Doherty, then me. 'Be brave,' she whispered in my ear.

'Does she know I'm coming?'

'Yes.'

'Does she know I'm here?'

'No. She's in the garden with Mrs Leary at the minute. Nia's in the kitchen, though. Will we go inside and reacquaint the two of you?'

I nodded and followed her. The living room was packed with people, but I kept my head down as I let my big sister lead me by the hand towards the kitchen. I had no idea who any of the people were; to me, they were just black blurs.

'Nia,' Aisling said.

A petite woman with shoulder-length, mousy-coloured hair had her hands in the sink. She jumped and turned, dropping her dishcloth onto the floor with a splat as she spotted me.

'Hi, Nia,' I said. 'Long time, no see.'

'Emm, hi, uh, Clare,' she stammered, pulling a shapeless, grey cardigan tightly across her tiny body. Her big, brown eyes kept flicking fearfully over my shoulder. 'You look a lot like I remember. But prettier. And taller. You're very tall, aren't you?'

I shrugged. 'It might be the heels?'

'There are people out here needing tea,' boomed a man's voice from the living room. 'Stop gossiping and get on with your work, Nia. It's embarrassing having people desperate for some basic hospitality and knowing it's my wife leaving them parched and starving.'

I cringed. So that was Nia's husband? What an absolute prick, shouting like that and humiliating her in front of all those guests. My fists clenched by my side and I bit my lip. I wanted to march into the living room and give him an earful, but I could tell from Nia's expression that it would only cause her more problems.

'Sorry, Jim. It'll be ready in a minute.'

'I shouldn't have to remind you, Nia. Should I?'

'No, Jim. Sorry, Jim.'

Nia swiftly retrieved the cloth from the floor, tossed it into the sink, grabbed the kettle and filled it.

'Charming,' I muttered.

'Shhh,' Aisling whispered. The doorbell rang. 'Nia, I'm needed out front. Will you let Clare help you?'

Nia dropped a teaspoon onto the worktop, and it bounced and clattered to the floor. 'There's no need. Really. I can manage.'

But I'd already put my bag down, rolled up my cardigan sleeves and put my hands in the sink. 'Will you sort out the drinks while

I finish this lot?'

Nia stared at me for a moment as if she were about to protest, then a flicker of something resembling relief passed across her face and she muttered, 'Thank you.'

'Don't mention it.'

The only problem with being stuck in the kitchen was that it was at the back of the house. Which meant it overlooked the garden. Which meant I could see Ma and Mrs Leary from the window above the sink. Ma looked angry, pacing up and down on the lawn. In one hand, she held a tumbler of dark liquid – brandy, perhaps? In the other, she held a cigarette. I didn't know she smoked. As she talked – or shouted – the liquid sloshed over her hand. Mrs Leary, seated on the garden bench, kept making calming gestures with her arms. I'd liked Mrs Leary as a child. She'd been a teacher at school and had always been friendly.

'How many's she had?' I asked Nia, who'd wandered back into the kitchen with a tray full of empty cups and glasses.

'Ma?' She placed the tray down next to the sink and peered out the window. 'I lost count after number six.'

'Jesus!'

'Clare!'

'Sorry. It just slipped out.' I loaded the dirty pots into the sink while Nia emptied a box of assorted shortbread biscuits onto a plate. 'The anger is because…?'

Nia stopped and looked at me with her eyebrows raised.

'Because of me,' I said. 'Of course. You think I should leave?'

'I, emm… I haven't really got an opinion on the subject.' She put the last handful of biscuits onto the plate and scuttled into the living room.

I picked up a tea towel when she returned and started to dry the pots. 'So, Nia, why don't you tell me about yourself.'

'What do you want to know?' She looked scared again.

'Anything. What you do for a living, for example?'

'Oh, I don't work,' she said. 'Jim likes me to keep house for him.'

Christ alive! The 1950s called and they want their protégée back. 'Hobbies and interests, then. What do you like doing?'

'I... uh... I cook.'

'Do you enjoy cooking?'

'Not really.'

'So, what do you enjoy doing?'

Nia shrugged. 'I don't really have any hobbies and interests. I go to Mass and I help out arranging the flowers for the altar every Sunday.'

'But you don't like either of them?'

She shook her head. 'Not really. But Jim says we need to be active at the church and I want to please God so...' She tailed off.

I decided to change the subject. 'How long have you been married?' I had to stop myself from adding '... to that arsehole'.

'Fifteen years.'

'Any kids?'

'No.' Her eyes seemed to plead with me not to explore that any further, before she turned away and busied herself loading some clean cups and saucers onto a tray. As I watched her, I found myself wondering whether she'd been unable to have children. She was a timid little mouse of a woman, all skin and bones, hollow cheeks and wispy hair. She didn't look strong enough to grow a baby inside her.

'So, what's your name now?' I asked, when I couldn't stand the silence any longer, yet couldn't face going into the living room.

'Cullen.'

'Jim Cullen?' I wrinkled my nose. 'Is he from around here?'

'He is.'

'Where?' I expected her to say one of the surrounding villages.

'Ballykielty.'

'Really? Cullen. Jim Cullen. How old is he?'

'Same age as me.'

I shook my head. 'I don't remember anyone of that name.'

'Yes, well, you moved away a long time ago, so you did,' she said. 'I'm sorry. I can't talk. I need to make more sandwiches.'

Conversation over, I turned back to the washing-up. If a stranger had walked into the kitchen and seen us together, they'd never have guessed that she was my sister; my older sister, at that. We were nothing like each other in looks or temperament. I hated that I so clearly intimidated her. She'd always been quieter than me, but I remembered playing with her as a child and there being genuine affection between us. Yet another thing Ma and Da had taken away.

I looked out the window. Ma had stopped pacing and had taken a seat on the bench with Mrs Leary. I noticed her glass was empty, which meant that she'd probably be coming inside any minute. Which meant that, if I wanted to do what I'd come to do – satisfy myself that Da really was dead – I'd better find him.

'Where's Da?' I asked Nia.

'In the small back bedroom.'

I gulped. Really? That was cruel! 'My old room?'

She nodded. 'Sorry.'

I shivered. This was going to be very strange. With another glance out the kitchen window to make sure Ma wasn't on her way in, I wiped my hands on the tea towel. 'Wish me luck.'

I had to walk back through the dining room, then the living room, to get to the stairs. A wave of whispers and nudges followed me, along with a few clear statements: 'She's got a nerve showing up here.' 'Where's her respect?' 'She brought such shame on the family, don't you know.' Head high, shoulders back. These people are small-minded and they mean nothing to you. I needed to see him, then get out of there. I glanced around the room brazenly. They weren't all hostile. I received a few smiles and a couple of nods. Which one was Nia's arsehole of a husband? There were only four men in the room including Father Doherty and all of them were 50 and above. Jim must have gone out. The men had probably retreated to the pub.

Aisling grabbed my hand as I reached the door to the hall. 'You're not leaving, are you?'

'Soon,' I said. 'But I'm going upstairs first.'

'Will you be wanting company?'

I smiled weakly at my sister. 'Thanks, but I have to do this alone.'

My legs shook as I took each stair and slowly made my way towards the back of the house. Nothing seemed to have changed. The carpet was still green, although it had probably been replaced. The swirly brown and cream wallpaper was definitely the same. I passed the hot press and paused to take in the white, glossed door with height measurements of the five of us as we grew. Only, there weren't five measurements anymore. Someone had scratched out mine. My eyes burned. I shouldn't have felt hurt or surprised, yet I did. Why not just paint over me? Why scratch me out? But I knew the answer to that: it was a cathartic act of scratching me out of his life. I could picture him sitting there for hours, carefully erasing me from his home and his world.

The next door was my bedroom door. It was wide open and I could see straight through to the window. The closed curtains fluttered in a slight breeze from the open window. A large mirror had been taken off its hook, turned around and propped against the wall. Most of the traditions observed, then. I heard the word 'Amen', then a couple of mourners appeared in the doorway. With barely a glance at me, they squeezed past and headed down the stairs. I hoped nobody was observing the tradition of sitting with the body constantly. I really wanted to be alone with him. I listened, but there was absolute silence, so I took a few steps forward and peered around the edge of the door. Empty. Except for the large, dark-wood coffin on the bed. I shuddered, then took another step closer.

I recognised his suit immediately: his Sunday best. He'd worn the same navy double-breasted jacket and trousers for as long as I could remember, so it shouldn't have surprised me that he'd never shelled out on another; he always was tight with money. Rosary beads rested in his left hand. I recognised them from childhood too.

'Hello, Da.'

I half-expected him to sit up and demand to know what the hell I was doing in his house, when he'd made it clear I wasn't welcome. But he just lay there. Still. Silent. I slowly reached up my hand and prodded him gently on the arm. Then a bit harder. Then harder still. I smiled and exhaled. It was safe to say that he was well and truly dead.

Staring at his body for a few more moments, I felt nothing. No sadness. No regret. And, importantly, no fear. I didn't want to say a prayer, ask for forgiveness or even tell him what I thought of him because, actually, I didn't think anything of him. In the same way he'd claimed I was nothing to him, I realised he was nothing to me. He wasn't my father; he was just someone I used to know. Someone who I'd never felt very fond of. Someone who caused me no end of pain. And, more importantly, someone who couldn't do that anymore.

I sighed. 'Goodbye, Da.'

Aisling met me at the bottom of the stairs. 'How was it?' she asked.

'Reassuring.'

She nodded. 'You'll be heading off now, won't you?' Her eyes showed sadness, but I knew she understood why I couldn't stay.

'I've done what I came to do. Me being here's awkward for everyone. Is there any chance you could run Father Doherty home? I know it's a big favour but—'

'It's fine. I'll see him home safe. I'm assuming you won't be back tomorrow but you will come on Saturday? To the funeral?'

'I might slip in at the back and shoot away before the end, but I'll come. I promise. I bought a new dress. I might as well wear it. It's bright red, shows my cleavage and only just skims my arse. Appropriate, don't you think?'

Aisling giggled as she hugged me. 'A tonic, so you are. An absolute tonic.' She opened the door.

'Bollocks!' I said. 'I'm such an eejit.'

'What?'

'I won't be getting too far if I don't have my handbag with me, will I?'

I reached for the door to the living room.

'Don't go—'

But her warning came too late. I opened the door and came face to face with my mother.

Chapter 38

'You!' she spat. Clumps of wiry, grey hair had escaped from her chignon and streaks of mascara down her face gave her the appearance of a coal miner. A very angry coal miner. 'I thought I made it clear that you aren't welcome here.' She staggered slightly, then lifted the glass tumbler to her mouth. She frowned and staggered a bit more when she realised it was empty, then dropped the glass on the carpet, where it rolled under a chair.

'I didn't come to cause a scene,' I said, my cheeks burning as I took in the curious faces around the room. They'd all stopped talking, eating and drinking, and were watching. Intently.

'Cause a scene? CAUSE A SCENE?' She laughed – a hollow, chilling sound. 'You've caused a scene your whole life, Clare. From the day you were born, you caused a scene.'

I wasn't exactly sure what she meant by this, but a few nods and murmurs of 'You tell her, Maeve' from around the room suggested that others knew exactly what she meant.

'I'm going. I just need to get my bag from the kitchen.' I tried to sidestep her but she blocked me.

'Where do you think you're going, missy? This is my house. MY HOUSE! And I don't want you in it.'

'I know that. But I can't leave without my bag.'

'I never wanted you, you know.' I felt my stomach clench at her words and heard an audible gasp go around the room. 'I thought two girls and two boys were enough,' she continued, 'but your da insisted on having you. The moment you were born with your blonde hair and big eyes, I knew you were trouble, and that's all you've been. You've brought shame on this family.' She lifted her hand towards her mouth, then must have registered she no longer had a glass in it. 'Nia! Bring me a drink. Now.'

'Don't you think you've had enough, Ma?' whispered Aisling.

'Siding with her, are you? I might have known she'd turn you against me.'

'Ma! You're being ridiculous. Clare hasn't turned me against anyone.'

'Nia! Drink!'

Nia scuttled into the living room, shot a terrified look at me, handed Ma a tumbler of brandy, then darted back towards the kitchen.

Ma took a couple of gulps, then exhaled. She was so close by this point that I could smell the fumes on her breath. I took a step backwards.

'You still here?' she demanded.

'I need my bag. As soon as I have it, I'll go. If you'll just let me past.'

'I'll get it,' Aisling said, but Ma blocked her way too.

'You see! You're siding with her. I knew it. She always gets what she wants. Just look at her. She's like a blonde Mary Magdalene. Bats her eyelashes and all men keel over and give her whatever she wants.'

'Ma!' Aisling cried. 'Stop it!'

Ma pointed at me, sloshing liquor over her hand. 'You were always his favourite, but I knew you were trouble. I warned him, but he never saw it until it was too late. When you left, you took a piece of him with you. He was never the same. *You* did that to him.'

'He threw me out. I had no choice.'

'You had lots of choices, but you chose whoring.' Another gasp went around the room. I flinched, but I'd heard it all before. Well, apart from being Da's favourite. I'd never have guessed from the way he treated me, even before Daran. And her not wanting me was new information too, although not surprising in the least. She'd never shown much tenderness towards any of us, but least of all towards me.

'Enough, Ma.' Keenan appeared by her side with Éamonn just behind him. They must have arrived while I was upstairs and been out in the garden.

She twisted around, slopping more brandy. 'Ah! Keenan. The other embarrassment. Soon to be divorced. Just like that one.' She twisted back around and pointed at Aisling.

'Don't be starting on Keenan and Aisling,' Éamonn said, stepping forward and taking the glass from her hand. 'Da's laid out upstairs and this really isn't the time or the place, is it now?'

'But he loved her more than me,' she cried.

I flinched again. Really? But I couldn't remember Da ever showing Ma any affection. Perhaps they'd stayed together to avoid the shame of divorce but actually hated each other.

'Nia,' shouted Éamonn. 'Can you get Clare's bag for her, please?'

Nia appeared from the kitchen a few moments later and handed me my bag. 'Thanks, Nia,' I said. 'It was nice to meet you today.'

'And you,' she whispered.

'Don't say that,' shouted Ma. 'Don't be making friends with her. She's an embarrassment to us all and I want her out of my house. NOW! Why's nobody listening to me? Why are you all on her side?'

'I'm going.' I turned towards the door.

'You're not welcome tomorrow or at the funeral,' Ma screeched. 'Don't you dare show your face. I'll call the Guards if you do. I'll have you removed. You ruined our lives, you little slut. I'll never forgive you for—'

I slammed the door on her shrieks and ran down the driveway as fast as my stupid heels would let me. I stumbled down the lane that ran alongside the house, where I'd parked the car, then leaned against the driver-side door, gulping in fresh air, waiting for the churning in my stomach to subside before I unlocked the door and left Ballykielty. For good. Forever.

Gradually, my heartbeat slowed and my breathing regulated itself. For a moment there, I'd thought I might pass out. I unlocked the door and grabbed a bottle of water from the door compartment. I took a few greedy gulps, keeping an eye towards the end of the lane, in case Ma decided she was ready to unleash another torrent of verbal abuse and I needed to dive into the car for safety. She'd said some nasty things in the past, but the venom with which she'd let go just now had been something else. Why did she hate me so much, though? I didn't buy that bullshit about Da loving me more, because he'd never behaved as though he did. I remembered my childhood and teenage years as being filled with lectures, punishments and expressions of disappointment.

I was just about to get into the car when a figure appeared at the end of the lane. Shit! I should have got away from the house and caught my breath outside the village borders. I squinted in the low sun. The figure was waving something. I shielded my eyes with my hand. Was that Nia? And was that…? I put my hand up to my neck. Of course! I'd removed my scarf in the kitchen because it kept dipping into the washing-up bowl. I closed the car door and headed down the lane towards her. She took a few steps closer to me too, then she stopped abruptly and looked to her right as a gruff voice shouted, 'Nia! What the feck are you doing? Get back in the kitchen, where you belong. Christ, woman, what the hell was I thinking when I married you?'

The sun in my eyes meant I couldn't see his face, but I could make out the silhouette of a large bulk of a man staggering towards my sister. So that was the gobshite of a husband, was it? Poor Nia.

'Sorry, Jim. It's just that… Well, I… It was Clare. She left her scarf behind. I just wanted… She was leaving and…'

He grabbed at her arm and she yelped like a puppy. 'I'll give her that.' He snatched my scarf out of Nia's hand. 'After all, Clare loves it when I give her things, don't you, Clare?'

I took another step closer, ready to do battle with Nia's arsehole of a husband, but the sun dipped behind a cloud at that moment and I gasped. Jesus Christ!

He released Nia and shoved her roughly in the direction of the house. Running one scabby hand through his greasy, ginger hair, he raised my scarf up to his nose and sniffed.

'You still wear the same perfume. I always did like that smell.'

I stared at him, then at Nia hovering awkwardly nearby. 'This is my husband, Jim,' she said. 'I think you knew him as Jamie.'

'Jamie Doyle,' I whispered, still staring at Nia. 'Cullen. You said your name's Cullen.'

Jamie laughed and I shuddered at the chilling sound. I knew that laugh. It reminded me of… What was it? I closed my eyes tightly, trying to think.

'The Guards took my da away again.' He lifted a bottle of whiskey to his mouth and took a swig. 'Ma changed our names to wipe us clean of him, stupid cow. Couldn't change my blood, though. Bad blood runs through my veins, doesn't it, Clare?'

He lifted my scarf up to his nose again and inhaled deeply, closing his eyes momentarily. 'Brings back memories, so it does. Good memories.'

Memories? My breathing quickened. The shadows. The shapes. It was…

'Jim? What are you doing?' I heard fear in Nia's voice, but I couldn't tear my eyes away from Jamie's face. There was something so familiar…

'None of your business. Get inside, Nia.'

'But, Jim…'

'NOW! Unless you want my fist to connect with your face again, you useless bitch.'

I heard the sound of gravel crunching as Nia turned and ran.

Jamie took another glug of whiskey, then let the empty bottle drop to the ground with a smash. He slowly wound my scarf around his left hand, then twisted it around his right, before pulling his hands apart so that the material was stretched between them. He laughed that sinister laugh again. 'This would make a good gag, wouldn't it, Clare? Not that we really needed the one we used before. Who was going to hear screams from a deserted farmhouse in the middle of a meadow?'

Oh my God! Sweet Jesus. The shadows. The shapes. The fear. It had been him. It had been Jamie Doyle.

Chapter 39

Seventeen Years Earlier

Daran pulled on his boxer shorts and jeans after we'd made love for a third time on my 16th birthday. The second time had been slow and tender, and the third more frantic and daring as we started to understand each other's bodies. 'I really don't want to leave you, but I have to get back to Mrs Murphy and see whether old Carrig is still with us.'

'I wish you could stay here all night with me, but I understand. They need you.' I reluctantly got dressed, cringing at the dampness in my panties.

'What's up?' asked Daran.

I grimaced. 'I'm a bit wet between the legs. I think some of your swimmers are making a bid for freedom.'

'Urgh. Sorry. Will you be okay to walk back like that?'

I shrugged. 'I might stay here a little longer, dry off a bit, and gaze at my gorgeous ring before I have to hide it from view.'

'I can wait for you.'

'No, you can't. You're already late for a dying man. I won't be the one who stops you doing God's work. See you here tomorrow night?'

Daran held me tightly. 'I can't. Remember I'm going away in the morning.'

I pouted. 'Shite! I'd forgotten about that. I don't know if I can last 10 days without you.' Daran was going on a school trip to Jerusalem, returning via Vatican City.

'I wish I didn't have to go, especially after what we've just done. I'll be thinking of nothing else for the whole 10 days.'

'I'll miss you.'

He kissed me tenderly. 'I'll be counting down the hours. Happy birthday, fiancée. Don't forget that I'll love you till the end of time.'

'And I'll love you for longer than that.'

'Don't stay long. It's a quarter to eight now, so you only have about half an hour till sunset.'

'I'll be grand. Ten minutes should sort things out.' I blew him kisses as he headed for the doorway, then disappeared into the meadow.

'Right, so, let's be having you.' I bent down and slipped off my panties again and grimaced as I wiped between my legs. 'Now, that's one side of having sex that I hadn't given any thought to. Ew.'

I dropped my panties onto the rug, removed the grape juice and beakers from the straw-bale table and sat on it, legs apart, wafting the skirt of my dress. A rustling outside made me jump. 'Daran? Is that you?' I stood up and cocked my ear. 'Could you not stay away, knowing I'm not wearing any panties?'

'You're not wearing panties? I always knew you were a dirty girl.'

I leapt up. 'Jamie Doyle! What the hell are you doing here?'

'Watching you.' He took a few steps closer, his dark eyes boring into my skin.

'For how long?'

'Long enough.'

My stomach churned. 'Long enough for what, Jamie?'

'To see you and the Father doing things a priest shouldn't even be thinking about, let alone doing.'

I shuddered at the thought of him being a voyeur. 'He's not a priest and it was private. You shouldn't have been watching.'

'And you shouldn't have been doing it.' He took another couple of steps closer. 'At least I know why you kept turning me down. You were already getting your needs serviced elsewhere.'

I backed away a couple of paces, my heart racing. 'I turned you down because I'm not interested in you in that way.'

'Why not?' He took another step closer. Too close. I could smell alcohol on his breath again and see that gross foam at the corners of his mouth.

I shrugged. 'I'm just not. I'm sorry, Jamie, but we can't control who we fall for. I need to be getting home now, so I'll say goodnight if you'll just let me pass.'

'You're not going anywhere.'

'Come on, Jamie. You don't mean that.'

He took another step closer and reached out. 'Such beautiful hair.' He ran his fingers down a blonde tress. I froze. 'Don't ever get it cut. Because, if you did, I wouldn't be able to do this.' He grabbed most of my hair and yanked it, pulling me down onto my knees in front of him.

I squealed as my left knee scraped against a stone and pain shot through my ankle. 'You're hurting me, Jamie.'

'Considering what I saw during your last go with the Father, you quite like it rough. It's my turn now.'

'No, Jamie, don't,' I whimpered.

But he unzipped his fly and released himself. 'Suck,' he ordered, thrusting my head towards his crotch. I gagged at the unwashed aroma and tried to clamber to my feet, but he had one hand entwined in my hair and the other on the back of my head, holding me down and pulling me towards him. I couldn't move.

'You take my dick in your mouth and suck it or I'll tell everyone in the village about your dirty little secret. You'll be ruined and your beloved Daran McInnery will be shipped abroad where you'll never see him again.'

'You wouldn't do that.' I knew he would. Even if I did as he demanded.

'Are you prepared to take the risk?'

Finding some courage from God alone knows where, I pushed at his legs, but he held his ground and laughed. I slapped at them, but he laughed harder – a cold, sinister sound. 'I'll tell you something really funny, will I, Jamie? You put that thing in my mouth and I swear to God I'll bite it off.'

Jamie looked down in horror. 'You wouldn't.'

'Are *you* prepared to take the risk?'

'You whore.' He released my hair and I tried to scramble to my feet, but the punch to my left eye sent me crashing to the floor. 'You asked for that,' he yelled.

I tried to scramble to my feet again, but my left ankle wouldn't hold and I fell to my knees again. Another punch knocked me onto my back. My dress flipped up, revealing my nakedness. Jamie's eyes widened and, before I had time to move, he'd pounced on top of me. Pinning my arms above my head, he laughed as I screamed. 'You're in the middle of nowhere, slut. There's nobody to hear you. But just in case.' He grabbed at my discarded panties. 'We'd better use a gag.' He stuffed them into my mouth. 'We don't want anyone disturbing us.'

And he was right: nobody disturbed us, and nobody heard as I cried for help while I staggered across the meadow and fields in the darkness. Nobody heard as I limped through the village. Nobody heard as I crawled into bed at home shortly before midnight. Yet they all heard when I claimed I'd 'tripped' in the darkness. They heard that I was a 'clumsy eejit' while the nurse bandaged my twisted ankle and stitched my cheek back together. They heard that I wanted to get my beautiful, long locks cropped into a short bob because I 'fancied a change, now I'm 16 and all grown up.' Because that was all they wanted to hear – the simple explanations muttered with fearful, downcast eyes and a tone that begged them to say, 'Are you sure?' But nobody really heard. Nobody asked. Nobody wanted to. Rape wasn't something that happened in a good God-fearing community like Ballykielty.

Chapter 40

Present Day

I could hear whispering. I opened my eyes, but the room was in darkness. I was laid on my back in a bed. I fanned my arms out either side of me. I soon touched the wall with my left hand and the edge of the bed with my right. It was a single bed, which meant I wasn't in my hotel room. So, where the hell was I? I tried to sit up, but my head hurt and I quickly lay back on the pillow again. I reached out my right hand and touched some sort of bedside table, which thankfully had a lamp on it.

A dull, yellowish glow lit the small room. It was a very feminine room. Three walls were painted a dusky pink and the fourth was papered with a delicate flowery pattern. A white wooden wardrobe stood opposite the bed, next to a tall white bookcase packed full of romantic and historical paperbacks. A couple of framed cross-stitches of cottages hung on the walls. It wasn't a room in Ma's house. Oh Christ, what if it was a room in Jamie Doyle's house and he'd…? No! Surely it was too feminine. I imagined Nia had no say in the décor of their home.

The door opened and a shadow crept along the wall. My heart raced uncontrollably. I could have wet myself with relief when Aisling's voice said, 'Is that you awake, Clare?'

'Where am I?'

She shuffled into the room. 'Mrs Shaughnessy's house.' She

placed a glass of water on the bedside cabinet.

'The Black Widow? Why?'

'She saw the whole thing. She's the one who called the Guards.'

I closed my eyes. 'What happened?'

She sat down on the end of the bed. 'Don't you remember?'

'I was about to leave, but Nia had my scarf. She… Jesus! Jamie Doyle!' I sat upright and grabbed Aisling's arm. 'You've got to warn her. She's not safe. He's violent.'

'I know. It's okay. The Guards took him after he knocked you out.'

'He knocked me out?'

'Mrs Shaughnessy says he struck you and you went down like a sack of spuds.'

Aware that my face was throbbing, I reached up and touched my cheeks, wincing as I felt the swollen skin. I gently moved my fingers and they made contact with what I assumed were some Steri-Strips.

'The doc came and patched you up.' She shook her head. 'You really don't remember him hitting you?'

'I remember him hitting me all right. On the night of my 16th birthday. Right before he raped me.'

The next several hours passed in a blur of visits from the doctor and the Guards. They took statements, they took photos, they took swabs from my nails and a sample of my saliva.

I discovered what had happened in the laneway. After wrapping my scarf around his hands and talking about it making a good gag, Jamie had lunged at me, thrusting the scarf across my mouth and grabbing both sides of my head. Nia, who'd obviously ignored his orders to go into the house, had screamed and hurled herself at him. Her tiny frame was no match for his bulk and he'd swatted her away as though she were a fly. Seeing my sister pushed to the ground, anger-induced adrenaline flowed through my veins and I finally unfroze. I tried to knee Jamie in the balls, but he was too quick and jumped back, knocking me off balance on my stupid heels. As I staggered to regain my stance, he drew his fist back and hit me square on the cheekbone. I was already on an unsteady footing, so the force sent me to the ground and I hit my head. Dr Ellory suspected that the blow to my head hadn't actually knocked me out but that I'd passed out as a result of the trauma of remembering what had happened on my 16th birthday.

The memory of what Jamie had done to me, which I'd somehow managed to bury deep in the recesses of my brain for more than 17 years, was now as vivid as if it had happened yesterday. Dr Ellory explained that it was normal for regressed memories to feel very recent at the point of their return. He suggested that Taz's attack at New Year had started to awaken them, which was why I'd been having bad dreams and seeing shapes and shadows. Then the sight of Jamie Doyle again, brandishing a gag and laughing that chilling laugh, had been the final turn of the key to unlock Pandora's box.

After I'd fallen to the ground unconscious, Mrs Shaughnessy had alerted the Guards, then ran across the road and into Ma's house, screaming for Keenan and Éamonn's help. Nia staggered to her feet and launched herself at Jamie, kicking, screaming and biting. She was no match for him, though. He grabbed her arms and bent one of them behind her back with such force that he actually broke it. Keenan and Éamonn managed to rugby-tackle him to the ground at that point, and several of the guests from the wake kept him pinned there until the Guards arrived.

The whole time he was pinned to the ground, he screamed and shouted about what a whore I was and how I deserved to be raped, and how Nia was just as bad, which was why he had to give her a damn good beating on a regular basis. I cried when I heard that.

She was tiny. What sort of monster would do something like that? But I pictured him pinning me down in the farmhouse and hurting me so badly that I knew exactly what sort of monster would do that. Jamie Doyle. A man whose father's bad blood flowed through his veins.

'Are you sure you want to be alone tonight?' Aisling said, as she drove my hire car towards the centre of Cork on Friday evening.

I twisted around in the passenger seat to see out the back window, where Mrs Shaughnessy was following us in Aisling's car.

'Mrs Shaughnessy's been grand, but I can't stay there. It's not fair on her and I've been so on edge.'

'Jim's locked up. He can't get to you.'

'I know. I was thinking more about Ma. I kept expecting her to storm across the road and have another go at me.'

'You could have stayed at my place.'

'I couldn't let Torin and Briyana see me like this. They'd have questions.' She couldn't argue with that. They'd want to know why their auntie Clare's face was covered in bruises. How could we tell them their uncle Jim had thumped me, then thumped their auntie Nia, then had to be pinned down by their uncle Keenan and uncle Éamonn until the Guards arrived to arrest him? Oh, and now he was in custody being questioned, not just about that incident but about 15 years of domestic violence and the assault and rape of a minor.

'I'm worried about you, on your own, after what you've been through.'

'You don't need to be. I could actually do with some time on my own to get my head around everything. Remember, I'm tough as old boots. It takes a hell of a lot to knock me down.'

'You and I both know you're not and that what's happened to you would be enough to push anyone over the edge. But we also know that you're stubborn and nothing I say is going to change your mind, is it now?'

'No, but I appreciate you offering.'

We pulled into the hotel car park and exited the cars. I thanked Mrs Shaughnessy for everything she'd done and was a little astonished when she pulled me into her arms and held me tightly. 'If you need anything... anything at all… you'll be sure to let me know, won't you?' She sounded as if she was about to burst into tears. I raised my eyebrows at Aisling over her shoulder but she shrugged, clearly as confused as me by Mrs Shaughnessy's reaction.

Twenty minutes later, I was in my PJs with the snuggly complimentary hotel robe wrapped around me. I curled up on the large armchair overlooking the River Lee, sipping on a large glass of wine. I'd hesitated by the bar as I crossed the lobby, wondering if it might be more sensible to have a hot drink instead of alcohol. Coffee wouldn't numb the memories, though. Wine would. And I wanted them to be numbed.

The return of my memories explained something that had been bothering me: why I hadn't told Daran when I found out I was pregnant, and how I'd got pregnant in the first place when I had a morning-after pill to take. Despite the trauma I'd gone through, I'd actually remembered to take the pill, but I'd been sick several times that morning – probably from the shock – so it clearly hadn't made it into my system. As for not telling Daran about the baby, I had no idea who the father was. I pictured Shannon. Anyone with eyes could see that she was my daughter. Personality-wise, she was very much like me too. I hadn't seen anything of Daran in her so far. Was there anything of Jamie Doyle in her? Jesus, I hoped not. What about the red hair on Luke? Had that been Jamie's but it had skipped a generation? If that violent rapist was Shannon's father, did that make any difference to how I felt about her and Luke? So many questions. No answers. I gulped down the rest of my glass, poured another and took a big gulp of that. I looked over at my suitcase and chewed my lip.

It was time.

Chapter 41

I stuffed the last letter back into its envelope. He'd never known I was pregnant. Daran said he'd wondered and had even asked Father Doherty, but he'd categorically been told I wasn't.

I poured another glass of wine. Bollocks! That was the end of the bottle. The second bottle. I glanced towards the phone by the bed. No! I couldn't order a third bottle, and I certainly couldn't move on to spirits. I'd be sick. Chances were, I was going to be sick anyway with nearly two bottles inside me. Oh well, couldn't feel worse than I already did.

I'd cried, and laughed, and cried some more as I read through Daran's letters. His early ones were filled with regret that he'd been the cause of my exile, but no regret about our relationship. He poured out his ongoing love and devotion to me, and his longing that we'd be reunited once more. As time progressed, his letters became more chatty. The expressions of eternal love were still there, but it was as though he were right next to me, chatting about his day and his hopes for the future.

When he moved to Sumatra, the letters had arrived less frequently. The love was still there, but there was also a resignation that we weren't going to see each other again. There was so much of God's work to be done over there that he couldn't ever see himself leaving, but he didn't think it was the right place for me.

I didn't need to read my letters to him, because I knew they followed the same pattern: hope followed by resignation that Da had succeeded and we'd never be together.

I rummaged in the pile for the second one, scattering the others to the floor. He quoted 1 Corinthians, chapter 13, verse 13 – a verse from the Bible that is heard frequently during wedding ceremonies: 'And now these three remain: faith, hope and love. But the greatest of these is love.'

I think of this verse constantly. It's so perfect for us right now. I HOPE that you're happy and are being treated well, wherever you've been sent. I have FAITH that God will reunite us when the timing is right because He was the one who brought us together. He believes in us. And, of course, my LOVE for you will last until the end of time and beyond…

The words, which were already blurred from the wine, became even more blurred as tears dripped onto the page. I swiped at them. I wasn't going to cry. If I cried for what we'd lost and what could have been, they'd have won. Da would still be controlling my life.

A knock on my door made me jump. I glanced at the phone. I hadn't ordered a third bottle of wine, had I? I staggered over to the door, bouncing off the bed, then overcompensating and ricocheting off the wall. I opened the door.

'Ben! How…?'

'Aisling called. I thought you might need a friend,' he said, reaching out his arms. 'I hope I've done the right thing.'

'I need a friend,' I whispered. As I fell into his arms, the tears started again. 'He raped me, Ben. He raped me.'

He stroked my back and held me tight. 'I know. I'm sorry, Clare. But I'm here now and nobody can hurt you anymore.'

At some point in the early hours, my eyes flickered open. My mouth felt as if I'd eaten sand, my cheeks were tight from unwashed tears, my eyes stung and my head thumped. I focused on Ben, fully clothed on top of the duvet, and smiled to myself. My knight in shining armour. Again. Yes, I felt terrible, but I felt safe.

When I awoke again, Ben was sitting by the window, reading a newspaper. 'How are you feeling?' he asked, folding the paper and placing it on the table.

'Hungover.'

'I'm not surprised.' He nodded towards the two empty bottles on the dressing table.

I rubbed my head. 'Was I coherent last night?'

'You were a bit slurred and very upset, but I got the gist.'

'Did I make an eejit of myself?'

He sat down on the bed next to me. 'You could never make an idiot of yourself. And, if you had, you'd have had every right to. You've had a heck of a few days. I'm sorry about your dad.'

'I'm not.' I looked away, reluctant to let Ben see the hate in my eyes. 'He wasn't a nice man.'

'What happens next?'

'It's his funeral today.'

'Are you going?'

I looked at Ben again. 'Ma ordered me not to.'

'So are you going?'

'I just said—'

'You just said that your mum told you not to. The Clare I know does her own thing, not what others tell her. In fact, the Clare I know is *more* likely to do something that she's told not to do.'

'What if that Clare is sick of fighting? What if they've broken her?'

Ben reached out and gently pushed a tress of hair behind my ear, revealing my bruised cheek. He looked at me with sadness in his eyes. 'No. She's not broken. She's been bashed about a lot, physically, mentally and emotionally, but she's not broken. She's too strong for that.'

'Do you really think so? I don't feel very strong at the moment.'

He smiled. 'That's because you're hungover, wearing your PJs and you have a bit of a panda-eye situation going on with your mascara. I guarantee that you'll feel better after a shower.'

'Have the leprechauns turned it into magic water that'll take away the memories of what Jamie Doyle did?'

'Of course. I ordered it especially.' Ben put his arm around me and I cuddled into his side as he kissed the top of my head. 'You and I both know that a shower is going to make sod all difference to the trauma that your mind had managed to bury. Only time can do that. I know a great counsellor who specialises in this field and I'd urge you to see her. Your friends will get you through this, your family will get you through this, and you'll get yourself through this. You could choose to let your mum and that rapist win, but you're not going to, are you? Having seen you going after that king with such determination, I know how competitive you are. You're going to win this time, aren't you?'

'Yes,' I whispered.

'Sorry, did you say something?'

'I said, yes.'

'I think I might be going a bit deaf in my old age. I'm sure I heard a noise, but I couldn't quite make it out.'

I laughed. 'YES! I'M GOING TO WIN!'

He hugged me tighter and kissed my head again before releasing me. 'And she's back in the room!'

'Thanks, Ben. I can't remember if I said it last night, but I'm glad you're here.'

'You did. About 20 times, as it happens, but it's good to hear it sober. You don't have to go through any of this alone anymore. I know you kept Daran and Shannon secret from everyone for 17 years, and that your mind kept what that Jamie Doyle did secret from you for all that time, but we know now and we're here to help you get through it. If you want to talk, we'll talk. If you want to focus your mind elsewhere, we'll do that. You know me. I can talk mindless bollocks any time you want!'

I laughed. He really was an amazing friend.

'Go on, get yourself in the shower, because the only thing you're going to win looking like that is a Halloween competition for scariest make-up.'

I rolled off the bed and looked in the mirror. My eyelids were black with mascara and eyeliner smudges, and my cheeks were covered in black streaks. 'Jesus! Would you look at the state of me? I'm surprised you didn't jump on the first flight home last night.'

'Believe me, it was very tempting.'

I shook my head in disbelief at my reflection. Had I really let them do that to me? Ben was right. I *was* a fighter and I *was* going to win. It was easy to think of it as a façade that I'd built up to cope with my exile and Shannon being taken away from me, but I'd *always* been strong and confident, even as a young child. It was just who I was.

'I'd better get myself ready for a funeral, hadn't I?'

Ben smiled. 'Will you be taking a handbag?'

'Of course. Why?'

He reached into his pocket and took out the king. 'Because you're going to need somewhere to keep this.'

Chapter 42

'Wow! You look amazing,' Ben said.

I smoothed down the sides of my straight black dress and adjusted the hot-pink belt slightly. 'You'll notice I'm not fully embracing the black-for-mourning concept,' I said, indicating the belt and the matching pink stilettos.

'Why should you? You're not in mourning, are you?'

'No.'

'I think more people should wear sparkly pink stilettos for funerals.'

'Men included?' I asked.

'Especially the men. In fact, you don't have a spare pair for me, do you?'

'I'd happily lend you a pair, but your enormous, hairy hobbit feet won't fit into them.'

'How rude!'

'How true!' I reached for my coat. 'You're sure you don't want to stay here?'

'And miss the fireworks when your mum sees you? No chance!'

I laughed, but my stomach churned. Despite the splash of daring colour, and all the bravado, I was absolutely bricking it, and I knew Ben knew that I was.

When Ma had thrown me out on Thursday, I'd told Aisling

I'd slip into the back of the church, but I'd changed my mind as I'd leant against the car. What was the point in attending? I'd already sought the reassurance I needed that he was really gone and I had no intention of crossing swords with Ma again. Yet, lying in the spare room at Mrs Shaughnessy's yesterday morning, I'd found myself wanting to attend again. I'd thought about Daran and what he'd say. He'd have acknowledged that Da was a cruel man who, on the face of it, didn't deserve my forgiveness, but he'd also have reminded me that Da had thought his actions – however selfish or wrong – were the right actions for Shannon. It could be argued that my actions in giving up Shannon were selfish or wrong, but they were also the ones I believed were right for Shannon. She'd (sort of) forgiven me. Well, God would judge Da and decide whether or not to forgive him; I didn't need to. My role was to say goodbye and perhaps even feel sorry for a man whose narrow-minded views had pushed aside his chance of a happy, loving family.

Aisling had made it clear that she visited as infrequently as possible and tried to keep his only grandchildren away from him. From what I could gather, Éamonn and Keenan weren't exactly close to him, and the attack following the divorce announcement certainly hadn't helped their relationships. It seemed that poor Nia had been terrified of him. Mind you, after what she'd probably been subjected to at the hands of Jamie Doyle over the years, Nia was likely to be terrified of most men, understandably so.

Nia. She was another reason I wanted to attend the funeral. Although she was older than me by two years, she seemed like a baby sister whom I wanted to protect. I needed to know she was safe and was going to be able to walk away from Jamie Doyle and start living her life at last. The funeral could be my only opportunity to talk to her.

My legs shook as I walked slowly along the path to the entrance of *St Mary's* in Ballykielty.

'Who's the winner?' Ben whispered.

I lifted my head and pushed my shoulders back. 'I am.'

'That's the spirit. So your mum doesn't want you here. What's the worst that can happen?'

'She creates a scene like at the wake and throws me out?'

'So what if she does? You'll have paid your final respects, you'll have shown support for your family – the ones who count, that is – and you'll have held your head high, showing that you won't be bullied or intimidated by a lonely old woman.'

He was right. What was the worst that could happen?

Éamonn and Keenan stood in the entrance, welcoming the mourners. Aisling had told me they'd both stopped by Mrs Shaughnessy's while I'd been sleeping and had been very concerned about me. Éamonn was deep in conversation with an elderly couple I didn't recognise, but Keenan looked up and spotted me.

'That's one of my twin brothers, Keenan,' I whispered to Ben. 'The other one's Éamonn. Oh bollocks, he looks angry.'

Keenan strode towards me. It took every ounce of strength not to turn on my pink heels and leg it. I stood my ground but was nearly knocked off my feet as he grabbed me in a tight bear hug. He didn't say a word, just squeezed me tightly. What could you say when you discovered that your youngest sister had been raped by the man who then married your next-youngest sister and beat her regularly?

Éamonn appeared by my side and tightly hugged me too. 'I'm sorry,' he whispered into my hair. 'We didn't know. We should have known. I'm so very, very sorry.'

When he released me, I could see pain and confusion painted across both of their faces.

'Don't be blaming yourselves for any of this. I never let on back then, and Nia never let on either. You weren't to know.'

They both nodded, but I could feel their guilt.

'Is Nia here?'

'She's at the front,' Éamonn said. 'With Ma and Aisling.'

Keenan's eyes widened. 'You're not going to...? Are you?'

'I'm not going to what, Keenan? Make a scene? Of course not! Oh, unless you'd call tap dancing on Da's coffin in my glittery pink stilettos making a scene.'

His eyes widened even further. Éamonn nudged him in the ribs. 'She's winding us up, you daft eejit.' Then he frowned. 'You are, aren't you?'

I smiled. 'It's tempting, but have you seen how straight and tight this dress is and how high my heels are? If I attempted to get up there, I think I'd end up laid out in a coffin myself.'

Stepping through the church doors again was like stepping back in time. My eyes were drawn immediately to the pulpit, where I could vividly picture Daran reading the Gospels during Mass, with so much passion for the message conveyed.

St Mary's felt cold and strangely empty without him, despite the packed congregation. I ushered Ben into a pew at the back and slipped in beside him. Another couple of people squeezed in next to me, but I didn't recognise them and they paid little attention to me.

Most of the Mass was uneventful. When the homily was delivered, I'd swear that the priest was talking about someone else entirely. If Keenan and Éamonn hadn't greeted me at the door, I'd have thought we'd walked into the wrong funeral. Loving father? Dedicated husband? Devoted to his family? Yeah, right, and I could sneeze butterflies from my arse!

'Pádraig's wife of 41 years, Maeve, would like say a few words,' said the priest.

I found myself shrinking a little further into my pew. The

church wasn't that big. If she stood up on the altar, she was bound to see me.

Ma, wearing a shapeless, ankle-length black dress, lace-up black flats and a baggy, long, dark-grey cardigan, slowly staggered towards the altar. Her long hair was pulled back into a severe bun, but she'd missed a bit. In fact, she'd missed a couple of bits. A long straggle of hair hung down the side of her face and another clump stuck out of her bun at a funny angle. She looked like a bag lady. She'd never bothered with her appearance much, but today she looked extra dishevelled. I tried to feel sympathy. She'd just lost her husband. Washing her hair and putting on nice clothes weren't going to be top of her priority list.

She lifted her foot to step up onto the altar and somehow missed, falling forward but steadying herself just in time. A gasp went around the congregation. She regained her composure and somehow made it up and over to the lectern, but as soon as she spoke, it was obvious why she'd lost her footing: the woman was blind drunk.

'Forty-one years,' she slurred. 'Forty-one long, long years. And for what? Look at them! Look at the state of them. Two divorces. Two! What a disgrace.'

A murmur went around the congregation. People started nudging each other and giggling. Jesus wept!

'Three of them incapable of producing offspring of their own. Wouldn't be surprised if those poncey twins prefer men to their wives, bloody disgrace to God and mankind.'

I closed my eyes, willing someone to shut her up, but everyone seemed rooted to their pew, no doubt shocked at what they were hearing.

'That one there!' She pointed to Nia, head bowed in the front row. 'That pathetic mouse of a woman with no idea how to please her man. No wonder he had to keep her in order. And don't even get me started on the other one. Biggest embarrassment of the lot. At least she's had the decency to stay away today after ruining the wake, the little whore.'

It seemed to happen in slow motion. Like a Mexican wave, heads turned from all directions to look directly at me. I could see Ma following the movement. And then she spotted me. 'You!' She turned and raced down off the altar. 'I asked you for one thing, but you couldn't grant me that, could you? Had to waltz in here, showing off, and showing everyone up.' She marched down the aisle towards me. Ben grabbed my hand.

Éamonn raced after her. 'Leave it, Ma. This isn't the time or the place.'

Keenan appeared by his side. 'Let's lay Da to rest. Clare'll go, won't you, Clare?'

I nodded, but I was trapped in the pew by the two strangers.

'I never wanted you,' she cried. 'Did you know that?'

I rose to my feet. 'Yes, because you decided to tell everyone at the wake and, even if you hadn't, it was obvious from how you treated me my entire life. You made it *very* clear that you never wanted me.'

'Is it any wonder, in light of where you came from? You're just like her, you know, with your big green eyes and your perfect blonde hair. Should have known you'd behave just like her too.'

'Just like who?'

'Her!' She spun around and pointed at Mrs Shaughnessy. 'Dirty Jezebels, the pair of you. Like mother, like daughter, so you are.'

Jesus, Mary and Joseph! I stared at Mrs Shaughnessy, who stood a little way behind Ma, open-mouthed and pale-faced, as I took in her bobbed blonde hair and green eyes. Aisling and the twins were brunettes like Ma, and Nia had mousy hair like Da. None of them had green eyes. How had I never questioned it before?

'Is this true?' I asked her, although I knew at that moment that it was. I could see the similarity.

Mrs Shaughnessy nodded. 'I'm sorry, Clare. I wanted to tell you, but not like this.' Suddenly, her kindness made sense, her insistence that I stay overnight, the huge hug and the request that I call her any time I needed anything. And a million comments that Ma had made over the years now had context too.

'You and Da?'

'We loved each other.'

Ma turned on her. 'Loved each other? What a pile of shite. You were just a tart who offered it up on a plate, and he was an eejit who couldn't keep it in his pants. A leg-over with consequences, that's what you were.' She turned around again and pointed to me. 'Bet you weren't expecting that, were you?' She swayed in the aisle and grabbed hold of the end of the pew to steady herself.

'It wasn't like that,' Mrs Shaughnessy cried. 'It wasn't just one night.' She clapped her hand over her mouth, as though she hadn't meant to let that slip.

Ma turned to face her again. 'Yes, it was. That's what you both told me. One drunken mistake on what would have been your dead husband's 30th birthday.'

'No, Maeve, it wasn't.'

Ma looked her up and down, contempt written across her face. 'So he came back for more, did he? Once? Twice?'

Mrs Shaughnessy pushed her shoulders back. 'Twice a week for about 20 years.'

Another gasp went around the congregation. When they'd woken up that morning, I bet none of them had expected a sombre funeral would descend into an episode of *The Jeremy Kyle Show*.

'You're lying,' screeched Ma.

Mrs Shaughnessy shook her head. 'I'm sorry, Maeve. We never meant to hurt you.'

The next moment, all hell broke loose. Ma let out a high-pitched shriek akin to a battle cry, then hurled herself at Mrs Shaughnessy, kicking and screaming, then trying to throttle her. The priest, who'd maintained a dignified distance until that point, sprinted down the aisle, begging them not to fight in God's house – a place of peace and forgiveness. Keenan and Éamonn tried to drag Ma off, but she was like a woman possessed, with the strength of decades of betrayal pushing her on. Mrs Shaughnessy didn't fight back. Poor woman probably thought she deserved it.

'I'm sorry you had to find out like that.' Mrs Shaughnessy leaned back in her armchair and winced as I placed a bag of frozen mixed vegetables against her neck. Ma had really gone for her. I could actually see handprints and nail imprints. Just as well Ma kept her nails short; long ones would have definitely punctured the skin.

'Were you ever going to tell me?' I asked.

'I wanted to tell you yesterday, but you'd had such a shock already. I didn't want to add to it. I was hoping I'd catch you before you returned to England and, if I didn't, I was going to fly over to tell you.'

'Why now?'

'Because Pádraig – I mean your da – begged me not to say anything while he was alive and I respected that. I might have taken the secret to my grave, but I heard what she'd said at the wake. It didn't seem right to let you go on thinking that she was your mother when she clearly wanted nothing to do with you.'

Ben came through from Mrs Shaughnessy's kitchen with two mugs of tea, plus a coffee for me. 'Would you rather I went?' he asked, placing the drinks on the coffee table.

'No.' I turned to Mrs Shaughnessy. 'If that's okay with you, Mrs Shaughnessy.'

'Of course it is. Ben, is it?' She looked at me. 'Your boyfriend?'

'No. He's a friend. An amazing one.'

Ben smiled and took a seat on the sofa.

'So, you and my da?'

Mrs Shaughnessy sighed. 'Yes. Me and your da.'

I shrugged. 'For 20 years?'

'Yes. Right until the day he told me he'd banished you to England. The Pádraig I knew and loved would never have been so cruel. He'd changed over the years, but he changed that day beyond recognition. I think it broke him.'

She shook her head, her eyes taking on a distant look, as though remembering what had happened. She looked back at me. 'I suppose I'd better start from the beginning. First of all, you must stop calling me Mrs Shaughnessy. Don't panic, I'm not expecting you to call me Ma, but I feel like a schoolteacher when you call me Mrs Shaughnessy. And I'd rather you didn't call me the Black Widow either.' She winked at my shocked expression. 'Or any of the other names the kids called me. Please call me Ellen.'

I sat on the sofa next to Ben, with a cup of coffee, on the morning of my Da's funeral, and heard how my parents had kept the secret of my birth.

Ellen had been brought up in a village about 20 miles from Ballykielty and met her husband, Cormac Shaughnessy, at a céilí held on the farm where he worked. It was love at first sight and they were married within six months. She was 19 and he was 23. Ma and Da had been married for a year at that point and had just discovered that Ma was pregnant with Aisling. Cormac and Da were best friends, so they used to double-date but the women never quite hit it off. Ellen said Ma was always very aloof, which didn't surprise me at all.

Tragically, Cormac was killed in a farming accident two years later, leaving Ellen a widow at only 21. They'd just bought a house over the road from Ma and Da, and had been planning to start a family, when their future was suddenly snatched away from them.

Naturally, Ellen was distraught, and so was Da. He and Cormac had been best friends since they were toddlers. Ma, on the other hand, told Da she never really cared for Cormac, and that he should get over it and focus on his own family instead. This didn't go down very well with Da and he stormed straight over the road to offer his comfort and support to Ellen.

It started off as support as they both grieved, but it quickly developed into a genuine friendship. Da would confide in Ellen about the difficulties he had at home and how Ma had become increasingly distant since Aisling was born.

On what would have been Cormac's 26th birthday, a couple of birthday cards arrived for him from overseas relatives who somehow mustn't have heard about his death. It tipped Ellen over the edge. She bought a load of strong painkillers, intending to join Cormac. Da went to visit, even though Ma tried to order him not to. He found her with a glass of brandy in her hand and 50 painkillers neatly lined up on the dining table.

'He asked me why I wanted to end it,' Ellen said. 'I told him that I had nothing to live for. I had no job, no children, no husband and no family in the area. I didn't even have any friends locally because all of mine were back home in Kellerpatrick. He said that he thought we were friends and that he needed me to stick around because he'd already lost one friend he loved, and he couldn't cope if he lost another.' She smiled at the memory. 'I got the impression that he meant "love" in a non-friendship way and I realised at that moment I was falling in love with him. We had a few drinks, we toasted Cormac's birthday and, well, one thing led to another…' Ellen blushed. 'Don't worry, I'll spare you the details.'

Within a couple of weeks, they both knew they wanted to be together. Even though Ma had no idea, things were getting worse at home. She always seemed to be angry or frustrated about something. She hadn't taken to motherhood and was constantly trying to farm Aisling off to friends or relatives. Da decided he was going to leave her, but Ma announced that she was pregnant again. With twins. Ellen had agonised over letting him break up the family unit when it was just Aisling, but she point-blank refused to let him when she knew about the twins.

'I gave him an ultimatum, so I did,' she said. 'Stay with his family and keep me, or leave his family and lose me. In theory, staying gave him the best of both worlds. He got to enjoy his children and still have me, but it wasn't that simple. Looking back now, I think your mother had postnatal depression, but it wasn't really a thing back then, so she went without the help and support she needed. The birth of the twins darkened her mood even further. When she fell pregnant with Nia, things hit rock bottom. She had a really difficult pregnancy and a very long labour. She nearly died, did you know?'

I shook my head. 'They never talked about things like that. All Ma would say was that Aisling screeched and gave her an instant migraine, the twins were the ugliest babies she'd ever seen, that Nia was pale and weedy and stayed that way as she grew, and that she knew I was trouble the moment I was born. She was such a wonderful mother.'

'You poor treasures.'

'So, how did I arrive on the scene?'

'Like your ma said, we got a bit drunk on Cormac's 30th birthday. Forgot the precautions. I was thrilled, though. I'd always wanted children of my own. As I said before, Cormac and I had been planning a family. I became very aware that time spent with your da was time I could have been building up a new relationship and having a family of my own, but I couldn't leave him. I'd been fortunate enough to be blessed with love twice. I didn't think it would happen again and, having seen your ma and da, I knew how destructive a loveless marriage was and what it could do to the children. I couldn't go through that. I prayed to the good Lord to find me a solution that meant I could keep your da and have a child. I knew it was selfish, and God obviously thought so too, because he gave you to me and he took you away.'

I frowned. 'Surely it was up to you whether you kept me?'

Da had apparently been ecstatic when Ellen told him she was pregnant. He wanted to leave Ma, but she wouldn't let him walk out on four young children. She'd bring up the baby on her own, keep the identity of the father a closely guarded secret, and let him visit as much as he wanted. They'd managed to keep the relationship quiet so far – helped by her reputation as a man-eater caused by some serious flirting to throw people off the scent – so why wouldn't they be able to keep it secret from then on?

Somebody in the village had other ideas, though. Somebody wanted Ellen for himself and had been watching her. He'd realised she was pregnant, had spotted Da visiting and had reached the right conclusion. He threatened to tell Maeve and to make Ellen's life hell. Ellen called his bluff, but strange things started happening. It started off as small nuisances: someone ordering 10 bottles of milk to be delivered instead of one, a copy of every national newspaper being sent to her and silent telephone calls. Then it became vandalism: all the heads cut off her prize roses, the word 'whore' daubed across her garage in red paint and her car tyres getting slashed. Finally, it became scary: a dead rabbit was strung up on her doorknob with a note attached stating: 'It's you next.'

'I was terrified,' Ellen said. 'I got to the point where I was scared to use the car in case he'd cut my brakes.'

'Who?' I asked.

'A man you don't want to ever mess with,' Ellen said, eyes downcast. 'You know, they said it was an accident, but I'm convinced that he killed my Cormac so he could remove the competition, so I am. I don't mean to sound like a big-headed eejit, but I'd been dancing with him at the céilí and he'd made it clear that he liked me. I found him a bit creepy, though. I was happy to dance, but it would never have gone further. And then I saw Cormac and I lost my heart. He'd turned on Cormac the next day and accused him of stealing his girl. Cormac laughed it off and said I wasn't property so I couldn't be stolen. He'd always been an awkward bugger to work with, but he made Cormac's life hell after that. Cormac would joke that if I ever got a call to say he'd been in an industrial accident, I should tell the Guards who to investigate.'

'Who was it?' I asked again, a coldness engulfing me. I knew the answer.

'Eoghan Doyle.'

'Oh my God!' cried Ben. 'He's not…?'

I turned to Ben and nodded. 'Jamie Doyle's da. Eoghan Doyle was in and out of prison when we were kids. Theft, assault, fraud. When I was about 15, he got into a pub brawl. His victim was so badly beaten that he died. Eoghan was put away for manslaughter. That was obviously what triggered his ma to change her and Jamie's names.'

'He's been in and out of prison ever since,' Ellen said. 'They never had the evidence back then to pin Cormac's death on him, but I knew.'

She went on to explain that the vandalism and threats continued until Eoghan himself cornered her in an alley one night, held a knife to her throat and told her she could either let the world believe the baby was Ma's, hand it over at birth and watch her baby grow into a fine young woman from across the road. Or she could keep the baby and know that it would never grow into a fine young woman because it wouldn't live that long.

'Could you not go to the police?' Ben asked.

'What could the Guards do? I had no proof and, if I told them, I'd have had to confess to the affair. I'd have been painted as the scarlet woman who moved on to a married man the moment her husband turned cold. I'd have ruined your da's family, I'd have ruined my reputation and, with no evidence to put Eoghan away, I'd have put my baby at risk. Besides, the Guards already thought I was crazy for my allegations about Eoghan's part in Cormac's death. I know they thought it was some sort of vendetta against him at the time.'

'What was in it for him?'

'I suspect that, after I had you, he was going to expect certain… emm… favours from me. Fortunately, he got sent to prison just after you were born. When he came out, he found someone else to hound.'

I had to ask the question. I knew she was a nasty piece of work, but could she really stoop so low? 'Did Ma know about Eoghan Doyle's threats?'

Ellen shrugged. 'I'd like to think not. I can't be sure, though. They were quite pally.'

'What does your gut tell you?'

'That he told her and she asked him to make a few threats, but she had no idea how far he'd gone. She's a nasty, bitter woman, is your ma, but she's not evil. Not like the Doyles. '

The doorbell rang 10 minutes later. Ellen got up to answer and returned with Aisling and an attractive fair-haired man of about the same age.

'I came to make sure you were all right,' Aisling said, looking from me to Ellen. 'Both of you.'

'We're just grand,' I said. 'I've been finding out all about the skeletons in the family closet. 'How's Ma?'

'Asleep. Dr Ellory gave her something.'

'I'll just pop the kettle on,' Ellen said, indicating that Aisling and her companion should take a seat.

I turned to him. 'My sister's being rude. This is Ben, a good friend of mine, and I'm Clare, youngest sister and trouble…' I stopped and shook my head as I looked at Aisling. 'Jesus! We're only half-sisters.'

'I don't care how much blood we have in common, you're still my sister and auntie to our children.'

I looked at her companion again. '*Our* children? Is this…?'

Aisling nodded. 'This is Finn, my ex-husband.'

'Lovely to meet you, Finn. Aisling didn't say you were coming.'

'That's because I didn't know he was coming, did I, Finn?'

'I thought she might appreciate some moral support,' he said. 'And I had to see if the old bugger had really gone.'

'I take it you were a big fan?'

'Founder member of his fan club, so I was.'

'Da had a go at him for not having the kids baptised immediately,' Aisling said. 'And for *allowing* me to work after I had the kids. And for bringing shame to the family by divorcing me.'

'Not forgetting the lecture I got for *permitting* you to go on a hen weekend to Ibiza and leaving me with the kids, which was, of course, woman's work.'

'He never used to be like that,' Ellen said, picking up the dirty mugs. 'I know he didn't always show it, but he really was a wonderful man. When you were babies, he was amazing with you all. He was like a mother and a father to you. She wore him down, though. He became tired and irritable. By the time he discovered you were pregnant, Clare, he was broken. He'd become nasty and bitter, like her.

The night he sent you away, he came to tell me what he'd done and why. I think he expected my support, but I was mortified. I demanded that he tell me where you were, so I could bring you back to live here and help you bring up the baby, or I could even bring up the baby for you, if that's what you wanted. He stamped and swore and blasphemed. I told him that he could either tell me where you were or he could walk out of my house and never return. He never returned and I never did find out where you were. It was…' Her voice cracked. She jumped up. 'Who's for tea and who's for coffee?' she asked, a little too brightly, darting into the kitchen before we could give our orders.

Chapter 43

The four of us moved to the village pub for a late lunch, leaving Ellen with her memories and the news that she was now a mother, a grandmother and a great-grandmother. I promised to see her again before I returned to England and she was keen to visit as soon as possible. I already liked her, and I suspected we'd become kindred spirits, united in having our daughters taken away from us, then being reunited with them years later.

I couldn't quite get my head around Ellen and Da being an item for 20 years. How hypocritical could one man be? After all the accusations he'd hurled at me about sinning, it turned out that Da had been the biggest sinner of us all!

'It was very lovely of you to rush to Aisling's side in her hour of need,' I said to Finn, after our plates had been cleared and we'd got another round of drinks. 'Not many exes would do that.'

Finn shrugged. 'She'd had a challenging relationship with Pádraig, but I knew she'd still be upset. I wanted to be there for her.'

I watched a tender look of adoration pass between them. My head might have been slightly fuzzy from a couple of afternoon drinks, but the love was definitely coming from Finn's direction as well as Aisling's. If I raised the subject, maybe they could both open up about their feelings. I thought about her meddling in my relationship with Ben based on non-existent looks. Well, this time there were definitely meaningful looks. Before I had time to think about the consequences, I said, 'You wanted to be here for her, or you were after another weekend of friendship with benefits?'

Finn nearly dropped his pint. 'You told her?'

'Yes. No. Yes. She's the only one who knows, though. I promise.'

'Perfect set-up you've got going there, Finn. Get to see the kids and have a shag every month or so, and date who you like in between. Whereas Aisling remains hopelessly—'

'Don't do this, Clare.' Tears pricked Aisling's eyes. Bollocks. I wasn't trying to upset her; I was trying to help her. But what did I know about love, anyway? I'd refused to let it in after Daran.

I smiled reassuringly. 'Sorry, both of you. Feels like it's all been about me for the last few days, so I'm resorting to dirty tactics to divert the attention.'

'Don't be doing it again,' Aisling muttered. 'Life's complicated enough without anyone else meddling, so it is.'

There was an awkward pause while everyone took a sip of their drinks. 'So,' Ben said. 'At the risk of keeping the attention on you a little longer, I have something you might like to see, and this is the first opportunity to show you.' He dug his phone out of his pocket and tapped the screen a few times. 'Let me just turn the volume up. Here we go.'

He handed me his phone. A close-up of Callum filled the screen. 'Hi, Clare,' he said. 'I'm really sorry to hear about your dad. Shannon and I wanted to tell you that we're thinking of you, and there's no need to, like, rush back from Ireland. Luke's fine. We're getting all the help we need at the hospital so you take your time and do whatever you need to do over there.' He grinned and gave a thumbs-up into the camera.

'She's going to think we don't want her to come back,' came Shannon's voice.

Callum turned away from the camera. 'I didn't say that. I just said not to rush back. I didn't say *don't* come back.'

'Well, she might think we don't want her to rush back and she might stay forever.'

'I hardly think she's going to—'

'Just give me that thing.'

Everything went blurry and I heard Shannon muttering, 'If you want a job done well, do it yourself.' Her face then appeared on the screen. She smiled and waved, 'Hi, Mum!'

I grabbed Ben's arm. 'Rewind it.'

'Why?'

'I think she called me Mum.'

He fiddled with the phone and handed it back to me.

'…well, do it yourself. Hi, Mum!'

Tears pricked my eyes. 'She did! She called me Mum. She usually calls me Clare.'

Aisling reached for my hand and squeezed it.

'What Callum was trying to say is that we know what happened and…'

I turned to Ben, eyes wide, my heart racing. 'They know?'

Ben shook his head. 'No! They know your mum had a go at you and asked you to leave the wake. That's all they know. I hope you don't mind.'

'That's grand. I just wouldn't want Shannon to know… other stuff. Sorry, Ben, can you rewind? I missed the rest.'

'…what happened and we hope you're okay. I've had a lot of thinking time while you've been away and I'm really sorry I've given you a hard time. Your mum sounds like a right cow, and I should be grateful that it's not hereditary and that you're really nice.'

'Really, really nice,' Callum shouted in the background.

A tear slipped down my cheek at that point.

'Anyway, I wanted to tell you that I'm going to make a special effort not to be such a stroppy cow when you get back and you have permission to send me to the naughty step if I am.'

The camera moved away from Shannon and focused on Luke asleep in a cot next to her bed. 'Luke misses his grandma,' Shannon said, 'and apologises that he fell asleep before he could tell you himself. And I miss you too.'

'So do I,' Callum cried. The phone turned around and focused on him giving the camera a stupid grin, then returned to Shannon.

'If you need a few more days or even a few more weeks in Ireland, we understand. We know you have things to sort out. When you get back, there are things we want to sort out. We still want to get married, but we don't think we need to run off to Gretna Green this time. We'd like something small, but I'd like you to give me away. We also need to decide where to live. I hear that Whitsborough Bay comes highly recommended. Neither of us has been so there are no guarantees, but if we do decide to make our home there, we'd like you to join us. If you want to, that is.'

Callum snatched the phone off her. 'What she meant to say is that you're still welcome to join us even if we don't move to Whitsborough Bay.'

'That's what I said.'

'No, it isn't! You said that she could join us if we decided to make our home there, which implied she couldn't join us if we settled anywhere else.'

'Bollocks!'

I giggled at the sound of Shannon using my favourite expletive.

Shannon snatched the phone back. 'Okay, so Mr Pedantic here has clarified things. I hope you'll join us wherever we settle. And we don't mean as a live-in babysitter or anything like that. I'm sure you'd want and need your own space. We just want to you to be around. Luke needs his grandma and I need my mum.'

'Only if you want to,' Callum called.

'Yes, only if you want to. Which we hope you do. But, like, there's no pressure or anything. Well, not much.' Shannon looked to her right and frowned. 'Sorry. Got to go. Tablet time. Say goodbye, Luke.' The camera panned onto Luke, still fast asleep, then onto Callum.

'Thanks, Ben, for coming to visit and filming this. Give Clare a big hug from us all when you see her. Keep us posted.'

They both chorused, 'Bye,' then the video stopped.

I wiped at my cheeks, but I couldn't speak. They liked me, they wanted me to live wherever they lived, and Shannon had called me Mum. After a very shaky start, today was shaping up to be the best day ever. I'd discovered that Ma – the woman I hated – was no blood relation to me; I'd discovered that Ellen Shaughnessy – a woman who'd always been friendly, despite knowing what I called her – was actually my mum, and I'd discovered that my daughter – the one who'd resented me all her life – actually wanted me around. I bet Daran was looking down and smiling.

Chapter 44

✉ From Elise
I'm so sorry. Melody had a temperature spike and I haven't touched my phone for days. She's fine now, but I've only just heard your voicemail. I'm sorry about your dad. I hope he was kind to you at the end. How were the wake and the funeral? I'll check my texts intermittently, but I'm not able to answer my phone on baby unit. Thinking of you xxx

I put my iPhone in my bag as Ben drove us back to the hotel that evening.

'What did Sarah say?' Ben asked.

Shite!

'You didn't call her, did you?' Ben said, when I didn't answer. 'You left a message with Elise but you didn't call my sister. I don't understand.'

'It wasn't deliberate. Elise had texted me with a Melody update so I rang and left a message on Tuesday night. I didn't think to call Sarah. You're annoyed with me, aren't you?'

'Not annoyed, but I *am* disappointed. I asked you to call her a week ago.'

'I know. I'm sorry. I've had a lot on.'

‘I know you have, but she could really use a friend right now.’

I twisted in my seat so I could see his face, albeit only occasionally lit by the street lighting. ‘Seriously, Ben, stop it with the cryptic stuff. What’s going on?’

‘I’m not telling you. Call my sister.’

‘Okay. I’ll do it now.’

‘Good.’

I held the phone to my ear. ‘Switched off and no voicemail.’

‘At least you tried. Try again later.’

‘Yes, sir!’ I saluted him.

‘Sorry. I don’t mean to lecture you. I’ll shut up about it now. What do you fancy doing tonight?’

‘I could do with a long, hot bath, then a lie-down on the bed with a film.’

‘Do you want some company? I mean, for the film, not in the bath!’

I laughed. ‘Just as well. The bath’s not that big.’

‘Do you think the hotel will be full, with it being a weekend?’

‘I doubt it, but why?’

‘I need a room.’

I nudged him. ‘Don’t be daft. It’s pointless you shelling out when I’ve got a kingsize bed. I think I can trust you for another night. I might even let you sleep under the duvet this time.’

A bath, followed by room service and a movie, was exactly what I needed. It felt more like our usual weekend together: safe and predictable. It would have been even better with an Indian or Chinese, but burgers and fries made a pretty good replacement. We didn’t register that the burgers would come with gherkins. Ben hates gherkins. The texture and smell of them make him gag. So, of course, I challenged him to eat his and mine without gagging, vomiting or even pulling a disgusted face. All credit to that man.

He rose to the challenge. I didn't even mind passing the king back to him on the day I'd won it, because it felt good to be exchanging him for something much more light-hearted than the previous couple of times it had changed hands.

I'd really needed that evening of stupidity, banter and a complete avoidance of talking about anything complicated, like my family or the rape. I knew I would need to talk about the rape, especially as it raised questions around Shannon's parentage, but I didn't need to do it at that moment. I already knew that I was going to seek the professional help that Ben had suggested because I suspected that, when I fully recovered from the shock about Ma and Ellen and everything that meant for my family, the rape would be the only thing I could think about. And it could destroy me. I didn't want to be that person. I wanted to get through it and I knew I couldn't do it alone.

The following morning, the bedroom phone rang as Ben and I were packing.

'Ms O'Connell, it's Cara on reception. There's a visitor for you. She says she's your sister.'

Aisling. 'Grand. I'll be down in five minutes.'

Only it wasn't Aisling in reception. It was Nia.

I cringed at the sight of her left arm in a sling. 'Nia! Hi.'

'Is there somewhere we can talk?'

'I could take you up to my room, but Ben's there. The bar's empty.' I indicated the entrance. Nia nodded and let me lead her to a table in the corner.

I winced at her black eye too. 'How are you feeling?'

'Sore. Not the first time. Won't be the last.'

'Nia! You're not taking him back, are you?'

She fiddled with a tassel on her scarf. 'What choice do I have? I've no job and no skills or experience, so who'd take me on? I've no home. The house is Jim's and I've no money of my own. I wouldn't want to move back in with Ma, not that she'd let me. I've no friends. Jim pushed them all away. I've got nothing, Clare. Jim says that, if I drop the charges, he'll keep a roof over my head and he promises not to hit me again.'

'Do you believe him?'

Nia didn't answer.

'Nia! Do you believe him?'

She shook her head. 'No. I'm scared of him, Clare. Really scared.' She looked up, her large, frightened eyes meeting mine. 'Were you scared?'

'I've never been so terrified in my whole life.'

'Did he hurt you?'

'Yes.'

'A lot?'

'Yes.'

'I'm so sorry, Clare. I didn't know. I knew he had a crush on you at school. He used to try to make out that you'd liked him too and he'd turned you down, but I knew you couldn't stand him. He said things about you over the years. Cruel things. Looking back now, they make sense but, you have to believe me, I had absolutely no idea that my husband had… I'm sorry, Clare, I can't even say the word. He's such a bad man.' She shook her head and lowered her eyes again. 'I'm so ashamed.'

'What are you ashamed for? He's the one who raped me. He's the one who should be ashamed. Unless… Jesus Christ! Did he rape you too, Nia?'

She played with the tassel on her scarf again.

'He did, didn't he?'

'It can't be rape if you're married.'

'Oh, Nia. It *can* be. Did he force himself on you when you said no? Make you have sex when you didn't want to? Force you to do other things?'

'Yes.'

'Then he raped you. Non-consensual sex, whether the man is a stranger, a neighbour, your boyfriend or your husband, is rape.'

Silent tears dripped onto the table. 'He hurts me,' she whispered.

'Then don't let him do it again. Escape from him properly. Come to England. Live with me. I know we barely know each other, but we have plenty of time to do that. We played well together as children. I'm sure we can get along nicely now that we're all grown up.'

'I don't have a passport.'

'You don't need a passport to go to England! Just a driving licence.'

'I don't have one of those either. Jim didn't want me learning to drive.'

'Then get a bloody driving licence! And a passport, while you're at it.'

Nia pulled a tissue out of her pocket, wiped her eyes and blew her nose. 'Thanks for the offer, but I can't. I have no money. I can't sponge off you, and I won't be able to find a job.'

'Bollocks. Are no ID, no money and no work experience the only things stopping you?'

'Aren't they enough?'

'We'll apply for a passport and a driving licence, and I'll give you a job. I'm out of work too and I might be moving to the coast. I'm thinking of going freelance. I could do with someone to do my admin and accounts.'

'I'm not sure I'd be much use.'

'Who does the shopping? You or him?'

'Me.'

'Who plans meals?'

'Me.'

'Who pays the bills?'

'Me. With Jim's money, but I sort it all out.'

'Grand. That's your admin and accounts basics sorted and I can show you the rest.'

Nia looked as though she were going to throw in another objection. I hoped she wouldn't. I was completely winging this, but I'd do anything to get her away from Jamie Doyle before he laid another finger on her or, even worse, killed her. I wouldn't put it past him for taking out his anger on her at being questioned by the Guards.

'I haven't worked out the details yet,' I said, 'so you don't need to make a decision just now, but I want you to think about it. Will you do that?'

'Yes.'

'And will you promise not to take him back?'

'I don't know. I—'

'Nia! He's a nutjob.'

'Where would I go?'

'I'm sure my mum – my real mum – would take you in.'

Nia smiled. 'That was unexpected, wasn't it?'

'Just a bit. But it was a hell of a relief for me, and it explained so much about Ma's behaviour towards me when we were young.'

'I wish Mrs Shaughnessy were my real ma too. She's always been nice to me.'

'And she will be again. I can ring her right now if you want.'

Nia shook her head. 'I need to think about it.'

'You can think about my offer for as long as you like, but don't take forever to decide about that rapist. If you let him come back to you, it could be the worst – or even the last – decision you ever make.'

She stood up. 'I've got to go.'

'Give me your number before you do.'

I typed her number into my iPhone and sent her a text to make sure I had it right. 'Please call me any time, night or day.'

'Thank you. And I really am sorry. That's all I came here to say. I didn't expect to tell you… you know.'

'That you'd been raped? I know it's a horrible, scary word because of what it means, but keep saying it to remind you of the horrible, scary thing that he keeps doing to you.'

'I suppose I should be grateful that we never had children. Imagine what he might have done to them.'

'Didn't you want children?' I asked, as we made our way out of the bar and into the lobby.

'I've always wanted kids, but Jim couldn't have them.'

I stopped dead. 'Why not?'

'He had a really bad case of the mumps when he was 15. It made him infertile, so it did.'

'You're sure he was 15?'

'Could have been 16. No, definitely 15. I remember him being off school for ages and him trying to make out that he failed his Junior Cert exams that year because of that. The eejit had loads of time to catch up, but he couldn't be bothered.'

I grabbed Nia in a huge bear hug and squealed. I didn't care that everyone was looking at me.

Shannon was Daran's daughter. There was no doubt about it.

Chapter 45

'What was the name of the farm again?' I asked Ben, early that afternoon as I drove down a narrow country lane with bushes on either side, hoping nothing would come the other way. I'd need to do a hell of a long reverse to the nearest passing point if it did. I hadn't actually been to Wicklow before. Stunning. Lots of rolling hills, green fields and pretty villages.

'Kylekerry Farm,' Ben said.

I looked at the colourful sign, swinging slightly in the gentle breeze, announcing it as a farm, B&B (currently with vacancies) and equestrian centre. 'This is it, then.'

I turned the car onto a gravel driveway and drove about half a mile up a steady climb, with nothing to see but meadows each side. The road then dipped and I smiled at the pretty stone cottage that revealed itself – what looked like a series of converted barns, which I suspected were the B&B business, and a collection of other outbuildings ahead of us. They were surrounded by fields containing sheep, cattle and horses. It was absolutely gorgeous.

'Are you nervous?' Ben asked.

'Very. I'm wondering if I should have rung ahead rather than just turned up.' Father Doherty didn't have Daran's mother's number, but it was a working farm so I could easily have found it online. I hadn't known how to broach the conversation: *You don't know me, but I'm the woman your son gave up his plans to go into the priesthood for, and I wanted to tell you that you're a granny.* Was it going to be any easier face to face, though? From what Daran had told me about his mother, she wasn't likely to scream abuse at me and order me off her land, but I knew she'd been incredibly proud of him for considering entering the priesthood, so she might not react well to the woman who'd ruined his vocation for him.

I drove carefully into the farmyard, avoiding a striped ginger cat and a few hens wandering around, pecking between the gravel.

'Do you want me to wait here or come with you?' Ben asked. 'I won't be offended if you'd prefer to do this alone.'

'No. Come with me. Please.'

A dog barked as we approached the large, wooden stable door. I rapped on the wrought-iron knocker, sending the dog into a frenzy. My stomach clenched as I pictured an enormous Alsatian or Doberman. I wasn't great around dogs, and big dogs with loud barks were even worse. I was therefore a little surprised when the door opened and an excitable Poodle ran out and playfully bounced around my feet.

'Sorry about that.' A slim woman in her early 60s with long silver hair in a side plait and twinkly grey eyes bent down to pick up the dog. 'This is Frodo. He loves visitors, don't you, boy?'

She tickled his belly, then looked up and smiled. 'Can I help?'

'I'm looking for Mrs McInnery,' I said. 'Is that yourself?'

'It is. Are you looking for a room?'

I glanced at Ben and he nodded in encouragement.

'No. I actually came to see you. I used to know your son, Daran.'

Mrs McInnery stopped tickling the dog. 'Oh my goodness! Clare? Is that you?'

'You know who I am?'

'Of course. What a beautiful young woman you've grown into. Come in! Come in! Kettle's just boiled and I've got some scones cooling. Do you like scones? I always say you can't beat them fresh out of the oven, so you can't.' She ushered us over the doorstep and my nerves steadied. Tea and scones were a good sign.

She led us into an enormous kitchen-diner. A Belfast sink, pale-blue Aga and a large fridge-freezer broke up sturdy wooden units. A preparation island stood in the middle of the room, on which racks of scones and a chocolate cake were cooling. At the other end of the kitchen, a pair of two-seater sofas covered in bright-coloured blankets flanked an open fireplace, and between them and the kitchen was a large, solid dining table.

'This is my friend, Ben,' I said, as she directed us towards the table. Mrs McInnery released the Poodle, who ran towards a dog basket on the hearth, where he rolled around with a knotted rope between his teeth.

'Pleased to meet you, Ben,' she said, shaking his hand.

She turned to me. 'God told me this day would come. Come here, child.' She reached out her arms and hugged me. 'I'm thrilled He brought you to me on a day I've baked. Sit at the table while I get you a bite to eat.'

A few minutes later, she was back with a tray laden with scones, butter, jam and cream, plus a coffee for me and tea for herself and Ben. 'Tuck in! There are fruit and cheese scones.'

'Thanks, Mrs McInnery.' I reached for a cheese scone. 'This looks amazing.'

'You must call me Laurel. My poor husband has been gone these past 20 years, the Lord rest his soul. Being called "Mrs" doesn't feel right, so it doesn't. I'm just plain Laurel.'

'I hope you don't mind us turning up out of the blue, but I was in Ireland for my da's funeral and—'

'Oh, my treasure. I'm sorry for your loss. Was it unexpected, God rest his soul?'

'Heart attack. I'm… Well, we weren't close, so…'

'Daran told me. It's still a sad thing when a parent passes, even if the relationship is an estranged one. I'll pray for his soul and that the good Lord grants forgiveness.'

I wiped my buttery fingers on a piece of kitchen roll. 'How much did Daran tell you?'

'Oh, he told me everything, my treasure. I do know that yours was a loving relationship in every sense of the word and that the good Lord gave His blessing for it to be so. I know that your da found out and sent you away, and that my Daran tried so hard to find you. He wrote to you for years, but he had nowhere to send the letters.'

'I know. Father Doherty kept them. He gave them to me recently.'

'And how is the good Father? We send cards at Christmas, but it's been years since I've seen him. I never have cause to be in Cork. It's so far away and there's so much to do here.'

'Father Doherty is just grand. I've seen him a couple of times. He's the one who gave me your address.'

I reached forward for my mug of coffee, and the light must have reflected off my Claddagh ring because Laurel put her tea down and reached for my hand. 'You still wear it, my treasure.'

'Wear what? Oh! The ring.'

'Did he tell you I helped him choose it? He was so excited. I've never seen a man so in love. It warmed my heart.'

'He never mentioned it. It's beautiful. You helped him make a good choice.'

'You wear it on your other hand, though.' She frowned, then shook her head. 'Of course you do. You've been separated these past 17 years. He'll be so happy that you still wear it.'

I smiled. 'I'd like to think he would be.'

'Oh, I guarantee he will be. Can I tell him? Or do you want to?'

'Tell him? What do you mean? By praying?'

'I could pray about it, but the conventional way would be when

I next see him.'

I exchanged a confused glance with Ben. Was Daran haunting his mother? A shiver ran down my spine. 'We *are* talking about the same person, aren't we? Daran McInnery, the eldest of eight siblings?'

'Yes. Such a good boy. Let me think. What day is it today?'

'Sunday,' Ben said.

'I'll be seeing him tomorrow, but I bet he'd jump in the car and drive straight over if I told him you were here.'

'I don't understand. Daran's dead.'

'What?' Laurel leapt up from the table, slopping her tea over her hands. 'When?'

Jesus! What had I done? Was it possible she had Alzheimer's and I'd just told her that her son had died, when, in whichever year she believed she was in, he was very much alive? I cringed as I said the next words. 'In the Thailand tsunami of 2004.'

She sat down again and breathed out loudly before reaching for some kitchen roll to mop up the spillage. 'Goodness me, my treasure. You scared the life out of me just now. Daran didn't die in that awful tsunami, though many did, God rest their souls. Terrible tragedy. Just terrible. And the day after Christmas too.'

'But there was a memorial service and everything. Father Doherty went to it. He said you were all there.'

She nodded and closed her eyes for a few moments. 'That was one of the most painful days of my life. I thought that burying my precious husband was just about the worst pain I could ever experience, but a parent should never, ever have to lay one of their children to rest. I thought the blackness would never lift but I prayed to the Lord and, not only did He help me to see the light again, He returned my firstborn to me. Daran's alive and well, and living five miles down the road from here.'

Chapter 46

'Are you sure you don't mind flying back on your own?' I asked Ben, an hour or so later.

'It's for the best. I need to be back at work tomorrow, and you need to spend time with Daran.' Ben's voice cracked as he added, 'You won't expect too much from seeing him, will you? It's been a lot of years. People change.'

'I'll be grand. I'm not really expecting anything. I don't think I'm quite over the shock of discovering he didn't really die.'

Ben and I had listened in stunned silence as Laurel told us how Daran had indeed been caught up in the disaster, but he hadn't died. He'd been swept along with the tidal surge but had managed to cling onto some debris and stay afloat. He awoke to find himself in hospital, with no idea who he was or how he got there. He had several broken bones so was laid up for quite some time.

In the meantime, a body had been found matching Daran's description, with Daran's wallet in their pocket, so his death was reported back home by the charity he was working for and the family never viewed the body because of the state it was in.

Many weeks later, a former colleague of Daran's happened to be visiting someone at the hospital where he was, and she recognised him. All it took was her telling him his name and some details about his family, and his memory started to return. He couldn't remember anything after entering the water, but he could remember the lead-up to it. He'd been demonstrating to a new recruit how to do some repairs on a shack. As he'd bent over, his wallet had dug into him and he'd passed it to that colleague, asking him to hold it until he was finished. Next moment, there were shouts and screams and they looked up to see a wall of water rushing towards them.

After the tsunami, Daran spent another four years in Thailand, helping rebuild communities, before returning to Ireland to live a low-key life. Laurel thought she'd told everyone he hadn't been killed, but she must have omitted to tell Father Doherty, for which she felt terrible.

'Don't rush into anything,' Ben said, opening the driver's door. 'Take your time. Just let me know when you're coming home. Assuming you do come home, that is.' His dark eyes fixed on mine.

'Don't be daft. Of course I'm coming home! I've got a daughter and a grandson, and the possibility of an exciting new life and career at the seaside. I'm not about to give all of that up. And, of course, I need to win that king back, don't I?'

Ben smiled, then hugged me tightly. 'Take care of yourself. Ring me any time.'

I hugged him back, closing my eyes at the safety I felt in his embrace. 'Thank you for everything this weekend. You've been my rock. Now, release me because you're crumpling my lovely new *Primark* T-Shirt.'

Ben laughed. 'I never thought I'd see the day when you went for the *Primani* look. I like the new, relaxed Clare, though. Apt slogan too.'

I looked down at my grey skinny-fit T-Shirt. Emblazoned across the front in white letters, it said: Life Begins After Coffee. Yes, very apt. I'd had my coffee. Was my life with Daran about to finally begin? After all of these years of wishing, and waiting, and wondering what if…?

As I stood in the farmyard with my suitcase by my side and a black and white cat weaving around my ankles, waving goodbye to the hire car disappearing over the summit, I felt quite overcome with emotion. A stream of tears rained down my cheeks.

'He's a remarkable young man, isn't he?' Laurel said, appearing by my side. 'A true gift from God.'

I couldn't answer her. Without Ben by my side, I felt very vulnerable.

'Let's get you inside, my treasure. Get those tears wiped away before Daran arrives.'

'Did you tell him I was here?'

'No. I told him he had a very important visitor and that he and the children should get over here immediately.'

My heart skipped a beat. 'Children?'

'Ah, yes. I might have left that part out. You see, Daran got married and had three beautiful children. They're not together anymore, though.'

'Oh. What happened?'

'I think I'd better let Daran tell you that. Come on. Let's get you settled in one of the guest rooms so you can freshen up and change if you want to. Not that there's anything wrong with what you're wearing, of course. They'll be here in about 40 minutes.'

Laurel settled me in a beautifully decorated guest room on the ground floor of one of three barn conversions. She told me that they had eight rooms in total: six doubles/twins and two family rooms. It had always been Daran's father's plan to convert the barns and, 10 years ago, she'd finally seen it through. The farm was very much a family business, with three of Daran's brothers working the land and tending to the cattle, two of his sisters running the equestrian centre, and his youngest sister managing the B&B

business. His remaining brother was a vet, so closely linked with the business too. Daran was teaching again, but he kept the accounts for the business.

I opened out my suitcase on my bed. Christ. What the hell should you wear for your first meeting after 17 years with the fiancé you'd thought was dead? I finally settled on a cute, soft-lemon dress that had taken my fancy in Cork when I'd shopped for my funeral attire. It had a baggy bodice with spaghetti straps and gathers around the neckline. The flared skirt was covered in pansies, cornflowers and some pretty yellow flowers I couldn't name. It made me think of the meadow outside our farmhouse. I wondered if Daran would make the connection. I'd bought the dress for the summer, but it was a beautiful spring day and, let's face it, I didn't have many alternatives.

I slipped my feet into a pair of beige Converse and pulled a soft, cream cardigan on. Staring at my reflection in the shabby-chic cheval mirror, I could vividly picture myself standing in front of my wardrobe at home, trying to see whether I looked innocent yet alluring on my 16th birthday, before I fully gave myself to Daran. I'd been wearing a pretty flowery dress back then too. I'd loved that dress. If only Jamie Doyle hadn't ripped it and my blood hadn't smeared across it. I closed my eyes and shivered. This was *not* the time for thinking about him. He was *not* going to ruin this for me.

'Goodness me, aren't you a vision of summer meadows and sunshine?' Laurel said, smiling as I slipped back into the kitchen.

'Do I look okay? I didn't really have much else to wear.'

'You look perfect.'

My heart jumped at the sound of a car crunching on the gravel. Laurel squeezed my hand. 'That'll be them. Don't you be expecting too much. Neither of you are the same people who fell in love back then.'

'Ben said something like that too.'

She smiled at me. 'He's got a wise head on young shoulders, that one. He sees things.'

Frodo started barking again and jumping up at the stable door. 'Why don't you go through to the sitting room and out onto the patio. I've put some iced lemonade out there. I'll keep the treasures amused. You and Daran can talk.'

She pointed me in the direction of the sitting room. I heard car doors slamming and the squeals of young children. What was I doing here? How would he react after all these years? Would he even recognise me? I shook my head. Of course he would. Laurel had recognised me and she could only have seen me as a teenager in a handful of photos.

Sliding patio doors at the end of the room opened out onto a stepped terrace with stunning views across the farm. What an incredible place to live, knowing that everything the eye could see belonged to them.

I looked at wrought-iron chairs but didn't sit down. I had too much nervous energy for that. I paced up and down the patio, waiting for Daran to appear. What would he look like? Fat? Grey? Bald? Or just as damned gorgeous as he'd been that first Sunday Mass when he'd stolen my heart?

The patio door slid open, and there he was. He'd filled out a little, his hair was receding slightly and he wore glasses; otherwise, he looked exactly how I remembered. My heart fluttered and a well of emotions threatened to overcome me. Daran was clearly shell-shocked. He didn't move or speak for several moments, and I found that I couldn't either.

Eventually, he said, 'Clare? Is that you? Or am I dreaming?'

'It's me, Daran. It's been a long time.'

The next minute, we were in each other's arms, holding on tightly. Tears streamed down my cheeks and I could hear Daran sobbing too as he stroked my hair and my back.

‘Where did they send you?’ he said, when we finally separated.

‘Cornwall. To my great-aunt Nuala’s house.’

‘I heard you’d gone to England, but nobody mentioned Cornwall. I heard London, the Cotswolds, Liverpool and Brighton, I think it was. Why did they do it? I know your da was angry that we were seeing each other, presumably because of your age and my vocation, but surely sending you away was a bit extreme.’

‘It wasn’t because we were seeing each other. It was because… Actually, I think you’d better sit down.’

Laurel was true to her word. She kept Daran’s children entertained and out of our way so Daran and I could talk. He was absolutely stunned to hear about Shannon, especially as the suggestion of my pregnancy had been vehemently denied.

I told him everything, from the moment my parents threw me out right up to the events of the last few days, including the return of my blocked memories.

‘I should never have left you alone that night,’ he said, as we ambled side by side through a field full of grazing sheep.

‘Don’t do that,’ I said. ‘I’d been alone at night loads of times. You had prayers to perform, and I told you to go. Jamie Doyle was determined to take me sooner or later. If it hadn’t been there, it would have been somewhere else.’

‘I remember you being distracted when I got back from the school trip, but you said you’d had a huge argument with your parents, and I believed you.’

‘Why wouldn’t you? My wounds had healed by then. Well, my physical ones had.’

‘When we made love that first night, you cried. You said it was with happiness at having me back. But it was because of what he’d done, wasn’t it?’

I nodded. ‘I’m sorry.’

'Oh, Clare! You have nothing to be sorry about. And you've only just remembered that this happened?'

I nodded again. 'I didn't block it out immediately, because I remember not telling you about the baby in case Jamie Doyle was the father, which, thankfully, he isn't because he's infertile. I'm wondering whether the loss of Shannon was the trigger for putting it in a box and hiding it in the back of my mind.'

'Like one traumatic thing wiping out another?'

'Something like that. I'll ask the counsellor about it when I get home.'

'I can certainly relate to lost memories,' he said.

Daran talked to me about his work in Thailand, before and after the tsunami, and the disaster itself. He hadn't planned to return to Ireland, but he'd received the news that one of his brothers was seriously ill and needed a bone-marrow transplant. Wondering if he might be a match, he started thinking about home and decided to wrap up his affairs in Thailand and set up home in Wicklow. He was a match so he donated and his brother recovered. While in hospital, he met a Finnish nurse called Freja. They married and had three children – two girls, now aged six and five, and a boy aged three. He awoke one morning to a note from Freja telling him that she'd gone back to Finland and he wasn't to follow her.

'Jesus, Daran! Why would she abandon her husband and kids just like that?'

'She never really took to motherhood. She found it difficult showing affection towards the children.'

'Yet you had three of them?'

Daran laughed. 'Still the same Clare – as blunt as ever. It's a valid point, so it is. I think she kept hoping she'd feel something different with each birth, but she just found it harder and harder. She said in her note that she couldn't stay, when she knew she'd never have the whole of my heart. She said I gave too much of it to our children and what was left had been given away a long time ago, leaving none for her.'

I stopped and faced him. 'You mean, to me?'

He nodded. 'Until the end of forever, remember?'

My breath caught in my throat. As I stood face to face with Daran, looking deep into his eyes, the years seemed to melt away. We could easily have been standing in our meadow 17 years ago. My heart thumped uncontrollably.

Daran reached out and tenderly cupped my face with his hand. 'We haven't reached the end of forever yet.'

He titled my head ever so gently as he moved closer and closer until his lips found mine. His kiss was so light and tender, and so full of love, that I couldn't help but respond. As I wrapped my arms around his neck and pressed my body against his, Ben's words came into my mind – Don't rush into anything – swiftly followed by Laurel's – Neither of you are the same people who fell in love back then. Was this a mistake? He was single. I was single. We were in a beautifully romantic setting. We were reminiscing about what might have been. The moment felt right. But was it just that: a moment? Could love really be rekindled after so many years apart, especially after what we'd both gone through during those years?

Obviously sensing my hesitation, Daran pulled away. 'Sorry. Probably too soon, isn't it?'

I nodded. 'I'm just a bit overwhelmed by everything. Until a couple of hours ago, I thought you were dead. Now you're right here and we're kissing, and you've got three kids and a life in Ireland, and I've got a home and family in England. Well, I don't actually have a home, but I will and… and I'm babbling and going to stop talking right now.'

Daran laughed and gave me a quick hug. 'You always did babble when you were nervous. I'm sorry if I'm the one making you nervous. I couldn't help myself.'

'You aren't making me nervous, as such. My feelings are. I don't know what to think or feel anymore.' I indicated that we should set off walking again.

'Is it because of him?'

'Who?'

'The one who you said brought you here today. Ben, is it?'

'Christ, no! He's just a friend. Well, I say "just a friend", but he's so much more than that. Not in a friends-with-benefits way or anything like that. He's just been incredibly supportive for… well, for pretty much the whole time I've known him.'

'Someone else, then?'

'There isn't anyone. Actually, there hasn't been anyone since you, Daran.'

'Anyone you've loved, you mean?'

'Anyone, full stop. A few kisses when I've let my guard down, but that's been it.'

'Really? Why?'

'Because the only two people I ever cared deeply about were taken away from me. Being sent away from you was heartbreaking, but I had our baby to focus on so I still had a little part of you, assuming she was yours. When I was told that she'd died, I'd never felt pain like it. I couldn't put myself through that again. So I didn't.'

We walked side by side in silence for a while.

'When do you have to go back?' Daran asked.

'Tomorrow, assuming I can get a flight from Dublin. It's pointless going all the way back to Cork.'

'Any chance you can stay a bit longer?'

I shook my head. 'I've been away for nearly a week already. I want to get back to Shannon and Luke. I need to explore where we're going to live and think about getting some work.'

Darren stopped and took my hand. 'You couldn't make it Tuesday, could you? I know it's a big ask, but I'd really like to see you again and I think tonight would be too soon for you. I think you need a bit of space to get your head around things, don't you?'

I considered for a moment. One more day? 'Okay. Tuesday it is, but I absolutely can't stay beyond that.' I glanced at my watch. 'Christ! We've been gone ages. Your kids will be thinking you've been kidnapped.'

'I heard rumours of chocolate cake, so they probably haven't noticed I'm gone.'

We turned and walked back towards the farmhouse. 'I like your dress, by the way,' Daran said. 'It reminds me of our meadow.'

'It reminded me of that too.'

We walked on a bit further. The farmhouse came into view. Laurel was pegging out washing on a lawn next to one of the hay barns. I could see three small children racing around, ducking between the sheets, presumably chasing Frodo, by the sounds of the excitable barks. How different their childhood would be from mine. They only had one parent, but he clearly adored them and made up for their lack of a mother. They were surrounded by aunties and uncles, and had a granny with a farm on which they could run riot.

'I noticed that you're still wearing my ring,' Daran said.

I held out my right hand in front of me but dropped it quickly when I realised it was shaking. I decided to pre-empt the question. 'I've never taken it off. Other than to swap hands, of course. If Great-Aunt Nuala had thought it was an engagement ring, she'd have confiscated it.' It had been the genuine reason at first, but I could have swapped it back at any point. Why hadn't I?

'Thank you for keeping it.'

'It was until the end of forever for me too, you know.'

'Was… or still is?' Daran paused by the gate.

I shook my head. 'I can't answer that at the moment.'

He smiled. 'Sorry. Far too pushy. I promised to give you time. Freja was right, though, my heart always was – and still is – yours.'

He pulled on the metal bar to open the gate and we stepped into the farmyard.

'Daddy!' Two dark-haired little girls rushed towards him.

'My princesses!' he cried, gathering them in his arms. 'Where's your brother?'

'Pretending he's a dog.' The taller one pointed to where a small boy was rolling around on the grass with Frodo.

'This is Clare, Erin and Ethan,' Daran said. 'Girls, this is an old friend of Daddy's. She's also called Clare. Say hello.'

Both girls looked up at me, squinting.

'Your dress is very pretty,' Clare said.

'I like your hair,' Erin added. 'It's yellow like the sun.'

'Thank you,' I whispered, as they ran off to join Ethan and Frodo.

I turned to Daran. 'You named your firstborn after me?'

He bit his lip. 'Freja wasn't too impressed when she found out. We were planning to call her Katelyn and I changed my mind at the last minute when I registered the birth. Freja went mad. She threw a vase at me.' Daran pointed to a faint scar close to his hairline.

'I think that if I'd been her, I'd have thrown 10 vases at you.'

'It wasn't one of my finest moments. It was probably the beginning of the end for us.'

Ethan launched himself at Daran's legs at that moment, and Daran picked him up and swung him in the air, ending the conversation. Poor Freja. I'd started off feeling bitterness towards a woman who could abandon her husband and three young children by leaving a note. Now I just felt sorry for her. The poor woman had been living under my shadow for the whole of her marriage. No wonder she'd fled.

Chapter 47

The next day, I awoke a little after nine to the sounds of birds chirping, cows mooing and sunlight streaming through my window. I rolled onto my back and stretched. It had been the early hours before I'd managed to fall asleep, although I'd slept soundly once I'd finally managed to stop my mind from whirring.

I showered and dressed before crossing the farmyard to the main house. The top of the kitchen half-door was open, and the delectable smell of bacon and eggs wafted out to me as I approached. My stomach rumbled.

'Good morning!' Laurel said, as I unlatched the bottom half of the door. 'The boys have just been in for their mid-morning snack and I'm about to put some more bacon on. Sit yourself down.'

'Can I help?'

'No, no!' She shooed me towards the table. 'You're a guest.'

I'd no sooner sat down than my phone started ringing. I glanced at the screen. Aisling. 'It's my sister. Do you mind if I take this?'

'Help yourself. Reception's not great in here. You're better in the yard. I'll wait till you're back before I put the bacon on.'

I accepted the call as I headed into the yard. 'Aisling! I meant to call you yesterday, but things got a little crazy. I'm so sorry for interfering between you and Finn. I shouldn't have said anything. I thought I was helping, but I should have engaged brain before mouth, as usual.'

'It's grand. I'm glad you interfered.'

I sat down on a wooden bench. 'Really? Has something happened?'

'Let's just say that it's taken two kids, a divorce, a few booty calls, as you put it, and a long-distance friendship to make my husband finally fall in love with me.'

'No! Oh my God, Aisling, that's amazing! What happened?'

'When *she* left him, he was devastated, but after a while he realised that he was more upset about her stringing him along and getting him to move to Manchester away from the kids than he was about losing her. He said he missed my company more than hers and, when the kids visited, he found himself looking forward to seeing me as much as them. Every time something happened at work that made him happy or sad, he wanted to tell me about it. He found himself watching TV programmes or films and wanting to hear my opinions on them.

'The first time we slept together again, he lay awake watching me for a while, and he said it was like he was really seeing me for the first time. He'd thought that love and friendship were two separate things and that our relationship hadn't worked because we'd started out as friends, but it struck him that he actually loved me because of our friendship.'

'So why didn't he say anything?'

'He was worried that I didn't feel the same way. He knew he'd hurt me and he'd expected me to shout and scream at him, demand more maintenance, make it awkward to see the kids, and generally act the part of the scorned woman that so many exes play. When I didn't, he assumed it was because I didn't really care. What you said in the pub and my reaction to it made him dare to hope.'

'Aw, Aisling. I'm so thrilled for you both. What happens next?'

'He had to be back for work this morning, but it's the Easter holidays starting next week. The kids were going over anyway so we're extending our trip and I'm staying the whole time and, well, a move to the UK wouldn't be off the cards. We're not going to rush into anything, though.'

'I bet you'll be living there by the summer.'

Aisling laughed. 'I bet you're right. I'm so happy and it's all thanks to you. If you were still in Ireland right now, I'd come and give you a huge hug.'

'Actually, I am.'

'You are what?'

'Still in Ireland, only you won't believe where.'

'The *Giant's Causeway*.'

'Why would I be at the *Giant's Causeway*?'

'I don't know. It was the first thing that came into my head.' A bell sounded in the background. 'Damn. Break's over. Can I call you back at lunch?'

'Okay.'

'Where are you, though? If you don't tell me, I'll spend the next two classes thinking about it.'

I giggled. 'If I tell you, you'll *definitely* spend the next two classes thinking about it. Are you sure you want to know?'

'Tell me!'

'Daran's mum's farmhouse in Wicklow. And Daran's still alive. I saw him yesterday.'

'Feck off!'

'I know! Enjoy your class. Speak to you later.' I hung up giggling. The unfortunate kids she was teaching next were probably about to have the most shambolic science lesson ever.

I'd run out of clothes. I frantically rummaged through my suitcase. Seriously. I had nothing suitable to wear. It was either jeans and my Life Begins After Coffee T-Shirt or the dress I'd worn to Da's funeral. Everything else was dirty.

'I've got a problem,' I said to Laurel, over a spot of lunch. 'I've got no clothes for tonight. Is there a town I can get to around here?'

She shook her head. 'Nowhere close with any decent clothes shops. I'm sure our Aoife will lend you something. She's about the same size as you. Bit shorter, perhaps. She'll be over to clean the rooms shortly. I'll give her a ring and ask her to bring you some options.'

As soon as she arrived, Aoife gave me a huge hug. 'So you're the one who stole my big brother's heart. I can see why. Come on, let's get you fixed up. I've got just the thing.' She grabbed my hand and pulled me over to a bright-yellow van. She opened the passenger-side door and rummaged through a pile of clothes. 'You're welcome to look at the others, but I think this one's you.' She thrust a navy dress on a hanger at me. 'Do you have shoes? Ma didn't say to bring any.'

'I have shoes,' I said, holding the dress out in front of me. It had a ruched bodice and a short, flared, lacy overskirt. Not too casual and not too dressy. My nude heels would be perfect with it. 'I love it. Thank you.'

'You're welcome.' She closed the door and leaned against it. 'He's still besotted with you, you know.'

'I know.'

'If anything, absence has made the heart grow fonder for him. It doesn't mean it's going to be the same for you.' She moved around me, opened the back of the van and lifted a vacuum cleaner out. 'The kids are staying with me so you won't be disturbed. Enjoy tonight. You'll look stunning in that.'

'Thank you for lending it to me.'

She walked towards one of the barn conversions, then stopped and turned around. 'I love my brother, Clare, but I know what he can be like. Don't let him talk you into anything that you don't want. Sometimes the past is called the past because it's already passed.' With a sigh, she turned and headed into one of the rooms, leaving me in the middle of the farmyard with a dress draped over my arm, wondering if I should have stuck to my original plan and caught a flight back to England instead of staying another night.

Chapter 48

'Was it strange, seeing him again after so much time?' Ben asked, as we tucked into an Indian takeaway the following night. It felt so good to be home and back to normality.

'Actually, it was. Sunday was grand. We had 17 years to catch up on, so lots to talk about.'

'And last night?'

I pushed a chunk of chicken around my plate with a piece of naan bread while I found the right words. It had started so well. We'd continued to reminisce about our time in Ballykielty. Daran had reassured me that giving up the priesthood had definitely been right for him. He'd still been able to do God's work, and continued to do so in his local community.

I told him about Da's claims that he'd been unfaithful to me. Although I was convinced that Da had just been a vindictive liar, it was reassuring to look Daran in the eye and hear him declare emphatically that I had been – and still was – the only one for him. Actually, I liked the 'had been' part, but the 'still was' concerned me.

After eating, we'd moved to the sofa. He held me and kissed me, and it was lovely, but something was missing. He whispered again that he still loved me, and I so wanted to be able to say that I felt the same, but I really wasn't sure, which made no sense, because I'd dreamed of a moment like this for so long. I closed my eyes and tried to focus on what it had been like when we'd been together in the farmhouse, hoping to recapture the passion and longing I'd felt for him back then, but my mind kept picturing Jamie Doyle instead. Looming over me. Laughing. Hurting me.

As Daran's hand slid up my bare leg and caressed my thigh, I froze. I was back in the farmhouse, pinned down by a man whose intentions were very clear. No! I had to stop thinking like that. This was Daran. He loved me. 'Pinned' was the wrong word. He was gentle. It wasn't forced. I could move. I could escape. I could say no. And I did. The moment his fingers touched my panties, I screamed. I actually screamed.

Daran had leapt off me immediately, absolutely distraught. He couldn't apologise enough for taking things too far, too soon.

'It's not that,' I whispered, sitting forward on the sofa with my head in my hands. 'I know it happened 17 years ago, but my memory has only just come back and it's like I was raped a few days ago. I'm sorry, Daran. I can't do this.'

He held me as I sobbed, then drove me back to the farm, apologising all the way. But it wasn't his fault. It was Jamie Doyle's for what he'd done. It was Da's for separating us. And it was mine for falling out of love with Daran and not being able to find the words to tell him.

'Clare?' Ben asked, bringing me back to the present.

'Sorry. Lost in my thoughts. It was lovely. He was lovely.' I put my unfinished meal on the coffee table. 'Can we watch a film?'

'Anything in particular?'

'Something that doesn't require much concentration.'

'Sounds good. I'll clear these away first. Another beer?'

'Another five, please.'

'It's like that, is it?'

'Be grateful it's not another 10!'

Ben stood up. 'I'll get you the number of that counsellor tomorrow.'

'Yes, please.'

I'd actually necked six bottles of beer by the time the film ended and was halfway down my seventh. I felt more relaxed than I'd felt in a long time, grateful for the slight fuzziness in my head to numb the bad stuff.

'Great, big, steaming pile of elephant shite,' I said, as the credits rolled.

'Really? I didn't think it was that bad. On a scale of shite, I'd say gazelle droppings.'

I laughed. 'A scale of shite? I think we might just have to create one of those for our future critiques.'

'Why did you hate it?' Ben asked, taking a glug on his lager. Despite his protests that he had to work the next day, he'd managed to match me drink for drink and he was slurring his words. I was too.

'Plot was okay. Couple of holes. Nothing major. What was shite was the chemistry between the leads, 'cos there was shag all! Weren't they meant to be dating in real life when the film was made? No wonder they split up.'

'Didn't think they were *that* bad. Pretty steamy sex scenes.'

I nodded. 'Yep. But the rest of it had zero chemistry, especially the kissing. It was like watching my parents kiss. Actually, don't think I ever saw them kiss, but that's what I imagine it would be like. Complete lack of passion. Surely any half-decent actor can convince an audience that they're in love. I reckon that even I, with no acting training at all, could fake a passionate kiss and have anyone believe I was madly in love with the man I was kissing, even if I hated him.'

'I bet you couldn't.'

'You *bet* I couldn't? Are you challenging me to win the king back?'

'No! Just a turn of phrase, but if you want to see it as a dare, Irish, that's up to you. Not sure who you're planning to kiss, though.'

It absolutely was a dare. Well, if he was stupid enough to dare me when he was the only man around… I leaned forward on the sofa and planted my lips on his, and held them there for a few moments, fully expecting him to laugh and pull away when it got too much. But he didn't. Ah! I knew what he was up to. The eejit was challenging me to be the first to pull away, then he'd say I'd lost the challenge and he'd get to keep the king – faked chemistry or no faked chemistry. Bollocks to him. No way was he going to win that easily. I opened my mouth slightly and gently kissed him. He responded. Mr Daring! I parted my lips a little more and cheekily slipped out my tongue, then gasped as he did the same. Most unexpected and most pleasurable. His kiss became more urgent and his hands found their way into my hair. I let out a soft moan as something stirred in me that hadn't stirred for so long. It certainly hadn't stirred with Daran over the last couple of days. Jesus, Mary and Joseph. What was he doing to me? Playing me at my own game, of course. He was showing that he could fake passion and chemistry too. Right. He'd asked for it.

I wrapped my arms around him and held him tightly, kissing him with more fervour. We lay back on the sofa, legs entwined, hands running through each other's hair. I knew one of us had to break soon, because the point had definitely been proved and this was going beyond a stupid dare. But I didn't want it to be me.

As I ran my fingers through Ben's hair and down his back, all I could think about was ripping his shirt off, liberating him of his jeans and surrendering myself to him completely. I didn't feel afraid, like I had when I'd screamed the night before as Daran touched me. I didn't feel anxious. I just felt… oh my God! I felt absolutely everything. Every nerve ending fizzed.

Ben began to trail light kisses across my face to my neck and ears. A shudder of delight ran through me as I arched my body in response to his touch. Why were we still kissing? We didn't fancy each other. We hadn't been flirting. How had we got to this point? This wonderful, amazing point? Because of a dare. Because we were both too stubborn to stop. I was determined to win the king and Ben wanted to keep him. What a pair of eejits we were. It made no difference to me in my fiercely single status, but he had Lebony. Dare or no dare, this was surely being unfaithful, and Ben wasn't that kind of man. I had to stop it. I had to… Oh Christ, Ben, just take me to bed!

A shrill ringing broke us apart. Saved by the bell! Ben pulled away looking completely shell-shocked, as if he'd expected it be Lebony opposite him, not me. What the hell had I done?

'I'd better get that. Sorry,' he muttered, dashing towards the sideboard and retrieving the phone from the cradle, then disappearing into the kitchen with it. I was sure I heard him say, 'Hi, Lebony,' but that could have been my guilty conscience.

I stood in the middle of the lounge, trying to recover my breathing, feeling suddenly very sober. I ran my fingers through my dishevelled hair, shaking my head. Feck! That was close. If that phone hadn't rung, we'd… Well, we might have… Surely not… No, one of us would have had the sense to declare that the dare had gone too far. I just wasn't sure it would have been me. Feck, shit, bollocks! I grabbed my beer from the coffee table, then slumped back onto the sofa, gulping the rest of it down in one.

When Ben returned to the lounge 10 minutes later, he looked pretty sheepish. 'Sorry about that. I… er… you know I can't stand ringing phones.' He returned the phone to the cradle and stood awkwardly for a moment, his hands in the back pockets of his jeans, nearly overbalancing as he rocked on the spot. 'Sorry.'

I needed to regain my composure and act normally. 'I think you need to give me something, don't you?' I held out my hand to him.

He gulped. 'You really want to do this?'

'Of course. I wouldn't have kissed you like that if I hadn't wanted it so badly.' I winked at him. 'Are you going to make me beg for it?'

'I… er… I don't know if this is such a good idea.'

'What do you mean? I won him fair and square. Unless you're going to try to make out that you didn't believe the fake chemistry.'

Ben closed his eyes for a moment and shook his head. 'The king. Of course. Well done! That was pretty amazing acting.'

'Thank you. You were pretty amazing yourself. Hand him over, then.' I put my hand out again and Ben dropped the king into my palm.

'I'm seriously impressed with how far you took that,' I said, 'especially when you're the one with the girlfriend. I've no idea why she spends her time abroad, when she's got that on offer at home.'

Ben stiffened. 'Yeah, well, life doesn't always turn out the way we'd like it to, does it?' He turned and left the room.

Awkward. I picked up my bottle and tutted. Eejit! I'd already emptied it. I placed it back down and waited. And waited. And waited.

It was a good 10 minutes before Ben reappeared. 'Sorry about that. My mobile rang while I was upstairs. Pete called.'

'Pete who threw the crappest New Year's Eve party in the history of the world?'

Ben nodded. 'Well, he and some of the lads had invited me down *The King George* tonight and I said no, in case you needed me. It's Pete's birthday and they're pestering me to come down…'

'Oh. So…?'

'Well, I said I'd go. I'd invite you but it's blokes only and, well, you've met some of them and they're not exactly… erm… It's just…'

I jumped to my feet. 'It's grand. You go. You were probably planning to before I demanded an Indian and a movie, weren't you? You should have told me.'

'You'll be okay on your own?'

'Of course. I'll unpack, then get to bed.'

Ben nodded. 'I'm at work early in the morning so I guess I'll see you tomorrow night.'

'Grand. See you tomorrow.'

It was only when he'd gone that I looked at my watch and realised it was 11.15pm. Who went out to join their mates at a pub at 11.15pm on a Tuesday night, when they had to be up early the next day? Arse! I'd completely bollocksed things up with that kiss, hadn't I? He couldn't get away from me fast enough. If that had been Lebony on the landline, I couldn't blame him for wanting out. That had been some intense kissing and he probably felt 50 shades of guilty. Ooh, speaking of 50 shades… I put my fingers up to my red cheeks. I had to stop thinking about that right now. All that had happened was that the trust and friendship I had for Ben had triggered some dormant feelings. Not for him, just for a relationship. Although, kissing Daran, the former love of my life, hadn't had the same effect, which meant... Stop it! It had been a one-off and, while extremely pleasurable, it would never happen again.

Chapter 49

'We've got, like, amazing news,' announced Shannon, the moment she spotted me the following day. 'They're letting me out!'

'That's just grand. When?'

'Friday!'

'Jesus! So soon? And that's Good Friday, isn't it?'

'I know. Very good Friday for me! Apparently, I've made great progress,' she said, grinning, then her face fell. 'How was the funeral?'

'Great craic! Ma was plastered, had another go at me and revealed the reason why she hates me so much. Turns out I'm not actually her daughter, which means you're not her granddaughter. My da had an affair with the woman over the road for 20 years and I was the unexpected output a few years in. She's lovely and can't wait to fly over to England to meet her new family.' I plonked myself down in the chair by the bed. 'And I have even more incredible news for you, Shannon. Your dad, Daran, is still alive and, if it's okay with you, he wants to meet you next week.'

I had a lovely day at the hospital with my family. Shannon squealed when I told her about Daran, promptly waking Luke up, so he added his own louder squeals to hers. She wanted to know all about him so I gave her the edited highlights, leaving out any mention of what had happened between us.

'We wanted to talk to you about moving,' Callum said. 'We've done some research and we think that Whitsborough Bay looks pretty decent. We want to explore before we commit to anything, so we've booked a holiday cottage for two weeks from Friday in a place called Little Sandby.'

Little Sandby. It rang a bell. 'Oh! That's where my friends Elise and Stevie live.'

'Is it nice?' Shannon asked.

'I've only been there once, but it's a lovely village.'

'We'd like you to stay with us. If, like, you're free,' Callum said. 'There are three bedrooms so Ben can stay, or Shannon's dad when he comes over next week. Luke'll sleep in our room.'

'I'd love to stay! What happens if you like the place?'

'Then we find somewhere to rent until we can buy next June, when my inheritance comes through,' Shannon said. 'Do you think we'll like it, Mum?'

My heart melted as she called me that. 'Yes. I think you will. But if you don't, we'll find somewhere else that's right for us all.' I didn't really care where it was, as long as we were together.

Luke was going to stay with Callum at *Jimmy's* until Shannon was discharged. It didn't make sense to disrupt the routine and bring him home with me, so I said my goodbyes and looked forward to seeing my family again the next day.

As I drove through Leeds later that afternoon, I found myself hoping that Ben wouldn't be late home from work so I could share the news with him. And so I could apologise for taking the dare too far the night before. My body fizzed again as I thought about lying on the sofa, kissing him. Why did it keep doing that?

The house was in silence, but that was fair enough, as Ben didn't usually get home till after six and it was only half five. I dumped my handbag on the kitchen worktop and looked around at the steriliser, bottle warmer, empty bottles and teats. I had better start packing, to be ready for our move. The kitchen could wait. I'd start upstairs.

Four hours later, I'd packed most of Luke's possessions and had even managed to disassemble his cot, despite not being able to find the instructions. I was pretty proud of my handiwork. There was still no sign of Ben, though. My stomach growled in protest at the late hour without food, so I padded downstairs and made some cheese on toast.

✉ To Ben
Where are you? Getting worried! Hope you're not avoiding me after last night. Pleasurable as it was, I promise not to force you to repeat it! ;-) xx

✉ From Ben
Forgot to say. Working really late. Back about midnight. Don't wait up

I frowned. Those last few words sounded like an order, i.e. he absolutely didn't want me to wait up because he was avoiding me. No! It was just a text. People are curt in texts. I shook my head. *I* was curt in texts, Ben wasn't. Bollocks. I should never have got drunk and thrown myself at him like that, dare or no dare.

I picked up the number of the counsellor he'd left me on the kitchen worktop. It was a Leeds landline. If we were moving to Whitsborough Bay, a Leeds-based counsellor wasn't going to work for me. I'd call her in the morning, though, and see if she could recommend anyone on the coast instead.

Time to return to the packing. I'd just turned towards the stairs when my phone rang and, as soon as I saw the name on the screen, I cursed myself.

'Daran! I'm so sorry. I completely forgot.' I was meant to have FaceTimed him at eight. Feck it anyway. How had I forgotten that?

I lay in bed, watching the clock, and listening for the sound of Ben's key turning in the lock. I hated that I hadn't seen him that day. Having previously found his home a haven, even when on my own, it had felt empty and lonely without his easy banter. Even though I'd had a good chat with Daran on the phone, I'd found myself wishing it had been Ben who I was talking to about my plans for the future. But that was only because Ben would have been excited for me about the move, whereas Daran suggested that if I wanted the coast and the countryside, I couldn't go far wrong with Wicklow. He was never going to move to England, and I was never going to move to Ireland. What did that mean? I definitely didn't love him, but I still cared for him deeply and he was the father of my child. Could my feelings come back? Would they ever be enough to bridge the distance? A long-distance relationship worked for Ben and Lebony. Could it work for Daran and me? As I drifted off to sleep, the last thought in my mind was: did I *want* it to work for Daran and me?

Chapter 50

I switched my phone back on as I left *Jimmy's* the following afternoon. I had the packing to finish before we moved the next day. I felt quite giddy with excitement at the thought of the fresh start with my new family.

My iPhone beeped, indicating a missed call from Ben from a little after 11am and a text advising me that I had a voicemail. Phew! He was still alive, then! He hadn't been around when I'd awoken that morning and a quick look in his bedroom suggested he hadn't been home all night.

Crossing the car park, I dialled into my voicemail: *Clare. It's Ben. My dad's just phoned. Auntie Kay's been in a coach crash. It's on the news. There are fatalities. We don't know if… We're hoping she's… Oh God! I can't bear to think about it. I'm going to Whitsborough Bay. Mum and Sarah are in bits. They need me… I'm sorry I didn't come home last night. I hope you were okay. It was… It doesn't matter. Look, call me when you get this, if you can.*

I ran across the car park, jumped into the car, attached my phone to the hands-free system with shaky hands, then sped towards the A1. As I waited impatiently at a red light, I speed-dialled Elise's mobile. Voicemail. 'Elise. It's Clare. Call me on my mobile the minute you pick this up. I'm on my way to Whitsborough Bay. We need to see Sarah.'

She rang back less than 10 minutes later, panic in her voice. 'Has something happened to Sarah?'

'No. Yes. Sort of. I don't know much. I've just picked up a message from Ben. Kay and Philip are in Italy on holiday, but their coach crashed and he doesn't know whether Kay's…' I couldn't bring myself to say the word 'dead'. '… one of the survivors.'

Elise gasped. 'Oh my goodness. I can't believe it. What about Philip?'

'Ben didn't say. I'm assuming they don't know about him either.'

'I only saw them a couple of days ago. They were so excited about the trip. How's Sarah?'

'Not good, by the sounds of it. I've just set off now. Do you want to go to Sarah's directly or will I pick you up?'

'Can you pick me up? Stevie will be here in an hour or so.'

I hung up after making arrangements to ring her when I pulled into the hospital car park. My heart raced. Poor Ben. And poor Sarah. Ben was close to Kay, but Sarah had an exceptional bond with her auntie.

As I headed north, I cursed myself for being so lax at keeping in contact with Sarah. She probably thought I didn't care. I did. I just wasn't very good at dealing with other people's problems when I had so many of my own to sort out. And it wasn't as if I hadn't tried. I'd made a couple of attempts to visit, and I'd called her on the day of Da's funeral when I was with Ben. I hadn't tried again, though. I should have. I'd promised Ben I would.

'Do you think she'll be pissed off at us for turning up together?' I asked Elise, as I rang the bell at Sarah's parents' house.

'No. I think she'll appreciate that we're here.'

Ben opened the door, and my throat constricted as I took in his pale face and red eyes. 'You got my message. I was worried you wouldn't.'

'I came as soon as I heard it,' I said, reaching my arms out to him. He hugged me, then Elise, and ushered us into the hall.

'Any news?' I asked.

He shook his head and opened the lounge door. Sarah's dad, Chris, was pacing up and down, talking in hushed tones on the phone. Sarah was curled up on the sofa, watching him intently. I frowned. She'd lost a lot of weight since I'd last saw her, and not in a good way. She actually looked quite frail. I glanced at Ben. He'd warned me something was up, but he'd insisted she wasn't ill. Had that been a cover-up?

At that moment, Sarah looked up and spotted Elise and me. She stood up. 'What are you two doing here?' was all she managed, before she broke down in tears.

'Did you think we'd let our best friend go through something like this on her own?' I said, giving her a hug. Elise put her arms around her too, and the three of us stood in the middle of the lounge, clinging onto one another.

'What's the news?' I asked, when Sarah had calmed down and we'd all taken a seat.

Sarah shook her head, clearly unable to speak. She looked at her brother. 'The latest news report said three of the five fatalities were British,' he said, 'but they also said that two thirds of the passengers were British.'

Chris walked back into the room. 'That was Adrienne from the tour operator. They've been able to confirm that Philip *isn't* one of the fatalities, although that doesn't mean he's not injured. They still can't tell us about Kay, though.'

'That's ridiculous,' Ben cried. 'The crash happened last night. How can they not know who's dead and who's alive?'

'Apparently, the crash site was between two hospitals, so passengers have been taken to one or the other with no particular logic. It's chaos out there. Families and couples have been split up so they're struggling to work out who's with whom and who's where.'

Ben sat forward in his chair. 'So, how can they confirm the nationalities of the dead, yet they can't confirm the names?'

'I don't know, son, I really don't know. She's going to call me again within the next two hours and promises me she'll do everything she can to get definitive information about them both.'

'Has anyone contacted Daniel and Michael?' Elise asked. 'I could call them if you like?' I could tell from the tone of Elise's voice that she didn't really want to, and I couldn't blame her.

'They know about the crash,' Ben said, 'but I'll call and update them on Philip now.' He headed into the kitchen.

'Where's your mum?' Elise asked Sarah.

'Asleep. She was beside herself. I called your Gary and he gave her something to settle her.'

'I think I'll just go and check on her.' Chris left the room.

'How are you holding up?' I asked.

She crumpled again. 'She can't be dead.' Big, fat tears tumbled down her cheeks.

I sat down beside her and held her tightly. 'I'm sure she isn't. She would have been sitting next to Philip and he's alive, which would suggest they weren't in the part of the coach that took the greatest impact. I also believe that, with these things, they do know who the dead are and they're letting those families know first. As Ben said, they know the nationalities of the dead, so surely they know the names. I really think that, if she'd been one of them, you'd have heard by now.'

The doorbell rang. 'Do you want me to get that?' Elise asked.

Sarah nodded.

Elise returned moments later accompanied by a tall, slim woman with long, blonde, tousled hair, the sides of which were swept back in fishtail plaits. She looked very tanned, despite it only being March, and was dressed for summer in a tight coral-pink t-shirt and floaty white skirt. There was something familiar about her. Oh Jesus, she had to be…

'Lebony!' Ben cried, returning from the kitchen.

She rushed across the room, arms outstretched. 'Oh, Ben! I'm so sorry.'

Ben gave way to his grief as he held onto her and she stroked his back. I felt as if I was invading a very private moment, but I couldn't take my eyes off the pair of them. I had to admit that Lebony was beautiful and, seeing them together, they looked so right. I was still staring at them when they finally pulled away and Ben composed himself.

'Er… This is Lebony. Lebony, this is Clare, and I think you've met Elise before.'

'Yes, I have, and she answered the door just now. Hi, Elise. Hi, Sarah,' Lebony said. 'And hi to you, Clare. Ben's told you so much about you. I feel like I know you already. I'm only sorry we've had to meet under these circumstances.'

'It's good to meet you too, at last,' I said. My voice sounded strange, as though I was struggling to say the words.

Ben sat back down on the armchair and Lebony perched on the armrest with her arm around his shoulder. We all jumped as the phone rang.

'I'd better let Dad get it,' Ben said. 'It was quick, though. I hope that doesn't mean bad news.'

We could hear pacing up and down the landing, then Chris ran down the stairs and burst through the door. 'She's alive! She's injured. They don't know the details, but apparently it's not critical. Adrienne's going to call me back as soon as she knows more. I think I need a cup of tea, after that,' he said.

'I'll make it.' Lebony jumped up and took drinks orders from everyone, then disappeared into the kitchen.

Chris slumped onto the second armchair, looking exhausted

but happy. 'I can't wait until your mum wakes up so I can tell her Kay's safe.' He smiled at Elise and me. 'Thank you both for coming over. You're such good friends. After what Sarah went through with the baby, this was the last thing she needed.'

'What baby?' I said.

'Oh no!' Chris put his hand over his mouth. 'Didn't you know? I'm sorry, Sarah. I didn't mean to… I think I'll just see if Lebony needs any help.' He jumped up and scuttled out of the room.

'Sarah…?'

She started sobbing again. 'Ben, I can't…'

'Do you want me to tell them?'

She hugged her legs to her chest and nodded.

'Shortly after getting back from Canada, Sarah discovered she was pregnant. She didn't want to say anything till she'd had her 12-week scan and knew the baby was okay. At about 10 weeks… Is that right, Sarah?'

Sarah nodded.

'At about 10 weeks, she started bleeding so was taken into hospital, where they discovered she had an ectopic pregnancy. She had to go in for surgery to remove the foetus, but they had to remove one of her fallopian tubes too.'

'Jesus Christ!' I said. 'Why didn't you say anything?'

'I couldn't… so ashamed… my fault.'

'Of course it wasn't your fault,' Elise said. 'These things happen.'

'No. My fault.' An agonised sob escaped from her.

'It isn't Sarah's fault,' Ben said. 'Sadly, these things *do* happen. However, Sarah and Nick wanted to spend a few years together before they started a family. She was a bit upset to discover she was pregnant so soon. When she started bleeding, she blamed herself for not wanting the baby, and now she can't seem to stop blaming herself.'

I took Sarah's hand in mine. 'You can't blame yourself, but I know how easy it is. At first, I blamed myself for Shannon dying because I thought God was mad at me for taking Daran away from the priesthood.'

'I might never be able to have children,' she whimpered.

'I thought Ben said they only removed one tube.'

'They found some scarring on the other one. They're running tests at the moment.'

Sarah blew her nose. 'I'm sorry I haven't been there for you both, but I couldn't be around babies and talk of babies. I know it's selfish but—'

'When you visited me in hospital before Melody was born and Clare was there…?' Elise asked.

Sarah nodded. 'I shouldn't have come. I thought I'd be okay, but I'd just found out that morning and I was booked in for my op that afternoon.'

No wonder she'd acted so strangely. What must have been running through her mind, seeing me and Elise all excited about Luke and about Melody's impending arrival, when she knew she was about to lose her baby? 'I wish you'd told us.'

'Yeah, like you told me about Daran and Shannon, and Elise told me about her pregnancy and having the hots for Stevie?'

Awkward.

'Do you know what I think?' Ben said.

I shook my head. 'Enlighten us.'

'I think you should all go for a long walk, and talk. Really talk. Get all your secrets out in the open and start supporting each other through some of the shit you're going through right now, because I know that you, Clare, need your friends around you to help you through the latest revelations.'

'Why? What's happened?' Elise asked.

'What hasn't happened?' I sighed. 'I hate to say it, but Saint Ben is right. Who fancies a walk along the beach?'

Elise and Clare muttered their agreement. 'You'll call me if there's any more news?' Sarah said, looking at Ben. 'And will you tell Nick where we are when he gets back from walking Hobnob?'

'I will.' He stood up. 'Dad! Lebony! It's safe to return. The girls are going for a walk.'

'We need absolute and complete honesty,' I said, as we piled out of my car and crossed the road, ready for a walk around The Headland to North Beach. 'It's going to hurt at times, but I think that the only way we can get this friendship back on track – bearing in mind that the dynamics have changed and it's a three-way friendship now instead of two pairs – is if we explore how we've all felt over the past year, when we've encountered certain hurdles or discovered certain secrets. Is everyone up for it?'

I don't think I'd ever talked so much in my life. Or listened so intently. We got it all out in the open, exploring the friendship shifts, the secrets, the lies, the misunderstandings and the lack of communication. We laughed, we cried, we had awkward moments where one or the other could happily have run off down the beach, but we got through it. I'd thought before that being in our early 30s automatically made us 'mature adults' but it didn't: it was the harsh realities of life that had been thrown at us all over the past couple of months, and talking about how we'd struggled to deal with them, that had matured us.

Chapter 51

I lay on my back on the sofa in the semi-darkness of Sarah's parents' lounge. Sarah had insisted on staying the night in case there was more news, given that we'd heard nothing since before our walk. Nick had joined us for a takeaway, then gone home to tend to their dog and cats. He'd offered me their spare bed, but I insisted I was happy with a sofa and a duvet. Elise had returned to the hospital and, as far as I knew, Lebony and Ben were upstairs.

That had been one hell of a conversation on the beach. A long-overdue one. Christ, we'd been through a lot recently. I felt like a right cow for not taking Ben seriously when he'd suggested – several times – that there was a reason for Sarah not being in touch. There certainly had been. I should listen to Ben more. He spoke so much sense.

Ben. An image flashed into my mind of Lebony and him clinging onto each other when she'd arrived. Tightly. Tenderly. She wasn't what I'd expected. I'd seen photos, of course, so I knew what she physically looked like, but I hadn't been prepared for her personality. She was so bubbly, so helpful, so damn friendly. She'd heard all about what I'd done for Luke and said I was an inspiration in the way I'd left my job and taken him on without question.

I'll admit that I wanted to dislike her. I knew that Sarah had mixed feelings about the woman; she liked her as a person but hated her for spending so much time away from Ben. I wanted to hate her too. But I couldn't. Why did I want to hate her? Out of support for Sarah? It had to be. Ben was just a friend, so what difference did it make to me who he chose as a girlfriend? If he wanted to see someone who lived overseas for 48 weeks of the year, that was his decision and he could live with the consequences. Sod all to do with me.

I kicked off my duvet and padded barefoot through the dining room and into the kitchen, gently closing the doors behind me. Coffee. I filled the kettle and opened a few cupboards before I realised the mugs were hanging on a mug tree right next to the kettle. Eejit! I made a strong black coffee, then turned all the lights off except the one on the cooker hood. The clock on the oven informed me it was 04.12. Far too early for the glare of spotlights. I sat at the small, round table, blowing on my coffee and reflecting on the events of the previous day.

I heard a slight noise upstairs and suddenly my mind was in overdrive, imagining Ben and Lebony on the bed together, kissing, undressing each other, caressing… Only, it wasn't Lebony I was picturing with Ben anymore. It was me! Oh God! What was going on?

The door from the hall opened and a dark figure stepped into the kitchen. I don't know who was more shocked, but I was the only one holding a cup of coffee. Only, I wasn't holding it anymore.

'Shit! Let me get a cloth.' Ben dived towards the sink and I numbly looked down at the dark liquid trickling off the edge of the table onto the lino. Bollocks! How had that happened?

'Did it scald you?' he asked, wringing out a cloth.

'I don't know.'

'Let me see.' Ben knelt down beside me. 'I think you might be okay, but just in case…'

He gently placed the cloth on my bare legs, his hand grazing against my thigh. A shudder of something zipped up and down my body, and I jumped.

'Does it hurt? Sorry!' Ben said, completely misinterpreting my reaction.

'Coffee wasn't that hot,' I muttered, very aware that the coffee might not have been hot, but I certainly felt hot with Ben so close to me, touching my legs.

'Are you sure?'

'Sure.'

He finished wiping my legs and feet, while I sat helplessly like a small child being cleaned up after a nasty tumble. I watched him dash to the sink and rinse out the cloth, then deftly wipe the table and lino. How was it that there'd only been half a cup of cool coffee left, yet there appeared to be about five pints of liquid on the floor? It reminded me of the bottle spillage I'd had the first night Luke stayed with me. So much had happened since then.

Ben sat down beside me when he'd finished. 'I didn't mean to scare you. I thought you'd be asleep, which is why I came through the other door.'

'I couldn't sleep. Too much on my mind.'

He nodded. 'Tell me about it. Tough day, eh?'

'I'm sorry I didn't listen to you about Sarah,' I said. 'I should've got in touch.'

'I'm sorry I couldn't tell you why, but it wasn't my news to share.'

'I know. And I respect you for that. We've had a full confession session. We should have been honest with each other right from the start. In fact, I can look back on pretty much everything in my life and say that I should have told the truth from day one: Daran, the baby, the rape, my past. Elise should have told Sarah about the baby, and Sarah should have told us about what she was going through. Even though the timing was challenging with all those pieces of news, they should have been shared, because the short-term discomfort would have been a lot better than the hurt that's been caused by the secrets. I don't think anyone should have secrets anymore.' I sighed. 'Hindsight's a great thing, so it is. Anyway, everything's sorted now. We're all friends again.'

'I'm pleased to hear it. I know Sarah was pretty devastated that you'd all pulled apart and I know that, despite the blasé comments, you were hurting too.'

'I'm not blasé about everything, you know.'

Ben looked me in the eye for ages, before he whispered, 'I know.'

It felt as if he could see into my soul. I couldn't hold his gaze any longer. I jumped up to get some tap water. I grabbed one of the mugs off the tree, unable to face hunting for glasses and having him come to my rescue again. 'Won't Lebony be wondering where you are?' I turned the tap on and let it run for a bit.

'No. She left earlier.'

'Oh.' I couldn't stand there with the tap running forever, so I filled the mug and returned to the table. 'She's lovely, Ben. I can see why you've kept the long-distance thing going for so long.'

Ben didn't say anything.

'Why didn't she stay?' I asked.

'She's going back to France tomorrow… today. She needed to get down to Dover.'

Silence.

'How's Daran?' he asked, after a while. 'Are you looking forward to seeing him next week?'

'Yeah. It'll be grand. I can't wait for him to meet Shannon.'

More silence.

'Do you really think that people shouldn't have secrets?' Ben asked, eventually.

I thought for a moment. 'Well, there are obviously things that you don't want the world to know, but I don't think there should be secrets between friends.'

'Even if revealing the secrets could affect the friendship?'

'If the situation with Sarah and Elise has taught me anything, it's how *not* revealing the secrets can have a massive impact on the friendship, so surely revealing them can't be any worse than that.'

Ben nodded slowly. 'Clare, I—'

'Looks like I'm not the only one who can't sleep,' Chris said, bursting into the kitchen. 'It's quite the party in here.'

'Is Mum okay?' Ben asked.

'She's fine. Thrilled to hear that Kay's alive and not badly injured. I've managed to book some flights to Italy. We're going this afternoon to find out how she is first-hand.'

Ben and Chris exchanged some small talk about flight times and travel arrangements, then Ben filled a glass and left the kitchen, followed by his dad.

I sat there for a few more minutes, thinking about the conversation we'd had just before Chris appeared. Had Ben been about to reveal a secret?

Chapter 52

I needed to get back to Leeds to finish packing, so I got dressed. I scribbled a note asking them to keep me posted and telling Sarah that I'd give her a call over the weekend once we were settled in Little Sandby, then left the house.

We had a moving dilemma. Callum wasn't allowed to drive yet, so I'd hoped to rope Ben into playing either taxi service or baggage-delivery service. Three adults, a baby, suitcases for a fortnight, a buggy, a cot and all the other paraphernalia Luke needed packed into my car? Not going to happen. However, Ben had offered to drive his parents to the airport and, even if he hadn't, it was inappropriate to ask in the circumstances. I had no chance of hiring a van on Good Friday and, even if I could, it wouldn't have had enough seats for us all. In the end, Shannon, Callum and Luke caught the train to Whitsborough Bay, taking the buggy with them, and I drove across with a packed car.

Stevie, the absolute star, stepped in to help. He picked them up at Whitsborough Bay station and got them settled into the holiday cottage – a lovely, old, stone detached property with a modern interior, set back from the main street – then helped me unload the car when I arrived 20 minutes later.

'Are you looking forward to exploring tomorrow?' I asked, as we sat down with a fish-and-chip supper that evening. It had taken us what was left of the afternoon to get unpacked and organised, so we hadn't ventured further than the village chippy. The cot was up, though, and it felt like home, albeit a temporary one.

'I can't wait,' Shannon said. 'I've got a good feeling about this place.' She glanced at the two wooden boxes she'd carefully placed on the wooden mantelpiece earlier. 'Hopefully, we've found our forever place and I can finally scatter their ashes.'

'I hope you have too, but shout if it's not what you expected. We can keep looking.'

My iPhone beeped as I finished my meal.

🖂 From Sarah

Mum and Dad have found Kay and Philip. They're covered in cuts and bruises and she's dislocated her shoulder and broken her collarbone. Both very shaken. Two of the people who died were seated opposite them and they'd been talking to them when it happened. So awful. Thanks for yesterday. Sorry I missed you this morning. Hope you're settled in OK. I'm at work tomorrow but free on Sunday and would love to meet your family if that fits in with your plans ☺ xx

🖂 To Sarah

Such a relief! Send them my best. Cottage is lovely. Stevie helped us unpack. Sunday would be great. Will text tomorrow to make arrangements. Hope you sleep well tonight after a couple of difficult days xx

🖂 From Ben

I'm staying in W'bro Bay for the rest of Easter weekend. Do you have any time to talk tomorrow?

✉ To Ben
We're going to explore North Beach tomorrow if you fancy joining us?

✉ From Ben
Sounds great, but I was hoping to catch you alone. Any chance you could meet me early evening?

✉ To Ben
I'm intrigued. 6pm? 6.30pm? Where do you suggest?

✉ From Ben
6pm. There's a bluebell wood a mile north of Little Sandby. Head north out of the village and you can't miss it on your right. Meet me by the pond. Sleep well xx

I was early, just in case I got lost, but Ben had been right (as always); it was really well signposted. Plus, his car was parked in a lay-by next to the entrance stile, which was a slight giveaway.

Birds chirped their evening song and butterflies fluttered past. As I clambered over the stile, thankful that I was wearing jeans and canvas shoes, rather than a dress and heels, butterflies also fluttered in my stomach. Strange. I hadn't had my dinner yet. It was obviously hunger pangs, not butterflies.

The woods were quite spectacular. The lowering sun penetrated through the gaps in the trees, like hundreds of spotlights on the bluebells. I followed a well-worn path through the flowers, rising slightly, then dipping back down towards the pond, where I could see Ben sitting on a bench, staring at the water with his chin resting in his hands. I paused, leaning against an old oak tree, and watched him. He looked troubled. Hardly surprising, given the situation with Auntie Kay. I must have trodden on a twig or something, because he suddenly turned around as I approached him and jumped to his feet.

'You're early!'

'So are you. Are you okay, Ben?'

He nodded. 'Just thinking. It's a good place for it.'

'It's beautiful,' I said, turning in a circle.

'Mum and Dad used to bring us here when we were little. Sarah and I played hide-and-seek between the trees. She was rubbish at seeking so I used to let her find me.'

I smiled. That was so Ben, letting someone else win.

'Come and sit down,' Ben said. He waited for me to take a seat on the bench before sitting down again. 'I'm sorry for being all mysterious and luring you here, but there's something I wanted to say to you on your own.'

'You're going to tell me I owe you £16,000 in back rent, aren't you?'

Ben smiled. 'It's £26,000, actually, but that's not it.' He bit his lip. 'Okay. Here goes. You know we were talking in the early hours yesterday about being completely honest with friends, no matter how that might affect the relationship?'

'Yes.'

'Do you still believe that?'

'Definitely.'

'Good. So, I haven't been honest with you about two things. Two pretty big things.'

Butterflies fluttered in my stomach again and I felt my heart quicken. 'Go on…'

'The first thing is my relationship with Lebony.'

My stomach churned at the mention of her name.

'We're not together. We split up.'

'Jesus, Ben! When? Was it Thursday night? Was that why she

didn't stay?'

He shook his head. 'No. It wasn't Thursday night. Lebony and I… We… Well, we split up about six months ago.'

'What?'

Ben lowered his eyes. 'We're just friends now.'

'But you Skype her and call her all the time. And she rushed to your side on Thursday. That was Lebony, wasn't it? Not some actress?'

He laughed. 'That was definitely Lebony and, yes, we do call and Skype regularly. She's a good friend. She's been giving me some advice recently.'

'I don't get it. Why make out that you're still together when you're not?'

Ben sighed. 'That brings me on to the second big thing I've been lying about. The reason Lebony and I split up was because I'd fallen for someone else. Lebony knew it before I even realised it.' He smiled. 'I was stunned the day she pointed it out but, as soon as she did, it was like the biggest light-bulb moment ever.'

'Do I know her? Or is it a he? After the Elise-and-Gary situation, I don't want to assume.'

'It's a she.'

'Does she know?'

'No, but her sister guessed.'

My walk along The Headland with Aisling popped into my head. 'Oh my God, Ben! Are you talking about me?'

'We used to have such great craic, as you call it, when you were visiting. For years, I thought of you as a friend, but it all changed when you moved in with me the first time round. I got to see the real you, the person who loves to remove her make-up and put on her PJs as soon as she's home from work; the person who gets all emotional watching a film and pretends she's bored by it so she doesn't cry, and the person who's spent years refusing to be beaten by a challenging past and can proudly declare herself as king of every moment.'

Tears pricked my eyes. I couldn't speak. In fact, I could barely breathe.

'I didn't think it was possible to care for you any more than I already did, but when I saw how you were with Luke and Shannon, I fell even deeper. I'd never have said anything while you were living with me. I'd never have risked you feeling awkward and uncomfortable. Lebony gave me a lecture on Thursday. She insisted I tell you how I feel, especially as you were moving out anyway. So, here I am, telling you that, last September, you didn't just become the owner of my spare room, you also became the owner of my heart.'

My heart raced. Oh. My. God! I didn't know what I'd expected Ben to say, but it certainly hadn't been that. So Aisling had been right about him! How did I feel? He was looking at me intently, waiting for me to speak. But what could I say? What could I offer him in return? I'd shut myself off to love for 17 years. I'd even struggled to let Daran back in, and he'd been the person I'd believed I'd love until the end of forever.

Ben reached across and tenderly caught a tear rolling down my cheek with his finger. I hadn't even realised I was crying.

'You don't have to say anything,' he said. 'I'm not expecting some grand declaration of love in return. I just wanted to be honest with you, in case there was the slightest possibility that you may feel something towards me at some point in the future. I just hope that I haven't jeopardised our friendship and you never want to see me again.'

The thought of not spending time with Ben filled me with panic. I shook my head quickly. 'You haven't jeopardised anything. I'll always want you in my life. It's just that…'

He nodded. 'I know. It's completely out of the blue, it's a lot to take in, and you've got so much going on at the moment.'

'I wish I could say I feel exactly the same,' I whispered.

He lowered his eyes. 'But you don't. And that's fine. It's good. I expected it.'

'It's not that I don't care. It's just that I swore I'd never love anyone ever again. The thing is—'

But I didn't get to tell him what the thing was. Someone called my name. I jumped up, startled. The next moment, Daran had hold of me and was spinning me around, just like he used to in our farmhouse.

Chapter 53

'I hope you don't mind me coming early,' Daran said. 'The kids were so excited about going on an airplane that I thought, "Why not change the flights?"'

'Where are they?'

'Shannon and Callum have taken them to the park. Our daughter's gorgeous, Clare, and our grandson is adorable. I'm so proud of you.' He certainly looked it, with a beam from ear to ear and his eyes sparkling. 'Oh my goodness, it's so good to see you!' He grabbed me and kissed me. Startled, I glanced over at Ben. He smiled, but his sad eyes told of his devastation. 'I'll go,' he mouthed.

Awkward. I pulled away from Daran, giggling nervously. 'Emm. We're being rude. This is Ben. He's…' I paused. How could I describe Ben? 'Friend' actually seemed so inadequate for what he really meant to me. My throat felt tight as I said, 'Well, he's just amazing.'

Daran grinned and shook Ben's hand enthusiastically. 'So, you're Ben. It's so great to meet you. I can't thank you enough for everything you've done for this one.' He flung his arm around my shoulder. 'She never stops talking about you. I thought you were her boyfriend at first, but she says you're just a friend.'

Ben nodded. 'That's me. Just a friend.'

'I haven't interrupted anything, have I?' Daran asked. 'Shannon said you were catching up about your auntie. There's been some sort of accident?'

I nodded. Of course. I'd told Shannon that I was meeting Ben to hear the latest on Kay and Philip. She'd had no reason to believe we couldn't be disturbed, and I could guarantee that Daran would have nagged her to let him surprise me if she'd tried to make him wait. I'd told her where I'd be and the woods weren't exactly hard to find.

'I'd better go,' Ben said. 'I'll leave you to it.'

'We'll walk with you,' I suggested.

Daran pulled me closer to him. 'No, you go on, Ben. There's something I want to speak to Clare about.'

Ben shrugged. 'Nice to meet you at last, Daran. You look after her.'

'I intend to.'

Ben looked at me and held my gaze. 'I guess I'll see you around.'

I swallowed hard as I nodded. 'Bye, Saint Ben.'

'Bye, Irish.'

'He seems like a good lad,' Daran said, once Ben had sauntered out of view.

'He is. The very best.'

'I've got something for you.'

'Oh yes?' My eyes were still fixed on the brow of the hill, where Ben had disappeared from view, a heavy feeling in my heart.

'Yes, but I need you to sit down.'

I reluctantly peeled my eyes away from the hill and sat down on the bench where Ben had declared his love for me moments earlier.

Daran knelt on one knee on the soft moss in front of me. Oh no! Oh shit!

He took my right hand and touched my Claddagh ring. 'I gave you this ring on your 16th birthday and told you that I'd love you until the end of forever. I meant it then and I still mean it now. I also told you that, one day, I'd buy you a real one.'

He paused as he reached into his coat pocket and opened up a box. A stunning platinum Claddagh ring, with a heart-shaped sapphire in the middle, gleamed as the last rays of sunlight filtered through the trees and bounced off it. 'I know we've only just got back together, but it feels to me like we've never been apart. If you feel the same way, please will you take this ring and be mine until the end of forever?'

I stared at the ring, my heart thumping uncontrollably. 'Daran. I'm genuinely touched but—'

'I know there are some logistics to sort out. We could move here, the kids and me. They have religious education teachers in England, don't they? I might have to retrain a bit because of the different exams. Or you could move to Ireland. We'd make it work. We would.'

I shook my head. 'It's not just the logistics, Daran.'

He gently stroked my face. 'I know it was difficult for you when I touched you. We don't have to rush the physical side of things. I'll wait for you. We'll get the support you need.'

'It's not that either. '

'Then, what is it?'

'Please will you get up off your knee?'

He slowly stood up and sat beside me on the bench. 'It was too much, too soon, wasn't it? Aoife and Ma warned me that I'd scare you off. Have I?'

I shook my head. 'It probably is too much, too soon, but I understood why you've done it. Your feelings for me have never changed over the years. You said so yourself, but…' I couldn't find a way of saying it without hurting him. There probably wasn't a way.

He twiddled with the open ring box. 'But yours have, haven't they?'

'I'm so sorry, Daran. I should have been clearer with you at the farm or on the phone, but I wasn't sure how I really felt until this evening. I genuinely did love you with all of my heart back then, Daran, and I did mean it when I said it was until the end of forever. But our forever ended when we were separated for so long. It wasn't your fault or my fault, but it happened, and I can't just pick up where we left off. I wish I could, but I can't.'

Daran nodded. He snapped the ring box closed and put it back in his coat pocket. 'If it's time you need, I can give you time…' He smiled ruefully. 'It's not time you need, is it?'

I shook my head.

'You've given your heart to someone else, haven't you?'

A tear trickled down my cheek. 'I'm sorry, Daran. I didn't realise it had happened.'

Daran stood up and gently pulled me to my feet. 'If you're quick, you might just catch him.'

'Who?'

'Who do you think? It's Ben, isn't it? He's your new forever.'

'No. Of course not.'

'You don't need to protect me, Clare. I saw the look on your face when he left earlier. You used to look at me like that when we said goodbye. I hoped I'd imagined it so I stupidly proposed anyway.'

'I didn't know,' I said, tears streaming down my cheeks. 'I'm sorry, Daran. I never meant to hurt you.'

'To be honest, Clare, I think I've done this to myself. You didn't promise me anything. I just assumed we could pick up where we left off, which was a bit of a ridiculous fantasy.'

'I'm sorry,' I said, again. It felt so inadequate, but I hadn't led him on. Yes, we'd kissed, but I hadn't told him that I still loved him, and I hadn't talked about a future together. That had all come from him. Perhaps I should have set him straight sooner, but I genuinely hadn't known how I felt about him, and I certainly hadn't realised that I'd fallen for Ben.

'Go on! Run!' he said.

'Will you be okay?'

He took a deep breath. 'Actually, Clare, I think I will. It's not what I wanted, but it's finally a conclusion to 17 years of dreaming and wondering and hoping and praying. I can finally lay the past to rest. God's been telling me to do that for years, but I haven't been listening to Him. I'll see you later. Run!'

He didn't need to tell me again. I sprinted up the slope, down the slope and leapt across the stile. Ben's car was still in the lay-by. I charged towards the window, but he wasn't there. I gulped in the evening air, trying to catch my breath, but my heartbeat just got quicker and quicker. Where the hell was he? I jogged a little way along the lane, away from the direction of Little Sandby, because there certainly hadn't been anywhere he could have gone closer to the village. A minute later, I came across another stile in the fence, with a wooden sign pointing towards 'Sea View'. It was a long shot, but it was worth a try.

I clambered over the stile and found myself in a wildflower meadow, just like the one surrounding the farmhouse where Daran had first declared his love for me. It seemed fitting that a meadow could be the setting for me letting love in for the second time in my life.

The meadow dipped and I stopped for a moment to catch my breath, as I took in the stunning view ahead of me. The meadow was on a clifftop, with the sea stretching out below. I scanned the edge of the fence, my eyes adjusting to the approaching twilight, but I couldn't see Ben. My heart sank. I was just about to turn around and go back to the car when something moved along the fence. It was him! I hadn't been able to see him because there was a bush in front of him and he'd blended into it, but his silhouette was clear now that he'd taken a couple of paces to the left. I ran across the field towards him. He must have heard my approach when I got closer because he turned around, and my heart skipped a beat as I saw his tears.

'Clare!' he said, wiping his cheeks roughly with his sleeve and sniffing. 'What are you doing here? Where's Daran?'

'Daran's gone back to the cottage. He asked me to marry him. Turns out I really am irresistible to all men, women and small furry animals.'

'Congratulations.'

'Here's the thing: I said no.'

'Really? But I thought…'

'So did Daran, but you were both wrong. I'm not the same person he fell in love with, and he isn't the same person either. It would never have worked.'

'It might have done. You could have got to know each other again. People do fall in love again after years apart.'

I shrugged. 'True, but it's not going to work for Daran and me. Too much time has passed and too much has happened.'

'I'm sorry,' Ben said. 'I know you might not believe me, in light of my earlier confession, but I really am sorry. I only want you to be happy.'

'I *am* happy. In fact, I'm the happiest I've ever been. I have a new family, and the potential for a new home and new career. It's all good. And a lot of it is thanks to you.'

'Me? What did I do?'

'You were there for me every step of the way. I've got a little gift to say thank you. Put your hands out and close your eyes.'

'Clare!'

'Quit your nonsense and do as you're told.'

Ben sighed, but closed his eyes and held out his hands anyway. I placed the king in his hands, my body fizzing as my hand connected with his. 'Open your eyes.'

'It's the king,' Ben said.

'For everything you've done for me over the past seven or eight months, and especially for putting yourself out there earlier and telling me how you really feel about me, I declare you king of the moment.'

'Clare, I…'

'Shh! I haven't finished. There's another reason why it would never have worked with Daran this time around. Even though I swore I'd never let anyone in ever again, somebody managed to wriggle his way in there without me noticing. Daran had no chance. My heart had already been given to someone else.'

Ben bit his lip. 'Does this person know?'

'Only if he believed what her sister told him.'

Ben grinned. 'What are you saying, Clare?'

'I'm saying that I didn't properly realise it until this evening but, somewhere along the way, my friendship towards you turned into so much more. It's not going to be easy, and I know I have a pile of shite from my past that I still need to address, but if you're prepared to take that rough road, then I'd like you to be king of all my moments from now on. I never thought I'd say this to anyone ever again, but I love you, Ben, more than I ever thought possible.'

Ben took a step closer to me and gently cupped my face in his hands. 'I'm prepared to take that rough road,' he whispered. Then he bent down and kissed me. Despite years of dreaming about Daran, the reality hadn't lived up to the dream when we'd kissed again. Kissing Ben, on the other hand, felt like a dream come true. The best dream ever.

Epilogue
New Year's Eve

'I now declare you husband and wife. You can kiss your bride.'

No! Not Ben and me! Philip and Kay, of course. I'm not quite ready for that sort of commitment. Actually, that's a lie because I'd jump at it, but he hasn't asked me. Yet.

I smile as Philip gently kisses Kay, and the guests whoop and cheer very loudly. Well, if you're going to have a wedding on New Year's Eve, you've got to expect a loud, rowdy bunch who've been on the beer all day.

Ben hands me another glass of Champagne and my heart melts. Wow! That man looks so damn sexy in a tux. He looks pretty sexy out of one too. It took six months and regular counselling before I felt ready to go all the way, but Ben showed the patience of a saint (naturally). We actually did the deed on my 34th birthday. I had a demon to exorcise from that same evening 18 years previously. It hurt, physically and emotionally, but it was absolutely worth taking that first difficult step. I still have moments where fear grips me, but Ben is so incredibly understanding. He knows it will take time to fully free myself of my demons.

Speaking of demons, I'm thrilled to say that Nia has exorcised hers too, and Jamie Doyle is currently serving time for assault and attempted murder. She'd gone home after our meeting on my last morning in Cork feeling inspired by our conversation. She packed some clothes, intending to seek refuge with my real mum, until she decided whether to take me up on my offer to join me in England. As she was walking down the driveway with her case, though, a taxi pulled up outside and Jamie got out. It was obvious she was leaving him, and there was no way he was going to let that happen. He thumped her in the stomach, then pinned her to the garage door by her throat. The taxi driver, an ex-Guard, pulled him off before he throttled her, and he made sure the book was thrown at him.

Two weeks after we'd moved into the holiday cottage, Ellen came to stay. I was so excited to have my real mum visit and have four generations of my family under one roof. After we hugged, she said she had a little surprise for me. Nia appeared from around the corner. 'I hear there may be a job going for someone with no skills or work experience,' she said. 'That sounds like something I might be able to do.'

I have to say that, for someone with no skills or experience, Nia was instrumental in helping me get my business off the ground. Jamie Doyle had stopped her from having ideas, opinions and even thinking for herself, so it took a lot of coaxing, but she tentatively came to me one day with a brilliant suggestion for how I could price my services. I loved it. That one piece of encouragement was like unleashing a party popper because the ideas streamed out of her from that moment. I secured a regular contract with *The Ramparts Hotel*, Whitsborough Bay's only five-star hotel, to do all their marketing and social media for two days a week, which acted as a brilliant platform for bringing in more local businesses.

Sarah proved invaluable in clinching the contract with *The Ramparts*. She runs a business club called *Bay Trade* with Nick and two of his friends, one of whom happens to be the sister of the hotel manager, so a bit of trading was done and I was in there. I provided my services for free at first, confident that they'd want to pay when they saw what I could do. They did.

I smile at Sarah across the room, looking stunning in her deep-red bridesmaid dress. She's put weight back on, thank God. She looks curvy and healthy now, rather than the gaunt woman she'd become after losing the baby. I convinced her to go for some counselling too, to help her accept that the loss of the baby and her fallopian tube wasn't her fault. She had some good news following the tests. While there is some scarring on her other tube, there's no reason why she shouldn't conceive again. The thing is, Nick and she aren't so sure they want children now. They've got a new puppy called Twix (with a dog called Hobnob and cats called Kit and Kat, spot the theme!) and they're still absolutely besotted with each other. Sarah told me that they'll give it a couple more years and they might try for a family then but, if it doesn't happen, that's fine.

She must have registered me watching her because she looks over, raises her glass to me with a grin, and continues her conversation with Elise and Stevie.

Aw, Elise and Stevie. Another fabulous couple. Melody was released from the special-care baby unit in late April and she's adorable. Daniel has seen her once. He's finally accepted that she's his but isn't bothered, which suits Elise and Stevie just fine because, let's face it, he'd have been a useless lump of a dad and Melody's better off without him in her life.

Stevie adjusts his hold on Melody, who is just about the cutest and smallest bridesmaid ever, dressed in a frilly ivory dress with a red sash to match Sarah's dress. I notice Elise place her hand on her stomach. There's no sign of a bump yet, but I know – and Sarah knows – that Elise is eight weeks pregnant. She gathered us both together a couple of weeks ago and said that, although she didn't want to announce it to anyone else until after the 12-week scan, she wanted to make sure that we both knew at exactly the same time, this time around. Good call.

'What are you grinning at, Mum?' asks Shannon, appearing by my side with a sleeping Luke in her arms.

'This,' I said, sweeping my arm around the room. 'This time last year, I was in such a different place. I hated New Year's Eve with a passion. And now I'm at the wedding of two good friends, surrounded by family I didn't know I had.'

'Are you crying?' she asks.

'No! Okay. Yes, I am! I swear that I've turned into an emotional wreck from the moment I knew you were still alive.'

And it's true. I cry at everything now. I cried when they moved out of the holiday cottage into a rental property with a year-long lease. I cried when Daran and I jointly gave Shannon away to be married to Callum on her 17th birthday in June. I cried when I waved them off on their honeymoon in Scotland for a few days, leaving me alone with Luke for the first time since Leeds. I cried when Shannon asked me to meet them at Lighthouse Point for a picnic, then sprinkled the ashes of Paul and Christine into the sea instead, telling me she'd finally found the place she could call her forever home. I cried when she secured a place at the local sixth-form college and when Callum secured another plumbing apprenticeship. And I cried when Shannon secured a part-time job at a school of dance and excitedly told me that the owner had plans to retire in the next five years. She's now grooming Shannon to take over within three years, knowing that Shannon already has the finances in place to buy her out.

'Auntie Nia looks lovely tonight and I reckon Philip's son thinks so too.'

I look across the room to where Nia is chatting animatedly with Michael. Wow! I can practically see the sparks flying off the two of them.

She really does look stunning. Her mousy appearance didn't

seem to fit with the confidence she found as she helped the business to grow and discovered her own self-worth. I'd marched her to the hairdressers in early September and ordered a full head of colour and a layered style. We went shopping for clothes, shoes and make-up, and giggled over glasses of wine one evening as she burnt her clothes from her former life. Actually, we just burnt one item – a cardigan she'd ripped a hole in and spilt paint on – and gave the rest to charity, as we couldn't bear the waste. She stood taller after that; she laughed more; she even gained the confidence to go out and join a Zumba class and a photography club, where Michael just happened to be a guest speaker in October, having returned from his latest overseas assignment. They've been inseparable since. I'm going to miss her when she moves out, which I fully expect she'll do within the next few months. We've been living together at Kay's cottage, *Smuggler's View*. Philip's house sold and that gave them enough funds to buy their new home together. Kay's had also sold, but the chain broke and the purchase fell through. I asked if they'd be willing to rent it to me instead, with a view to me buying it a few years down the line, when my business was more established and I could secure a mortgage. I absolutely love living there.

Ben stays as much as he can, but he still has his job in Leeds. He's been trying to convince them to set up a branch in North Yorkshire, but there've been so many stumbling blocks and funding problems that we don't think it's ever going to happen. Ben's been looking for other jobs in the area, but he loves what he does, and I won't let him leave because of me. We've managed with the commute so far and we'll continue to do so. Somehow.

'Are you looking at Michael and Nia?' Elise asks, joining us. 'That's one seriously smitten pair.'

I nod. 'I think they're perfect for each other.'

'So do I,' she whispers. 'Michael certainly deserves to find love at last, and so does your sister.'

As for the rest of my family, Aisling, Torin and Briyana moved over to Manchester during the summer holidays, and the kids have settled nicely into their new schools. Finn sold his house because, although it was a family home, he wanted their home together to be one they'd both chosen, rather than the one he'd intended to buy with *her*, even though she never actually lived there. Torin and Briyana came to stay with me for a weekend in October while Finn took Aisling away to Venice for her birthday. They came back married!

Éamonn's wife is expecting a baby in March, but it turns out that Ma was actually right about Keenan: he does prefer men. He isn't in a relationship, as he's struggling to come to terms with his sexuality, but he's hoping to make this coming year the year he explores a same-sex relationship. I hope he does. After a slightly awkward start, I've grown to really like my brothers.

I haven't seen or heard from Ma. The twins tell me she's very bitter and blames everyone except herself for everything that's happened in her life. She's pushed them all away. She'll end up a lonely old woman. Couldn't have happened to a nicer person!

We see Daran and his kids regularly. They've been over here three times, and Shannon, Callum and Luke have been there twice. I joined them the second time. Daran's kids think it's brilliant having a big sister and brother-in-law to look up to, and Shannon loves being able to spend time with her dad. I'd stayed away from Daran for the rest of the Easter visit. He needed time to get to know our daughter, and to get over me. Things were slightly awkward at first when he came over for the wedding, but I made him sit down and drink a bottle of wine or two with me, and I finally got him to admit that he hadn't really been in love with me for all these years; he'd been in love with the memory of what we'd had together. Although, it had taken a stern talking-to from his mum and sister Aoife after I turned him down to get him to realise this. He's actually met someone else through his church. It's early days and I've made him promise not to rush into anything, but I met her when we went to Ireland in November and I think they have a good chance, especially as she's not trying to compete with a ghost of girlfriends past.

Luke wakes up so Shannon excuses herself to feed him, as Sarah makes her way over.

'This time two years ago, things were quite different, weren't they?' she says.

I laugh. 'Christ, yes! I was staying with you at *Smuggler's View*, questioning why the hell you weren't chasing after Nick when you knew he was the one for you.'

'I was out with Gary and his work colleagues,' Elise says, 'with no idea that he was gay and that I was heading for a divorce.'

'And you were hiding some pretty big skeletons in your closet,' Sarah says to me.

I glance around the room again. 'Some of whom are in this room right now! What a difference a couple of years make.'

Elise nodded. 'I can't believe how much has changed, how painful it was at the time, but how much better everything is now.'

'To love, friendship and no more secrets,' I say, clinking my glasses with them both.

'To love, friendship and no more secrets,' they repeat.

'What's this about "no more secrets"?' Ben asks, putting his arm around me.

'We're just reflecting on the past couple of years,' I say, 'and how much better life is with everything out in the open.'

'You don't like secrets, do you?' Ben says.

I shake my head. 'You know I don't.'

'Would you be mad at me if I said that I have another little secret? Wait here.'

'Ben!' But he disappears into the crowd. I glance at Sarah and Elise, but they shrug. They know something, though. I can tell by the mischievous twinkles in their eyes.

A spotlight illuminates a microphone on the stage at one end of the function room and Kay steps up to the mike. 'Good evening, ladies and gentlemen. Philip and I have had an incredible day and would like to thank you all for celebrating New Year's Eve and our wedding with us. We know that many of you might have had other plans, but Philip proposed to me on this night last year, so it seemed fitting that we married on the anniversary of our engagement.' She pauses for applause and cheers. 'The last time I stood in front of a microphone and made a speech, it was at my 60th birthday party a year gone in June, only I'd lured everyone there under false pretences. It was actually an engagement party for my wonderful niece, Sarah, and her gorgeous husband, Nick, who I'm delighted to say that I fixed up. I can't take credit for this one but, tonight, I'm hoping I've done the double…'

She moves aside and Ben steps into the spotlight. 'Hi, everyone. For anyone who doesn't know me, I'm Ben, Kay's nephew. I won't take up much of your drinking time, but I have an exciting announcement that I want to share with you. As many of you know, I work for a charity that helps find and support missing persons, particularly children. It's based in Leeds and I helped set up a new branch in Birmingham at the start of this year. I've been trying for months to convince them to let me set up a branch in Whitsborough Bay. There've been all sorts of funding problems, and it looked like it might never happen, but at the start of December I got an early Christmas gift when they confirmed the go-ahead. From February, I'll be heading up a new branch right here in the Bay and living here permanently.' Ben pauses for more cheering and I'm aware that I'm grinning from ear to ear. That is the best news ever. We really didn't think it was going to happen.

Being able to curl up beside Ben every night will be such a dream come true.

Ben holds his hands up to calm the audience. 'There's something I've wanted to do for a while, but I didn't think it was fair while I was back and forth between here and Leeds. Now that I'm moving here permanently, I think it's time. Clare? Can you join me for a moment?'

Oh. My. God! My legs are shaking so much, I don't know how I manage to put one foot in front of the other. I step onto the stage and smooth down my dress. Ben is kneeling and he's holding the king between his fingers. My heart is beating so fast, I feel quite light-headed, although that could be the Champagne.

'In March, you presented me with this and asked if I would be king of all your moments. I hope I've lived up to your expectation of what being your king would mean.'

I nod, tears swimming in my eyes.

He reaches into the pocket of his tuxedo jacket. I laugh as he pulls out a white king. 'You will make me the happiest man alive if you agree to be the king of all my moments too. And, because you can't exactly wear this, I've got you one of these as well.'

A gasp goes around the audience as he delves into his pocket and holds out a ring. 'Will you marry me, Clare?'

I reach out my left hand towards him, tears streaming down my cheeks. He looks into my eyes, then slips the solitaire diamond onto my finger. 'Yes,' I whisper. 'Yes!'

Ben stands up and kisses me gently, as the audience erupts.

I used to hate New Year's Eve. Not anymore. And I used to dream about Daran all the time but, for the past 10 months, all I've done is dream about this day with Ben.

At Sarah's wedding just over a year ago, Elise had suggested I wasn't as cynical about weddings as I liked to make out, and that I simply hadn't met the right person yet. She was right about the cynicism; it had just been an act to protect myself. As for the right person, I'd already met him. I'd met him when I was 14. It had been real, it had been passionate, it had been amazing and, if things had been different, it probably would have lasted until the end of forever. But, as Daran's sister Aoife had said: *Sometimes the past is called the past because it's passed.* The time for Daran and me to be together had definitely passed and it was time for us both to build a new life.

After losing Daran and my daughter, I'd built a protective bubble around myself. I hadn't let my friends in, I'd denied my family and I certainly hadn't let love in. My mission in life had been success in my career and I couldn't imagine anything – or anyone – being more important than that. How wrong I was! I'd discovered the value of friends, I'd found the importance of family and I'd realised that a career gave the financial means to live, but it wasn't what life was all about. I can honestly say that I've never felt as happy and fulfilled as I have since running my own business, based locally, and not working every hour that God sends.

But, more than that, I'd let love in. I hadn't looked for it, yet it had unexpectedly found me, and I was so glad that it had. I'd found my king of every single moment and I knew that, for Ben and me, it really was going to last until the end of forever.

The End

Did you like this book?

Les us know and leave your review!

Want to read more now from the series?

Searching for Steven - Book 1

When Sarah finds a clairvoyant reading that's been missing since her teen years, she discovers that she's about to meet the man of her dreams. And she even knows his name: Steven! Let the search commence...

Getting over Gary - Book 2

It was supposed to be the perfect fairy-tale. Elise married her childhood sweetheart, Gary, straight out of college, and they've been happy together for over twelve years. Elise is now desperate to start a family, but Gary doesn't seem to share her enthusiasm anymore. Arriving home early from a party, she discovers why: Gary's been keeping a secret from her. A very big secret.

Acknowledgements

I can't quite believe my third full-length novel has just been released. What an amazing fifteen months since my debut novella, Raving About Rhys was released, followed by the trilogy (Searching for Steven in June 2015, Getting Over Gary in March 2016, and now Dreaming About Daran).

All the books are romance stories, but the trilogy includes a further theme of friendship and how it changes over time and circumstances. Friendships fascinate me. How is it that some friends stick around, no matter what different paths their lives take, yet others move on like a changing season?

Susan, to whom I've dedicated this book, is to the friend I've known the longest. We can't remember exactly when we met. Maybe age 8-10? We lived in different parts of town, went to different primary schools, were only in one GCSE class together at senior school, attended different colleges, and went to different universities, finally settling in completely different parts of the country. Yet we stayed in touch for all that time which, in the days before social media, included writing long, descriptive letters to each other whilst at university. Oh, the excitement of going to the pigeon holes and finding a letter had arrived from my best friend!

Susan's been there for me during dodgy haircuts, questionable fashion choices, and boyfriend disasters. We've drunk far too much cider together before going out clubbing, stunk out every shop in Middlesbrough after drenching ourselves in Body Shop Vanilla, Dewberry, and White Musk perfume, and spent sleepless nights on Ranger Camp when our supposedly heat-reflective "moonbags" turned out to be the coldest, flimsiest sleeping bags in the history of the world ever. Good times! She's read all of my books, even though romance isn't the style of book she'd normally choose, which I find really touching. She even beta-read Daran for me and provided some really valuable feedback, so it's definitely fitting that I dedicate this book to her and thank her for her support both now and over the past thirty-six years or so! I'll also take this moment to say "hello" to her mum, Beatrice, who has also read all my books and been a massive supporter of my writing. Thanks, Beatrice!

The second person I want to massively thank is my cousin, Lisa. (Actually, she's my cousin's daughter so I believe that makes her my first cousin once removed, but that sounds ridiculous so let's stick with cousin!) Anyway, Lisa is a nurse and she's given invaluable guidance on everything from how a nurse would introduce themselves to a patient, to medical terminology, to how quickly a patient would be encouraged to walk after an accident. Google is a good friend to a writer, but there's nothing to beat real life knowledge. If there are any mistakes in any of the medical aspects of this book, I can guarantee it's me being a muppet and misinterpreting what Lisa told me rather than her inaccuracies! Thanks, Lisa. Hope there's a family get-together again soon so we can drink wine and have a giggle about sleepy bees! ;-)

As always, thank you to my wonderful beta-reader team – Joyce (my mum), Clare, Liz, Sharon, Jo and newbie Susan – for taking the time to read Daran and giving me honest and helpful feedback to help make him even better. Sorry I kept you up till the early hours reading again, Clare, although that's such a massive compliment that you couldn't put Daran down!

Thanks go to my husband and daughter for not moaning about the hours I've spent with my fictional friends instead of them, my writing family 'The Write Romantics' for being there through the highs and lows of writing and life in general, and So Vain Books for publishing my trilogy and turning me from an aspiring writer into an actual writer. Dreams do come true!

My final thanks go to everyone who has bought/borrowed/read/reviewed any of my books, promoted my writing, and/or attended the various library talks I've delivered across North Yorkshire. Your support and encouragement is amazing. I hope you enjoy the final chapter of the trilogy and that you're ready to meet a new cast of characters in the next book.